Jack's hopes sank with the sight of the pistol. The escape plan and the life vest seemed all for nothing now. Jack figured they were about to suffer the same fate as the crew of the *Adele Bristol*.

"Guess we're gonna get to play captain and go down the ship," said Virgil.

"Yeah," said Jack. "Right now I'd trade places with two first-class ticket holders on the *Titanic*."

TWO LONERS—IN THE MOST AWESOME ADVENTURE ON LAND OR WATER!

RENDEZVOUS 2.2

Another Fawcett Gold Medal Book
by Robert D. Bennett:

SECTOR 12

RENDEZVOUS 2.2

Robert D. Bennett

FAWCETT GOLD MEDAL • NEW YORK

A Fawcett Gold Medal Book
Published by Ballantine Books
Copyright © 1985 by Robert D. Bennett

Library of Congress Catalog Card Number: 85-90829

ISBN 0-449-12833-4

Manufactured in the United States of America

First Edition: January 1986

Chapter One

ONE NIGHTER

THE CIGARETTE boat cut its way across the swamp, weaving the wake of a water moccasin. The Spanish moss hung down from the cypress, patterning the water with abstract shadows that added to the boat's camouflage. Black electrician's tape covered the cigarette's Florida registration number, and air moss nearly shrouded its name. The *Emmy Lou* was nearing the western edge of the Everglades.

The skipper of the cigarette passed by the skulls set atop stakes that loomed above Skeleton Lagoon, reminders of a bygone era of running liquor under the shadows of the Thirteenth Amendment and the men who prospered under Prohibition. Now the competition was even more fierce, for the dead did not rest atop stakes, but beneath the still water, ghostly sentinels rotting to the legacy of the deep six.

The skipper cut his speed, eased up on the throttles of the cigarette, and let the boat coast. Phil Lanard drifted. He was lost not in the swamp but amid his own thoughts. *Was this the right thing to do?*

Lanard, the youngest son of a New England salesman, had mustered out of the Air Force and taken a Cajun bride. As with most young couples, their lives had been a struggle; two children and never enough money. But that was all going to change.

At first Phil had avoided the drug trade. "Dope is for

dopes," he had always said. But when his friends passed him in the Naples Canals manning the wheels of their paid-for forty-footers, Phil began to have second thoughts. Why not? Hell, everyone he knew was in the trade. Besides, he wasn't going to become a career smuggler. It was just going to be one quick sting, no more. Then he'd buy the land, and build the home they'd always wanted.

The cigarette was on loan from Red Pardee. Pardee had made all the arrangements for Phil, including supplying the two hundred thousand in cash necessary to complete the score. Pardee's activities of late had come under the surveillance of the Naples Sheriff's Department and the Florida State Drug Task Force, and with them monitoring his every move, Pardee had offered the run to Phil on a sixty-forty split of the profits.

At first Phil had declined, until Pardee had pointed out that the two-hundred-thousand-dollar buy of cocaine would return three times the figure when they cut the coke for resale to a Miami dealer. Two hundred and fifty thousand dollars for about twelve hours' work. Whatever hesitation Phil might have harbored melted with the thought of all that money.

"All ya gotta do is make the run out from the swamps, meet the mother ship about twenty miles out, and make the run back," said Pardee. "If anyone sees ya, just give the cigarette its head, shove them throttles forward, and let 'em eat your rooster tail. Ain't nothin' on the water can touch my *Emmy Lou.*"

The six hundred horse mills of the *Emmy Lou* rumbled to the beat of Cutter hemihead pistons. The heavily modified cigarette could outrun any Coast Guard cutter and drew little water, which made it ideal for escaping through the Chokoloskee Pass and into the labyrinth of cypress that was the Everglades.

Sweat poured off Lanard's brow. He wiped his face clean with his forearm. Beads of perspiration now covered the half-finished tattoo just above his wrist. Phil kept mumbling his margin of profit as he neared the edge of the Everglades, but the ploy did not settle his anxiety. His stomach was so knotted he felt seasick.

A cool breeze from the sea gave Lanard a sudden chill. He hung his hand over the side and cupped a handful of water, which he splashed on his face. The water was tepid, but refreshed him and tasted of salt. He would be in the Gulf soon, halfway home.

Lanard came out of the swamps just north of the border with Everglades National Park and took a new heading westnorthwest through the Gator Straits and on to his rendezvous near Ten Thousand Islands. Phil followed Red's instructions and cut the cigarette's running lights before he came out into the Gulf.

The rumble of his engines sent flocks of white ibises flying out of their rookeries. The coastline was crawling with perennial breeding grounds, and the scrub trees were laden with nests. The shrieks of protective parents compounded Lanard's nervousness. Suppose someone heard the birds, he thought.

Phil angled the cigarette away from the rookeries, though he knew he should hug the coastline for camouflage. He kept looking aft, nagged by the feeling of being followed. Several times he had to swallow his heart when he thought he saw the silhouette of a cutter pulling out of a darkened inlet.

The moon was dangerously full, but it could have been pitch black and they would have seen him. Starlite sniper scopes, surplus army stores from the Vietnam era, turned night into an eerie green daylight.

The cigar boats kept their distance. Like half-submerged submarines, they paralleled the heading of the cigarette. The two cigars were not part of the Coast Guard or any other provincial authority, but of a much more lethal force, for they were not governed by the complexities of the judiciary. Their code was the smuggler's code: the law of the jungle. The cigars stalked their prey, waiting for the right moment to strike.

Phil swore he heard other engines, then remembered how the sea can play tricks with your ears. Besides, with all the sand bars and half-acre islands dotting the coast, it would be easy to hear his own engines. He checked his compass heading and entered the mouth of the Gator Straits.

The cigars lay off Lanard's stern, starboard side aft. There they could cut off any run he might make for the swamps and force him out deeper into the Gulf. There, even the speed of the *Emmy Lou* was no match for the cigars' twin jet drives and hydrofoils.

Phil spotted the light in the Gator Straits. It couldn't be the mother ship, he thought. Not this close to shore. It's a cutter! No, a cutter wouldn't sit with its running lights on. It had to be something else. Maybe it was the mother ship. Phil changed his course to veer past the mysterious light.

The *Ice Bucket* out of East Naples had broken down again. She wallowed in the Gator Straits like a bloated sperm whale. The forty-six-foot sportfisherman was the livelihood of Jack Grigsby and Virgil Fullenkamp. Charter fishing trips—cheap. An easy way to turn a quick buck, the transplanted midwesterners had thought. That was before they had bought the *Ice Bucket*.

Virgil stood on the broken catwalk above the *Ice Bucket*'s bilge. Oily water seeped between his toes as he sloshed about the twin Cummins diesels searching for the gremlin that had left them dead in the water.

Jack Grigsby held a second torch above Virgil, hoping the additional light might help him locate the problem. "What do you think?" asked Jack.

"I think when we bought this tub," said Virgil, skinning his knuckles, "we should have looked at the lousy engines, instead of the teak inlay and radar!"

"Wonderful," said Jack, giving Virgil a friendly thump on his swabby cap. "Do you think you can get us back to port?"

"Sure," said Virgil. "Just reach in your back pocket and see if you've got some new injectors."

Jack pulled his torch off the diesels. "You hear something?" he asked.

"Hey," snapped Virgil. "Shove that light back down here. I can't even *see* the injectors, much less clear them."

"Quiet!" said Jack. "I think I hear a boat."

"Great! Signal them down and see if they'll give us a tow," said Virgil, climbing out of the bilge.

Phil Lanard kept a wary hand on the throttles. He maneuvered the cigarette starboard of the lights and the faint silhouette of a ship wallowing in the Gator Straits. There were more lights on deck now, and they appeared to be signaling.

"You see anything?" said Virgil.

"No," said Jack. "But I can hear the bastard. Where the hell is he?"

Phil nursed the throttles of the cigarette back and squinted in the dark. He still could not make out the full shape of the ship and continued his cautious approach.

Jack waved his torch in the direction of the approaching engines. "Ahoy!" he shouted. "This is the *Ice Bucket* out of East Naples. Engines are dead. We need a tow. Do you copy?"

The answer was a roar of the cigarette's engines. The *Emmy Lou* came about and tore up the Gator Straits, heaving geysers of water off its stern as it headed up the channel and out to sea.

"Goddamn dopers," snarled Virgil Fullenkamp. "The only fuckin' boat on the water tonight and it's some clown runnin' coke. Shit!"

"Now what?" asked Jack.

"Well, I don't think I can clear the injectors. They're shot. You might as well call the Coast Guard."

"Oh, no, not that. Not again," said Jack. "I don't want to listen to their flak," he continued, saluting their imaginary rescuers. " 'Why don't you boys wise up and scuttle that tub?' Christ, if I hear that one more time."

"It's either the Coast Guard or we swim back," said Virgil.

"All right," said Jack, heading for the radio.

"I hope that sonofabitch gets caught," said Virgil, listening to the sounds of the engines fading in the distance.

"Me too," said Jack, switching on the radio.

Phil's nerves were worse than ever after his unscheduled rendezvous with the *Ice Bucket*. He felt guilty about not stopping. After all, the owners were his friends. Still he continued on course. He couldn't stop, not this night. Not with so much at stake.

No more deviations from Red's itinerary, he thought. If he saw anything other than the mother ship, he'd steer clear. Phil brought the cigarette out of the Gator Straits and into the Gulf.

The Gulf was calm. Moonlight shimmered across the water and the cigarette heading out to sea. Phil shot his azimuth and monitored the heading out beyond the twelve-mile limit. The coastal lights were barely visible when he made contact with the mother ship, anchored just on the edge of international waters.

Phil was surprised. He had expected a much larger ship. The Colombian vessel was like many of the ships that made the run up from the coast of South America, ready for the marine scrap yard. A heavy squall might send her to the bottom. Still, there was no point in investing money in a ship that sooner or later would be confiscated by the Miami Drug Task Force.

Phil came up amidships and cut the engines of the *Emmy Lou*. Suddenly two search lights hit Phil from the ship's bow and stern. Momentarily blinded, he waited for his eyes to adjust to the harsh glare. Silhouetted against the light he could see men pointing M-16's at him. "Buenas noches, mi amigo," came a voice out of the light. "What are you doing so far out this early in the morning?"

"Pardee sent me," Phil said, gagging on his own saliva. "I'm making the run for Pardee."

The man on the bow pulled the bolt back on his M-16. So did the man on the stern.

Phil threw up his hands so fast he nearly fell out of the boat. "Don't shoot!" he shouted. "I'm not a cop!"

Phil could hear men talking to each other above him. They spoke in Spanish and one of them seemed very angry. It sounded like he was cursing, and he spat over the side to enunciate his disdain for the change in routine.

"We know you're not a cop, señor. And you are not who we expected either."

"Didn't Pardee contact you? He was supposed to tell you that I was making the run tonight."

"No one told us shit, señor."

Another man was speaking now. Phil recognized the voice. It was the man who had cursed and spat over the side. "Shoot the sonofabitch," Phil heard him say.

"No!" screamed Lanard. "I've got the money. All of it. It's all here—see?" Phil held the suitcase full of cash up into the light and fumbled with the latches. Bundles of bills fell out and into the deck of the *Emmy Lou*.

"We can take the money after you're dead, señor."

Phil lost control of himself. He wet his pants. Then, just as he was about to wither into a state of shock, he was stricken with a moment of fear-generated courage. "Yeah," he said, sitting down to pick up the spilled money. "Then who will you do business with next week?"

There was more conversation in Spanish from above. This time the tone was more subdued.

"I got the money," Phil said, trying to keep his voice from cracking. "Now where's the snow?"

Still there was hesitation, then the voice of the man who had spoken first. "We have the snow, señor. Send up the money."

"The goods first," Phil snapped. His adrenaline was flowing now, and it countered the hollow-gutted feeling he had had when he thought they were going to shoot him.

"As you say, señor," Phil heard the first man say.

In the light, Phil could see a suitcase being lowered down from the mother ship. It was made of aluminum and appeared watertight. Phil took the suitcase and unfastened it from the line. He picked up the case of money and had started to make it fast to the line, when he remembered Pardee's instructions: *Take samples from both kilos before paying off.*

Phil set his suitcase full of money down and opened the latches of the aluminum case. Inside, he found two round bricks of cocaine, each wrapped in translucent blue plastic. He took out the small bore probe Pardee had given him and took a sample from each brick.

The samples tasted bitter, and in his dry mouth they made Phil gag. It tasted right, but Pardee had been adamant. Phil was to *sample* both kilos. If he came back with two kilos of baby laxative, there'd be no sixty-forty split and Pardee would probably kill him.

Phil held up his palm and took one sample into his right nostril. The coke pinched his nasal passages, and the urge to sneeze was overwhelming. He managed to shake off the sneeze and felt the coke-laced mucus slide down the back of his throat. The second hit went much easier, and now Lanard realized why people paid so much for the drug.

The stimulation he felt was almost orgasmic. His temperament changed instantaneously. His fear evaporated and he felt in charge, invincible. "All right," Phil said with complete aplomb. "Damn good shit," he continued as though he had snorted a a thousand lines before. "Cash coming up."

Lanard tied off the line to the suitcase containing the money and gave a tug on the rope to signal it to be hauled away. He watched the suitcase disappear into the darkness beyond the spotlights. "I'll thank you to take those guns off me now," he said, glaring into the lights fore and aft.

"As soon as we have counted the money, señor. We don't trust you any more than you trust us."

A few moments passed, and Phil could hear men counting out the bills in Spanish. *"Bueno,"* said the first man. "It is all here."

Phil heard the men clear the rounds from the chambers of the M-16's, and he sat back down in the *Emmy Lou*. "See you around," he said, firing up the engines.

The cigarette came about and headed back for the dim lights of the coastline. Lanard hadn't gotten more than a quarter mile from the mother ship when the coke began to wear off. Maybe it was the recognition of how close he had come to dying, the roll of the waves, or the coke-riddled mucus that had hit his stomach. Phil wasn't sure. All he could do was hang over the side and retch his guts out.

The sound of Lanard's vomiting carried across the Gulf, back to the mother ship. The captain listened as he picked up the suitcase of money. ''Goddamn one-nighters,'' he said, then gave the order for getting under way.

Phil washed his face in the Gulf. He blew the residue of vomit and coke out of his nose and washed his face again. Almost home, he thought. He'd cut south now, past the Gator Straits, and make a run through the Chokoloskee Pass and into the Everglades. By morning he'd be at Red Pardee's hammock, where he'd turn over the coke. The dealer from Miami would be there and they would get paid. Then Phil would take his own skiff home and forget all about this awful night.

The cigars began to close on the *Emmy Lou*. They were riding low in the water now, their abbreviated bridges, like the half-high conning tower of a submarine, breaking a wake through the Gulf. They began their flanking maneuver and came up port side aft of the *Emmy Lou*.

Phil seemed to sense he was being followed. He kept looking back, yet he could not see the cigars, now only a hundred yards off his stern. His nervousness bred a new-found fear and he pushed the throttles of the *Emmy Lou* forward.

The cigarette's bow raised out of the water with the increase in horsepower. A rooster tail plumed up off the Gulf as Phil increased knots. A fine spray came off the bow as he blasted through the waves, leaving a frothy wake.

The cigars broke formation and gunned their engines. Blasts of jetted water blew off their sterns as they raced across the sea. The hydrofoils lifted the cigars out of the water as they came up to flank speed.

Phil did not hear the approaching cigars over the roar of his own engines. He was caught up with the exhilaration of speed and buried the throttles. Twelve hundred turbo-charged horses reared to life. The *Emmy Lou* put some distance on the cigars.

The commander of the lead cigar signaled his companion to

match the speed of the cigarette. Both cigars were now full out of the water, riding smoothly above the Gulf on hydrofoils. The commander deployed his forward 7.62 mm Gatling gun. The flanking cigar followed the commander's lead. The Gatling guns came to bear.

The Gulf exploded in crimson light. Tracers from the flanking cigars tore up the water both port and starboard of the cigarette. Two lines of plumed water flew into the air as the slugs slammed into the sea.

Phil ducked, as though he could escape the fire of the Gatling guns. In desperation he shoved forward on the throttles of the *Emmy Lou*, but the engines were red-lined and would go no faster.

The lines of fire from the cigars began to squeeze in on the *Emmy Lou*. Phil dared not weave off his present heading lest he drive straight into the fire of the Gatling guns.

The commander coordinated his attack perfectly. The Gatling guns' cross fire cut an axis across the stern of the *Emmy Lou*. Slugs slammed into the transmissions, which detonated like bombs from internal pressures and the massive torque of the engines.

Phil was lucky. The blast blew the gas tanks of the *Emmy Lou* down into the Gulf and only an oil fire was started. The *Emmy Lou* went down fast. Its engines, with throttles locked on full, continued to run until seawater smothered the blocks. Then piston and rod blew what was left of the mills into jagged pieces that headed for the bottom.

The cigars cut their speed. They retracted the hydrofoils and their keels settled back into the water. They arrived at the sight of the sunken cigarette and found its skipper clinging to some debris and the suitcase full of coke.

The hatch of the lead cigar opened and the commander climbed out of the abbreviated conning tower, brandishing a Baretta SC 70 Short machine gun. "Out for a little midnight swim?" he said.

A light from the flanking cigar zeroed in on Phil. "That's not Pardee," Phil heard a man say.

"Who the hell are you?" snapped the commander.

"Lanard. My name is Lanard. I'm making the run for Pardee."

"Not doing too well, are you, one-nighter?"

Phil shook his head. "No."

"Hand it over," said the commander of the cigars.

Phil pushed the suitcase of coke toward the nearest cigar and clung to a seat cushion from the *Emmy Lou* to stay afloat. In the spotlight he could make out some detail of the ships that had blown the *Emmy Lou* out of the water.

The cigars rode low in the Gulf. They looked like miniature submarines with a small conning tower that rose forward of midships. Phil could see the Gatling gun protruding from the conning tower and below it the barrel of an even larger weapon. Phil's Air Force background told him what it was. "My God," he thought, "that's a twenty-millimeter cannon!"

The commander held his 70 Short on Phil while the crewman stepped down from the conning tower and came forward with a gaff. The cigar's deck forward of the conning tower was very narrow, no more than five or six feet wide, and the crewman used the gaff to stabilize his movements. He fished the suitcase out of the water and opened it on the deck.

A flashlight illuminated the contents of the suitcase. "Not much," said the crewman. "It will barely pay for a week's worth of fuel for the fleet."

"It's not worth we're after," said the commander. "It's the example we must set."

The commander's statement sent a chill up Phil's spine. "Wait a minute," Phil said, holding one hand out of the water in surrender. "I'm not part of the trade. I'm just a one-nighter like you say."

"No, son," said the commander. "You're just in the wrong place at the wrong time."

The burst from the Baretta 70 startled Phil. He clung to the seat cushion, pulling it to his chest as though it might offer some protection.

Some of the rounds were flattened when they hit the water

and penetrated only an inch or two into Lanard's chest. Other rounds caught him through the neck, and blood from these wounds poured down into his lungs.

Phil began to drown in his own blood and from the seawater drawn in through the holes in his chest. He made a few pathetic efforts to swim, gagged himself into convulsions, and died.

Lanard listed over face-first into the Gulf. The water was stained with his blood as a stubborn heart pumped its last few beats. The crewman tossed the empty suitcase toward the corpse.

"Take care of him," said the commander.

"Aye-aye, sir," said the crewman, gaffing the body to the side of the cigar. It took some effort to pull the body onto the deck, but soon the crewman had the remains of Lanard sprawled across the foredeck. The commander kept watch on the horizon as the crewman finished his grisly detail.

The crewman pulled an autopsy knife from a sheath he wore on his hip. He made his entry into the warm corpse just below the sternum and laid the abdomen open all the way to the crotch. The entrails steamed in the cool night air.

Next the crewman returned to the conning tower to retrieve a piece of pig iron, which he lashed to Lanard's ankles with a length of nylon rope. The crewman stood up and saluted the commander. "Ready, sir," he said.

"Give him the deep six," said the commander.

The crewman shoved the pig iron over the side. The body was pulled off the deck and fell into the Gulf with a resounding splash.

"Make all preparations for getting under way," said the commander.

"Aye-aye, sir," said the crewman, returning to his station at the helm of the cigar.

The team of cigars came about and took a course that would take them back to their hidden base inside Ten Thousand Islands, leaving the debris of the *Emmy Lou* to mark Lanard's watery grave.

The currents of the Gulf seemed to give movement and life to the corpse as it sank toward its final resting place in a lurid underwater canyon some fifty fathoms below.

Jack Grigsby strode down the dock of the East Naples marina with his battered Coleman cooler resting on his shoulder. The planks of the wharf bowed under the weight of his stride. Jack was still cursing the Coast Guard for all the wiseass cracks they had made about the *Ice Bucket* during the tow back to port. Jack and Virgil had been up all night making the necessary repairs to the engines so they could keep their charter for the following day. "Have you seen Phil Lanard?" Jack asked the dock master.

The dock master was splicing a length of hemp and did not look up. "Nope," he answered.

"He was supposed to loan me some tackle. Said he'd be here early. You sure you haven't seen him?"

The dock master spit out the window of his shanty. Brown saliva ran down his chin and stained his salt-and-pepper beard. "Ain't seen him," he said.

Jack hoisted his cooler higher on his shoulder. "Thanks," he said. "You've been a big help."

The dock master watched Jack continue down the wharf. "Pay your docking fee, ya deadbeat. Then see if I know somethin'."

Jack was troubled over the lack of equipment—his charter was a party of three, and he only had two rods—but was more concerned about the whereabouts of Phil Lanard. It wasn't like him to leave Jack hanging. They were good friends and had bailed each other out of tight spots. Phil had been acting strange of late, Jack thought as he continued down the dock. He seemed to be caught up with some kind of inner turmoil. Maybe it was business, but then business was bad for everyone this time of year. It was odd of him not to show up.

Jack was a displaced midwesterner who had settled in Florida purely by chance. He and some college cronies had made the annual spring pilgrimage south. After spending half the vacation in jail—drunk and disorderly—Jack decided not to return. His Veterans' benefits were due to run out, and he was far short of the necessary credits to graduate. Besides, eking out a living teaching English and physical education did not interest him. Owning a fleet of charter fishing boats was more to his liking.

Jack had been joined in his business venture by Virgil Fullenkamp. Virgil's VA benefits were also running out, and he didn't see much future in getting his bell rung every Saturday afternoon as a wide receiver on the football team, especially since his chances for turning pro were all but nonexistent.

Virgil and Jack had rekindled their military-born friendship during first-semester orientation. The campus VA crisis center had been opened to appease deans who were convinced that every Vietnam vet was a drug-crazed maniac ready to go on a search-and-destroy mission during half time at homecoming.

Virgil was Jack's wiry sidekick. A Dutch-descended scrapper who spent the greater portion of his time avoiding work and responsibility, Virgil, the perennial schemer, was forever on the lookout for a fast buck. And forever in Jack's debt for bailing him out of one campus flimflam operation after another. Virgil was slight of build, with an impish face and always-wrinkled clothes. A bit of an extrovert, Virgil captured the friendship of most who ever met him. He was a lecher, measuring women's beauty solely on bust measurements. He was also a bit of a blowhard, whose idea of a fight was to get in the first punch and run like hell.

Virgil and Jack had served with each other in the rice paddies and jungles of Vietnam. Both had grown bored with campus activities that engaged some people ten years their junior, and both jumped at the chance to enter the world of big business.

Four years later, their fishing empire was still wallowing in the shallows. The boat was barely afloat, their clientele anything but well-heeled, and if they didn't pay the docking fees soon, they'd lose the lousy tub anyway.

Jack continued down the dock, mulling over his options. Jack still had an athletic physique, despite his addiction to Canadian ale. In a T-shirt his broad shoulders vectored down to a defined waist that was still twelve inches narrower than his chest measurements. He kept himself in fair condition, nothing like the monster who used to maraud the gridiron, crushing the pretty-boy faces of quarterbacks, but still strong enough to handle himself in a brawl. As long as he didn't have to fight more than two guys at once.

Jack pushed his faded skipper's hat back and wiped the sweat from his brow. Most of his light brown hair was still intact, though it was thinning at the temples from too much worry over the arrival of his next few dollars. Like most Floridians, Jack was tan, with a face that was etched with white crow's-feet where his wince against the sun prevented the tissue from being browned. Jack's eyes were green and protected under sun-faded brows that nearly met on the bridge of his nose.

He turned down the wharf and saw that his charter was waiting for him halfway down the dock. A Mother Superior and two nuns of the holy order. "Well," Jack mumbled to himself. "One day's charter is better than none."

"Good morning, Mother Superior," said Jack, doffing his cap. "And how are you this morning, sisters?"

"Fine," they chorused.

"Mr. Grigsby," said the Mother Superior, "were you able to obtain the additional fishing equipment?"

"Well, a friend of mine was supposed to meet me here this morning, Mother Superior. Doesn't look like he's going to make it."

Mother Superior shrugged her shoulders. "Sometimes these things can't be avoided," she said. "Perhaps you could show me something of the operation of the boat while the good sisters fish."

"Why not," said Jack, with a smile. "Right this way, sisters."

Jack lead the sisters down the dock. He was surprised by Mother Superior's attitude. For a short period in his youth Jack had attended parochial school, and the experience had not been pleasant. Most of the Mother Superiors he had known were short on temper and long on discipline.

"Isn't it a wonderful day?" said Mother Superior. "The Lord's blessings must be upon us."

"Yes, Mother Superior," said the two novitiate nuns accompanying the senior sister. It was her first vacation in over twelve years.

The novitiates had yet to take their final vows, so their dress was less formal than the traditional summer white habit of Mother Superior. Both wore light blouses and shorts that revealed tourist tans, which would peel within a week of their return to the north.

"Are the fish biting?" asked Mother Superior.

"Yeah," said Jack. "Fishing has been pretty good for this time of year."

"I do hope we catch something," said Mother Superior. "It would be such a disappointment to the sisters if we didn't."

"Well, we'll see what we can do for you, Mother Superior," said Jack, gesturing down the dock. "That's the *Ice Bucket* just ahead."

Virgil Fullenkamp rolled over and got a faceful of breasts, Maggie Donohue's breasts, the eighth and ninth wonders of the world. Virgil made a few laps around her bosom before Maggie woke up. "What time is it?" she asked.

"You don't have to go yet," said Virgil, his words muted by boobs. "Jack is always late. You know Jack," said Virgil, pulling himself away from Maggie's chest. "Oh, God, they're even more beautiful in daylight."

"I know, ducky," said Maggie, trying to wrestle away from Virgil. "But give it a break, luv. Your whiskers are chafing my chest."

"I'll rub ointment on them later," said Virgil chasing Maggie up the cabin's steps and onto the afterdeck.

Virgil hadn't made such a nifty tackle since they had lost the conference championship, but then the referee would have called him for illegal use of hands. Maggie didn't seem to mind. They tussled off some deck furniture and into the supports of a sun tarp that came flopping down upon them. Maggie surrendered, and the pair's lust was consummated under twelve square yards of canvas. Another dubious first for the *Ice Bucket*.

Jack led his cost-plus-ten percent charter down to the end of the dock. Mother Superior stopped at the stern of the *Ice Bucket*. At first she thought the object poking out from under the tarp was some rare variety of fish. A large grouper, perhaps, and the thought of landing such a prize filled her with excited expectation. Then the remainder of the mysterious fish flopped out from under the canvas and Mother Superior was greeted by Virgil Fullenkamp's posterior.

"Virgil! What the hell are you doing?" bellowed Jack.

Mother Superior seemed somewhat surprised, but not shocked by the snow-white buns waving before her. She had served in hospitals, and the sight of a man's bottom was nothing new.

Virgil stood up and pulled the tarp about him. "Hi," he said lamely.

Just then, Maggie crawled out from under the tarp. She saw Mother Superior, ducked behind the tarp, and stammered an embarrassed "Good morning."

Mother Superior turned to Jack with a wry expression. "I gather she's the social director," she said.

"No," said Jack, leveling a withering glare on the naked pair standing on the afterdeck. "She's not supposed to be here at all!"

"Just give us a minute," said Virgil, ushering Maggie and the tarp below decks. "I've got a feeling you'll land a really big one today, Sister."

The novitiates hid their snickers behind their hands while Jack saw them aboard. Mother Superior gave the girls a scolding look but couldn't help smiling herself. "Well," she said. "Where do we go from here?"

"Make yourselves comfortable," said Jack, gesturing toward the seats on the stern of the *Ice Bucket*. "Now hear this!" Jack shouted below decks. "Make all preparations for getting under way."

"Do what?" said Virgil, poking his head up on deck.

"Ditch the broad," muttered Jack.

The *Ice Bucket* belched a cloud of noxious blue smoke as it pulled out of the marina. Jack nursed the engines up to half speed as he headed out into the Gulf.

"Would you like to take the wheel?" said Jack to Mother Superior.

"Is that allowed?" she asked.

"Absolutely," said Jack. "I'm the skipper, and it's okay with me."

"What do I have to do?" said Mother Superior.

"Just take the wheel," said Jack. "Watch your compass, and keep the needle pointing in this direction."

Mother Superior took the wheel. Jack showed her how to maneuver and how to correct her heading, and she took to the boat like an old salt. Jack took a pair of sunglasses off the bridge and fitted them to Mother Superior's face while she continued to monitor their heading.

"You'd better wear these, Mother," said Jack. "The glare off the water can give you a helluva headache!"

Mother Superior glanced at Jack with a raised eyebrow.

"Sorry about that," said Jack.

"It's all right, Mr. Grigsby," said Mother Superior. "Headaches in Hell are quite common."

Jack smiled and began to instruct Mother Superior in the operation of the boat's instrumentation. She eagerly picked up on Jack's instruction and was soon making navigational corrections on her own.

The sun climbed into the sky as the *Ice Bucket* neared the twelve-mile limit. Virgil instructed the novitiates in the art of deep-water trolling, while Mother Superior and Jack looked after the operation of the bridge.

"This is most invigorating," said Mother Superior. "I've never experienced anything like it. I can understand why you chose a life on the sea, Mr. Grigsby."

"Well, it's not all fun and games, Mother. I thought it would be at first, but I had all the wrong ideas about the charter fishing business. Figured all you had to do was buy the boat and wait for the money to roll in.''

"The dreams of all youth," said Mother Superior.

"The dreams of fools," said Jack.

Just then the deck was cut by the whine of a Johnson reel paying out line at breakneck pace.

"Now!" shouted Virgil to one of the novitiates. "Set the hook!"

The novitiate nun followed Virgil's instruction and in no time was battling the brute on the end of her line.

Jack took the helm and Mother Superior watched as he rode the engines to tire the fish, which was quickly sapping the novitiate's energies.

For over an hour the battle was waged, each novitiate spelling the other in what became a backbreaking ordeal. But with each turn of the reel, the fish was pulled closer to the *Ice Bucket*.

"Wow!" said Virgil. "Look at the size of that hammerhead!"

The shark came up out of the water, thrashing and throwing spray across the afterdeck. "Do I bring him aboard?" bellowed Virgil.

The novitiates were in no position to make a decision. Both fought the fish while Mother Superior watched from above.

"Is is necessary to kill the fish?" asked Mother Superior.

"No," said Jack, "but most of my clients do bring them in for trophies."

"I don't think the sisters will mind," she said. "Ask Mr. Fullenkamp if he can cut the fish free."

"It's your charter, Mother," said Jack. "Hey, Virge! Bring it alongside, then cut it free."

The novitiates concurred with Mother Superior's decision. They watched from a safe distance as Virgil gaffed the hammerhead to the side of the *Ice Bucket*. Virgil was just about to cut the shark free when he noticed something lodged in its teeth. "Hey, Jack!" Virgil shouted. "Come down here."

Jack left the helm in Mother Superior's hands and leaped

down to the afterdeck. There he joined Virgil, who pulled on the gaff to reveal the object of his concern.

"Look at that," said Virgil. "See? There, wedged in between the teeth on the lower jaw. It's a man's ID bracelet!"

"It sure is," said Jack, opening an aft locker. Jack reached inside the locker and pulled out a Smith & Wesson .357 magnum revolver. He shoved six slugs in the weapon and joined Virgil at the gunnels.

The blasts from the magnum startled the sisters. Jack pumped four rounds into the hammerhead before it flailed its last. It took a moment to lash a loop of hemp about the hammerhead and the boat's block and tackle so they could pull the fish from the sea.

"Cut your engines, Mother," said Jack, "and come on down."

Mother Superior followed Jack's instructions and cut the engines. She climbed down the steps to the afterdeck, where Jack and Virgil were already dressing out the shark.

"I thought you said we could let the fish go," said Mother Superior.

"We were," said Jack. "That's before Virgil spotted this."

Jack handed Mother Superior the ID bracelet they had pried from between the shark's teeth. It bore the inscription P. LANARD.

"This won't be pretty," said Jack, producing a six-inch knife from a sheath on his hip.

"We're all trained as nurses," said Mother Superior. "Do what you must."

Jack nodded and turned to Virgil. "Do it," he said.

Virgil's knife slit the fish from gill to bowel, and entrails poured about the deck. Virgil shook his head, as though he didn't want to continue his grisly detail.

"Keep goin'," said Jack.

Virgil set the knife inside the shark's stomach. He swept it along the blue-veined vessel and when Virgil saw the mixture of half-digested fish disgorged at his feet, he nearly vomited. In it was a man's arm, severed just above the elbow. Virgil backed away from his find and the novitiates gasped.

"Sisters!" shouted Mother Superior. "Help him!"

"Oh, my God," said Virgil, recognizing the half-finished tattoo on the severed arm. "It's Phil Lanard's arm! I'd know that tattoo anywhere."

"Mr. Grigsby," said Mother Superior. "Do you have any ice?"

"Yeah," said Jack. "But what do you—"

"Get it," said Mother Superior.

"All right," said Jack, pulling his cooler from a storage locker.

"We won't need the beer," said Mother Superior, peering inside the cooler.

"Yeah," said Virgil. "Well, *we* might!"

"Sisters," said Mother Superior. "Place the severed appendage inside the cooler." The novitiates followed her instructions.

"What is that for?" asked Jack. "The autopsy?"

"We don't know that the owner of the arm is dead," said Mother Superior. "If he is alive, there's a chance the limb may be saved."

"Take a closer look," said Jack, pointing at the arm in the cooler. "If I'm not mistaken, that's a bullet hole in what's left of his arm."

Mother Superior looked again at the arm. She saw the wound and concurred with Grigsby's diagnosis.

"The damn fool," said Jack, his eyes welling up with tears. "Suckered in on a Rendezvous two-point-two."

"I don't understand," said Mother Superior. "Is that some kind of map coordinate?"

"No," said Jack, shaking his head sorrowfully. "That's what the smugglers call a meeting with a mother ship. Two-point-two is the pound equivalent of a kilo of cocaine or marijuana. That's how it's sold, in kilos. Two-point-two pounds to the key. You can make a lot of money on a rendezvous," continued Jack, no longer able to look at the remains. "You can also get killed!"

"Yeah," said Virgil. "They even have a name for the burial. They call it the deep six. It's what happens to people who get in on the wrong end of the dope business."

"Then we can still give the remains a Christian burial," said Mother Superior.

"Granted," said Jack, closing the lid on the cooler. "Jesus," he continued, looking toward the shoreline. "Who's going to tell his wife?"

"We will," said Mother Superior, placing a comforting hand on Grigsby's shoulder.

"We'd better call the Coast Guard," said Jack, heading below decks.

"Yeah," said Virgil. "And while you're at it, get me a drink. Make it a stiff one!"

Chapter Two

A POUND OF FLESH

JACK RADIOED ahead and alerted the authorities of their find. Mother Superior and the novitiates said prayers for the remains during the return trip. Jack pulled the *Ice Bucket* into their berth and was shocked by the mob waiting on the dock.

"Damn!" said Virgil, joining Jack at the helm. "Who are those clowns?"

There were about fifty people on the dock, including a contingent of officers from the Naples sheriff's office, six men from Tobacco and Firearms, a full team from the Drug Task Force, and several FBI agents. They were all ignoring the clamor of questions from three competing news teams who had helicoptered down from Fort Meyers. The mob had attracted any passerby at the marina, and they all pressed toward the *Ice Bucket* as Virgil made her fast to the dock.

Virgil cleared a path through the mob for the sisters, who came under a barrage of questions as they departed. "Hey, we'll want to talk to them!" shouted one of the police authorities.

"They were just along for the ride," bellowed Jack. "We can answer all your stupid questions."

Mother Superior and the novitiates waved good-bye to Jack and Virgil. "God be with you," said Mother Superior, ushering the novitiates up the dock.

"Understand you pulled a torso out of a shark?" said one of the newsmen.

"Torso? Who said anything about a torso?" said Jack, being pushed back on the afterdeck by their onslaught.

"Richard Biggs," said a guy wearing a blue nylon windbreaker with DRUG TASK FORCE written across his back. "Let me see your manifest," he said.

"Manifest?" said Jack. "Hell, we're not hauling anything but some nuns and a dead fish!"

"Did you exceed the twelve-mile limit?" asked one of the guys from the FBI.

"Connie Boone, Newsflash Five. Just where did you find the body?" asked a newswoman from Fort Meyers.

"All right, that tears it!" roared Jack. "Everyone off this bucket, or I'll heave the lot of you overboard!"

"Now, just a damn minute," said the guy from the sheriff's office. "We're here on a felony investigation!"

"I don't give a shit if you're down here looking for Jimmy Hoffa," roared Jack. "Now, I'm master of this tub, and I'm telling you that you're trespassing! And unless you want me to have *you* arrest yourself in front of all these cameras, I suggest you get the hell off my boat!"

The authorities considered the situation for a moment. No one had had time to get a search warrant, and all knew that Grigsby was well within his rights to press the pinch for trespassing. And when he did, it would be all over the six o'clock news.

The long arm of the law began a discreet withdrawal. Jack waited for the lot of them to climb back on the wharf before making his address.

"All right, first things first," Jack began. "I want one, and only one, representative from each of the county, state, and federal authorities to come on board."

"What about the press?" piped up Ms. Boone.

"You clowns from the press can take a long walk off a short pier!"

Ms. Boone made an obscene gesture, which was later edited out of the news story she presented at six.

"Now, gather 'round," said Jack, taking the police authorities below decks. "I'm only going to say it once, so listen up."

Jack recounted the details of the day's activities, culminating with the landing of the hammerhead. Virgil watched the forensic specialists bag the arm and take tissue samples of the shark's flesh and digestive track. After an hour of answering questions and signing statements, Jack and Virgil were left to mop up the *Ice Bucket*.

Jack and Virgil stood on the afterdeck and watched the throng of policemen march up the wharf. They were glad to be rid of the meddlesome group but knew they hadn't seen the last of their number.

There were two men still standing on the *Ice Bucket*'s bridge. They were examining the instruments and pointing out irregularities, which seemed to amuse them.

"Hey! What the hell are you doing up there?" yelled Jack.

The men turned and faced the skipper. Each wore a well-tailored suit, had hair cut short, and wore chrome-lensed sunglasses. The taller of the pair reached into his coat breast pocket and pulled out a gold shield. "Dickerson," he said. "FBI."

"Am I supposed to be impressed now?" Jack sneered.

"This is my partner," said Dickerson, pointing to the sandy-haired fellow standing beside him, "Mr. Ames. We'd like to talk to you for a moment."

"Look," said Jack, striking a disgusted pose. "I just gave fifteen versions of the same story to all those other guys. Where were you when I was making my speech?"

"We have it all on tape," said Dickerson. "But that's not what we'd like to discuss."

"We ain't running dope," said Virgil. "And if you want to shake down this ship, you'd better have a warrant."

Both of the FBI men climbed down from the *Ice Bucket*'s bridge. They continued to examine the ship as though it had to pass some kind of inspection. "You make very much money with your business?" said Dickerson.

"That's none of your fucking business," said Jack.

"You're absolutely right," said Dickerson. "But from what I understand, if you don't make three boat payments, pay your dock rental and fuel costs, you're going to lose this tub."

"You guys don't miss much," said Jack.

"If you'd like, we can give you your combined bar bill at the Wharf Rat Saloon," said Ames. "They'd like to get some money out of you also."

"Okay," said Virgil. "What do you want?"

"Oh, we're looking for some volunteers," said Dickerson.

"Had enough sense not to do that in the Army," replied Jack. "What makes you think I want to do it now?"

"A fifty-percent share of all impounded goods sold at auction," said Ames.

"Impounded goods?" said Jack. "Dopers' goods?"

"The same," said Dickerson. "We have reason to believe that the owner of the arm you found was a one-nighter who didn't fare so well."

"And you figure we'll do better?" said Virgil. "Look, mister, I don't want to end up barracuda bait at the bottom of the bay."

"We don't want you there either," said Dickerson.

"Forget it," said Jack. "There can't be that much dough in selling a few light planes and a couple of cabin cruisers."

"Oh, you might be surprised," said Dickerson, following Ames off the *Ice Bucket*. "I just figured you fellows could use a quarter of a million bucks."

"How much?" said Virgil.

"A quarter of a million," said Ames. "And that would be the minimum. It could run much higher."

"Tell the truth," said Jack, walking across the afterdeck to get closer to the federal men. "And take off those sunglasses when you talk so I can see your eyes."

Dickerson came back on board and took off the reflective shades. "We're not exaggerating," he said. "Naturally we could not pay you on the value of the contraband. But the equipment necessary to import it, and the subsequent investments made with the drug money, would stagger your imagination."

"Stagger it a little," said Jack.

"Last year the Department acquired jewelry stores, grain silos, dry docks, a collection of Picassos, fifteen tons of sugar, twelve hundred cases of perfume, numerous businesses, thirty-seven airplanes, one hundred and twenty-two cars, and some prime real estate, worth a total of roughly eight or nine million dollars," said Dickerson.

Jack and Virgil looked at each other, dumbfounded by this revelation.

"You've got to be kidding," said Jack.

"No," said Dickerson. "This year we expect to do even better."

"We gotta kill anybody?" asked Virgil.

"Only if you feel your life is in jeopardy. And then you'd better have a damn good reason."

"Okay," said Virgil. "Make your proposition. Not that we agree. We'll just listen."

"We're looking for some informants," said Dickerson.

"Stool pigeons," said Jack. "Squealers."

"Call it what you like," said Dickerson. "It would be necessary for you to enter the trade, and the information we're after would require that you remain in the trade for some length of time."

"How long?" said Jack.

"A year," said Ames. "Perhaps longer."

"And during this time, what are we supposed to live on?" asked Virgil.

"We would pay all your old and future bills and grant you a monthly per diem," said Dickerson.

"What about the quarter of a million you mentioned?" said Jack.

"Commensurate upon the capture and conviction of the people we're after," said Ames.

"Capture only," said Jack. "I don't want some dipshit prosecutor fouling up the payoff with an overlooked legal technicality.''

"Capture *and* conviction," said Dickerson. "Without the conviction, we can't confiscate any goods."

"Wait a minute," said Virgil. "Why can't you place your own people inside?"

"Locals only," said Dickerson. "No one in these waters will accept any outsider. You're established residents. Besides, you've been approached to enter the trade before."

"Damn," said Virgil. "You boys do get around."

"Here's the name of your first contact," said Ames, handing Jack a small card. On it was the name of Red Pardee.

"Pardee," said Jack.

"Yes," said Dickerson. "We know he's contacted you before. We want you to get in touch with him again. Tell him that you've changed your minds. Business is lousy, and you've got to make some real dough fast."

"Wait a minute," said Virgil. "I don't remember agreeing to do anything."

"Let us give you the entire pitch," said Dickerson. "Then you decide."

"Fair enough," said Jack. "Go on."

"You aren't to make a move unless you contact us first. We will monitor all your activities and act as your guardian angels. However, I must add that there will be some situations when you'll be entirely on your own. You might be able to radio for help, but there's a good chance we'd never get there in time."

"That's comforting," said Virgil.

"We will supply all the equipment," Dickerson continued, "as well as the training necessary to handle the various hardware we will provide. Radios, weapons, and 'buy' money. Both of you served in Vietnam, so I think only a refresher course in weaponry will be needed."

Again Virgil and Jack looked at each other. "What do you think?" asked Jack.

"I dunno," said Virgil. "What do *you* think?"

"Give us a little time," said Jack.

"I can appreciate that," said Dickerson. "I would have some doubts about your ability had you reacted otherwise."

"Can you give us some more information?" asked Virgil.

"No, I'm afraid that's all I can say for now. And I must insist on having an answer by Monday. If you accept, we'll have to get your weapons and scuba training started right away."

"Scuba training?" said Jack.

"Yes," said Dickerson. "We're trying something new with this operation. We want informants who can act as liaison agents if possible. The fellows in D.C. were rather keen on that idea."

"Informant-agents?" said Virgil.

"Keen on the idea?" said Jack.

"Yes," said Dickerson. "Do let us know as soon as possible," he continued. "If you won't take the assignment, we'll have to make other contacts."

"We'll let you know by Monday," said Jack.

"Thank you," said Dickerson. "And do keep this conversation quiet," he continued. "It seems that Mr. Fullenkamp accepted Veterans' Administration benefits for periods when he was not attending college. It would be a shame to turn that evidence over to the Justice Department."

"Why, you dirty sonofabitch," mumbled Virgil.

"Have a good day, gentlemen," said Dickerson.

Virgil and Jack watched the two men from the FBI move up the dock and get into their car. They drove off, leaving the crew of the *Ice Bucket* to ponder their predicament.

Virgil was already looking for an avenue of escape when Jack turned on him. "You told me," he began in the snarl that used to turn quarterbacks white with fear, "that those checks were *back* payments. That the money was *owed!*"

"Anybody can make a mistake," said Virgil, feeling himself lifted off the deck by the lapels of his windbreaker.

"How much?" said Jack, his eyebrows smashing together.

"Two grand," said Virgil, shrugging his shoulders. "Got us by the balls, haven't they?"

"*Us?* You got a mouse in your pocket?"

"Okay, they got *me* by the balls. But I own half the boat."

"Don't remind me," said Jack, letting Virgil's feet return to the deck.

"Shit!" said Virgil, trying to change the atmosphere. "Did you hear those guys? The fellas in D.C. are really keen on the idea? Christ! They're more gung-ho than some of those assholes that nearly got our heads shot off in 'Nam."

"Tell me about it," said Jack. "Come on. Let's go over to the Wharf Rat. I'll buy you a beer and we can think things over. There's got to be another option."

"Sure," said Virgil. "We say no, we lose the boat. We say yes, we get killed and lose the boat."

"That's what we need on this operation," said Jack. "An optimist."

The Wharf Rat Saloon sat in the center of the old Naples waterfront. It had been erected in the twenties, and prospered under the name of The Seaman's Social Club. Two dollars for the woman and one for the room brought many a seaman a pleasant evening's entertainment.

During the thirties the building stood empty, but when Prohibition was repealed, Violet Monet reopened the club under a French name none of the locals could read. The most common mispronunciation was "Wharf Rat" and the name stuck.

Vi was a Cajun from Louisiana who had migrated to west Florida after being forced out of New Orleans for running the same business she would open on the Naples waterfront. Vi was a grand old dame, and dressed and acted the part of a madame of the late nineteenth century. She dressed in period costumes and insisted that all her girls do the same.

Vi didn't allow any hooligans in her house and inspected each client personally. During a strip search she would examine a man through a jeweled lorgnette that hung about her neck and that had a habit of getting wedged between her ample breasts. The strip search relieved the men of any weapons, liquor, and drugs, none of which she ever returned, and ferreted out those who were, as Vi diplomatically put it, "of bad credit." No one ever got a dose at the Wharf Rat Saloon.

It was said that Tommy Three Toes used to play cards there. He and No Neck Norris supposedly ran rum up from Havana and hid out at the Wharf Rat when things got too hot for them in Miami. Tommy was thought to have sired Vi's only offspring, though the madame never did admit who the father might be. Dominique Monet was perhaps the most beautiful woman in all of Florida. Her blue-black hair she must have inherited from her father, as Tommy did have a good deal of Seminole Indian in him. The blue eyes were her mother's, as was the complexion. Her figure was visionary. Full but not exaggerated, somewhat athletic, yet most feminine.

Dominique had studied French to augment her fluent, but bastardized, Cajun. She was a bit of a dreamer, spending many afternoons on the beach, fantasizing romantic scenarios in which she always played the heroine. Dominique was sometimes demure, honestly coy about some subjects and discreetly honest about others. She was an enigma, but a pleasant puzzle any man would love to unravel.

Vi had died of natural causes in the early seventies, and Dominique continued to run the business, but she abandoned the brothel, as she thought it too demeaning to women, not to mention the hassle with the law. Domino, as she was known to her friends, maintained the graciousness of the upstairs. The grandeur of the nineteenth-century motif lived on amid the salt air of the seedy waterfront.

Domino loved the contrast between the sawdust floors of the bar below and the grandness of the old brothel above. It was like living in a Humphrey Bogart movie. At any moment she expected "Rick" to come walking through the front door. What she got this day was Jack Grigsby and Virgil Fullenkamp. "The bar's closed, you bums," said Domino.

Jack and Virgil were about to begin their usual plea for an extension of credit, when they saw someone moving toward them out of the shadows under the staircase. "Look out," said Virgil. "Here comes Cody."

The man stepping out into the light was the bouncer at the Wharf Rat, a monster of a man named William Cody Carnes. Cody was an ex-professional wrestler who had grown tired of memorizing fight scripts and living in Holiday Inns. He had bought himself a percentage in the Wharf Rat and settled down in East Naples to watch over the Cajun princess as her adopted big brother.

Pity the poor slob who ever forced his attentions on Dominique. Cody would then demonstrate to the idiot why he had wrestled under the name of "Wild Bill." The lucky ones got a bum's rush out the back door and into the bay. Anyone stupid enough to try and duke it out with the ex-heavyweight champ got a quick trip to the hospital.

But Cody was not a muscle-bound moron. He was strangely refined for a man who had been voted by *Wrestling Monthly* "the roughest man in the ring." Cody enjoyed good wines, fine music, Brahms in particular, most of Shakespeare, and punching people out once in a while.

Cody had to suppress a grin as he approached the deadbeats at the bar. Virgil had already run around behind Jack, whom he shoved toward the now-closing bouncer. "You bums got any cash?" said Cody.

"Yeah," said Jack. "I guess I can come up with a few bucks for beers."

Jack and Cody shook hands. Their viselike grips closed as each titan tested the other's strength.

"Still keeping in shape," said Cody as the handshake turned into a bit of upright arm wrestling.

"You must pump a bit of iron yourself," said Jack, countering Cody's moves.

This tussling was routine, for although Jack and Cody were good friends, their competitive spirits never missed an opportunity to test each other.

"All right," said Domino, setting the beer on the bar. "You can stop shaking hands now."

"How about us exchanging some greetings," said Virgil, grabbing Domino's outstretched hands.

"Watch it, buster," said Cody.

"It's all right, Cody," said Domino. "He's harmless."

"Thanks a lot," replied Virgil.

"You boys are starting a little early today," said Domino.

"Depends on what you want to start," said Virgil.

"You never give up, do you," said Domino.

"Never," said Virgil.

"Heard you had quite a crowd down on the dock this afternoon," said Cody.

"What happened?" said Domino.

"We pulled Phil Lanard's arm out of the belly of a shark," said Jack, taking a gulp of beer.

"Oh, my God!" said Domino, covering her mouth with her hands.

"Yes, it's a damn shame," said Jack.

"Didn't he have a wife and a couple of kids?" asked Domino.

"Sure did," said Jack. "I don't know what they're going to do."

Domino reached out and took Jack's hands. "If there's anything I can do," she said.

"There's not much anyone can do. Take up a collection for his wife, I guess," said Jack.

They all stood silently for a few moments, paying homage to the dead. It was an odd sort of wake, but necessary nonetheless.

Domino caressed Jack's hands. She thought it best if she changed the subject. "I want to thank you for Sunday night," she said.

"Sunday night?" said Virgil.

"It was nothing," said Jack.

"Yes, it was," said Domino. "It was very special."

"Sunday night?" said Virgil. "You said you were going to Bonita Springs to visit your grandmother!"

"Best birthday present I ever received," said Domino, exchanging fond glances with Jack.

"But I didn't have any money for a gift," said Jack.

"You gave me the night on the beach, Jack," said Domino. "I'll always remember that."

"Night on the beach," wailed Virgil. "Why, Grigsby, you rotten sonofabitch. You snuck off so you could—"

Virgil's remarks were cut off by Cody's hands clamping about his throat. "You know I don't allow that kind of language around Domino," he said.

Cody choked Virgil until he started turning purple, then dropped him on the floor. Virgil was just regaining some of his normal color when Domino asked them if they'd like something to eat.

"Sure," gasped Virgil , climbing up to find Domino opening a cooler behind the bar.

The conversation halted as the trio of men watched Domino turn and bend over to reach the sandwich ingredients.

Domino's bikini-clad derriere wiggled before them. She had just recently come back from the beach and her daily swim. She wore a light blue frock over her bathing suit, and the view of the back of her thighs was absolutely breathtaking. She was tan, and still covered with suntan lotion, which highlighted the curves of her legs. She swung around to face them, her arms laden with cold cuts and three varieties of bread. The front of her frock opened, revealing the top of the bathing suit. Her ample breasts undulated as she cut up the roast beef for the almost drooling men watching her. "Those Federal fellas talk to you yet?" she asked, setting some sandwiches on the bar.

"Two creeps with chrome-lensed shades," said Jack.

"They were here just after you radioed in your report," said Domino, giving Jack a wink as he grabbed a beef on rye.

"I suppose the Feds want you to go to work for them," said Cody.

"Yeah," mumbled Virgil, through a mouth full of food. "How'd you know?"

"You ain't in jail," replied Cody. "If they didn't want something from you, they'd have hung you out to dry the minute they stepped on the *Ice Bucket.*"

"You guys aren't going to enter the trade, are you?" asked Domino, with some concern.

"Doesn't look as if we've got a whole lot of choice in the matter. Bastards are putting the squeeze on us," said Jack.

"What for?" said Domino. "You're not in the trade."

"For pinching college tuition money out of the VA," said Jack, glaring at Virgil.

"So it wasn't such a good idea," said Virgil with a shrug.

"How much?" said Domino.

"With interest and penalities, maybe two thousand," said Virgil.

"Over and above what you owe on the boat?" Domino asked.

"Yeah," said Jack, picking up a sandwich.

"Not counting what you owe us," said Cody, taking the sandwich out of Jack's hand and placing it back on the tray.

"We'll lend you the money," said Domino, handing the sandwich back to Jack.

"The hell *we* will," said Cody.

"All right, I will," said Domino.

"Can't let you do that, Domino," said Jack.

"Why not?" asked Virgil.

"Because I said so," replied Jack.

"Good reason," said Virgil, stuffing another sandwich in his face.

"It's a mistake, Jack, and you know it," said Domino.

"Not really," said Jack. "We've been in tougher spots before. Besides, the Federal boys will be playing lifeguard. We'll be okay."

Domino studied both Jack and Virgil, her worry obvious. She was quite fond of the vagabond boatmen, especially Jack.

"You'd better be careful," said Domino, taking Virgil and Jack by the hand. "Promise me you won't take any unnecessary chances."

"We promise," said Virgil.

Jack gave Domino a grin. "Okay, Mom," he said.

"Yeah, take care of yourselves," said Cody. "Sure

wouldn't want you clowns gettin' killed before you paid your bar tab.''

"Thanks," said Jack. "I didn't know you cared."

After some deliberation and a case of beer, Jack and Virgil decided to go to work for the FBI. "It's always best to begin any business venture on a firm foundation of careful thought," said Virgil, begging another case of beer on credit.

"Damn right," said Jack. "What do we owe you for the brew? We'll start paying off what we owe right now."

Jack dug around the pocket of his jeans and pulled out the charter fee given to him by the Mother Superior. He paid for the beer and wobbled toward the front door of the Wharf Rat, hanging on Virgil for support.

Domino dashed ahead of the drunken volunteers and cut off their exit. "Listen," she said, imploring both of them with her doleful blue eyes. "Are you sure you want to do this?"

"Hell no, we're not sure," said Jack.

"Yes we are," said Virgil. "Airborne all the way."

"Promise me you'll sober up before you call the Federal boys."

"We promise," chorused the drunks.

"I'd rather see you lose the *Ice Bucket* than see either of you get hurt," said Domino.

Domino's concern penetrated their inebriated fog. Virgil and Jack were touched by her worry. "Oh, you're much too good for us," said Jack, picking up Domino in one arm and Virgil in the other.

"She sure is," said Virgil, who began kissing Domino. "She's just a dream girl," he continued between kisses. "To put up with all of our crap and still love us."

"You will be careful," said Domino, giving Virgil a friendly stiff arm.

Jack gave her a sloppy, drunken grin. "Yeah. We'll be careful."

Domino reached up and grabbed Jack by the hair on the back

of his head and tried to shake some sense into his alcohol-sodden brain. "I mean it," she said.

"Okay, okay," said Jack, wincing in her grasp.

"Good," said Domino, releasing her grip and wrapping her arms around Jack's neck.

Jack felt Domino's mouth press against his. Even though he was three sheets to the wind, he still responded with a hard-on.

Virgil was dropped to the floor as Jack wrapped his arms around Domino's back and waist. They would have held the embrace and kiss had not a cooler head prevailed.

"All right," said Cody, prying the pair apart. "Sooner you get to work, the sooner we get paid."

Cody lifted Virgil off the floor by the scruff of his shirt and pulled Jack away from Domino by the arm. As Cody ushered them to the door, he glanced back and noticed that Domino looked as if she was going to cry. "Ahh, shit," he said. "You're not going to start bawling, are you?"

"No," said Domino, though her chin was already beginning to quiver.

Cody gave out a great piqued sigh. "All right," he said. "I'll keep an eye on these bums. I ain't joining the FBI, but I'll see that they keep their heads above water. Okay?"

"Thanks, Cody," said Domino, wiping the tears from her eyes.

"Don't mention it," said Cody, hauling the drunks out the door. "I suppose I'll have to drive you bastards home, too, in that bucket of bolts you call a car."

Chapter Three

NEVER VOLUNTEER AND STAND IN THE MIDDLE

WHEN JACK awoke, he was back aboard the *Ice Bucket*. His face was stuck to the mattress ticking, and his mouth tasted like the bottom of a pickle vat. Virgil was in about the same condition.

Jack rolled over and fell onto the deck and several empty beer cans. He was still too numb to feel much pain, but he did manage to roll off the bent aluminum and get to his feet. Thereafter followed a series of grunted monosyllables only a wino could appreciate. Jack's groaning stirred Virgil from his coma.

Somehow they both arrived at the *Ice Bucket*'s head at the same time. Neither Virgil nor Jack seemed aware of the other's presence until they became wedged in the door and began bickering over who was going to go first. Virgil lost out to Jack's size, and decided he couldn't wait. He staggered through the maze of discarded beer cans and crawled up on deck.

Virgil unzipped his pants and was about to relieve himself over the side, when he realized he was not alone. Two men stood on the dock above him. Virgil tried to shake some sense into his head and closed one eye to get a fix on their location.

Virgil thought he had tuned in on three test patterns at once. Each of the men standing above him wore enough contrasting plaids, stripes, and Hawaiian print to make them poster children for the color blind. "Yeah?" said Virgil. "What can I do for you?"

"Like to charter your boat," said the fellow in the stripes and prints.

There was something familiar about his voice, but Virgil couldn't place it. "Come aboard," said Virgil. "My partner will be with you in a minute."

Virgil disappeared below decks, and the polyester twins sat down on the afterdeck.

Jack wasn't long in coming up on deck. He had splashed some water over his head and was toweling himself down as he greeted the would-be charter.

"Can I help you gentlemen?" he asked.

"Yes," said the first man, tipping back his straw hat. "Have you come to a decision yet?"

"Decision?" said Jack, swabbing his face.

The man lowered a pair of cheap plastic shades, then quickly covered up again. "You remember us, don't you Mr. Grigsby?"

"Oh, yeah," said Jack. "I remember you. Well, Virgil and I have thought it over and . . ."

"Lovely day," said the second of the polyester twins. "Do you suppose we could take the boat out for a spin to see how she runs before we decide on whether we want to charter it for a full day?"

"Sure," said Jack. "Only take a few minutes to get under way."

The *Ice Bucket* ran south out of Naples and stayed within sight of the coast. After fifteen miles north of Big Marco Pass the federal men took off their tourist disguises and got down to business.

"In case you've forgotten, my name is Dickerson, and this is Mr. Ames," said the federal man, replacing the plastic shades with the now familiar chrome-lensed shooting glasses. "Have you come to a decision?"

"Yeah," said Virgil. "You got us by the balls, you bastard. What'd you expect us to do?"

"Gentlemen, we're not forcing you to do anything," said Dickerson.

"No, but you've got a damn good way of persuading people," said Jack.

"It was Fullenkamp's choice to accept VA checks for periods when he wasn't attending classes. You certainly can't blame us for that," said Ames.

"Cut the bullshit, buster," said Jack. "What the hell are we getting into?"

"To be quite honest," said Dickerson, "a real hornets' nest."

"All right, let's have it," said Jack.

"As I said before," Dickerson began, "we'd like you to enter the trade. We'll supply all the necessary hardware in addition to money to make the buys."

"Yeah," said Jack. "Suppose somebody gets curious as to how we came by all this stuff so fast."

"Tell them you've been nickel-and-diming it with the *Ice Bucket*. Small scores of hemp. Say that instead of fishing for marlin, you've been landing square grouper. But now you're ready for the big time."

"Cocaine?" asked Virgil.

"Exactly," said Dickerson. "We'll put the word out through our other informants that you're ready to enter the trade."

"Who do we deal with?" said Jack.

"Red Pardee," said Dickerson. "He'll get you started."

"He on your payroll too?" asked Virgil.

"No," said Dickerson.

"What do you want us to find out?" asked Jack.

"Someone has moved into the area," said Dickerson. "We don't know who they are. We haven't been able to find out much about them. We think they might be from South America. Colombia maybe, although we haven't been able to trace any members directly to the Colombian Mafia."

"Oh, they're a nice bunch of fellas," said Jack. "Read about them in the papers all the time. They rub out anybody who gets in their way. Men, women, and children. They don't draw the line anywhere.''

''True, but we don't think they are the bunch that's trying to take over. Some of their people have disappeared, and they don't know who's doing it either.''

''I suppose you've got informants there too,'' said Jack.

''I'm sorry,'' said Ames, ''but we're not at liberty to discuss that.''

''I think we can make an exception here,'' said Dickerson. ''Yes, we have some contacts with the Colombian Mafia, but it's at a very low level, and we can't be sure of all the information we're fed. But one thing is for sure. Their people are getting hit, and hit hard. They'd just as soon see us clear out this third party as do it themselves.''

''I'm beginning to get cold feet,'' said Jack. ''This operation sounds more and more like a good way to get killed.''

''Not if you follow our instructions,'' said Dickerson, ''and remember our arrangement. Fifty percent of all goods confiscated. An operation of this size could net you a million dollars.''

''Fat lot of good that will do us, dead,'' said Virgil.

''Look,'' said Dickerson. ''If things get too hot you can always bail out.''

''Yeah,'' said Jack. ''And you forget about the two grand Virgil owes the VA.''

''Yes,'' said Dickerson.

''And we can keep the boat?'' asked Virgil.

''Yes,'' said Dickerson. ''But that doesn't mean you make one run and back out. We have to obtain useful information, or it's no deal.''

''And who's to decide what is useful and what isn't?'' asked Virgil.

''We will,'' said Ames, with a grin.

''Wonderful,'' said Jack. ''Okay, what do we have to do?''

''We'd like you to take a week or two of training,'' said Dickerson.

''Training?'' said Virgil.

"Weapons, radio, scuba, explosives," said Ames. "That sort of thing."

"Oh, yeah," said Jack. "I remember. The boys in D.C. are really keen on having informants acting as liaison agents."

"Yes." Dickerson smiled. "Quite keen."

"Right," said Jack, giving Virgil a dour look. "What was it my father always said? Never volunteer for anything and always stand in the middle."

Jack and Virgil spent the remainder of the day with the "tourists." Dickerson and Ames took the *Ice Bucket* south past Cape Romano and Ten Thousand Islands, pointing out places frequented by the dopers. They provided Jack and Virgil with a detailed map of each location, the best escape routes from the sea marked in red.

They cruised by Lostman's River Patrol Station, which they were told would serve as a relay station should they get into any difficulties so far south of port. They continued on down the western coast of Florida, and Jack and Virgil became aware of the enormity of the problem of trying to stop the smugglers.

"Christ," said Jack, studying the coastline. "You could hide an army in there."

"You're right," said Dickerson. "There *is* an army in there."

"What?" said Virgil.

"The Cuban nationals have got quite a militia operating in there. Just a wild guess, but I think they're planning to invade Cuba. And I wouldn't want to be the guy to try to stop them."

"Training grounds?" asked Jack.

"Exactly," replied Dickerson, shaking his head in admiration. "If you can survive in there, you can survive anywhere."

The *Ice Bucket* continued its southerly heading, rolling past Shark Point and Ponce de Leon Bay.

"I thought this was all a National Park," said Virgil, pointing the length and breadth of the coastline.

"It is," said Ames. "Ask any Ranger if he wants to try to

apprehend a doper in a cigarette with an M-sixty machine gun mounted on the deck.''

"No," said Virgil, "guess he wouldn't."

The *Ice Bucket* rounded the Horn of Florida and kept heading south toward the Keys. About twelve miles due south of Flamingo, Dickerson brought the boat about.

"Here's where the mother ships will anchor," said Dickerson. "They'll work their way north from here. Might make as many as twenty drops before heading back into the Gulf and the return run to South America."

"You'll get to know the drop points as you work your way into the trade," said Ames. "They change the locations all the time to prevent capture, so there's no specific information we can give you concerning their movements."

"Don't rush yourselves once you get in. I mean, don't ask too many questions too soon," said Dickerson. "If you do ask any questions, ask something really stupid. Rookie questions, no specifics, everything strictly business."

"This group we're supposed to infiltrate," said Jack, "you must have some hunch as to who they might be."

"We're not sure," said Dickerson.

"The Cubans?" asked Jack.

"No, they wouldn't risk their cause by getting nailed in the cocaine trade. It's someone else. And we want to know what they're buying with all that money."

"Terrorists?" said Jack.

"No," said Dickerson. "They keep a very low profile, and we've had no threats, bombings, or kidnappings, that sort of thing."

"This is a wonderful group I'm with," mumbled Virgil.

"Then *what*?" said Jack.

"That's what we want you to find out," said Dickerson.

Jack and Virgil returned to port and left the "tourists" at the marina. Dickerson and Ames had said the arrangements were being made to have their docking fees and back boat payments made, and they could expect the first per diem check in a few days. No money would change hands. Their joint checking account would simply show a new balance.

Dickerson emphasized that there would be no further direct contact in public. He instructed Jack and Virgil to drive to Miami the following day and go to the airport. Tickets would be waiting for them at the Delta counter, and they were to pick them up and fly to their destination.

"And where the hell will that be?" asked Jack.

Dickerson had just smiled. "Enjoy yourselves, gentlemen," he said, leaving the dock. "We'll be in contact."

The drive to Miami the following day was passed in speculation. Jack and Virgil proposed one preposterous scheme after another, until even their vivid imaginations were exhausted.

Traffic was unusually heavy for a weekday, and Jack carefully nursed their backfiring Chevy through the cloverleafs where the interstate flowed into the airport. They parked their junker and took overnight bags with them inside the terminal.

"You know, I don't ever remember actually saying I was going to do this," said Virgil.

"We're doing it," said Jack. "We've got no choice."

"So, big deal. We lose the boat," said Virgil. "We could get regular jobs, save up some dough, and buy another one."

Jack stopped in the lobby of the Delta Terminal. "You know that liability lawyer friend of mine?"

"Whiplash Wally?" asked Virgil.

"The same," said Jack. "Well, he may be a crook, but he knows his stuff. He says if the Feds want to get shitty about that VA deal of yours, you could do two years and get a ten-thousand-dollar fine. How'd you like to work *that* off?"

"Guess I just volunteered," said Virgil.

"Right," said Jack. "It's this way."

"You know," said Virgil. "Those Federal guys got no sense of humor. Hell, you read all the time how the government loses millions on bombers that don't fly, graft, corruption, payoffs. And here they go getting shitty about a measly two grand. Man, I mean, we're Vets. Is that anyway to treat a veteran?"

Jack shook his head and grinned. He had always enjoyed

Virgil's misplaced sense of honor, ever since they had met, in Danang. At the time Virgil had been stealing ice from the Marines, a mission more deadly than taking the point in the Mekong Delta. Virgil had explained while Jack held open a duffel bag to cart the ice away. "Sure, the Marines've got it a lot tougher than the regular army sometimes, but ain't we over here defending truth, justice, and the American way too? And ain't that the same as capitalism? You gotta turn a buck somewhere. Hold the shovel while I get another bag."

Jack recalled how he and Virgil had kept in touch after ETS-ing out of Oakland upon their return to the States. Both had taken jobs in a plant that supplied parts for the Detroit auto industry. Frequent layoffs made them grow restless, and they applied for admission to a small college in northern Ohio.

They roomed together and spent the next four years playing football, drinking beer, and burning up their veterans' benefits. It was just an extended vacation, and Virgil loved every minute of it. He was a free spirit who was accepted by most of the collegiate cliques. From the freaks to the frats, Virgil always made friends.

Perhaps it was the larceny in his soul that made so many people like him. He was forever working up some mad scheme to make money, and if a few rules had to be bent in order to turn a profit, so much the better. From scalping rock 'n' roll tickets to silk-screening bootlegged T-shirts in his dorm room, Virgil always had some kind of action going. The scheme to rip off the VA he had considered his crowning achievement. Now it looked as if he was being given a penance for all his previous sins.

"Where do you think we're going?" asked Virgil.

"We've been over this a hundred times," said Jack. "Let's just get the tickets and go."

"Okay," said Virgil. "You know, this may not be such a bad deal after all. We make enough, hell, we could retire."

"Yeah," said Jack, stopping at the ticket counter. "It might just be permanent!"

"I don't like the sound of that," said Virgil.

"Name's Grigsby," said Jack to the ticket agent. "You're supposed to have two reservations booked for me and Mr. Fullenkamp."

"Yes," said the ticket agent, handing Jack the boarding passes. "You're to go to gate sixteen A. That's sixteen *A*. You understand?"

"Sure we understand," said Virgil. "We ain't stupid, you know."

"Have a pleasant trip," said the ticket agent, disappearing into an office behind the counter.

"What's the big deal about the gate?" said Virgil.

"I don't know," said Jack. "Let's go find out."

The finger of the Delta terminal angled out onto the tarmac. Jack and Virgil took the conveyor walk to save time. They passed stretch DC-9's, 747's, and DC-10's, yet when they reached gate sixteen A, it was empty.

"What is this?" asked Virgil. "We're on time, aren't we?"

Jack checked his watch. "Yeah, we're early. And this is the gate all right."

Virgil looked around. There were groups of passengers being boarded at all the surrounding gates, people dashing up and down the finger to make flights or beat the lines at the rental services. It was the normal airport hubbub, yet no one was at sixteen A. "Ah, somebody screwed up," said Virgil.

"Party of two?" came a voice from behind Jack and Virgil.

He was what the airline personnel called a Ramp Rat. A Bag Crusher par excellence. He wore Delta-issue everything, from his crushed cap, headset and shades down to his boots. Blue and white Delta corporate logos abounded. He pulled off his Delta gloves and stuffed them inside his Delta overalls. "You Grigsby and Fullenkamp?" he asked.

"Yeah," said Jack. "Who might you be?"

"Never mind," said the Ramp Rat. "This way, please."

Jack noticed the picture on the Ramp Rat's ID card. It looked strangely familiar. "Where are we going?" asked Jack.

The Ramp Rat pulled a half-smoked cigar out of his mouth and smiled. "Just follow me, fellas."

Jack and Virgil looked at each other. "Let's do what the man says," said Virgil.

"Lead on," said Jack.

The Ramp Rat took Jack and Virgil down the "flight personnel only" steps and through a door that led to a small operations office. There he opened a locker and pulled out two pair of mechanics' overalls. "Put these on," he said.

"What for?" asked Jack.

The Ramp Rat checked his Delta watch. "Hurry up, will ya, bud? We ain't got much time."

Virgil grabbed his overalls and pulled them over his sport coat and slacks. Jack did the same. The Ramp Rat pinned airport ID's on the both of them. Fictitious names, but their faces. "This way," said the Ramp Rat, handing headsets to Jack and Virgil.

They pulled the headsets on and followed the Ramp Rat out onto the tarmac. "Toss your bags on the cart, boys, and jump up in the tug," said the Ramp Rat.

Jack and Virgil did as they were told. The Ramp Rat fired up the engine and pulled the train of carts out to a stretch DC-9 being loaded on the tarmac. He pulled the train of carts up beside the DC-9 and backed it into place. "Okay, boys. Hop out and let's get her loaded up."

Jack and Virgil looked at each other with confused expressions. "Let's go," said Virgil. "We might learn something."

Jack and Virgil got out of the tug and trotted around to the carts, where other Ramp Rats were loading bags into the forward and aft cargo bins. None of the other men paid any attention.

"You boys jump up there in bin number one and start crushin' bags," said the Ramp Rat.

"Do what?" said Virgil.

"Get in the bin, dummies," said the Ramp Rat, "and just stuff them bags in the best way you can."

Jack and Virgil obliged. They found the confines of the cargo bin cramped and had to squat, coolie-like. They had finished loading the last of the bags when they saw the Ramp Rat reach up to the top of the cargo hatch and trip the inside door. "Enjoy the trip, fellers," he said, dropping and latching the door.

"Hey!" roared Jack. "What the hell are you doing?"

Virgil started kicking the hatch and bellowing at the top of his lungs. Suddenly the hatch swung open. "What the hell are you doing, stupid?" snapped the Ramp Rat. "You want to scare the passengers to death?"

"Let me out of here, you sawed-off bastard," said Jack, stiff-arming the Ramp Rat away from the hatch.

"You better get back in there," he said, pulling off his Delta sunglasses.

Jack stared at the Ramp Rat. "Say, aren't you—"

"Ames, FBI," said the Ramp Rat. "Dickerson's partner. Remember?"

"Oh, yeah," said Jack.

"You want to climb back inside?" asked Ames, pushing his shades in place.

"Okay," said Jack. "I guess so."

"Now, it'll be all right," said Ames. "I'll have the captain turn on the air and the lights. Hell, the airlines ship guys out of here like this all the time. By mistake, of course. Hang on a second. We got some more stuff to load."

Ames ducked out of the hatch and returned with four cardboard boxes with mesh screen covering one side. He tossed them in the bin with Jack and Virgil and grabbed the inside hatch once again.

Jack caught a whiff of the stench coming from the cardboard boxes. "Jesus," he said, covering his mouth and nose, "what the hell is in there?"

"Laboratory rats," said Ames. "Don't worry," he continued, "They won't hurt you. It's the raw potatoes they put in the boxes for them to feed on that stink. But you'll get used to that. Have a nice flight," he said, closing the inside hatch.

Jack and Virgil listened as the outer hatch was sealed. They were plunged into darkness, and groped about in the black.

Ames connected his headset to the female plug in the side of the jet's fuselage. He contacted the flight engineer and told him to turn on the pressure and lights in bin number one. The engineer complied, and Jack and Virgil let their eyes adjust to the dim utility lights.

"Ugh, that smell," said Jack, still cupping his hand over his mouth. "That's awful."

Just then the bin began to pressurize. Jets of fresh air were pumped in, and Virgil and Jack pushed their faces toward the relief. The jet fired up its engines and began to taxi out toward the main runway. Jack and Virgil crawled around and braced themselves for takeoff.

"What *is* this?" said Virgil. "Coach economy class?"

"Shut up," said Jack, piling up some mail bags to sit on. "It could have been worse."

"How could it have been worse?" asked Virgil.

"They could have taped us to the wing," said Jack.

"Don't give them any ideas," said Virgil.

During the flight Jack and Virgil bounced around with the baggage. The laboratory rats went into fits every time the plane hit an air pocket. Jack and Virgil found that the best way to ride was lying on their backs with their feet pressed against the ceiling of the bin. This prevented them from bouncing around like the luggage. The flight lasted a little over an hour, with touchdown bringing a relief from the stowaway passengers.

The cargo bin doors opened, and another Delta Ramp Rat awaited them. "Have a nice flight?" he asked.

"Marvelous," said Jack, easing his stiff body out of the cargo bin.

Virgil followed, and both took to stretching their cramped muscles on the tarmac.

"You'll have to help us unload the flight," said the Ramp Rat.

"Why not," said Jack, pulling the boxes of laboratory rats out of the bin. "Did you have a nice flight?" Jack said to the rats.

"Wonderful," said Virgil, grabbing luggage and tossing it onto the waiting carts.

With the plane unloaded, Virgil and Jack hopped into another tug. This time their destination was not the terminal but the freight center.

"Where the hell are we?" said Virgil.

Jack tapped Virgil on the shoulder and pointed to the sign above the freight building. SAVANNAH GA. FREIGHT, it read.

"Savannah? What the hell are we doing in Savannah?" asked Virgil.

The Ramp Rat didn't say anything. He just smiled, pulled up behind the freight building, and told Jack and Virgil to get out. "Gotta go now," he said. "Passengers get pretty pissed if they don't get their bags right away."

The Ramp Rat, towing his train of luggage carts, drove back to the main terminal, leaving Jack and Virgil alone behind the freight building.

"Now what?" said Jack, picking up their bags.

"How the hell should I know?" said Virgil.

The UH-1 "Huey" helicopter came in low over the trees and hovered above the tarmac next to the freight building. Jack and Virgil covered their faces to shield them from the wash of its rotors and turned their backs as the pilot set the chopper down. The man who dropped out of the side doors was all too familiar. It was Dickerson of the FBI.

"You boys have a nice flight?"

"Swell," said Jack. "Just swell, smartass."

"Yeah," said Virgil, unzipping his Delta overalls. "Why couldn't we fly with the other passengers?"

"Couldn't risk you boys being seen moving about by regular channels," said Dickerson. "Your destination had to remain classified. Follow me, please."

"Sure," said Jack. "Where else are we going to go?"

"Home would be nice," quipped Virgil.

The trio boarded the chopper and lifted off. Jack and Virgil were seated on one side, and Dickerson opposite. "Where are we going?" asked Jack.

"You'll see," said Dickerson.

"Oh, boy," said Jack, "another surprise."

Virgil looked around the Huey. "Kinda brings back old memories," he said thinking about the dust-offs in Vietnam.

"Yeah," said Jack. "All of them bad!"

The Huey flew north-northeast out of the Savannah airport. They hadn't been in the air more than thirty minutes, when their pilot began his descent. Jack peered out the side window and became wide-eyed at his discovery. "Holy shit!" he said. "Is that what I think it is?"

"Good God, I think you're right," said Virgil.

The Huey set down at the heliport, and Grigsby and Fullenkamp leveled looks that could kill at the man from the FBI.

Dickerson smiled. "Enjoy your stay here on Parris Island," he said. "You'll find it most informative."

"You dirty sonofa—"

"Temper, temper, gentlemen," continued Dickerson. "We don't expect you'll have to remain here more than a few days. That is, if you cooperate. But then the Marines know a few things about cooperation. I sincerely hope you won't give them any trouble."

"We're not going to give them any trouble, wise guy. But you just made the top of my shit list!"

"Yeah," said Virgil. "You're underlined on mine."

"Your drill instructor is waiting," said Dickerson, pointing out the door of the Huey.

"God, I hate Marines," said Jack, stepping out of the chopper.

"Me too," said Virgil. "Almost as much as I hate Dickerson."

"Well, if it isn't two of the army's worst," said the tall black noncom.

"Semper, fuck you," said Jack.

The DI bristled. "All right, now that we understand each other, let's get one thing straight. If either of you fuckups foul up during any phase of training, the Justice Department is going to fry your young butts. You got that?"

"Yeah, we got that," said Virgil.

"Then let's not waste any time. The sooner I get you trained, the quicker you get outta here. Follow me."

"What do we do with the overalls?" said Jack, sweating under the extra clothing.

"Take them off," said the DI. "But hang on to them. You'll need them for the return trip."

"Wonderful," said Virgil. "First-class accommodations going home too."

"My name is Sergeant Smith," said the DI.

Jack noticed that he wasn't wearing a name tag. "Sure, whatever you say."

Jack and Virgil followed Sergeant Smith to a nearby jeep. They tossed the overalls and their bags in the back and climbed aboard.

"What we're going to give you is a refresher course in weaponry," said the sergeant. "Sharpen you up."

They drove to a remote section of the Parris Island Complex, passing platoon after platoon of recruits going through the rigorous physical training required of the Corps. Jack watched the young recruits and thought back to a time when it was he who was sweating on the physical training field.

Jack remembered the constricting feeling of being forced into a situation he could neither control nor escape, that nightmare of being trapped that used to haunt his sleep. The feeling was returning, perhaps stronger than ever, and Jack's stomach began to turn.

On they drove, passing the propaganda billboards that dotted the compound. Each billboard portrayed Marines in heroic charges or bayonetting Orientals, with graphic emphasis placed on gore.

It was all coming back to Jack now. Only the places had changed. Instead of trying to stay alive in the mud of the Mekong Delta, it would be the swamps of southern Florida. And there were no options, no way out. The government was still calling all the shots. Jack swore a silent oath. This would be the last time the authorities would use him. He'd jump to their tune just this once more, but God help the bastard who ever tried to draft him again.

The jeep pulled to a stop at a small rifle range on the seaward side of Parris Island. There the sergeant instructed Jack and Virgil to get out of the jeep and accompany him to the firing line. The sergeant disappeared into a concrete ordnance bunker and reappeared, carrying three peculiar weapons. They looked similar to .45-caliber pistols, though they were obviously more sophisticated.

"What are these?" asked Jack.

"These are Big Mack Attacks," said the sergeant. "More properly a MAC 11/9. Little brother to the old Ingram M-10. Nasty little weapon. Fires nine hundred rounds of three-eighty ammunition per minute. Punch a hole in a concrete wall if necessary."

"Marines don't use these things," said Virgil.

"Some of them do," said the sergeant. "Counterterrorist forces use a variety of weapons. Uzi's, Macks, Rugers; even AK-47's. Plus a variety of explosives. You're gonna get a crash course in all of it."

"Let's start shooting," said Jack.

"Not so fast," said the sergeant. "Here's how they break down. There's not much to them. Fewer moving parts than your old M-16," continued the sergeant, breaking the MAC-11 down.

Virgil and Jack tore down their weapons in the same manner. When they had reassembled the components, the Sergeant produced an odd accessory. A Cobray "Sonics" suppressor. It was nearly as long as the weapon itself.

"These might come in handy," said the sergeant. "Won't cut the muzzle velocity too much and quiets the weapon down to a whisper."

"We going to get to fire these things?" asked Jack impatiently.

"We'll begin on semi-automatic," said the sergeant.

For the next hour Jack and Virgil got used to the ultra-lightweight weapon. They learned how to retract its collapsible stock, and dealt with the thirty-two–shot plastic magazine. They fired at silhouette targets and hungered to release the weapon's awesome firepower. The sergeant finally allowed them a few bursts, and they cut down one target after another in a hail of lead.

Jack and Virgil spent the remainder of the day firing the MAC-11 from a variety of positions, learning how to load and fire the weapon in the least amount of time, and mastering the function of the suppressor. By the end of the day, firing the MAC-11 had become quite boring. Jack and Virgil longed for a trip into town, some steak and ale, and a good night's rest at a three-star motel. What they got was a meal carried out of the mess hall, and a night alone in an abandoned barracks.

The following morning the sergeant took Jack and Virgil to another firing line. This firing line was unique, nothing like the shooting galleries they had trained on prior to their shipping out to Vietnam. This firing range was set entirely on the water.

The jeep stopped at the end of a wharf. The sergeant got out and climbed down into a waiting swift boat, the kind that used to operate in and around the Mekong Delta. He took MAC-11's from the skipper and dropped out of the swift boat into a thirty-foot cigarette moored nearby. "Get in," he shouted.

Jack and Virgil came down the wharf, climbed down into the swift boat and over into the cigarette. "Now comes the hard part of your training," said the sergeant. "Here, you'd better put these on."

The sergeant handed Jack and Virgil life jackets, crash helmets, and Marine deck shoes. They donned the equipment as the sergeant fired up the engines of the cigarette. The sergeant led out first and the swift boat followed after. They ran about a thousand yards off shore, then changed their course for the run through the firing range.

The swift boat moved down range. "Only one of you will fire on each pass we make," said the sergeant. "You are to stand on the afterdeck and fire in short bursts at the targets as they pass by our starboard beam. Take care with your trigger finger. If you lose your footing, take your finger off the trigger. I don't want you yo-yo's shootin' holes in the boat.''

"Where are the targets?'' asked Jack.

"The swift boat is towing them," said the sergeant. "And take care you don't shoot the swift boat. The captain is just likely to shoot back!''

The sergeant brought the cigarette around. Now he lay at one end of the range, and the swift boat at the other. Jack and Virgil donned speed goggles provided by the sergeant, and the boats began to make their runs toward each other.

The cigarette lifted out of the water as its engines thundered to life. They raced across the water at breakneck pace as they closed on the swift boat.

"You fire first," bellowed Jack over the roar of the cigarette's engines. "I'll spot you. Make sure you don't fall.''

"That's the idea," said the sergeant. "Buddy up.''

Virgil stood up. The wind and the wash off the bow of the cigarette made it difficult to see. He braced his knee against the starboard gunnels and brought the MAC-11 to prefire position, barrel pointed skyward.

The swift boat and the cigarette blew past each other. Their crisscrossing wakes blasted against the bows, and Virgil was nearly tossed overboard. Only Jack's hand, clenched around Virgil's belt, kept him from going over the side.

"Fire!'' bellowed the sergeant.

Virgil let go with a burst. Lead poured out of the MAC-11. Hot shell casings flew into Jack's face as he held on to Virgil's belt. The target being towed by the swift boat flew past Virgil in a yellow blur. The MAC-11 was already empty when the target passed. "Nice shot!'' yelled the sergeant. "Okay, big guy. You think you can do any better?''

"Bring her about," bellowed Jack. "We'll get the hang of this yet.''

"I doubt it,'' said the sergeant.

The cigarette and the swift boat set up for another pass. Jack stood up, took the smoking MAC-11 from Virgil, and shoved in a fresh magazine. The boats came up to speed and Jack readied himself. He too braced against the gunnels, but he crouched low, so that his knees would act as shock absorbers when the boats' wakes crisscrossed.

The wash off the bow of the cigarette pelted Jack's face with droplets of water, which beaded on his speed goggles and partially obscured his vision. Jack picked up the rhythm of the boat's bow as it bounced over the waves, and let his legs soak up the undulations until he was able to hold his weapon almost motionless. Jack flicked off the safety on the M-11 as the swift boat bore down on him for its passing run.

The swift boat barreled past the cigarette. This time Virgil had to keep both of them from going overboard. Jack cut loose with the MAC-11. He sprayed the sea in front of him but completely missed the target. "Christ, we're gonna be out here all day," groaned the sergeant.

"Bring it around again!" bellowed Jack. "I'll blow that thing out of the water or know why not!"

The sergeant obliged. The boats made pass after pass until Jack and Virgil had mastered the timing and agility necessary to stand up on the stern of a boat moving at seventy miles an hour, hold a gun on a target moving at twice that speed in the opposite direction, and dump the entire clip of MAC-11 ammunition on bull's-eye.

The sergeant was indeed impressed. "Hell," he said, "I figured we'd have to be out here at least three days. You saved Uncle Sam a whole lot on fuel and ammunition."

"Thanks," said Jack. "What's next?"

"Couple days' training on explosives and counterterrorist tactics."

"Counterterrorist tactics?" said Virgil.

"Gentlemen, I don't know what the FBI wants you to do. I was just told to give you training in specific areas. Now, let's make a few more passes while we still have some daylight."

The next two days Virgil and Jack spent with the sergeant learning the mysteries of C-4 plastic explosive. The dos and especially the don'ts. Most of it was a review, for both had become extremely adept at the uses of C-4 during their tour in Vietnam.

The counterterrorist training was an all-new and gruesomely fascinating experience most of which concerned motivation and negotiation with the various groups. It was not the shoot-first-and-ask-questions-later tactics Jack and Virgil had expected, but subtle, psychological diplomacy. Sergeant Smith doubted they would employ negotiations in their dealings for the FBI, but he gave them the instruction just the same.

By the end of their three days of training, Jack and Virgil had gained a good measure of respect for the DI and the Marines in general.

"Thanks for everything," said Jack, shaking Sergeant Smith's hand. "If you're ever in Naples, stop at the Wharf Rat. We'll show you a good time."

"I'd like that," said the sergeant, watching the pair board the helicopter for the flight back to Savannah. "Hey!" he said as they were closing the door of the Huey.

"Yeah?" said Jack.

"Try not to get killed," said the sergeant, with a broad grin.

The Huey took off before Jack could respond.

Chapter Four

THE ROOKIE RUN

JACK AND Virgil arrived behind the Savannah freight terminal again and were driven back to an awaiting DC-9. They took up their dubious accommodations in the forward cargo bin and waited for takeoff.

The return flight was longer than expected, and touchdown did not bring an immediate opening of the cargo bin doors.

"Do you think they forgot about us?" asked Virgil.

"They'd better not," said Jack, giving the hatch a few swift kicks.

Still, no one opened the hatch. The DC-9 wasn't on the ground more than fifteen minutes before it was airborne again. Another twenty minutes passed and the plane began its descent.

"Now where the hell are we?" asked Virgil.

"How should I know, Hiawatha?" said Jack.

The jet taxied up to a small terminal. A man dressed in the conservative black suit of Delta supervisory personnel walked out to guide the jet into its berth. He signaled the captain to cut his engines, and he went to the forward cargo bin. There he opened the hatch and peered inside.

"I should have known," said Jack, recognizing the Delta supervisor.

"Me too," said Virgil. "Hey, Agent Dickerson," he continued, "where the hell are we?"

"Welcome to Key West," said Agent Dickerson.

"Key West?" said Jack. "What are we going to do down here?"

Dickerson smiled. "Trust me, gentlemen," he said. "You'll enjoy it."

" 'Trust me,' he says," said Virgil. "Trust you my ass."

"This way, gentlemen," said Dickerson, climbing into a nearby tug.

They drove across the tarmac to a remote part of the Key West Airport. Another helicopter was waiting for them, this one belonging to the Navy.

"Oh, hot damn," said Jack, boarding the chopper. "They're going to make us swabbies."

The chopper set down inside Key West Naval Air Station, and Dickerson drove them to a small training center. The center was located on the eastern side of the Key, with a magnificent view of the sea. The view of their instructor was even more magnificent.

She was a redhead, tall, and wearing a vest wet suit with the zipper open down to the cleft in her breasts. Her naval-regulation-length hair blew in the early-morning breeze, and she stood with her hands on her hips, eyeing the new arrivals with some disdain.

"This is Lieutenant Shively," said Dickerson. "She will complete the final phases of your training."

"More like Lieutenant Shapely," mumbled Virgil to Jack.

"I heard that," said the lieutenant. "Any more smart remarks and I'll dump you out in the Gulf, and you can swim home."

"Feisty, isn't she?" said Jack.

"Yeah," said Virgil. "Maybe she'll teach us how to wrestle."

"Good luck," said Dickerson, walking toward the chopper. "See you in a few days."

"Listen up, you clowns," said Lieutenant Shively. "I'm in charge here. You mess up once and I turn in a bad report. Do we understand each other?"

"Damn," said Virgil. "Hard-hearted Hannah."

"This way, gentlemen," said the lieutenant. "I don't want to waste any more time."

Jack and Virgil followed Lieutenant Shively to a nearby jeep. They boarded the Navy-gray vehicle for a short ride to the base swimming pool. The pool was deserted, and Lieutenant Shively took masks, snorkels, and swim fins out of the jeep and tossed them to Jack and Virgil.

"You can change in the locker room over there," said the lieutenant.

"Some dish," said Virgil, walking beside Jack.

"Yeah," replied Jack, though his thoughts were elsewhere.

"What's wrong?" asked Virgil.

"Nothing," said Jack.

Jack and Virgil entered the locker room and found black naval-issue swimsuits of all sizes. They slipped out of their civvies and into supporters and swimsuits. As the two men dressed, Jack's thoughts drifted back to the Wharf Rat and Domino.

Jack thought about the night they had spent on the beach. The way Domino's face appeared, bathed in the light from the fire. Her smile. The long looks they exchanged. How she felt when he pulled her on top of him. Of all that blue-black hair as it cascaded down the sides of his face while they kissed. He could almost feel his hands on her again. The soft flesh at the back of her thighs. . . .

"Come on," said Virgil. "Lieutenant Shapely is waiting!"

"Yeah," said Jack. "Go on ahead. I'll join you in a minute."

Virgil left the locker room and hurried outside. Jack remained with his thoughts. Domino still commanded his mind, but the restrictions of his involvement with the FBI tainted the vision.

Jack wondered if he could handle being involved with Domino and still maintain the high level of concentration necessary to survive the ordeal that lay ahead. Jack came to a decision quickly. He would be a fool to lose Domino. Thoughts of her would not confuse his thinking but sharpen it. Jack's lifestyle of late had been simple. No involvement, no pain. But no feeling either. Now he would have a reason to persevere, to survive. And Domino would be the impetus, the driving force behind him.

Jack started outside, then stopped and smiled. A newfound confidence welled up inside of him. He thought about it a moment. It wasn't overconfidence. He still felt smothered by his situation and concerned over what lay ahead, but now there was a goal to achieve. And no one, not the FBI or the dopers, could keep Jack from attaining his goal. And his goal was Domino!

Virgil Fullenkamp flew ass-over-elbow into the pool. His resounding splash brought Jack Grigsby back to reality.

"You try that again, wise guy, and you'll get even worse," said Lieutenant Shively.

"I'll give you a three on the dive," said Jack, "and nothing for your entry into the water."

"Watch out, Jack," said Virgil. "She's a purely dangerous person," he continued, climbing out of the pool.

"Look, you guys," said Lieutenant Shively. "I don't like this assignment any more than you do. So let's try to get along while you're here."

"That's what I was tryin' to do, Lieutenant," said Virgil.

"Put a lid on it, will you," said Jack with a grin.

"During training, yes," said Virgil, striking a comical leer, "but later this evening at dinner—watch out!"

Now even Lieutenant Shively had to suppress a grin. "Into the water," she said. "We'll start your scuba training right away."

For the remainder of the day Jack and Virgil got a crash course in scuba-diving. They began with snorkeling, learning how to clear their masks underwater and develop the controlled breathing necessary to come up from depth without contracting the bends.

By the end of the day, Shively had them donning tanks and taking a swim around the pool. She was genuinely impressed with their progress. They learned remarkably fast, and by the end of the session, she felt confident enough to let them take a dive inside the training tank in an adjacent building of the training center.

Jack and Virgil descended with Shively to a depth of fifty feet. There they remained for ten minutes while Shively reviewed the underwater hand signals she had taught them. At the end of the ten-minute dive, she brought them up and went through a mock decompression run. The session ended with their surfacing and swimming to the side of the tank.

"Did we pass, Teach?" asked Virgil.

"Don't get cocky, wise guy," said Shively. "You can easily drown in a tank like this."

"What's next?" said Jack, climbing out of the tank and slipping out of his aqualung.

"You'll get some training in high-speed navigation," said the lieutenant.

"High-speed navigation?" said Virgil. "Hell, lady, we own a boat!"

"Not like the one you'll be operating for your work with the FBI," said Shively.

"And who's gonna give us this training?" said Jack.

"I am," said the lieutenant.

"*You* are?" chorused Jack and Virgil.

"Damn right I am," said the lieutenant, somewhat piqued. "Mr. Dickerson will be bringing the boat down tomorrow. Follow me. I'll show you where you sleep."

"Hopefully with you," mumbled Virgil.

"Don't push it, fella."

The naval accommodations were hardly more glamorous than those that the Marines had provided. Virgil spent the night flopping about the top bunk, lost amid his nasty fantasies. Each time he made love to Lieutenant Shapely, a chorus of groans echoed off the empty barracks walls.

Jack didn't sleep well. It wasn't Virgil's moaning that kept him awake but the bargain they had struck with the FBI. Jack knew they were in over their heads. Granted, the training and expertise both he and Virgil had acquired in Vietnam would give them an edge, but would it be enough?

Jack tossed for over an hour before drifting off. His dreams were a mass of confused visions. One moment he was surviving a fusillade of bullets from some dopers, and the very next he was lost in the ecstasy of Domino's embrace. It was a recurring set of dreams that would haunt Jack for some time to come.

The morning dawned with cirrus clouds billowing in off the Gulf. Virgil's most erotic fantasy was interrupted by Lieutenant Shively shoving him out of his bunk.

"Good morning, gorgeous," said Virgil.

"I can see you're in rare form this morning," said Lieutenant Shively, noticing the bulge in Virgil's shorts.

Virgil shrugged. "It's got a mind of its own."

"Hit the deck," she said. "I want you two in and out of the mess hall before the regular cadre arrives."

"Yes, Lieutenant Shapely," said Virgil, watching her walk out of the barracks.

"You'd better watch how you mouth off to that broad," said Jack.

"Why?" asked Virgil.

"She's liable to clean your clock," said Jack, pulling on his faded stovepipe jeans.

"Promises, promises," said Virgil.

Navy chow was no different from Marine. Not bad. Virgil had his usual voracious appetite. Jack picked at his food, still plagued by thoughts of what lay ahead.

Lieutenant Shively accompanied them down to the dock, where Dickerson was already waiting. "Good morning," he said.

"How're you doing?" said Jack.

"Got something for you," said Dickerson, pointing to the end of the dock.

It was one of those boats Jack had passed up before they had bought the *Ice Bucket*. A hundred grand easily, thought Jack as he walked down the dock to inspect the sea blue catamaran.

"Picked this up just last week," said Dickerson. "Helluva nice boat. Here, let me give you the specifications."

"Damn!" said Virgil, raising his eyebrows to Jack. "Nice rig, huh?"

"Yeah," said Jack, momentarily enthralled with the appearance of the catamaran. "Damn nice boat."

"Its centerline overall length is thirty-nine feet two inches," Dickerson began. "She only drafts about eighteen inches. Got a cruising range of about two hundred miles. You'll be at home in the open sea as well as the swamps, although I wouldn't take it too deep into the Everglades. Props will foul, and you'll end up rowing home."

"What about power plants?" asked Virgil.

"She's got two standard five hundred and forty-horse Mercruisers, both of 'em beefed up. With the modifications, the engines should rate over seven hundred horses each. At red line you'll pull an even fourteen hundred."

"Holy mackerel," said Virgil.

"That's right," said Dickerson. "I wouldn't open this thing up until you're comfortable with her feel. She rips from zero to seventy without even breathing hard."

Virgil watched Lieutenant Shively slip out of her uniform, under which she wore a modest one-piece tank suit. She pulled on a life vest and crash helmet, and climbed aboard the catamaran.

"Let's go on board," said Dickerson. "The department authorized some special modifications to the boat you should know about."

Virgil and Jack donned their life jackets and carried their crash helmets as they climbed aboard.

"We cut back on the boat's fuel capacity to allow for the armor plating. It's a new ultralight alloy, product of the space program. We've had it inserted at key locations about the boat, around the fuel cells, and have had wafer walls constructed about the passenger area. It'll stop a rocket-propelled grenade."

"Wonderful," said Jack. "And what are we supposed to

shoot back with if we take fire like that? Those peashooters we trained with on Parris Island?''

"Hardly," said Dickerson. "Those are your personal weapons. You'll carry them at all times during any transactions you make with the dopers. We have had something entirely different installed for use on the catamaran.''

Dickerson walked aft and hit a trip latch near the stern. Up popped a familiar weapon, an M-60 machine gun. "There's another one mounted forward," he said. "I think you know how to use them.''

"He knows how to use 'em," said Virgil. "Saved my bacon more than once with one of those things. At a thousand yards, he'll lay down a pattern so tight you wouldn't believe it.''

"Good," said Dickerson. "But I don't want you getting trigger-happy just because you've got all this firepower.''

"I know what I'm doing," said Jack.

"Look, Grigsby," said Dickerson. "I know you've got little respect for authority. You think everyone in a position of power is a goddamned idiot. But there are a few of us who know what we're doing, and all I'm trying to do is keep you from getting your ass shot off!''

"Sorry," said Jack. "Didn't mean to act so high and mighty.''

"Now, I've checked your service records," said Dickerson. "Pretty colorful 201 files. Couple of heavyweight commendations, and not those medals the army issued for publicity. The real thing—bona fide heros.''

"Ah, cut the crap," said Jack. "What's this all about?''

"What I'm driving at, Grigsby, is that you guys were good. Really good. Now you've got a chance to do good again. Do something worthwhile.''

"Oh, well, let's hear it for Mom, apple pie, and the flag," said Virgil.

"Hey, wise guy," said Dickerson. "You can make sport of this all you want. To you this little escapade represents beating a stretch in the slammer and picking up a lot of dough. The department looks at in an entirely different perspective.''

"And what might that be?" asked Jack.

"Our goal is to nail the ruthless bastards who are running white poison," said Dickerson. "I really don't care about the pot; it's the cocaine that's the killer. Now, we could stand here all day and debate the ethics of drug use, but I've seen what cocaine can do, and there's no such thing as recreational use. It's poison. I want the traffic stopped. And I want you to help me do it."

Jack thought for a moment. He knew Dickerson's description of his attitude was correct, yet he hated to put any trust in the guy. Jack had been burned by too many West Point grads who called artillery fire in on their own positions to rely on credentials anymore. Still, Dickerson was more candid than any field commander he'd known in Vietnam.

"All right," said Jack. "We'll cooperate. But you'd better tell us everything we need to know. I don't want any of that top-secret shit. You keep us in the dark about something we should know about, and mister, I'll beat the living hell out of you."

"We understand each other," said Dickerson. "Now let's take this new boat out for a trial run."

Lieutenant Shively fired up the engines. The Cyclone Mercruisers rumbled to life, and Virgil was enthralled by the thought of commanding such awesome power. Jack cast off and pushed the bow of the catamaran away from the dock before leaping on board.

The lieutenant guided the boat out of the docks and took a northeasterly heading along Sugarloaf Key toward Loggerhead.

"Better put your crash helmets and goggles on," said Dickerson. "You guys ride up front with Lieutenant Shively. I'll be in back, in the rumble seat."

Jack watched Dickerson strap himself in aft, then took up a position in the starboard contour couch. Virgil climbed in the port couch, beside Shively, who stood centerships.

"This is a USA thirty-nine *Blue Water* Catamaran," shouted Shively over the roar of the engines, "designed by the same guy that came up with the idea for the cigarette. Only these are even faster. The hull design is such that the boat rides on a cushion of air, somewhat similar to a hydroplane.''

"What's the top speed?" shouted Virgil.

"She'll do a hundred and forty in a pinch, but she will handle poorly at that speed. Run all day at a hundred."

"Hot damn!" said Virgil.

"Your instrumentation is a mix of standard marine and space-age technology," said Lieutenant Shively. "Your trim, throttles, and tach are here. Z–two thousand satellite navigational system and VHF radio. We've also installed radar and sonar. Your antenna is forward. Take care you don't tear it off when you run in the swamps."

"What, no TV?" said Virgil.

"All right," said Shively. "Let me show you what she can do."

The lieutenant eased the throttles forward and the bows of the catamaran came up out of the water. Jack watched the tachometer as the needle eased upward until it registered 5,800 rpm's.

"The boat will handle like a sports car with rack-and-pinion steering, so watch your oversteer," said Shively, gently moving the wheel of the catamaran back and forth. "If you run into heavy seas, one of you will drive while the other monitors the throttles. You take too much air on a jump and the engines will bury the tach and probably blow."

"Isn't she wonderful?" said Virgil.

"Now I'll demonstrate evasive tactics," said Shively, pushing the throttles forward.

Jack watched the tachometer. They were now running at 6,200 rpm, and the only things still in the water were the boat's transom and the props.

A fine froth blew off the bows as Shively ran a zigzag course up the coast of Sugarloaf Key. Jack and Virgil stood on Shively's left and right as she maneuvered the boat into the wakes of the current, causing the catamaran to leap out of the water, taking fifty- and hundred-foot airborne bounces at a jump. She expertly rode the throttles so the engines did not damage themselves, then brought the boat back on its north-easterly heading.

"I'm going to show you some hot-dogging," said the lieutenant with a grin. "Now suppose you've got some clown on your behind and you want to ditch him fast."

They were running right at a hundred miles an hour when Shively began her maneuver. "Hang on!" she screamed.

Shively whipped the wheel hard to port, set her trim, then rammed the throttles on max. Fourteen hundred horses reared to life and the catamaran came about inside a distance equivalent to three times its own length. Virgil and Jack fought the foot-pounds of inertia and grabbed the sides of their couches in a death grip. Shively simply rode the momentum, as though she were part of the boat, and let the wheel snap back to reverse their previous course.

"Jesus Christ!" said Virgil.

"That's about as tight a turn as you can make," said Shively.

"Any tighter and you'd lose your teeth," said Jack.

"Okay, fellas," said Lieutenant Shively, "it's your turn."

Virgil took command first, and he showed a knack for handling the catamaran. He had piloted offshore power boats before and kept up on the exploits of Rocky Aoki. But never had he experienced such power. The engines had a way of pulsing the deck beneath his feet. The throb of the pounding pistons charged Virgil with rush after rush of adrenaline.

Virgil took the catamaran closer to shore. Here the water was dotted with sand bars, which made navigation dangerous. Virgil cut back his power and kept a wary hand on the trim. Lieutenant Shively was impressed with his marine savvy. She monitored his progress and made only passing remarks concerning his seamanship.

Virgil's sun-blond hair trailed out the back of his crash helmet and into the wind wake of the catamaran. He chewed on the ends of his zapata mustache as he angled the boat onto a new heading.

Lieutenant Shively saw the line Virgil was taking and pounded him on the shoulder. "Break it off!" she shouted.

"Don't worry, lady," said Virgil. "I know what I'm doing. Now let me show you how I peel barnacles off the bow and bastards off my ass!"

Virgil took the catamaran on a collision course for a sand bar. He upped his speed, set his trim, and bore down on the sand bar dead ahead.

The catamaran came up out of the water, riding on a cushion of air, and flew up onto the sand bar. The props rode safely on a level with the transom as the boat streaked up a ridge of sand and became airborne. There was a feeling of momentary weightlessness just before the catamaran began to nose over.

The catamaran cut a splash wake as it reentered the ocean. Virgil dropped his trim and rode his throttles to prevent the boat from losing momentum. "You can keep that one-hundred-and-eighty-degree-about jazz," said Virgil. "I want some clown off my ass and I'll take him out *my* way!"

"Do what you want, then," said Shively. "Okay, Grigsby, you're next."

"The hell with driving," said Jack, popping the aft M-60. "Virgil will do the driving, I'll do the gunning."

"Suppose Virgil gets hurt," said Shively.

"If he gets hurt, it'll be because I'm not doing my job," said Jack. "Virgil," he continued, "bring this thing around and make another run at that sand bar."

"Aye-aye, sir," said Virgil. "Hang on!" he bellowed, matching Shively's high-speed turn but in a third less the distance.

Shively was caught off balance and nearly lost her footing. She reached out and grabbed Virgil by the arm.

"Later, baby," said Virgil, continuing his maneuver.

"Why, you impertinent—"

"Make a strafing run!" shouted Jack, pulling back the bolt on the M-60.

"Roger," said Virgil. "Take you in at five hundred yards."

The catamaran flew across the ocean. The water turned into an aquamarine blur. The wind no longer brushed past them; it tore at their skin and billowed pocket parachutes in their clothes.

Jack stood on the aft deck next to the mount of the M-60. A belt of 7.62 ammunition snaked out of the hatch below the weapon's mount. Jack drew down on the sand bar and let go with burst after burst.

Agent Dickerson watched with open-mouthed awe. The patterns Jack laid down were incredibly tight. Fifteen rounds a burst, at one-second intervals. Shell casings littered the deck as Jack tore up the shores of the sand bar.

"That'll do it," said Jack, clearing the weapon.

Virgil eased off the throttles. "Can this guy shoot or can he shoot?"

"Yes," said Dickerson. "It would seem you've both had enough training. Think you can find your way back to the Naval Station?"

"Ace Navigator, at your service," said Virgil.

On the return trip, Jack and Virgil were given instructions as to the operation of the boat's radar and sonar. The devices were the latest in microcircuitry, and ridiculously simple to operate.

Virgil brought the catamaran back to the docks at Key West Naval Air Station, where Lieutenant Shively and Dickerson departed. "You're on your own," said Dickerson.

"What?" said Virgil.

"Take the boat through the Keys, up the coast, and back to Naples," said Dickerson.

"But what about our first run?" asked Jack. "When do we make it? Where do we go?"

"Agent Ames and I will be in contact with you," said Dickerson. "We'll use the Wharf Rat as a meeting place. It's usually crowded, so we should be able to blend in with the mob."

"Okay," said Jack. "When do we meet you?"

"In two days," said Dickerson. "The Wharf Rat is always busy on Saturday night."

"How will we find you?"

"We'll find you," said Dickerson, waving them off.

"Good luck," said Lieutenant Shively.

"Thanks," said Jack. "We're gonna need it."

Cody Carnes was not thrilled with the idea of watching the Wharf Rat while Jack and Virgil took Domino for a spin in their newly acquired boat. "You watch out," Cody said to Domino. "Those two bums are up to something."

Jack and Domino ambled down the dock, heading for the catamaran. Virgil and Maggie Donohue walked ahead of them.

"Are you sure you want to do this?" asked Domino.

"Not really," said Jack.

Domino's look of concern bothered Jack. "Oh, hell!" he said. "We'll be all right. Come on. Let's go look at the boat."

Domino reluctantly followed Jack down to the end of the dock. There she saw the sea-blue catamaran with white trim riding magnificently on the water. "Wow!" said Domino. "That is some boat!"

"Sure is," said Jack, dropping down on the aft deck and grabbing on to the canvas tarp draped over the boat's transom. "Here, take a look at this."

Jack pulled up the canvas and the name on the transom came into view. DOMINO, it read. "Hop in," said Jack, producing a bottle of champagne. "We'd like you to christen it."

"Oh, Jack," said Domino, blushing with embarrassment. "You shouldn't have."

"Why didn't you name it after me?" Maggie Donohue pouted, giving Virgil a stiff clout.

"Because he's bigger than I am," said Virgil between his teeth.

Domino took the bottle and then gave Jack a warm kiss. Jack helped her with the kissing.

"Hey, you two," said Virgil. "Come on up for air."

Domino grinned and broke away from Grigsby. "How can I thank you?"

"Oh," said Jack with a sly look, "we might be able to work something out."

"I christen you the *Domino*," said the Cajun princess, smashing the bottle over a cleat in the transom. The white bubbly sprayed over the stern. Virgil fired up the engines and the *Domino* pulled away from the dock.

Virgil took the *Domino* south, out of the Naples harbor, ran the boat through its paces for the ladies, then made a landing on Cape Romano, east of Ten Thousand Islands. There the group went ashore to enjoy a picnic lunch.

"So, when do you start?" asked Domino.

"Day after tomorrow," said Jack, spreading out their blanket.

Domino seemed lost within her thoughts. She watched Virgil and Maggie wrestling with each other down the beach. Maggie's breasts threatened to bounce out of her bikini. "Virgil always did like the healthy ones," said Domino wanly.

"What's wrong?" asked Jack.

"I don't think this is a good idea, Jack. I really don't," said Domino, taking Jack's hand and pulling him down beside her.

Jack took Domino's head and pressed it against his shoulder. "We'll be all right," he said.

His words did not convince Domino. She had a nagging premonition that something disastrous was going to happen.

"Hey," said Jack, "we're supposed to be having fun today."

"I'm sorry," said Domino, forcing a smile. "I'm just so worried."

"Hell," said Jack, "you know what they say. No guts, no glory."

Jack stifled Domino's next comment with his mouth. He pushed her back on the blanket, and for the moment they were caught up with each other's passion.

The cigar lay off the Cape with only its conning tower above the water. The captain and gunner stood on the abbreviated bridge, watching the couples on the nearby beach through Tri-X field glasses.

"It's nothing," said the gunner. "Just some locals out necking."

"You think so?" asked the captain. "Take a look at their boat. It's a doper's boat, one I've never seen before."

"You're right," said the gunner. "Fast, from the looks of her."

"Yes," said the captain. "I venture to say we'll see it again."

"I hope we do," said the gunner. "I could use a new challenge."

Chapter Five

TURNING PRO

THE WHARF Rat was crowded, unusually crowded. At first Jack and Virgil didn't understand the heavy turnout, but then they recognized the clientele.

"Ah, shit," said Jack, "spring break again?"

"Look at it," said Virgil. "The place is crawlin' with frat rats and freaks."

Two coeds, reeking of baby oil and coconut butter, wiggled past Virgil. The girls' string bikinis left swaths of untanned skin to catch Virgil's eye. Virgil took a step toward the tender, taut flesh, but Jack redirected his attention.

"We don't have time for that tonight," said Jack. "Let's take our usual table and wait for our friends to show up."

"Damn," said Virgil. "You always were business before pleasure," he continued, giving the coeds a last glance. "You run interference."

Jack waded into the mob crowding the Wharf Rat. "Look at these idiots," he said. "All these horny bastards down here thinking the place is still a bordello."

Another set of coeds jiggled past Virgil. "Oh, I don't know," he said. "Things could be worse."

"They are," said Jack. "Some surly-looking dudes are sitting in our seats."

Jack led Virgil across the dance floor. It was crawling with students engaged in some kind of fertility rite. They seemed out of place in the Wharf Rat, the French motif clashing badly with football jerseys and cutoff jeans.

All the Wharf Rat regulars holed up on the perimeter of the unwelcome horde, sipping their drinks and giving disgusted looks as Cody threw drunken freshmen out the back door. Jack and Virgil arrived at their usual seats at the bar. There, two frat rats were making a run at a couple of coeds.

"Why, yes," said the first frat rat. "The cost of tuition in the Ivy League is just skyrocketing."

"Ivy League?" gushed one of the coeds. "You're in the Ivy League?"

The frat rat never got time to explain. The stool was yanked out from under his Ivy League ass, and he lay sprawled across the floor.

"You're in my seat," said Grigsby.

The frat rat, co-captain of the lacrosse team, leaped to his feet to defend his honor and impress the broads. "Your seat?" he snarled. "I don't see your name on it!"

Jack slowly turned the stool over, grabbed the co-captain by the scruff of his neck, and pointed to the name painted on the bottom of the seat. GRIGSBY, it read.

"So what?" said the frat rat.

"All right," came a guttural voice from behind the frat rat, "what's the problem?"

The frat rat turned and ran his face into Cody Carnes's chest. He looked up into the narrowing eyes burning down on him. Grigsby closed in from behind, sandwiching the frat rat between biceps that could crack Brazil nuts.

"No problem," said the frat rat, beating a hasty retreat from the bar.

Virgil and Jack sat down in the seats vacated by the frat rats. The two coeds seemed impressed and coyly inched closer to Jack and Virgil. "Gee," said the first coed, "that was really something."

"Ah, beat it, sister," snarled Jack. "Your face is breaking out."

The coeds left in a huff.

"Hey!" said Virgil, "they were all right. What'd ya do that for?"

"We have no time for that tonight," said Jack, turning to find Dominique standing behind the bar.

"Yeah?" said Virgil. "What were you saying?"

"Yeah," said Jack, giving Domino a warm, loving smile. "She doesn't count."

"What do you mean I don't count?" asked Domino.

"Nothing," said Jack. "A play on words," he continued, looking about the bar. "Seen anyone unusual tonight?"

"As a matter of fact," said Domino, pointing to a refrigeration repairman climbing up from under the cooler behind the bar.

"There ya go, miss. That ought to take care of the Freon leak," said Agent Dickerson. "Hey, fella," he said to Jack. "Give me a hand, will you? Gotta take this compressor out."

"Sure," said Jack, hopping over the bar.

Dickerson stooped down behind the bar to pick up the compressor and spoke quietly with Jack. "Red Pardee will be here tonight," he began. "You know him. He's approached you before to enter the trade."

"Yeah," said Jack, "I know him."

"He's looking for someone to make his runs now. He lost most of his working capital plus his boat the other day with that one-nighter."

"You mean Phil Lanard," said Jack.

"Yeah," said Dickerson. "Why didn't you tell me you knew him?"

"You didn't ask," said Jack.

"Well, from now on I suggest you offer information," said Dickerson, somewhat piqued.

"Deal," said Jack. "What else?"

"Go ahead and make arrangements to make Pardee's next run, but hardball him for the rates. You sixty. Him forty."

"Gotcha," said Jack.

"If he asks where you got the new boat, just tell him you've been nickel-and-diming it for a while with pot, but now you're ready to move up into the big time. If he presses for details, tell him to go to hell!''

"What?" said Jack. "Then we won't be able to make the run?"

"Yes, you will. This is a hard-nosed business, but Pardee's out on a limb. You've got to take advantage of him; otherwise he'll smell a rat.''

"Oh, I see," said Jack.

"Now, here's the number where we can be reached," said Dickerson, handing Jack a grimy piece of paper. "Memorize it, have your partner do the same, then destroy it."

"What do we do after we finish the run?" asked Jack.

"Simple," said Dickerson. "Bring the money back here."

Jack grabbed Dickerson by the front of his lapels. "Here?" he said through clenched teeth. "I don't want Domino involved in this!"

"Well, you'd better talk to *her* about that," said Dickerson. "I'm afraid she volunteered to help."

Jack looked up at Domino, who was standing above them. "Somebody has to save your bacon," she said with a smile.

"No!" said Jack emphatically.

"There's no time to argue," said Domino. "Red Pardee just walked in."

Dickerson lifted his tool chest up on the bar, gave a glance at Pardee as he entered the back door of the Wharf Rat, and dropped back down beside Jack. "You're on, kid," he said.

"All right, asshole," said Jack. "But if anything happens to her, I'm gonna take you out first."

"Agreed," said Dickerson. "Give me a hand with this, will you, son?" he asked, grabbing the compressor.

Jack and Dickerson lifted the compressor and set it on the two-wheeler Dickerson had brought with him. Dickerson zipped up his repairman overalls and wiped his hand across his grimy face.

"That other unit I installed should work fine," he said to Domino.

"Thank you," said Domino, watching Dickerson wheel the compressor across the crowded bar and out the front door.

"I don't want you involved," mumbled Jack to Domino as he hopped back over the bar.

"We'll talk about it later," said Domino. "You'd better go see Pardee."

Jack gave Domino an aggravated glance, then slapped Virgil on the shoulder. "Come on," he said. "Here's where we turn pro."

Red Pardee had taken a booth on the upper tier of the Wharf Rat. He had unscrewed the booth lamp, leaving only the conversation candle burning in the center of the table. The flickering flame highlighted Pardee's features. He scratched at his scraggly beard, flicking bits of snuff out of the snarled thatch and onto his lap. He pushed the bill of his ragged ball cap back where the brim met his bald brow and wiped the sweat off on his hand. Pardee's gaunt cheekbones were pockmarked and marbled with blue veins that were hemorrhaging. He coughed repeatedly, the dry rasp of emphysema-ravaged lungs, then reached into his pocket for his cigarette pouch.

Pardee spread the Bull-Duram makings out on the tabletop, laced the pungent tobacco with a bit of hashish, and rolled himself a cigarette. He took a long puff, suppressed the urge to cough, and waited for the drug to take effect.

The hash numbed his lungs and mellowed his mood. Pardee was still seething over the loss of his *Emmy Lou*. "That idiot Lanard!" he thought. "How could I have been so stupid as to turn my boat over to a rank amateur?"

Pardee began to scour the bar. It wasn't often that he came in from the swamps, and his bib overalls and sweat-stained T-shirt did not blend well with the collegiate crowd dancing below.

A barmaid climbed the stairs to reach the balcony horseshoeing the Wharf Rat. She approached Pardee apprehensively, intimidated by his looks. Pardee's leering eyes squinted at her out of the dim light. He licked his lips as she came closer to his booth.

Pardee watched the barmaid's legs. She was in the costume

of a Paris streetwalker, and the hip-split skirt gave him a breathtaking display of thigh with every stride. The barmaid stopped at his booth. "May I help you?" she asked.

Pardee's leer now broadened. Light from the candle reflected off his stump-toothed smile, made more offensive by the bits of black snuff that clung to his gums. "Yeah," said Pardee, running his eyes the length and breadth of her body. "Whiskey. I want whiskey."

"How would you like it?" she asked.

Another set of skin-crawling glances washed over her. "Just bring the bottle, honey," said Pardee. "We'll discuss the fun later."

Pardee's cackle accompanied the barmaid down the stairs. She cut across the dance floor and stopped at the bar, where Jack and Virgil listened in as she voiced her reluctance to serve the filthy swamp rat.

"No sweat," said Jack, taking a bottle of Jack Daniels from Domino. "We'll do you the favor."

"Thanks," said the barmaid, with a sigh of relief.

Jack felt Domino grab his arm. "You be careful," she warned.

"Don't worry," said Jack, glancing up toward Pardee. "I'm not afraid of that slimy bastard."

"Maybe you aren't," mumbled Virgil, "but I am."

Jack and Virgil made their way around the perimeter of the dance floor. They passed a few regulars who were waiting for the campus crowd to leave.

Jack and Virgil climbed the stairs leading to the balcony and walked over to greet Pardee.

"How ya doin', Grigsby?" said Pardee in his gravelly rasp. Jack just nodded a hello.

"See ya brought your little shit friend," said Pardee.

"Hey, right there," said Virgil, giving the swamp rat the finger.

Pardee was getting out of his seat when Jack's arm shoved him back into the booth. "Like to talk some business with you,'' said the ex-linebacker, sliding in beside Pardee and pinning him to the back of the booth.

Virgil eased in on the opposite side of the table.

Pardee's body odor was almost unbearable and made Jack's eyes smart. "Don't you ever wash?" he complained.

"Don't you smart-mouth me, boy," said Pardee, taking a drag on his specially rolled cigarette.

Jack got wind of the dope and gave Pardee a Cheshire-cat grin. "Better not let Cody get downwind of what's inside that home roller," he said.

"I ain't afraid of Cody," said Pardee, opening the sides of his bib overalls. A black-handled Bowie knife came into view. "I'll slice him from crotch to Adam's apple."

"Well, you can try," said Jack. "But I wouldn't advise it."

"And what *do* you advise?" said Pardee, placing his hand on the handle of the knife.

"That you take your hand off the blade," said Jack. "I want to talk some business."

"Business?" asked Pardee with a gleam in his eye. "What kind of business?"

"Big business," said Jack.

"Yeah," said Pardee. "Wouldn't have somethin' ta do with that new boat of yourn?"

"It might," said Jack.

"And jes' how did a couple of nickel-and-dimers like you come by such a fine machine?" Pardee said, squinting.

"We're working for the FBI," said Jack. "They gave it to us so we could catch assholes like you!"

Virgil nearly swallowed his tongue.

There was a moment of silence, then Pardee's face broke into a broad grin. "Now tell me the truth, sumbitch," said Pardee.

"You had us pegged," said Jack. "Like you say, we've been nickel-and-diming it, but I'm tired of running pot. We want to get into the white gold."

Pardee thought a moment. " 'Tain't easy," he said, "but I might know a fella who can help you."

"Yeah?" asked Jack. "Where is he?"

"Oh, he's around," said Pardee, grabbing the bottle of Jack Daniels. "You know where Royal Palm Hammock is?"

"We can find it," said Jack.

Pardee sneered in Virgil's direction. "You mean the little shit's in on it too?"

"He is," said Jack.

Pardee gave out a guttural growl. "All right," he said. "You boys meet me tomorrow afternoon in Royal Palm. I'll see what I can do."

Jack got up to let Pardee out of the booth. Jack reached into his pocket and pulled out a dollar bill. "Here," he said, handing the bill to Pardee. "Buy yourself some soap."

"You go fuck yerself," said the swamp rat, cutting down the back stairs.

"Jesus, I wish you wouldn't push him like that," said Virgil.

"Why not?" asked Jack. "He doesn't scare me."

"Damn!" said Virgil. "You're gonna give me an ulcer."

"Come on," said Jack. "I want to say good-bye to Domino before we go."

She was waiting for them at the bottom of the stairs. Domino's dress was something straight out of Billy Wilder's *Irma la Douce*. Black, hip-split skirt, green stockings, a black brassiere, and a chiffon blouse open nearly to the navel. The outfit drove the tourists mad and always gave Jack a stiff-legged walk.

"Well," said Domino, "how did it go?"

"We meet Pardee at Royal Palm Hammock," said Virgil.

"That's right," said Jack. "You'd better go gas up the boat," he continued, taking a quick glance at Domino's figure.

"Me?" said Virgil. "But what about all this young stuff?"

"You don't want to get arrested, do you?" said Jack, glaring down at Virgil.

"No, I guess not," said Virgil. "All right if I bring someone along to help?"

"Sure," said Jack. "Tell Maggie Donohue the boat comes first!"

"Whatever you say, Captain Bligh."

Domino giggled as she watched Virgil head out the front door.

"That's quite a getup you've got on," said Jack. "Isn't it a bit too revealing?"

"It's good for business," said Domino, coyly pulling the top of her blouse together. "Besides, you never notice."

"The hell I don't!" said Jack.

A group of drunken football players from some college in Georgia began to tussle on the dance floor. The hubbub disturbed Jack and Domino's conversation, and as Cody waded in to stop the fracas, Miss Monet asked Mr. Grigsby to join her upstairs.

It was the first time Domino had asked Jack up. In fact, it was the first time any man had invaded her domicile, and when Jack stepped through the mahogany doors he was awed by what awaited him. It was all ornate French provincial, with red the dominant color. Antiques abounded, in an elegance Grigsby had never before encountered. The room was dominated by a spiral staircase that led to an immense brass bed set in an open loft.

Domino went to a small bar set in a corner of the room. "What's your pleasure?" she asked.

"You know me," said Jack. "But ordering a glass of suds in here seems completely out of place."

"Well, then," said Domino, "how about some champagne?"

"Yeah," said Jack. "That'd be all right."

Domino put a bottle on ice, then stepped out from behind the bar. Jack still hadn't taken a seat. "Sit down," said Domino. "Make yourself at home."

Jack looked down at his ragged deck shoes, faded jeans, and windbreaker. He looked back at Domino. "I feel out of place," he said.

Domino shook her head and smiled. "And to think that a great bear of a man like you is intimidated by a place like this."

"Can't help it," said Jack, shrugging his shoulders.

"Maybe I can," said Domino. "Come over here."

Jack followed Domino to an ornate wooden wardrobe. "Mother kept all these things," said Domino, opening the doors. "I hung on to the stuff. Silly, I suppose. Most of these things are over forty years old."

Jack looked inside. There were sets of men's evening clothes, apparently of all sizes, but in the style of the 1930s.

"Mother kept these," said Domino, "in case she ever ran into someone special and wanted to step out."

Jack's ego got a boost from her remark, and he watched Domino ferret out an old tuxedo that appeared to be his size.

"You can change in there," said Domino.

"Okay," said Jack. "Might be good for a few grins."

The bathroom was an event in itself. Gold and porcelain were lavished everywhere. The fixtures could have been hocked for a king's ransom. There was a deep marble bath, a separate shower, and an old-fashioned whirlpool tub that seemed to be in good working order. Jack stood before the oval gold-rimmed mirrors above the vanity and took off his seaman's clothes.

He examined himself in the mirror and decided to wash up before donning the costume. He washed his face and wet his hair. He found a brush and combed his hair differently. Instead of his usual single part, he brushed it straight back. Then he slipped into the socks and shoes that came with the tux.

Jack had some difficulty with the cummerbund and a horrible time with the tie. After a major struggle he was in the time-capsule regalia. He looked at himself in the mirror and slicked back his hair again. "Eat your heart out, Humphrey Bogart." He grinned, shutting off the light in the bathroom.

Domino was waiting. She too had changed into a period costume, an old evening gown of her mother's. The man who stepped into the room literally took her breath away. "Rick" had finally arrived.

"Got a light, sweetheart?" said Jack, mimicking Bogie's famous lisp.

"I have indeed," said Domino, walking toward Jack.

It was one of those moments that few people ever experience.

An almost ethereal atmosphere seemed to pervade the room. Jack and Domino became like visions in some dream. They came into each other's arms and danced silently to "As Time Goes By," though no music could be heard.

Jack and Domino moved about the room, gazing into each other's eyes. The touch of their hands seemed charged, as though a force greater than the both of them was at work. They stopped dancing.

Jack picked up Domino and kissed her. He carried her across the room and began to climb the spiral staircase. There was no effort involved in the carrying. Jack reached the top of the stairs and took Domino to the bed. There he eased himself down and pulled Domino across the length of his body. Domino could feel him rising beneath her and wrapped her arms around his neck.

It was a slow, building passion that engulfed them. They eased each other out of their clothes and let their hands linger about their bodies. Jack drew stimulation from the softness of Domino's skin, Domino from Jack's rock-hard musculature.

They made love and the dreamlike atmosphere prevailed. They rode each other through the fantasy, reaching climaxes neither had ever experienced. Then with their energies spent, they fell asleep in each other's arms.

Jack was awake before dawn. He lay beside Domino, watching her sleep. Her lips were parted slightly, and her blue-black hair billowed lavishly across the pillow. He wanted to take her again as he had the night before, but he stopped himself. Jack rested his head on his arm and just watched Domino. It was not the stare of a voyeur but a lover's gaze, the fascination with every facet of a person and the ultimate pleasure it can provide.

Domino stirred. She groped about the bed, reaching for Jack. Grigsby taunted her momentarily by pulling away and watched the reaction on her face. Domino seemed concerned that she could not find him. Then she opened her eyes.

"Hi." Jack smiled.

"Jack," she said.

"Yeah?"

"I love you."

Jack was startled by her remark. A gut-wrenching feeling swept over him, yet he felt infinitely serene. "Do you?"

"Yes," said Domino. "I've been in love with you for a long time."

Jack pulled her closer to him. "It's been a long time," said Jack. "A long time since I've said that to anybody."

"Well, do you, Jack?" asked Domino.

Jack smiled. "Yes, Domino," he said, "I love you too."

Domino drove Jack to the dock, where they found Virgil waiting for them on the deck of the catamaran. "Get a good night's sleep?" groaned Virgil. Jack just glared at Virgil as he turned to bid Domino good-bye.

"You will be careful," said Domino.

"Hey, you know me," said Jack. "I can take care of myself."

"Damn it, Jack! This isn't some football game," said Domino. "I don't want the authorities pulling pieces of *you* from the inside of a shark."

"I told you," said Jack. "I can take care of myself."

Domino shook her head. She knew she was wasting her words, but she had to voice her concern. "Why do you always have to live life right on the edge?" she asked.

"I don't know," said Jack. "Get kind of boring if I didn't."

"Please," said Domino, her eyes welling up with tears. "For me. Promise me you won't take any unnecessary chances."

"Ahh, shit!" said Jack. "You're not going to cry, are you?"

"No," said Domino with a quivering chin. "Well, maybe."

"Woman," said Jack, taking Domino's face into his massive hands, "I'll be fine. I know what I'm doing."

"You always say that," said Domino, starting to tremble.

"Are you going to kiss me good-bye?" asked Jack.

"No," said Domino, starting to whimper. "Oh, yes I am,

you bastard. You know I am. God, I wish I didn't love you so much.''

Jack kissed her, not the kiss spouses exchange at the train station, but as though the kiss had to last forever.

''Come on,'' said Virgil, firing up the engines.

Jack bade Domino good-bye, and she managed to suppress her tears until the catamaran was pulling away from the dock.

Virgil took the *Domino* down the western coast of Florida. He set a course through Big Marco Pass to save time, then south-southeast along the southern tip of the Seminole Reservation. Once past the Reservation, he headed north, toward Royal Palm Hammock and their rendezvous with Red Pardee.

Big Cypress Swamp lay northwest of the Everglades. It was only in the late 1970s that anyone in Florida knew the difference between the two. To the locals, it was all the Everglades, and for fellows like Red Pardee that was just fine. The less anyone knew about Big Cypress Swamp, the better for Pardee to run cocaine.

Virgil took the *Domino* into the estuaries, where the sea stained the earth with salt. Here mangroves had replaced the cypress where the loggers of the 1950s had gutted the forest. The rainy season was already flushing nutrients from Big Cypress Swamp into the estuaries, and as a result, the mangroves lining these waterways were thicker than ever.

Jack and Virgil had to duck below the foredeck at times to keep from being swept overboard by the limbs of the overhanging mangrove trees. Virgil took care to avoid the mangrove's prop roots lest he tear the cleaver propellers off the *Domino*'s transom.

After traversing some miles through the mangroves, Virgil came into a stretch of dwarf bald cypress. They rose like hundreds of knarled, arthritic hands above the infertile limestone bottom. Some of the trees were eighty or ninety years old yet stood no more than a foot tall. Virgil carefully avoided these navigational hazards as well. It would be easy for one of the dwarfs to punch a hole in the boat's Kevlar hull.

They passed by the snake-infested pinelands and palmetto thickets. The thought of losing power in this labyrinth of diamondback and water moccasin did not sit well with Virgil. He kept the boat away from tree limbs, fearing that a sunning snake might drop down onto the open deck.

Jack took their M-11's out and they placed them inside their shoulder holsters. He strung five clips of ammo aross the small of his back in the bandoliers provided by the FBI. The weapons gave both men a sense of security inside the swamp.

Jack pulled on a camouflaged ranger bush hat and a pair of polarized shooting glasses. He screwed the suppressor onto his M-11 and threw a burst into nearby stump. The weapon hardly disturbed the serenity of the swamp. "Guess we're ready," he said. "You know where we are?"

"Yeah," said Virgil, altering his course. "Used to go hunting in here all the time. Be another hour before we get there."

The *Domino* now entered the most dangerous portion of the swamp. Here the cypress trees were so thick and cloaked in Spanish moss that the men might have to get down on their bellies and slither.

The air grew thick and pungent with the aroma of algae and rotting plants. Water moccasins cut back and forth across the twin bows of the *Domino* as they swam to safety. Egrets and herons watched the *Domino* from above, their darting eyes and ear-piercing shrieks warning the inhabitants of the swamp that men were dangerously close.

Royal Palm Hammock was a maze of mounds deep inside Big Cypress Swamp, and finding Red Pardee's shanty was no easy task. Virgil maneuvered the *Domino* carefully as the boat's keel began to touch bottom. They were drawing eighteen inches of draft in twenty-five inches of water when they sighted Pardee's shanty. Any deeper into the swamp and Jack and Virgil would have to get out and push.

"See anyone?" asked Virgil nervously.

"No," said Jack, scanning their suroundings. "Better tie up at the dock."

"Is *that* what it is?" said Virgil.

Virgil brought the *Domino* to the dock, which was more in the swamp than out. He tied her fast, took out his M-11, and shoved a magazine home. "Where is he?" he said.

"Fan out," said Jack. "We'll find him."

The earth beneath Jack and Virgil's feet was rich with humus, which cushioned their stride and smothered their stalk. They crept up on opposite sides of Pardee's shanty, using tactics they had learned in the Mekong Delta.

The shanty seemed in place for the swamp but out of character for a man who could easily produce several hundred thousand in cash. Jack and Virgil traversed the small island in the swamp but could not find Pardee.

"I'll thank you ta put them weapons down," came Pardee's voice out of the swamp.

Jack and Virgil pivoted, landing back to back with their M-11's brought into firing position.

"Put them pieces down, God damn it!" snapped Pardee. "Elst I'll splatter yer insides all over the swamp."

"You see him," hissed Virgil.

"Yeah," said Jack sadly. "He's up in that tree over there. He's got a double-barreled shotgun on us."

"Wonderful," said Virgil. "What do we do?"

"Put our pieces down, like he says."

"That's better," said Pardee, watching Jack and Virgil set their weapons down. "Now walk toward me, and put yer hands on top of yern heads."

Jack and Virgil walked toward Pardee until they reached the edge of the small hammock. There they waited while Pardee climbed down from a blind he had built about twenty feet up in a nearby cypress tree.

"Well, if it ain't the great killers of the Viet Cong," said Pardee, grinning. He spat his chew into the swamp. "You fellers're kinda of stupid if ya ask me."

"Didn't ask you," said Jack, taking his hands down and reaching for his M-11.

"You jes' hold a minute, son," said Pardee, bringing the shotgun to bear.

"We're here to do business," said Jack, wiping peat off his weapon. "Now let's cut the crap and get to it."

"All right," said Pardee. "Time is a–wastin'. But don't you sass me, boy. This here is *my* domain. I blow a hole in the side of that fancy boat of yourn, and I'll leave you out here to die more miserable than you can imagine."

"All right," said Jack. "We understand each other. But hear me. You shoot a hole in that boat and I'll cut you in half with this!"

Pardee gave a guttural laugh. Tobacco-stained saliva dribbled down his chin as he spoke. "This way, gentlemen," he said. "As it be, you'll just have time to make the rendezvous with the mother ship."

The interior of Pardee's shanty was a monument to filth, old billboards and tar paper held together with spit and bailing wire—a palace befitting the old swamp rat. Pardee had spent most of his life haunting the backwaters of Big Cypress Swamp south to the Everglades. When poaching gators was no longer profitable, he had turned to running dope. His second occupation was a thousand times more profitable, but despite the riches, Pardee couldn't get the swamp out of his system. Though he had access to enough money to buy the most lavish property in Palm Beach Shores, he remained a hermit holed up in his Spanish moss fortress. The calls of the herons and egrets were far more soothing than the wretched sounds of the city, and so Pardee remained a welcome captive inside his temperate hideaway.

Pardee paced off a few steps from one wall, then two more to his left. He picked up a spade and dug a small hole in the floor. He uncovered an old Maxwell House coffee can, which he carried to a homemade table in the center of the room.

"Here's the buy money," he said, pulling two hundred thousand in cash out of the can. "And don't go a-losin' it like that dipshit Lanard."

Jack and Virgil looked at each other, realizing they were in the presence of the man who had indirectly taken their friend's life. Virgil's hand reached for his M-11. Jack restrained him and shook his head.

"Now, here's where you'll make the rendezvous," said Pardee, pointing to a spot on a map of the western coast of Florida. "Be thar at twelve sharp. Can ya find that, boy?"

"I can find it," said Virgil. "Now you answer me a question."

"Maybe," said Pardee.

"If you've got all this cash, why ain't *you* makin' the run?"

"Cops is watchin' me," said Pardee, rubbing his black beard. "Bastards hardly let me breath anymore. Got some goddamned court injunction to impound all my boats. All I got left is my johnboat fer swampin'."

"Yeah, life is tough all over," said Jack, picking up the map and the coffee can full of money.

"Use my name at the rendezvous," said Pardee, "and sample that coke. You know what it tastes like, don't ya?"

"We know," said Virgil. "Now, what's the captain's name?"

"You jes' never mind the captain of the mother ship, boy. You be where ye're supposed ta be, and be back here tomorrow."

"We'll be here," said Jack.

"Ya better be," said Pardee. "Or ya better be dead."

Virgil was visibly shaken by Pardee's statement.

"Don't try'n cross me, boys. Tougher fellers than you have tried. I sure would hate to see you both end up gator bait."

Jack held his M-11 under Pardee's whiskers, tickling his chin with the end of the suppressor. "Take care the same don't happen to you," he said. "Come on, Virgil," he continued, heading for the door. "We'd better get out of here before I get scared to death."

Pardee watched them from his doorway. Jack and Virgil pushed off from the dock and headed back for the Gulf.

"You jes' make sure you're back here by sundown tomorrow," Pardee shouted as they left. "You hear? Sundown tomorrow!"

Chapter Six

BEGINNERS' LUCK

THE *DOMINO* came out of Big Cypress by the same route she had entered. Jack and Virgil said little to each other before reaching the Gulf. It wasn't the serenity of the scenery that lulled them but the realization of their predicament.

The *Domino* cleared the mangroves and came out into the mosaic of Ten Thousand Islands. Virgil took a southeasterly heading while Jack watched the sun set.

"I feel funny," said Virgil. "It's like the feeling I used to get over the pond, only different."

"Me too," said Jack. "It's like all those damn dust-offs in 'Nam. You always knew Charlie was waiting. You just never knew where."

"Think somebody's waiting for us now?" asked Virgil.

"I don't know," said Jack. "It's like you say, a funny feeling, but not quite the same."

Virgil took his hands off the wheel of the *Domino* and looked at his palms. "Fuckin' hands are sweatin' again," he said. "Used to get so bad I could hardly hang on to a weapon."

"That's all right," said Jack, popping the aft M-60. "I'll do the shooting for both of us."

Jack's aplomb seemed to calm Virgil. He watched Jack ready the weapon before pushing it back inside its concealed hatch.

Virgil angled the *Domino* out into the Gulf while Jack

climbed forward of the helm to ready the forward M-60. With this accomplished, Jack climbed back to join Virgil beside the wheel.

"Hit the radar and sonar," said Virgil. "It'll make locating the mother ship easier in the dark. No moon tonight, you know."

The glow of the setting sun kept the ocean illuminated with its reflection off the atmosphere, but soon its rays would be swallowed by the black of the night. The *Domino* ran at half throttle, cutting a wake through the Gulf, a tiny white speck dwarfed by the great expanse of sea.

The cigar ran steady at fifty feet below the Gulf. It was a new ship, finishing its shakedown cruise and heading for its home base. The captain was on orders to avoid all contact with any vessel, yet the temptation was overwhelming. A lone blip on the sonar. The prize was easily within range as it cut across the horizon.

"Bring her up to periscope depth," said the captain.

The helmsman gave the captain a concerned glance, then followed his orders. The captain waited for the cigar to reach periscope depth, then swung about in his couch to peer through the aperture. In the failing light he could just make out the silhouette. It was a doper all right, and making a run for the mother ship.

"Come to a new course," commanded the captain. "Intercept on target."

Now the helmsman hesitated. "That's against orders, sir."

The captain swung about in his couch to glare at the ashen-faced helmsman. "Come to a new course," he repeated.

The helmsman complied, wishing he were on another vessel miles away. The captain continued to monitor the progress of the powerboat on the horizon. He was anxious to test the armaments of the newly assembled cigar, and the dopers' boat would be a worthy target.

The helmsman glanced at the captain as he corrected the course. Strutting egoist, he thought, who else but Vicente Villa could be so reckless?

Villa was a distant descendant of Pancho Villa, and he too was involved with rebellion. His goals were perhaps more grandiose than his long-dead relative, but no less dispassionate.

Villa sat wedged into the surrounding consoles of the cigar, bathed in the eerie green light of computer screens. His black eyes and goatee took on a sardonic appearance in the contrasting light. Villa was perhaps the finest cigar captain in all the fleet; a man who could pilot one of the twentieth century's marvels nearly by instinct. Even when most of the navigation controls had been knocked out, Villa could still navigate.

Perhaps his strength of expertise was born out of a heavily cloaked inferiority complex. It was not his mind or ego that was lacking, but his sickly body. Villa's body had been ravaged by boyhood diseases unheard of in most western civilizations. Rickets had left his legs stunted and bowed, and malnutrition had ravaged the rest of his frail frame. But then that was the lot of many children of central Chihuahua, where the lack of a staple diet was the rule, not the exception.

He had drifted east with a migratory family that abandoned him in his early teens. Villa continued his nomadic ways until his early twenties, when he met the comandante. Then his life changed, as had those of all others who came in contact with the charismatic father figure.

Now Villa commanded the comandante's fleet, the ultra-secret flotilla operating under the very noses of the authority they were sworn to humble. Truly a tribute to the comandante's genius.

Villa watched as the helmsman brought the cigar onto its intercept heading.

Virgil glanced at the radar and sonar. The screens showed only the mother ship, about six miles ahead. Virgil looked at Jack then off their stern. "Remember when we were in 'Nam," Virgil said, "and how I used to say I could feel Charlie? Even though we might not see him, I just *knew* he was there."

"Yeah," said Jack. "I said you were full of shit, until I saw you always kept us from walking into ambushes."

"Well, there's somebody back there," said Virgil, gesturing toward their stern.

Jack checked the sonar and radar. The devices seemed to be functioning correctly, but still only the mother ship in the distance registered. "You sure?" Jack asked. "Nothing is showing up on either screen."

"I don't give a damn what those screens say!" said Virgil, looking back across the black of the ocean. "I tell you there's somebody back there!"

This time Jack didn't question Virgil's statement. Jack popped the aft M-60 and kept a close watch on their stern.

In the cramped quarters of the cigar, Villa and the helmsman manipulated their hydraulically operated couches. Now the helmsman sat below and forward of the captain, who took his position behind the weapons console of the cigar. The helmsman brought the cigar on a new course to flank the *Domino* and began to increase speed.

The blip registered first on the *Domino*'s sonar. Virgil could not hear the beep over the rumble of the engines, but did see the electronic pulse on the screen. "Jack!" shouted Virgil. "Look! I told you there was somebody back there!"

Jack left the aft M-60 and came forward. He studied the screen and confirmed Virgil's sighting. "Guess you haven't lost your touch," he said, returning to the machine gun.

The cigar came up to periscope depth, and Villa picked up the image of the *Domino* in his sight. Their quarry was beginning to increase speed. Villa ordered the helmsman to overtake them.

"We can't match their speed underwater," said the helmsman. "We'll have to surface and exceed their velocity on the hydrofoils."

"Then do it," ordered Villa.

Jack and Virgil pulled on flak jackets and full-face bulletproof Bell racing helmets. Virgil increased their speed to exceed that of their pursuer while monitoring the sonar. The blip on sonar began to fade, while another blip appeared on radar. "Jesus!" said Virgil.

"What is it?" asked Jack.

"Would you think I'd flipped if I said I thought we are being tailed by a fuckin' *submarine*!"

"A what?" said Jack.

"Hey," said Virgil. "I'm tellin' ya, the blip I had on sonar just disappeared, and another blip at the same range just appeared on radar!"

Jack flipped up his face shield and peered through a set of binoculars. "You're right," he said. " I can't make it out completely, but something is tailing us."

"Not for long," said Virgil, laying a heavy hand on the throttles.

The bows of the *Domino* came up out of the water as the tremendous torque of the engines came to bear. The *Domino*'s twin power plants began to pound out the horsepower that would soon have the catamaran running at well over a hundred miles an hour.

Virgil was about to give out with a rebel yell, when he noticed that the blip on the radar screen was keeping pace with their increasing speed. Virgil took his eyes off their course momentarily to give a closer examination to the radar screen. The blip wasn't maintaining its distance anymore. It was beginning to close in on the *Domino*.

"You'd better get ready," yelled Virgil over the roar of the engines. "Whoever that bastard is, he's gainin' on us."

Jack didn't waste time asking questions. He set the sights on the M-60 and drew back the bolt. If their pursuers came any closer, he'd fire a warning burst right in front of their bow.

Virgil was about to take evasive action when a third blip appeared on the screen. The *Domino* was closing fast on the mother ship, still a mile or so in the distance, and the strange vessel was still closing on them from their stern, but now this new blip registered. It came at the *Domino* and its pursuer from their starboard beam.

"Who the hell is that?" shouted Virgil, over the thunder of the *Domino*'s engines.

A blinding searchlight answered Virgil's question. A Coast

Guard Cutter was closing on the *Domino*. Using an old ploy, the cutter had masked its presence on the radar by mirroring the course of the mother ship. Now they were signaling the *Domino* down, and Virgil had no choice but to cut back the throttles.

"Hey, look," Virgil said to Jack.

Jack unloaded his M-60 and dropped the equipment into its hatch before joining Virgil at the helm. There they both watched as the image of their pursuer faded from radar to sonar, then turned one hundred and eighty degrees about. Momentarily the blip left the sonar.

"Damn!" said Virgil. "What the hell was that?"

"I don't know," said Jack. "Better stash that coffee can full of money," he continued. "Looks like we're going to be boarded."

Virgil stowed the cocaine buy money and stood to while the cutter came alongside. In the harsh light it was difficult for Jack to see, but he recognized the voice immediately.

"All right, where's the fire?" said Agent Dickerson.

"In your eyes," said Jack, watching Dickerson and the captain of the cutter climb down onto the *Domino*'s deck.

"Did you catch what was following us?" asked Virgil.

"Yeah," said Dickerson with a grin, "we were."

"No," said Jack. "We think we were being tailed by a submarine."

"A submarine?" questioned Dickerson. "Have you boys been drinking?"

"No, we haven't been drinking, goddamn it!" said Jack. "We both saw it, and there's nothing wrong with the equipment."

The captain of the cutter checked their sonar and radar. "He's right about one thing," said the captain. "The equipment is okay."

"Sure you weren't monitoring ground clutter?" asked Dickerson.

"I might have thought that if we were still inside Ten Thousand Islands," said Virgil, "but we're well out to sea!"

"We'll have someone check the equipment when you get back to port," said Dickerson.

"Then you don't believe us?" said Jack.

"I didn't say that," said Dickerson. "We'll just have the equipment checked. For now, you'd better make your rendezvous with the mother ship."

"How the hell can we do that," asked Virgil, "with you hangin' around?"

"You're not alone on the water tonight," said Dickerson. "Look," he said, pointing at the radar.

Another blip had appeared. This was a surface ship, angling in and out of radar range.

"Looks like a hungry wolf stalking a sick deer," said Dickerson. "They'll run like that until they think it's safe to contact the mother ship. Then they'll make their rendezvous and make a run for the swamps. We'll hassle them while you make your pickup."

"Is this the way things are usually done?" asked Jack.

"Unfortunately," said the captain of the cutter. "If we had more ships we could catch more of them. We hassle a few and catch a few," he continued. "Our boarding of your boat is strictly routine. Hell, I've stopped the same guy three times in one night."

"Did the guy make his rendezvous?" asked Jack.

"Yeah," sighed the captain.

"Did he get away?" asked Virgil.

"Yeah," said the captain, "he sure did."

"Well," said Jack, "maybe you'll catch him tonight."

The captain gave Jack a piqued look as he and Dickerson climbed back aboard the cutter. "Don't worry," said Dickerson as the search light was cut out. "We'll be in touch."

"Thanks a lot," said Jack. "Good luck."

"Good luck to you, too," said Dickerson.

The cutter pulled away from the *Domino* in pursuit of other dopers trying to make their rendezvous with the mother ship anchored safely beyond the twelve-mile limit.

Virgil brought the engines of the *Domino* back to life and ran a skirting course around the perimeters of the cutter's radar. He did so to satisfy any wary eyes that might be watching. Virgil did not want to give the impression that he was receiving any favors from the authorities.

"I'd still like to know what was tailing us," said Virgil.

"Me too," said Jack. "You don't suppose it was one of the Navy's vessels?"

"Maybe," said Virgil. "They might be runnin' the damn thing out of Key West Naval Station."

"Possible," said Jack. "I noticed a lot of experimental craft down there during our training."

"I got it!" said Virgil.

"What?"

"It's Lieutenant Shapely. She's still got the hots for my body," said Virgil.

"Bullshit," said Jack, giving Virgil a friendly clout. "Come on. Let's make a run for the mother ship before the cutter comes back in our direction."

Virgil brought the *Domino* onto a heading for the mother ship anchored in the Gulf Stream. She was a surly-looking ship. Even the darkness of the night could not shroud the rust and neglect. Virgil brought the shiny new catamaran alongside and signaled topside with a flashlight.

At first there was no response, then both Virgil and Jack heard an all-too-familiar sound—the chambering of rounds into M-16's.

"*Cómo están, mis amigos?*" said Jack. "*Qué hora es?*"

"Cut the shit, Anglo," came the response from the darkness of the upper deck. "We do not know you."

"You know Red Pardee," said Jack.

"*Sí*, we know señor Pardee," came the voice. "Why does he send so many in his place?"

"The police have impounded his boats," replied Jack, searching the deck for the source of voice.

"You have the money?"

"The goods first," said Jack.

Thereafter followed the same routine that Phil Lanard had

experienced, only this time it was Jack Grigsby and Virgil Ful-lenkamp who learned the meaning of smuggler's sweat. They followed the routine detailed by Pardee, sampling the bricks of cocaine while feeling the barrels of loaded rifles pointing at the backs of their heads.

Satisfied with the quality of the coke, Jack spat the residue into the sea. He took the coffee can full of money and tied it off to the line lowered from the upper deck.

"When do we meet you again?" asked Jack.

An awful silence fell over the sea. It was as though Jack had violated some sacred taboo, and the sounds of more machine-gun bolts permeated the air.

"You are bold, señor," came the voice from above. "Per-haps too bold. In this business that can be a fatal mistake."

"I don't want to be Pardee's errand boy forever," said Jack.

There was some hushed conversation in Spanish while Virgil gave Jack some anxious looks.

"Es your pilot a good navigator?" came the question from the mother ship.

"He is," said Jack.

"A week from today," said the Colombian seaman. "Twenty-five degrees ten minutes north, eighty-two degrees fifteen minutes west. Jou got that, Anglo?"

"We got it," said Jack. "What time?"

Now the tense atmosphere was shattered by laughter. It seemed as though the entire mother ship had erupted, and those who did not speak English were quickly informed of the blun-dering remark.

"What time?" roared the Colombian seaman. "When de fucking cutter is chasing one of your stupid friends, Anglo."

"Right," said Jack, nodding his head.

"Well," Virgil whispered, "Dickerson told us to ask stupid questions. I guess that qualifies."

"Cast off, Anglo," said the Colombian seaman, whose irri-table demeanor had returned.

Jack and Virgil pushed off of the mother ship, fired up the

engines of the *Domino*, and set a course back for Ten Thousand Islands and the trip to Royal Palm Hammock.

"I didn't know you spoke Spanish," said Virgil.

"Didn't flunk it three years running for nothing," said Jack. "I know just enough to get by. How to order a drink, how to find the can, and how to find the back door."

"That would cover it," said Virgil.

Virgil took the *Domino* on a skirting course around where he guessed the cutter might be sweeping. No sense in acting any differently from any other doper out that night.

The *Domino* was running at half throttle when the cigar picked her up on sonar. Villa had ordered the helmsman to set a circular course in hopes of picking up the catamaran after it made the rendezvous with the mother ship.

The helmsman brought the cigar up to periscope depth and Villa searched the surface for their target. "Bearing two twenty-five," he said.

The helmsman reluctantly brought the cigar onto the intercept heading.

"Bring her about smartly," snapped Villa.

"With the capitan's permission," said the helmsman. "This is a shakedown run. Our orders were to avoid intercepting any vessel."

Villa's upper lip drew into a horrific sneer. "We have completed the necessary adjustments to the machine's main operational systems. I see this maneuver as a means of fine-tuning the entire system."

"But Capitan—"

"Whether you agree with my decision or not is irrelevant. Now, steady on heading two twenty-five."

"Yes, Capitan," said the helmsman.

"Five degrees up angle on the bow planes," said Villa.

The helmsman brought the cigar up to a depth of twenty-five feet.

"All ahead full," said Villa.

The helmsman brought the cigar up to speed and began her attack run on the *Domino*.

Jack was about to pull off his helmet when he caught the blip on sonar. He gestured to Virgil to look at the screen.

"I see it," said Virgil. "What's his heading?"

"Two twenty-five," said Jack, "and closing fast."

"It's gotta be a sub," said Virgil. "Check the radar."

Jack watched the line sweep. The radar showed all clear. "Nothing," said Jack. "Jesus, where's the Coast Guard when you need them?"

"Is he still closing?" asked Virgil.

"Yeah, picking up speed, from the looks of it," said Jack. "If it's a sub, what do you think it'll hit us with—torpedoes?"

"No," said Virgil. "We're running too fast and draw too little water for them to do that. If it's a sub—and I'm damn sure it is—then she'll have to surface."

"That'll be just fine," said Jack, climbing forward to release the bow M-60, "because I'll be waiting for them when they do."

Virgil rested his hand on the throttles. He pushed them forward and the *Domino* began to pick up speed. A cushion of sea froth and air suspended the twin hulls of the catamaran as it tore up the Gulf. Two plumes of salt water blew off the *Domino*'s transom as it passed the one-hundred-mile-per-hour mark and kept on accelerating.

As Lieutenant Shively had warned, the boat handled stiffly with the increase in velocity, but Virgil was up to the task. He ran a course perpendicular to that of the closing mystery ship, then gave the engines their head.

Fourteen hundred turbo-charged horses reared to life as the *Domino* put some distance on the cigar. Villa ordered the helmsman to surface and bring the minisub up out of the water onto its hydrofoils.

Jack was just pulling the bolt back on the forward M-60 when he heard a burst from off their starboard beam. This burst came not from a light or medium machine gun but from a heavy gun, fifty-caliber probably, and the tracers cut a swath across the heading of the *Domino*.

"Jesus Christ!" said Virgil, cutting their speed and veering off his present heading. "Who the hell is that?"

Another burst from the heavy machine gun cut across the *Domino*'s bows. Virgil angled away from the heavy guns and got back on the throttles. The cigar had made a high-speed turn upon sighting the first burst of heavy machine gun fire. Their sea savvy was such that they knew who was gunning for the dopers, and their night's itinerary did not include a rendezvous with the Coast Guard.

"Run away, this night," said Villa, watching the catamaran outrun the cutter. "You live only because of the gringo authorities, but I swear, another night and you will be mine."

"That should convince any doubters as to whether our operatives are really in the business or not," said Agent Dickerson. "Hope they don't get too upset about your men taking pot shots at them."

"We fire warning bursts like that once or twice a month," said the captain of the cutter. "They weren't in any danger of being hit."

"Who was that other target we monitored on radar?" asked Dickerson.

"Another doper," said the captain. "They'll run like that sometimes. One of them will find a hole in our surveillance and a whole damn flotilla of them will race side by side, back into the swamps. Our shooting must have scared him off, too."

"Didn't do much for your capture percentage tonight," said Dickerson.

"There'll be other nights," said the captain.

"I hope so," said Dickerson. "I hope so for them too," he continued, listening to the fading sounds of the *Domino*'s engines.

Navigating the mangrove estuaries in the dead of night was no simple task. Jack rode the *Domino* belly-down on the forward bow with a small flashlight, calling out the navigational corrections to Virgil. Virgil kept their speed down to a crawl as they zigzagged along the estuaries.

Finally the navigational hazards became too great and Virgil cut their engines and trimmed the props up out of the water.

"We'll have to paddle until first light," said Virgil. "If we catch one of those dwarf cypress, it could punch a hole in the hull."

Jack agreed, and they spent the next four hours paddling the hundred-thousand-dollar powerboat through the reeds and mosquitoes. By daybreak both were exhausted and covered with mosquito bites. They tied off to a nearby cypress and broke into Jack's cooler for some food.

Tuna salad sandwiches and beer for breakfast were a welcome relief, even if they were soggy. Jack and Virgil used the ice from the cooler to soothe their insect bites, then continued deeper into the swamp to keep their rendezvous with Red Pardee.

Fog banks began to form with the rising of the sun. These pockets of ethereal mist rode on breaths of breeze, anointing the flora with a slick of dew. The sunlight reflected off the moistened plant life, christening each leaf with crystalline sparkles that gave the swamp a diamond-like aura.

The *Domino* moved through this surreal splendor like some fabled ship in search of its lost crew, perhaps drawn by the lure of the Fountain of Youth and the ghost of Ponce de Leon.

"We must be getting close," said Jack. "I'm beginning to pick up a few landmarks."

"Yeah," said Virgil. "Should I fire up the engines? I'm sick of this paddling."

"No," said Jack. "I don't trust that old bastard Pardee. No sense letting him know we're coming."

Virgil agreed, and they continued paddling the *Domino* toward Royal Palm Hammock, and Red Pardee's shanty. They were about four hundred yards from Pardee's island in the swamp when Jack signaled Virgil to stop paddling.

"What's wrong?" whispered Virgil.

"I'm not sure," said Jack, peering through his Tri-X field glasses. "I didn't expect a brass band welcome, but I did figure on seeing that old swamp rat."

Virgil took out a pair of the powerful field glasses and scoured the swamp around Pardee's shanty. Virgil paid particular attention to the trees, remembering how easily the old man had ambushed them before. Still no sign of the drug runner.

"What now?" asked Virgil.

"Search-and-destroy mission," said Jack, reaching into the pocket of his windbreaker. Jack began to smear army-issue OD greast paint onto his face and arms. He pulled out an old jungle-weight camouflaged blouse with the sleeves cut off and took off his shooting glasses.

"Where the hell did you get the war paint?" asked Virgil.

"Kept it as a souvenir of Vietnam," said Jack, handing the two hued sticks to Virgil.

Virgil painted up, then hung a hand over the side of the *Domino* to grab a handful of muck. This he spread liberally about his T-shirt and pants until his camouflage was complete.

Both Jack and Virgil took extra clips of ammunition before taking their M-11's out of their holsters. They pulled back the bolts, set the safeties, and slipped over the side of the *Domino*. The water was waist-deep, and their deck shoes were quickly sucked off by the mud. They moved away from the *Domino* as they flanked in toward the island. They both squatted down in the water until only their eyes, hands, and weapons were above the waterline.

Jack and Virgil took cover behind stands of cabbage palm and began to stuff the broad leaf into their belts and down the back of their shirts. In a few moments they both took on the appearance of the floating debris that riddled the swamp's waterways. The two clumps of deadly debris began to close on opposite sides of Pardee's island and the shanty they had visited before.

Pardee was waiting in a blind just behind his shanty. The blind was sinking into the peat bottom, and Pardee stood ankle-deep in water. Beside him on the ramshackle shelves lay a Winchester pump shotgun, and in his hands was a 9mm Uzi submachine gun. He listened for the sound of the approaching engines.

The clump of floating cabbage palm drifted with the current and came up against Pardee's island in the swamp. Jack Grigsby poked his nose out of the cabbage palms and surveyed the island. Still no sign of Pardee.

Jack was about to crawl up on the island when he noticed something odd about the footpath to the left of the boat dock. Peat had been hastily cast across the footpath, thrown there to deliberately hide something.

It was a clumsy booby trap, crudely concealed and stupidly planted. Hell, Jack could see the chain leading to what must have been an old bear trap. Jack noted its location and continued his stalk toward the rear of the island.

Virgil found a similar trap on the right side of the island. This bear trap was positioned as poorly, and Virgil noted its location before closing in on the rear of the island.

Both Jack and Virgil located Pardee's blind at about the same time. Their little walk through the swamp had refreshed both their memories, and now they closed in on the target in the same manner they had applied with deadly success in the Mekong Delta.

Pardee's first mistake was sighing with the boredom of waiting. His second mistake was sticking his head out the front of the blind to grab a breath of fresh air. Jack exploded out of the water, and caught Pardee squarely across the jaw with the Cobray sonics suppressor screwed onto the front of his M-11.

The force of the blow knocked most of Pardee's few remaining teeth out and left him unconscious, but not before he had flinched and thrown out a quick burst from his Uzi. A few rounds tore up the blind in front of Pardee. He fell face-first into the swamp water engulfing the floor of his blind.

"I should leave you there and let you drown, you sonofabitch," said Jack, peeling the rest of the cabbage palm out of his clothes.

Virgil came out of the swamp on the right flank of the shanty, with his M-11 still at the ready. Virgil saw Jack standing over Pardee, whom he picked up and threw over his shoulder.

"Nice work," said Virgil. "You took him just like you took

that NVA captain. Clean and quiet. Bet old Pardee here is going to have a helluva headache when he comes to.''

"Better get the boat," said Jack. "I'll keep an eye on him."

Some ten minutes later Virgil returned with the *Domino*. Jack had dragged Pardee to the front of the shanty. Virgil was just pulling into the dock when Pardee regained consciousness.

"Ugh," said Pardee, spitting blood and tooth fragments. "I think you broke my jaw."

"You're lucky I didn't blow your head off," said Jack, shoving the muzzle of his M-11 in Pardee's face. "Now, get up and tie that boat off at the dock."

Pardee got to his feet and staggered down the footpath. When he reached the point where he had buried the bear trap, he started to step around the potential leg breaker.

A burst from Jack's M-11 tore up the side of the footpath next to Pardee's feet. "Stay on the path," said Jack.

Pardee turned and looked back at Grigsby. There was no compassion in Jack's eyes. "You know I can't do that," said Pardee.

"In Vietnam I knew a fourteen-year-old Viet Cong who could slice you to pieces using no more than seven feet of bamboo, and you came after us with a bear trap? Man, you really are stupid."

"What do you want me to do?" asked Pardee.

"Keep walking," said Jack, drawing a bead on the back of Pardee's legs.

"What do you want?" whined Pardee, whose speech was garbled by blood and swollen lips.

"Answers," said Jack, taking a few steps toward Pardee.

"Okay," said Pardee. "But first gimme some water."

"Give him a bucket of swamp water," said Jack.

"Sure thing," said Virgil.

Pardee stood in front of the bear trap while Virgil fetched a bucket of water from the swamp. "Here ya go, pops," said Virgil, tossing the water in Pardee's face.

"Who tailed us in the Gulf last night?" snarled Jack.

"How should I know?" said Pardee. "Coast Guard maybe."

"Coast Guard doesn't run submarines," said Jack. "Now, tell me. Who was shadowing us?"

"Submarine?" repeated Pardee.

"That's probably how you took Phil Lanard out, isn't it?" said Virgil, bringing his M-11 to bear.

"I don't know nothin' 'bout no submarines," said Pardee.

"Then keep walking," said Jack.

Pardee looked into the jaws of the bear trap, then back to Grigsby. "I tell ya, I don't know nothin' 'bout no damn submarine!"

"Keep walking, you sonofabitch!" said Jack, "or so help me I'll shoot both your legs out from under you where you stand."

Pardee lifted his left leg and began to lower his foot into the trap. He was sweating profusely when he felt the ball of his foot gently touch the trigger of the bear trap. "I cain't," Pardee screamed, dropping down to his knees. "Go ahead and shoot," he cried. "Ah swear, I don't know nothin' 'bout no submarines."

Jack and Virgil looked at each other. Virgil shrugged his shoulders. "Maybe he is tellin' the truth."

"Ah swear I am!" said Pardee. "Look, I'll give you anythin' you want! Jes' don't kill me!"

Jack thought a moment. Perhaps the old swamp rat was telling the truth. There was no way of really knowing, unless Jack wanted to employ some of the tactics he'd seen used on communist sympathizers by South Vietnamese regulars, and he never could stomach that sort of action.

"Give him a shovel," said Jack.

"What you gonna do?" cried Pardee. "Make me dig my own grave?"

"Not a bad idea," said Jack, "but you see I've grown kind of thirsty. I want some coffee. So you'd better be digging up a lot of coffee cans," said Jack, lowering the muzzle of his M-11 against the back of Pardee's skull. "Or by God you *will* be digging your own grave!"

For the next hour Pardee dug up his dope profits of the last six months. Jack forced him to name every contact he had in the drug trade, hoping one of the names might give their friends at the FBI a clue as to who might have been trailing them in the Gulf.

Jack and Virgil left Pardee on his island, but not before they had taken the firing pins from his shotgun and the Uzi. They paddled back away from the island with only one more task to complete. Jack let a burst go into the bottom of Pardee's johnboat.

The garbled curses of Pardee accompanied Virgil and Jack until they reached deeper water, where they fired up the engines and continued toward the coast. Pardee had left them with over five hundred thousand in cash and a wealth of information. Still, both Virgil and Jack were troubled by the mysterious craft that had tracked them the night before.

"Who were those guys?" asked Virgil.

"I don't know," said Jack, "but I've got a bad feeling they're the guys the Federal Boys are after. And you know what that means."

"Yeah," said Virgil dolefully. "We get to volunteer again."

Chapter Seven

THE HIDDEN CITY

VICENTE VILLA left his helmsman to complete the shakedown checklist on the cigar. The ship had performed well, yet Vicente knew that the comandante had not sent for him to offer congratulations.

Villa entered the lift that would take him from the cigar docks to the top of Triangle Island, to Rudolfo Cordova's headquarters, where he would have to explain his break in routine to a man who was a fanatic about following orders.

Villa was not afraid of Rudolfo Cordova. Intimidated, perhaps; he knew it was wise to respect the comandante. Those who misjudged Cordova's often-psychotic changes in temperament did not often get a chance to repeat the mistake.

Rudolfo Cordova had been born in Cuba and reared under the Batista regime. He had joined the then-unknown revolutionary Che Guevara, to stalk the mountains of Cuba as a guerilla fighter. It was Guevara who had introduced Cordova to Castro. Castro had been impressed with Cordova . . . had found the self-educated Cordova to be a brilliant innovator and master tactician; a man who could take the meagerest supplies and turn them into lethal weapons, which were often used to decimate Batista's troops. He was a master of munitions, improvising, from a variety of ordinary chemicals, explosives of devastating quality. Cordova soon had become known as "El Cerebro" or

"The Brain," a title that only swelled Cordova's already inflated ego.

It was Cordova who planned the mining of the sewer system of Havana. The mines were built in Havana basements and planted at strategic locations around the city right under the eyes of provincial forces they were designed to kill. This system of mines enabled Castro's forces to delay or destroy key convoys sent to reinforce the provincial troops fighting around the city.

But with the fall of Batista had come the fall of Cordova from Castro's favor. Castro saw Cordova's growing ambition as a threat to his own power base, and Cordova's ambition was not restricted to the island of Cuba. Cordova saw Cuba as the dominant force in Latin politics and, along with Che Guevara, beseeched Castro to continue his revolution throughout Central and South America.

Castro had not agreed with their grandiose plans and had let both Che and Cordova go their separate ways.

Cordova had fought with Che until his death, then had gone into self-imposed exile. He schemed for years to implement the plan that would foster his dream rebellion. Eventually he had settled on Triangle Island and set about raising the vast amounts of money necessary to fuel the small army he wanted to raise to fulfill what he considered his destiny—the control of one of the smallest countries in Central America.

Cordova sat before his surveillance screens, waiting for Vicente Villa to arrive, monitoring the construction inside Triangle Island. Even he was impressed with the progress they had made over the last ten years. The Anglos' passion for the drug cocaine had grown even greater than he had imagined. The cash he stripped from the smugglers had raised his power level to the point where he was now almost ready to begin his attack.

Everything he viewed on his surveillance screens Cordova himself had designed, and yet he was perhaps most proud of the fact that he had built the megalithic underground complex under the noses of the very authorities he would soon hold in the palm of his hand.

The door to his quarters opened, and Vicente Villa stepped in.

"You sent for me, Comandante," said Villa.

"Sí," said Cordova, gesturing toward a row of wooden chairs set before his Spartan desk.

"Thank you, Comandante," said Villa, bowing to Cordova's authority but remaining standing behind the row of chairs.

"The progress with the island goes well," said Cordova.

"Sí, mi comandante," said Villa. "Your plans are sheer genius. Even the engineers praise your expertise."

The necessary compliments stuck in Villa's throat. He knew the comandante was primarily responsible for the construction, yet his demands were often impractical, even outrageous.

"Thank you, Vicente," said the comandante. His demeanor suddenly changed. "I'm glad it meets with your approval." The tone was sarcastic.

"Comandante?"

"You directly disobeyed my orders!" shouted Cordova, slamming his swagger stick on his desk.

Villa did not reply. His only response was to hang his head, like a little boy being shamed by his father. Villa had learned to weather these outbursts by letting the comandante rant and rave, sometimes for twenty or thirty minutes, until either his ego or his madness was satisfied.

This day Villa was lucky. The comandante's diatribe lasted only a few minutes, during which period Villa stood mute.

"You are absolutely right, Comandante," said Villa. "I let emotion get in the way of better judgment. To give chase to one of the Anglos with the Coast Guard so close was not only dangerous, but reckless as well."

Cordova studied Villa. Granted, he was his favorite, but he did not want their friendship to interfere with his purpose. Cordova could not stand insubordination, even from his favorite.

"You will, of course, refrain from such activity in the future," said Cordova.

"You have my assurance, Comandante," said Villa, knowing that the situation would still dictate his movements, and not some blind allegiance to a sometimes neurotic despot.

"Excellent," said Cordova. He began to pace before the huge map of Central America behind his desk. Again his mood changed radically, and Villa stood by, waiting for Cordova to complete his thoughts.

The comandante was revered by his compatriots as a demigod. Cordova charisma *was* his command, the sense of control and authority he could muster from within the souls of his followers. Cordova's influence was like some aphrodisiac, an almost hypnotic spell he could cast over those within his sphere of influence. A modern-day Napoleon, he had ambition that was no less grandiose.

Cordova favored his old mentor Castro in many ways. He had adopted Castro's olive-drab wardrobe as well as his full-face beard, but there was no benevolence about Cordova, as there was with Castro. Cordova had a wildness in his eyes, the same mania that possesses most psychotics; however, the mania was a subtle, manipulative control that produced results.

Cordova stood six feet tall and was of slightly larger than medium build. The gaunt frame that had haunted the mountains of Cuba had filled out, the funds from the cocaine having padded what was once an athletic physique. His eyes were burning brown and carried with them a piercing penetration, the kind of withering stare that made many suspect him of being clairvoyant.

Cordova chained-smoked Cuban cigars and had a metabolism that kept him running eighteen hours a day. Perhaps it was his ambition that fueled his stamina. In any case, he could stay up longer and perform better than men twenty years younger in his command.

Cordova, a devout Catholic, believed that his quest was somehow divinely decreed, yet he would violate any rule of the church to see that his long-range goals were achieved.

Cordova beckoned Villa to join him in front of the map of Central America adorning the wall behind his desk. Cordova placed his arm over Villa's shoulders, and the two men paced back and forth in front of the map.

"Soon, Vicente," said Cordova. "Soon we will be ready to move. It is only a matter of time now. Even the trial run has been scheduled."

"Magnifico," said Villa, though he still harbored some doubts as to the plan's real potential for success.

"The flagship is nearly completed," continued Cordova. "I hope you will excuse me for chastising you so, but your reckless move might have endangered my entire timetable."

"I was wrong, mi comandante," said Vicente.

"Bueno," said Cordova. "See that it doesn't happen again."

Villa nodded.

"Come," said Cordova, pointing to a pile of computer printouts on his desk. "We now have intelligence on all the shipping that will enter the Canal for the next six weeks. Let me show you how they will be used."

The Gulf was ablaze with the new morning sun. The turquoise of the sea contrasted with the white cumulus clouds rolling in over the Florida peninsula. The morning exhibited the kind of still that sells lots of airline tickets to residents of the northern latitudes during the winter.

Jack and Virgil weren't interested in their surroundings, only the rendezvous they had with the Coast Guard. Dickerson had contacted them at the Wharf Rat concerning their next run, and both Jack and Virgil had been adamant. They weren't moving anywhere until someone explained about the submarine that had stalked them in the Gulf.

Dickerson agreed to a meeting, specifying a point in the Gulf at approximately where Jack and Virgil's sighting had occurred. That way he felt he could clear up any doubts the two neophytes might harbor, and check the equipment aboard the *Domino* as well.

"Here they come," said Virgil, pulling in his fishing pole.

Jack turned and saw the cutter closing on them from the port beam. "Yeah," said Jack. "And isn't that our friend from the FBI there on the bow?"

"Sure is," said Virgil. "Look at the bastard wave, would you?"

"Friendly cuss," said Jack, pulling a beer from his cooler.

The cutter came alongside the *Domino*, and Virgil tossed a line to Dickerson. Calling out a greeting, Dickerson came aboard the *Domino* with the captain of the cutter and an electrician's mate.

"Sorry we're late," said Dickerson, extending his hand. "Couple of vacationers had some engine problems."

"No problem," said Jack, shaking Dickerson's hand. "Where do we start?"

"Is this where you sighted the 'submarine'?" said the captain of the cutter, his voice heavy with sarcasm.

Jack didn't like the captain's manner at all. "I'll bet you think we're both a couple of idiots," said Grisby.

"Jack," said Dickerson, trying to intervene.

"Well, I got news for you, swabbie," Jack went on, ignoring the interruption. "We know what the hell we're doing out here, and what we saw the other night was a goddamn submarine."

"Is that so?" asked the captain. "Well, I've had just a few years on the sea, son. Now, I realize my expertise may not exceed yours, but I do know a bit about navigation and navigational equipment and what it shows and what is really there. So if you don't mind, perhaps my electrician's mate could examine your hardware. Then maybe we'll get some answers. That is, if that's all right with you."

"All right, gentlemen," said Dickerson. "Simmer down. I'm sure we're all on edge this morning."

"Who is this clown?" asked the captain, still steaming about Jack's remarks. "I don't have to listen to—"

"Perhaps the captain would like a beer," said Dickerson.

Jack and the captain exchanged glances, then he broke into the cooler.

"Not while I'm on duty," said the captain. His tone now was sanctimonious.

"Well, hell," said Virgil. "I ain't on duty."

Virgil grabbed a beer and then led the electrician's mate to the *Domino*'s sonar and radar. The sailor bent down and opened a reinforced chest that held a variety of electronic gear. He began to search the sonar and radar systems for some kind of glitch that might have registered an object that really wasn't there.

"These things can be tricky," said the mate. "I've seen some sonar systems that send out echoes that bounce off their own hulls and look like targets. All the system is doing is tracking itself."

"Is ours like that?" asked Jack.

"Nope," said the mate. "But there could be one of a hundred different reasons why you registered an underwater target. Clear me up on one point, will you?"

"Name it," said Jack, more comfortable to be dealing with a subordinate than with the captain.

"Didn't you say that this sub surfaced?"

"Sure did," said Jack.

"Then kept pace with this boat?" asked the mate. The skepticism was clear in his voice.

"Damn right it did," said Virgil.

"Well, gentlemen," said the mate, "my specialty is electronics, but I've never heard of any sub that could do eighty or ninety miles an hour on the surface."

Jack and Virgil looked at each other sheepishly. For a moment the mate had both men wondering whether they had been hallucinating.

"Look," said Jack. "I know I saw a conning tower behind us."

"It was dark, wasn't it?" asked Dickerson.

"Yeah, it was dark," said Jack. "But I know what I saw."

"I tracked the damn thing on both radar and sonar," said Virgil. "Jack saw the blip register, too."

"Gentlemen," said Dickerson, "we don't deny that you saw

something. Our contention is that it might have been a false image."

Again Jack and Virgil looked at each other, each searching for an expression of doubt. They both remained adamant.

"Hey, man," said Jack. "I'm sorry. But we *both* saw it!"

"All right," said Dickerson. "We'll continue with our investigation. Bur promise me this. If we can show you where either the equipment failed or you interpreted the information incorrectly, you will give up on the idea of being trailed by a submarine?"

Jack and Virgil thought about it a moment. Both were having relatively the same thoughts. Perhaps they *were* wrong. After all, the equipment was all new to them and their interpretation could have been wrong.

"Okay," said Jack after a pause. "Let's make the run just like we did that night."

"Good idea," said the captain of the cutter. "I'll leave Dickerson and my mate on board, and we'll pull off out of radar contact so we don't dirty your screens with our image."

"Fine," said Jack, glad to be rid of the captain.

The cutter broke off with the *Domino*, and Virgil brought the boat about to begin the run in approximately the same location as their first sighting of the submarine.

As Virgil brought the *Domino* up to speed, the electrician's mate studied the sonar and radar. The mate ran a gamut of tests on the systems, yet everything registered normally. "Is this where you made your sighting?" asked the mate, making an adjustment to his testing gear.

"Yeah," shouted Jack over the roar of the engines.

"Did it look like this?"

Jack and Virgil looked at the screen, and there, right where the submarine had registered, was a blip on the sonar screen.

"Yeah! That's it!" said Virgil. "That's right where it showed up, too!"

Jack didn't reply. He kept watching the electrician's mate, who once again adjusted the test equipment hooked into the *Domino*'s radar and sonar screen.

"And when the image appeared to rise above the surface, did it look like this?"

Now the image, as it had the night of their sighting, rose and registered on the radar. It appeared off the *Domino*'s stern as before, and trailed the boat in its every move.

"Damn," said Virgil. "That's what I saw, all right."

Then Virgil's excitement changed. He looked at Jack, then at Dickerson, who offered an apologetic look and shrugged his shoulders.

"Oh," said Virgil, cutting back on his engines.

Jack remained silent, watching the electrician's mate. It was plain he could manipulate the image on the radar and sonar screens, but the image's movement wasn't the same as it had been the night they had sighted the submarine. The image now on the screen mirrored the movement of the *Domino* exactly. The image that had tracked them had not reacted as fast.

Though Jack knew little of electronics, he knew there was nothing wrong with their radar and sonar systems. What they were viewing was merely the wizardry of electronics and the mate's expertise with the test gear. Common sense told Jack that no two boats moved at exactly the same time. Only electricity, moving at the speed of light, could do that. And captains of two different vessels don't think faster than the speed of light. And they certainly couldn't match each other's reactions at the same speed, either.

"That's very interesting," said Jack.

"You still don't believe it, do you?" asked the electrician's mate.

"No, I don't," said Jack.

"Well, there might have been a time when I wouldn't have, either," said the mate, closing up his test gear. "But you see, the semiconductors and microcircuits today have personalities of their own. Some react just the way they are designed. Others," he continued with a quizzical expression, "well, others just have a mind of their own."

"So what's the bottom line?"

"I think you ought to have the entire system replaced," said the mate.

"Consider it done," said Dickerson, "and thanks for your help."

"Anytime," said the mate.

"Better radio the cutter to pick us up," said Dickerson.

The cutter was back within fifteen minutes, and the mate climbed back aboard. Jack still did not believe his explanation, but kept his opinion to himself. Virgil wanted to believe it was a glitch in the system.

"So you'll make your run tomorrow night?" asked Dickerson.

"Sure," said Virgil.

"We'll dispatch a repair crew to fix the electronics. They should be on the dock when you return."

"Fine," said Virgil. "Where do we contact you next?"

"You've got our number," said Dickerson, climbing aboard the cutter.

"Sure have," said Virgil, casting off.

Jack and Virgil watched the cutter angle back toward the coast. The captain gave a disdainful look back at the *Domino*, which was drifting in the Gulf. "Submarines?" sneered the captain. "And in these waters? Submarines that can do seventy knots? Christ, I never heard such shit in all my life!"

The Wharf Rat was deserted, save for Jack, Virgil, and Domino, who holed up in front of the bar. Sundays usually passed lethargically at the Wharf Rat, at an easygoing pace, but this Sabbath was an exception. The atmosphere was charged, the clientele anxious, with no avenue to vent their frustration.

"I don't like this," said Domino. "You guys are getting in way over your heads."

"We've been in tougher spots before," said Jack, taking a slug of beer.

"Damn it, Jack!" said Domino. "Don't give me that Marvin Macho routine. It's not like you."

Jack smiled wanly. "Can't fool you, can I?"

"I still say there's nothin' wrong with the instruments," slurred Virgil, climbing around the bar to pour another round. "I don't care what that clown from the Coast Guard said. I saw a submarine."

Domino placed her hand on Jack's leg. "Please don't go tomorrow night," she said. "I can lend you the money to get the government off your back."

Jack reached over and took Domino's hand. "I let a woman pay my way once," said Jack, shaking his head. "It was a mistake. I swore I'd never do it again."

"Oh!" replied Domino in that disgusted tone women reserve for their man's stubborn behavior.

Domino started to bolt away from the bar, when Jack's massive arm caught her around the waist and pulled her back between his legs. She struggled in his embrace while Jack calmly finished his beer with his free hand.

"You're not going to change my mind," said Domino, straining to free herself. "Nothing you say or do is going to have any effect on my opinion."

Virgil ignored the tusseling and tried to squint his double vision into focus. He rediscovered his bottle and poured a triple shot of Jack Daniels into a beer mug. This he smothered in cracked ice and crowned with whipped cream and a cherry.

Jack pulled Domino closer to his bar stool. She seemed to struggle less, and Jack took advantage of the situation. Dropping his feet onto the floor, he pulled Domino in toward his chest until he felt the softness of her abdomen against his crotch.

Domino gasped as she felt the bulge inside Jack's jeans. Seeing her mouth slightly parted, Jack moved in for the kill. He pressed his mouth around hers, then gently bit her on the lower lip. The bite was not painful but playful, and Domino found herself quickly aroused.

Virgil was still trying to lick the whipped cream off his nose. He settled for chewing the cracked ice until the gnawing of molars on frozen water sent chills up Domino's spine.

She pulled away from Jack and glanced in Virgil's direction. "Not now, Jack," she said, "not here."

"Thanks a lot, partner," scowled Jack.

"What'd I do?" Virgil smirked drunkenly.

Jack was about to give his good buddy the bum's rush when Cody Carnes walked in the front door. Cody was dressed in a tailor-made "After Six" and looked rather elegant, a complete contrast to his usual pugnacious appearance.

Virgil cupped a hand over his right eye so he could discern the visitor. "Jesus Christ!" he said, astonished. "It's Cody!"

Cody ignored the stares and walked behind the bar. There he began to mix himself a milkshake. The shake was a health food store special, a nightmarish concoction of pills, powders, and oils, which had the aroma of rotten eggs.

"Care for some?" asked Cody, waving the disgusting brew under Virgil's nose.

One whiff sent Virgil staggering for the bathroom.

"Hurumph," said Cody, watching Virgil's world-record run. "I think it tastes rather good."

"And what are you dressed for?" asked Jack.

"The opera," said Cody haughtily.

"Uh-huh," said Jack, "and just where might that be?"

"Miami," said Cody, adjusting his tie. "Mother and I are going to see *Carmen*."

Jack took his index finger and twirled it a couple of times.

Cody sighed. "Sometimes the opinions of the bourgeoisie bore me to death," he said, downing his shake in a few gulps.

"Hey, how about dumping off Virgil on your way down Route Forty-one?" asked Jack.

"Oh, I suppose so," said Cody, continuing his contrived, stuffy mannerisms. "Will you be locking up, Domino?"

"Yes, Cody," said Domino with a grin. "As soon as you leave."

"Very good, madame," said Cody, heading for the men's room. "I shall deposit yon drunken lout on my way to the theater."

"Thanks, Cody," said Domino.

"Where am I going to get deposited?" asked Jack with a wry grin.

Domino's eyes began to well up with tears, and Jack was puzzled by her reaction. Cody was just hauling Virgil out the front door when Domino broke down and began to cry uncontrollably.

Jack took her in his arms and tried to console her. "What's wrong?" he said.

"Oh God, Jack," said Domino, her chin quivering so much it garbled her speech. "I've got an awful feeling something terrible is going to happen."

"Nothing is going to happen."

"Yes, it is!" said Domino, thumping him on his chest.

"I can see it's time to put *all* the drunks to bed," said Jack.

"I'm not drunk," said Domino, "just scared. Scared that something is going to happen to you."

"Come on," said Jack, picking her up in his arms. "It's time to get you to bed."

"I don't want to go to bed," said Domino. "I want you to get out of this awful business."

"I will," said Jack, kissing Domino on her forehead.

"You will?"

"Yes," said Jack, carrying Domino up the stairs toward her living quarters.

"Promise me," said Domino.

"I promise," said Jack. Just as soon as we finished what we started, he thought.

Domino fingered the hair on Jack's chest as he carried her up the stairs leading to her loft bed. Jack set Domino down on the floor and placed her hands on her hips.

"Now, don't move," said Jack.

"What?" said Domino, turning toward Jack, who was now behind her.

Jack gently pushed her head so that she again faced forward, looking out over the fabled upstairs of the Wharf Rat Saloon.

"Don't talk either," he said.

"But Jack, what are you . . ."

Domino felt Jack's mouth on the side of her neck. Her shoulder rose in reaction to the stimulation. She felt his hands slide down the sides of her ribs, over her stomach, and down inside the waistband of her slacks. Domino's breathing became irregular as Jack's hands eased the slacks away from her hips and let them slide to the floor.

Jack unbuttoned the back of her blouse and let the garment tease Domino's flesh as it too found its way to the floor. Domino could feel him behind her. She heard him pull his shirt over his massive shoulders, and she yearned to feel his arms lock about her. But Jack was just beginning.

Gently he eased Domino out of her bra, taking care to pull the flimsy material down across her breasts so the friction would heighten her arousal. Another garment joined the growing pile on the floor. Jack noticed that Domino was trembling and soothed her anticipation by grasping her about the shoulders and slid his hands down her sides until he knelt behind her with his face squarely in the small of her spine.

Jack's hands came up the sides of Domino's legs. His fingertips were barely touching the surface of her smooth skin, and the sensation was as though her every nerve ending were screaming for satisfaction.

Jack swept his hands around inside Domino's upper thighs until they caught the top of her bikini panties. Here Jack took care to harden his grip around the underwear, an indication of what was already happening to him.

Jack stripped her naked and let his arms linger on Domino's exposed flesh like two constrictors snaking about her erogenous zones. She could feel Jack's breath on the base of her back. The brush of his lips across her spine was almost too much to bear, an agonizing promise of pleasure.

Jack began to rise, and as he stood he wrapped his tensing arms around Domino's trembling body. Grigsby had a way of using his awesome strength, but not in a manner that would physically hurt a woman. He would surround his lover with a sense of power, tensing biceps and pectoral muscles until the woman was inundated by an overall feeling of *hard*.

Jack's hands crisscrossed Domino's breasts, his fingertips closing about the soft white flesh until the stimulation was such that she thought she was going to faint.

"Oh, God, Jack, I can't stand it. My knees are buckling."

It was a lecherous smile that greeted Domino. "That's the idea," he said, coming around to face her.

Now Domino felt Jack's right arm slide between her legs. He lifted her off the floor, holding her in the crook of his arm. Jack deliberately flexed the bicep so the bulge would keep pressure where it counted, and began to kiss her breasts.

"You're really enjoying this, aren't you."

"Uh-huh."

"You're sick, really sick, Grigsby," said Domino, grabbing handfuls of Jack's hair.

"I know," said Jack, letting his teeth rake over the tips of Domino's breasts.

"Oh, you bastard," said Domino, writhing in the crotch of Jack's arm. "Nobody ever made love to me like this."

Jack gave a low chuckle as he eased Domino down on the bed. "How about that?" he said. "And to think, I'm just getting warmed up."

Dickerson had come down to the docks to see Jack and Virgil off. It seemed strange to Jack that he came undisguised.

"Be sure to watch out for the submarines," Dickerson said with a smile.

It was an odd look that Dickerson gave Jack as they pulled away from the docks, almost as though he knew something important yet was deliberately withholding the information.

The *Domino* cut a wake across the Gulf, a vector of froth sliding across an almost silent sea.

Jack's movements seemed animated as they neared the rendezvous with the mother ship. Jack looked at Virgil, who manned the helm with his usual aplomb, yet he was still troubled by the gut feeling that something was wrong.

The mother ship lay on the horizon, its actual distance distorted by the setting sun. The rigging of the ancient tramp

steamer moved with the wind or the rock of the waves, beckoning Jack like some Flying Dutchman. Jack had an overriding
feeling of foreboding, a desperate sensation of déjà vu, yet
could not not bring himself to call out the order to go back.

Virgil seemed to move in slow motion as they reached the
side of the mother ship. Virgil appeared upset with Jack for not
responding more quickly to his orders to dock alongside the
tramp steamer.

Jack caught one of the lines dropped over the side of the
mother ship and made it fast to the bow. Jack went aft on the
Domino to retrieve the cache of money for the drop and froze in
his tracks when he reached the stern.

There was a gaping hole in the aft locker where the M-60 machine gun had been. Only a few rounds of ammunition dotted
the empty gun mount. Jack was turning to yell a warning to Virgil, when he noticed the water just aft of the *Domino*'s transom.
It was bubbling, as though some great leviathan was about to
swallow up the boat.

Jack tried to move, but his feet seemed locked in place.

Suddenly the water exploded. Men leaped out of the water,
buoyed up by some superhuman force. They leaped onto the
stern and began an assault toward Jack. There must have been
twenty of them, and the weight of their bodies threatened to
capsize the *Domino*.

Jack tried to grab a nearby gaff, but he could not seem to
grasp the makeshift weapon. Jack's eyes swelled with horror.
Those men coming in over the stern. They weren't Spanish—
they were Oriental. And what was that they were wearing?
Black pajamas?

Jack turned to bellow at Virgil, but when he did he found the
bow inundated with more VC. They had come up on Virgil
from behind and were strangling him with piano wire.

Jack jumped over the side of the *Domino*. The water was
warm, full of animal feces and night soil. Jack tried to run, but
the muck of the rice paddy held him to a crawl. The VC lined
the banks of the paddy, each taking turns firing their AK-47's
and using the bursts to herd Jack from one bank to another.

Jack's feet would no longer move. He stood sinking into the paddy as he watched the approaching burst from the AK close on him. Each slug sent a plume of paddy water high into the air as the line of spent death roared in upon him.

It was a horrific scream that awoke Domino. She hardly recognized the man beside her. His face was contorted with fear. His eyes seemed about to pop out of their sockets, and the tendons in his neck protruded so much she expected the flesh to tear.

Domino tried to comfort Jack, yet only became another threat inside his nightmare. Domino was trying to scream louder than Jack, and she had to dodge the blows he threw, for if one landed, she would end up in the hospital.

Finally Domino managed to slap Jack in the face. She hit him as hard as she could, and the reaction was almost instantaneous. Jack gasped for breath and seemed momentarily unable to comprehend his surroundings.

Domino reached out for him, trying to console the man who had only moments ago been a raving madman.

Jack turned and saw Domino. He recognized her, but was it still a dream?

Now Domino felt confident enough to touch Jack. She extended both her hands, and Jack grabbed them as though he still didn't believe what he was seeing was real.

"It's me, Jack," said Domino, pulling his head into her bosom. "It's all right. You're here with me, Domino."

Jack buried his face in Domino's bosom, not out of sexual ardor but for comfort.

Domino caressed Jack's head the way mothers have done with their children for a thousand years, and with this comfort, the giant of a man drifted off, exhausted by his ordeal.

Jack stirred and groped about the bed in a half sleep. Domino sat watching him from the far end of the bed. Jack found a pillow and pulled it toward his chest. The pillowcase against his mouth registered. Jack woke up.

"What are you doing down there?" he asked.

"Watching you," said Domino.

"Watching me do what, sleep?"

"Uh-huh."

"That's dumb," said Jack, rubbing the sleep from his eyes. "Come here. You can watch me make love to you."

"Uh-uh."

"Well, what do you want?"

Domino's look of worry told Jack everything he needed to know.

"Can't do that," said Jack, jumping out of the bed and pulling on his pants.

"Come back to bed," said Domino, letting the sheet drop to her waist.

Jack's mouth fell agape. "That's not fair," he protested.

"What's not fair?" asked Domino innocently, letting her fingers slide rhythmically across her chest.

"I'm not going to give it up, you know," said Jack, climbing back into bed. "I'm seeing it through, no matter what you say. No matter what you do."

"Of course, darling," said Domino, unfastening Jack's belt. "What ever you say. I'll go along with whatever you decide."

Chapter Eight

CONFIRMATION
VERIFIED

THE *DOMINO* worked its way south, hugging the coastline. Virgil ran at half throttle to conserve fuel. Jack seemed oblivious of his surroundings, and rode in the copilot's seat, gazing blankly out to sea.

"Something bothering you?" asked Virgil.

"Yeah," said Jack, returning to reality. "Domino is pretty worried about the business."

"No kidding. Well, it ain't doin' much for my nervous system either."

"She thinks I ought to get out."

"What?"

Jack let Virgil sweat for a moment, then gave him a wry grin. "Don't worry. I'll save your bacon. I want to keep the boat as much as, maybe more than, you do. Besides, things were getting a bit dull anyway." ·

"Dull? Well, next time, I think we ought to pick something a little less exciting than maybe getting our asses shot off."

"Hmm," pondered Jack facetiously. "Maybe we could invade Cuba."

"The man's crazy," said Virgil, speaking toward the heavens.

128

"Yeah! And while we're there, we could kidnap Fidel. That would be good for a few grins."

"I'm bookin' you into a rubber room the minute we get back."

Virgil held his course until he reached Gordon Pass, then cut his engines and nursed the *Domino* into an inlet, toward an old fishing shack and a ramshackle wharf.

"Why are we stopping here?" asked Jack.

"Got to pick up some supplies," said Virgil. "Go forward and dock us, will you, Jack?"

Jack waited on the dock while Virgil disappeared into the shack. He emerged a minute later, carrying two ten-gallon gas cans. A withered old man standing in the doorway of the shack waved good-bye.

"What the hell is going on here?" asked Jack.

"Here," said Virgil, handing the gas cans to Jack.

Virgil ran back to the shack and retrieved two more ten-gallon cans. He came aboard and waved back at the old man in the shack. "Thanks, Ned," shouted Virgil.

The old man gave Virgil another quick wave and closed the door of the shack.

"That's Ned," said Virgil, hoisting one of the gas cans and taking it aft to the fuel cells.

"That's nice," said Jack, watching Virgil dump the clear liquid into the fuel cells of the *Domino*. "I thought you topped off back at the dock."

"Took a ninety-percent load," said Virgil. "Had to leave room for this."

"And just what is this?" said Jack, sticking a finger in the familiar-smelling fluid. "That's alcohol!"

"Damn right!" said Virgil. "We'll be runnin' twelve-percent soon as I empty this. It'll beef up the octane of the gas. Might give us a few more miles an hour out of this rocket. You know, in case we run into that *submarine*."

"Ah, you're a sneaky bastard, Mr. Fullenkamp," said Jack.

"I try," said Virgil with a shrug. "Shall we proceed?"

"Yeah," said Jack, checking the sonar and radar. " 'Into the valley of death rode the six hundred.' "

"What?"

"Just drive."

The *Domino* kept a heading parallel to the coast. They kept moving on course 138 past Marco and Goodland and around the Cape of Romano. This was to give them the appearance of a pleasure craft. When the *Domino* reached Ten Thousand Islands it came to a new heading: 270, which would take them to the longitude and latitude of the mother ship.

The cigar lay in one of the many deep-water canyons off Ten Thousand Islands. It had picked up the sonar echoes of the catamaran as it came down the coast. The track of the vessel hadn't fooled Vicente Villa. He knew their destination and gave the order to his helmsman to shadow the *Domino*'s course.

The cigar cruised at a depth of fifty feet when it came about on the *Domino*'s stern. There she would hold steady until the dopers made their rendezvous. Then they were fair game. This was no shakedown cruise, and Villa wouldn't be shackled by any restrictions laid down by the comandante.

"All ahead two-thirds," said Villa, easing back into the captain's couch. "Steady on course 270."

Jack scanned the horizons with field glasses, while Virgil monitored the sonar and radar. The *Domino* appeared to be alone on the Gulf, save for a few hungry gulls that swooped about their stern.

"See anything?" asked Virgil.

"Nope. Anything on the marvels of modern technology?"

Virgil studied the crimson and lime screens. "Nothin'."

The cigar stayed astern of the *Domino*, running right on the limit of their detection devices. In the cramped confines of the conning tower, Villa and his helmsman began to sweat. The bandannas about their brows quickly became soaked, yet neither man had time to wring them out. The demands of operating the cigar were too complex to allow for such luxuries, and each man sat sweltering in his own stink.

"You're getting too close!" snapped Villa, his temper shortened by the heat. "They'll pick us up on sonar."

The helmsman glowered and eased up on their speed.

The turbines of the cigar hummed a lower tune, answering to the lessening of the fuel supply, yet the whine of the engine still filled both men with anticipation. It was as though the awesome horsepower were teasing them, begging them, beckoning them to unleash its pent-up desire for speed. It was a narcotic that did not develop tolerance levels.

"Stay on the limit of their radar and sonar," said Villa, realizing the dopers were nearing their rendezvous. "We will pick them up on the return run."

"Aye-aye, my capitan," said the helmsman, keeping the cigar positioned perfectly.

Virgil kept glancing aft, then glimpsing at the sonar, before returning his concentration to the helm.

"Something bothering you?" asked Jack.

Virgil shrugged his shoulders and took another look aft.

"Got a pain in the neck?" asked Jack.

Virgil nodded belatedly. "Yeah."

"Anything on those screens?"

Virgil again searched both sonar and radar. "Nothin'."

"Well, fuck the equipment," said Jack. "You have a better track record."

Virgil smiled, then his concern quickly erased his mirth. They were being shadowed again. Virgil just knew it. And no matter what the electronics specialist said, the equipment wasn't recording their stalker.

Jack continued to scour the ocean, including their stern. Some ten minutes passed before they picked up the mother ship, and by then, both Jack and Virgil were pretty jumpy.

Their invisible adversary was beginning to take a toll on both their nervous systems.

Virgil brought the *Domino* alongside the mother ship, and they concluded their business quickly.

"You seen any other ships in the area?" Jack asked the captain of the mother ship.

There was an ugly pause before the voice came from above deck. "That es none of jour beesness, señor," said the captain. "Now jove off!"

Virgil obliged, and they left the mother ship behind, carrying a triple load of coke, all purchased with the money they had lifted from Red Pardee.

"I'm headin' for the barn," said Virgil, increasing their speed.

"Shotgun!" shouted Jack, popping the stern M-60 and loading a belt of ammunition.

The bows of the *Domino*'s catamaran hulls buffeted over the water. The chop gave the boat a kind of rhythm as it sliced across the Gulf. The engines too caught the beat. A harder pull and torque with each touchdown into the sea, an angry snarl as the props tore at the ocean, as though the ship longed to be airborne once again.

The props of the *Domino* began to register on the instrumentation of the cigar. The haunting electronic blips that echoed off the bulkheads charged both Villa and the helmsman with expectation. The sensation was always different, always unique, and individually special.

"All ahead full," said Villa.

The helmsman pushed the throttles of the cigar forward, and the turbines reacted eagerly.

"Three degree up angle," said Villa.

The cigar began to close on the *Domino*, the comandante's dream machine making up the distance fast, as was her design. In a few minutes the dopers' boat would be sunk. Her precious load of cocaine would be carried on board the cigar and the hapless crew of the catamaran given the deep six.

The blip on sonar had made both Virgil and Jack jump toward the viewing screen. Virgil snarled as he shook his finger at the mechanism.

"You stupid fuckin' machine! You're tellin' me somethin' I already knew, you worthless sack of shit!"

Virgil was about to give the sonar a smash with his fist when Jack intervened. "Lose 'em!" said Jack, glancing back at their still-unseen adversary. "Lose 'em good!"

"Damn right," said Virgil, resting a heavy hand on the throttles. "Choke on my smoke!" shouted Virgil, giving the engines their head.

The alcohol-laced fuel now poured into the *Domino*'s hungry engines, the turbochargers gulping up the octane and turning it into power on a ratio that threatened to shatter the blocks.

The bows of the *Domino* rose out of the water as the man-made leviathan roared across the Gulf. Two huge plumes of wake blew off the transom.

"We cannot match their speed underwater, my captain," said the helmsman. "We must surface or they will soon be out of range."

"Prepare to surface," said Villa. "Full ahead on course 050."

The helmsman blew negative, and the bow of the cigar began to break the surface of the Gulf.

This maneuver registered on the radar of the *Domino* and gave Jack an estimate of his target's approximate range, heading and speed. Jack adjusted his sight accordingly and pulled the bolt back on the M-60 machine gun.

The helmsman set the bow planes and triggered the hydraulics to lower the hydrofoils into the water when the cigar reached the surface. The speed of the turbines was now adequate to lift the cigar nearly out of the Gulf, where it rode on its forward and aft hydrofoils.

"Jesus Christ!" said Virgil, monitoring his tach and speedometer. "They're closin' on us!"

The cigar was running wide open, cutting across the Gulf on the razorlike edges of its computer-corrected hydrofoils, and exceeding the speed of the *Domino*, which was now falling back into range of Villa's arsenal.

"Open the forward firing doors," said Villa. "Prepare to open fire with miniguns."

The forward doors on the cigar's conning tower slit open. Salt water beaded off the cigar's skin with the force of the wind, now registering well over one hundred miles an hour. The hideous muzzles of the miniguns poked out of the firing doors so the blasts would not damage the interior hydraulics. Villa brought his starlite sniper scope to bear. It would not be an easy target, for the doper had already begun to take evasive action. No matter; the miniguns would soon silence his engines.

The tracers came out of the firing doors of the cigar like slag blistering out of a blast furnace. Each line of fire was a ray of phosphorescent red, tearing up huge plumes of seawater as they raced toward their target, but before the lurid line of death could converge on the fleeing target, the quarry opened up with a sting of its own.

Jack Grigsby laid into the M-60 with one controlled burst after another; he too was blazing the night sky with a line of crimson lead, but his shooting had an advantage. Jack could react with the evasive action of the *Domino* almost instantly, whereas their attacking adversary had to wait for the movement to take place. It was an edge Grigsby would use to great advantage.

Spent 7.62 mm brass littered the afterdeck of the *Domino* as Jack laid down a murderous barrage. The tracer ammunition acted like spotter flares, and Jack could clearly make out the silhouette of the attacking cigar.

"What is it?" Virgil shouted over the roar of the engines and the blasting of the M-60.

"It's a sub!" said Jack, quickly reloading a fresh belt.

"My ass!" screamed Virgil. "Subs can't do a hundred and thirty!"

"Well, this one does. Now lose the sonofabitch," bellowed Jack.

"That's what I'm tryin' ta do!" said Virgil.

Slugs from Jack's M-60 began to bounce off the conning tower of the cigar, yet did little damage. So far the hull weathered the fusillade.

"The Anglos are armed," said the helmsman, trying to match the evasive maneuvers of the catamaran.

"So it would seem," said Villa, easing up on his firing. "Can you close on them?"

"No, my capitan," said the helmsman, monitoring his gauges. "We are faster, but they are more maneuverable. The best I can do is maintain contact."

"You must overtake them!" demanded Villa. "We cannot allow them to escape. The Anglos must not know of the existence of these boats. Not until the comandante puts our plan into action."

The helmsman shook his head. He knew that to exceed their present velocity would increase the tremendous pressures on the hydrofoils, to a point where even the computers could not make the necessary adjustments to keep the struts from being ripped out of the superstructure.

"As you wish, my capitan," said the helmsman, and the cigar began to narrow the margin separating the two blurs streaking across the Gulf.

"Goddamn it!" screamed Virgil, grabbing a glance at the radar. "He's gainin' on us again! Blow him out of the water, Jack!"

Now the target was even closer. Jack could see the miniguns spitting fire from the conning tower, and he concentrated his aim on the port delivering the crimson death. His first burst was a bit high, but the second threw six slugs of 7.62 mm ammunition inside the firing doors of the cigar.

Bullet fragments from Jack's firing slammed into the

minigun's belt feeders, yet the mechanism grudgingly continued to try to force ammunition, hopelessly jamming the
weapon.

"The port minigun has been crippled, my capitan," said the
helmsman, wondering who they were chasing.

"I'll keep firing with the starboard gun," said Villa. "Keep
increasing your speed."

The firewalls around the turbines of the cigar began to
scorch. Soon the insulation would begin to smolder, and the engines would have to be shut down, yet the helmsman kept the
throttles running the rpm well into the red. They couldn't allow
the dopers to escape with what they had seen.

Virgil monitored his tachometer. They too were running in
the warning zone, and oil pressure was dangerously high. If he
kept up this speed much longer he'd blow the engines.

"We can't hold this speed much longer!" bellowed Virgil.

Jack nodded and loaded another belt, but while his gun lay
silent, the remaining minigun aboard the cigar began to get the
range.

The first of the slugs punched a hole in the port quarter of the
transom, and the flying pieces of Kevlar hull being pulled off
the *Domino* nearly ripped the wheel out of Virgil's hands. Jack
fell over on his side as the *Domino* veered hard to port, but the
maneuver pulled them out of the firing that would have quickly
chopped the boat to pieces.

Jack leaped back behind his M-60, threw in a fresh belt, and
opened up again, while Virgil struggled to maneuver the *Domino*. This time Jack did not fire in bursts but rode the trigger,
knowing what the consequences would be. No matter; he had to
knock out their attacker's firepower, and if he had to sacrifice
the barrel of the M-60, so be it.

Villa could hear the rounds slamming into the conning tower
just above his couch. Now almost every round found its mark,
and the reverberating metal of the hull told him the doper was
doing a lot of damage. Villa started to fire his remaining

minigun when a tremendous explosion ripped the upper portion of the conning tower.

Villa pounded on the controls of the minigun. Nothing responded. Villa cursed their bad luck. Undoubtedly, the doper had hit the second minigun's mechanism, and the weapon had blown up.

"Open the firing door on the twenty-millimeter cannon," ordered Villa.

The helmsman reluctantly complied. He knew what this meant. The boat would be blown to bits and all its precious cargo would be lost. The firing door just below the miniguns yawned opened and the heavyweight weapon of the cigar came into view.

The lull in shooting almost made Jack think the fight was over, but his legacy from the Mekong Delta told him otherwise, and he tossed the useless aft M-60 with its fused barrel over the side and climbed forward to retrieve the bow machine gun. It was quite a feat, yanking the M-60 off its forward mount in the wash of the boat. The hundred-plus-mile-an-hour winds ripped at Jack and threatened to tear him right off the deck. Somehow he managed to hang on and slid back across the froth-slickened prow to the helm, then on the deck and back to the aft mount, where he quickly set the fresh gun in place.

Jack was just locking in a belt of ammunition when the cigar opened up. This time both Jack and Virgil had enough sense to duck, for they knew the sound blasting at them from behind, and it was no light machine gun. It was heavy stuff, and had it not been for their wafer armor plating they would have been blown out of the water.

"Jesus Christ!" said Jack, poking his head up just over the gunwales. "Get us out of here, Virgil! I can't stop that!"

"All right, motherfucker," screamed Virgil, shaking his fist at the cigar bringing its 20 mm to bear once more. "You want me? All right, you bastard, then come and get me!"

Virgil's hand shoved the throttles into a speed they were

never designed to sustain. He could see the tachometers bury themselves in the red, and he prayed the engines would hold together just a little longer. They were nearing Ten Thousand Islands now, and the water was dotted with sand bars and tiny atolls.

If that bastard wants us, thought Virgil, then he better be crazy enough to drive where I'm goin', and only a madman would go there.

The *Domino* veered hard to port. Virgil let the hole in the transom aid his high-speed turn, and as they completed the maneuver more of the boat's Kevlar hull tore way. The drag coefficients were taking their toll on the *Domino*'s speed now, and Virgil knew they'd get only one chance to peel the pursuers off their stern.

Virgil kicked on the forward flood lamps, and the ocean in front of him came alive in a blaze of white light. It lay dead ahead of them—an island, a good-sized island, quite long but very narrow, no more than nine feet out of the water and ringed with scrub palm.

"Hang on!" screamed Virgil, placing a ready hand on the throttles.

Jack dived into the aft couch and had just managed to snap his seat belt when Virgil made his final approach.

The *Domino* was doing a hundred and forty when she came up the island's sandy beach. The hull threatened to shatter upon impact, but the angle of attack was just within the guidelines of the design physics, and the boat held together.

The *Domino* lifted off like some majestic missile being photographed in slow motion. Its twin bows acted like airfoils, lifting the boat into an angle of climb that let them clear most of the scrub palm. Only the rotors touched the trees, and they chopped up the snarled branches into twigs.

The *Domino* leveled off. Its bows rode the cushion of air as they had been designed, yet the seawater was no longer on the stern, only more air, and Virgil held his breath, hoping the boat wouldn't nose too far over before coming back into the Gulf.

The *Domino* glided back earthward, the cushion of air now pushing the twin bows up, as though the forces of nature realized the danger and corrected the boat's trim.

The landing tore Virgil from the helm and threw him against the gunwales with such force he hairline-fractured some bones in his wrist. With an aching in his arm, he jumped back at the helm, reset his trim, and shoved the throttles back to full. Virgil sneaked a glance back at his adversary as he cut off the forward floodlights.

The helmsman had cut the turbines even before Villa gave the command. They knew they could not follow the dopers over the island. To do so was to rip the hydrofoils off the bow planes and invite certain death in a crash that would have splattered the cigar all over the island.

The cigar settled back into the water. Now the ground clutter of the surrounding islands made it difficult to plot the heading of the escaping dopers' boat on radar. Villa cursed the dopers' luck and ordered the helmsman to come about. Perhaps they could cut off the catamaran by second-guessing his approximate heading.

Virgil eased off the throttles of the *Domino*, but not very much. They were still running light at one hundred miles an hour when Jack joined Virgil at the helm. Jack monitored the gauges dotting the forward control panel.

"Jesus Christ, are you running hot!"

"I know it," said Virgil, rubbing his injured wrist. "We ain't out of the woods yet, and I'll be damned if I slow down before I put some distance on that bastard."

"Run her into the ground, then!" said Jack, returning to his aft M-60.

Jack took an abestos glove out of the ammunition locker and tried to free the barrel of the M-60, but the heat of his firing had swelled the metal and temporarily fused the pinions. He would have to wait for the barrel to cool before mounting the spare.

"Who *are* those guys?" asked Virgil.

"If you ask me that same question again, I'm going to think you're Butch Cassidy and I'm the Sundance Kid. How the hell should I know? Whoever they are, they're very good."

"Now who's quoting the movie?"

"Just drive the boat."

The *Domino* hugged the coast, staying in waters where it would be difficult for their adversary to follow.

"Well, one thing's for sure," said Virgil, poking at the bullet holes in the *Domino*'s forward wind screens.

"What's that?"

"They're gonna *have* to verify our confirmed sighting this time."

"I wouldn't be so sure," said Jack. "They're just liable to blame it on another doper."

"But we both saw—"

"I know what we saw," said Jack. "And I know what I shot, but getting the Feds to buy it may be quite another story."

The cigar made several more sweeps with its sonar and radar, but the proximity of the islands made location impossible.

"We must return to base," said the helmsman.

Villa hesitated. He kept hoping they would find the dopers and keep them from reaching port. The sighting of the cigar could threaten the comandante's entire plan, and the thought of facing his wrath upon their return was something Villa wanted to avoid.

A sudden blip on the radar screen sent Villa's heart jumping, but it was just another small island showing up on screen.

"They are gone," said the helmsman. "We must return to base."

Villa nodded in agreement but remained deep in thought. The dopers might have to keep their mouths shut. After all, they weren't the type who would go running to the authorities.

Villa realized that his troubles were only beginning. For now Villa had the unenviable task of explaining not only the loss of the coke but the escape of the dopers as well. The problem was further compounded by the fact that the cigar had sustained damage from the dopers. The news was sure to send the comandante into a blind rage. Villa shook his head and sighed as the cigar began its dive and corrected its course for the final approach to Triangle Island.

Jack was stowing the remaining M-60 inside the forward mount when the seizure began. Jack's left arm began to quiver as though he had been stricken with some rare variety of palsy. Jack clenched his fist in an effort to fight off the affliction. The spasm stopped, but only for a moment, then it returned, even worse than before. He pulled his arm into his gut and tried to massage the spasms away. As he squeezed the muscles in his forearms, Jack had a moment to reflect back to the time the spasms had first begun the second month he spent in the Mekong Delta.

"It's a nervous release," one of the field surgeons had said. "Nothing to worry about."

Jack squatted on the foredeck, rubbing his arm and hoping Virgil hadn't noticed. Virgil rode the wheel of the helm, suffering from a similar malady. With him it wasn't palsy but a locking of the muscles. The arm he had injured during their high-speed escape now seemed frozen to the wheel. Virgil had to make a course correction soon, and he couldn't get his hand to let loose of the wheel. Finally he put some pressure on the injured wrist, and the pain shocked the hand into a clumsy release.

Both Jack and Virgil nursed their wounds of nervousness, yet neither made any mention of the problem. It was the strange code of ethics that had seen them through the worst parts of the Tet offensive in Vietnam. The odd rituals and superstitions of GI's, dating back to "three on a match."

"You all right?" said Jack, getting up but keeping his left arm tucked behind his back.

"Fine," said Virgil, sticking his frozen fist in his pocket. "Just fine."

Chapter Nine

ABANDON SHIP

THE *DOMINO* was listing badly to port when she limped back into the Naples boat docks. Jack had been monitoring the bilge pumps while he stuffed their cocaine inside a modified aqualung with a false bottom. Now Grigsby's attention was drawn to the docks. There were some familiar faces waiting for them.

"Oh, man!" said Jack, waving a wan hello to Domino and Cody. "When she sees this boat she's going to throw a fucking fit!"

"No shit," said Virgil, eyeing the bullet holes in the wind screen. "And I'm gonna enjoy watchin' you try to calm her down."

"Thanks a lot," said Jack, stowing the aqualung.

"What are friends for?" said Virgil, bringing the stricken vessel in to the dock.

Jack tossed Cody a line, and the bouncer made what was left of the *Domino* fast to the dock.

Domino was so shocked by the appearance of the boat she could hardly speak. The forward windscreen caught her eyes first. There the effects of the miniguns were hideously visible. Most of the screen had been shot away, as had the headrests on the pilot's couch.

Domino walked aft to the boat along the dock, remaining mute as she assessed the damage.

The stern of the *Domino* was a shambles. The 20 mm cannon had turned the transom into "Shredded Wheat." Even the wafer armor had been chopped up. The hatch covers above both engines had been blown away, and below them the quarter panels punctured. Only the bilge pumps kept the boat afloat.

Jack stood on the aft deck with a sheepish look on his face. "Hi, honey," he said with a feeble wave, "I'm back."

Domino's reaction surprised Virgil. She brought her hands up to her face and began to cry. She was almost hysterical when Jack jumped up on the dock and took her in his arms.

Domino's crying made her words almost unintelligible.

"You said nothing like this was going to happen!" said the Cajun princess, thumping Jack on his chest. "You promised me! You said not to worry. God damn you, Jack! You *knew* this was going to happen! You lied to me!"

"No, I didn't, Domino," said Jack, trying to console her. "Christ, do you think I'd go out on the Gulf knowing I might get my head blown off?"

Domino's wailing was catching the attention of everyone in the immediate area. Curiosity seekers began to move down the dock, where they were headed off by Cody.

Suddenly Domino tore away from Jack, her shock now turning to anger. "You bastard! You sonofabitch! I was sick all the time you were gone. Do you hear me—sick! Sick with worry, and the only thing that got me through it was when I thought of what you said. You said not to worry. Well, look at that boat! Just look at it! You lied to me, you sonofa—"

Domino tore away from Jack and looked wildly for somewhere to run, but the end of the dock was now swollen with onlookers, and Jack blocked her other escape route. She stood where she was and continued to cry until she started to collapse. Jack caught her and took her into his arms.

"Oh, God, Jack," said Domino, burying her face in his chest. "I was so worried, so scared. I just knew something awful had happened."

"Nothing awful happened," said Jack. "I'm here. I came back."

Domino looked up into Jack's eyes. For an instant Domino's cry was of happiness and relief. She squeezed Jack and began to get control of herself. Jack kissed her forehead, her eyes, her mouth, yet his consolation was short-lived.

Four cars pulled up at the dock, four of those bland sedans that are bought at group rates. The no-frills specials disgorged a group of men all wearing windbreakers and baseball caps with the same identification: FDTF. Several members of Florida Drug Task Force came storming down the dock.

Cody blocked the authorities' onslaught. "And just where do you gentlemen think you're going?"

One of the Drug Task Force officers shoved two warrants in Cody's face. One was for the search and seizure of the *Domino*, the other for the arrest of Jack Grigsby and Virgil Fullenkamp.

"It's those two clowns at the end of the dock. I'll take care of the girl," said Cody, pointing at Domino.

The Task Force galloped down the dock. Three members nabbed Jack, reading him his rights and handcuffing him simultaneously.

"Jack!" said Domino, wiping the tears from her eyes. "What's going on?"

"It's probably all those parking tickets," said Jack.

"Hey, we got a comedian," said one of the officers.

"You don't know what you're doing!" charged Domino, wading into the narcs. "These guys work for—"

Cody's massive hand clapped over Domino's mouth. "Come along, dear," said Carnes, hoisting Domino off the dock. "I think it's time we found an attorney."

Jack watched Cody haul Domino down the dock. He could understand Domino's hysteria, but not her stupidity.

The Task Force poured onto the listing deck of the *Domino*. Virgil gave a casual glance to the aqualung containing the coke, then stepped away from the stash. Several officers grabbed Virgil, swung him about and began to frisk him.

"Oh, officer!" gushed Virgil, wiggling in his grasp. "I'll give you about an hour to cut that out."

"Another smartass!" said the Task Force member, feeling the hard lump under Virgil's left arm. "Oh-ho! What's this?" He pulled the M-11 out from under Virgil's torn windbreaker.

"It's made by Mattell," said Virgil with a toothy grin. "Cunningly lifelike."

"Yeah," said the officer, pulling two clips of .380 ammunition from Virgil's back bandolier. "And what are these—caps?"

"You wish to say anything at this time?" the leader of the Task Force asked Jack.

"Nope."

"You want a lawyer?"

"Nope."

"Well what do you want?"

"To go home and go to bed with that woman," said Jack, watching Cody carry Domino away.

"Jokes, always with the jokes," said the leader. "Book these bastards."

The bare walls of the detention cell were peeling several layers of paint. The floor reeked of vomit and disinfectant, and though Virgil had to move his bowels, he couldn't bring himself to use the cracked, seatless toilet.

"Jesus, what a pit!" said Virgil, squatting on the bare floor. "How long they gonna keep us down here?"

"Not much longer," said Jack, watching the jailer come walking down the corridor.

The jailer stopped at Jack's cell. He handcuffed both Jack and Virgil, then let them out of the cell. He said nothing, merely pointed in the direction they should go.

Jack, Virgil, and the jailer came out of the detention complex and into the Fort Meyers police station. It was a new addition to the old building, paid for with confiscated drug money. The jailer took Jack and Virgil to an interrogation room and opened the door. There, waiting inside, were the men Jack expected. Ames and Dickerson of the FBI.

The jailer tossed the handcuff keys to Dickerson and closed the door as he left. Jack and Virgil looked around the room. There was another man with Ames and Dickerson. It took a moment for Jack to recognize him. It was the captain of the Coast Guard cutter.

"Hi, guys," said Virgil. "How's tricks?"

"You mind?" said Jack, pushing his cuffed hands toward Dickerson.

"What the hell happened?" asked Dickerson, uncuffing Jack and Virgil.

"We told you before," said Jack, glaring at the cutter captain. "Nobody seemed to believe us."

"No one sighted any submarines last night," snarled the captain.

"Well, we sure did!" said Virgil, kicking a chair out from under the table.

"Did you see our boat?" asked Jack.

"They've been going over it for the past four hours," said Ames.

"And you kept us locked up all that time, just so you could check out the goddamn boat?" said Virgil.

"We kept you down there," said Dickerson, "so we could maintain your cover. Didn't want to make it appear as if you were getting special treatment."

"You're all heart," said Jack.

"Look," said Ames with a piqued sigh. "The sooner you help us get this mess cleared up, the sooner you two can go back to your drinking and whoring."

Ames was knocked nearly breathless by Jack, who plowed into the agent and lifted him off the floor by the lapels of his new suit.

"Now, listen to me, you sawed-off little prick! You ever talk to me like that again and I'll play handball with your fucking brains!"

"Jack!" said Dickerson, trying a more sympathetic tone. "We need you as much as you need us. Let him down."

Jack eased the visibly shaken agent back to the floor, and

shoved him into a chair. "I meant what I said!" continued Jack, pointing a finger at Ames.

The air of confrontation was broken by a knock at the door. Dickerson bade entry, and the electronics expert from the Coast Guard entered the room.

"Oh, boy," said Virgil. "We got another one."

The electrician's mate scowled at Virgil and saluted the captain.

"'Lifer,'" mumbled Virgil.

"Do you have the report?" asked the captain.

"Yes, sir," said the mate, pulling some papers from a briefcase. "But these are only the preliminary findings."

"Let's have it," said the captain.

"Sir," said the mate, examining the hastily scribbled documents. "Well, the boat sustained heavy damage. We found seven-point-six-two–millimeter infire fore and aft. The wind screen, couches, and engine hatches sustained the heaviest damage. The transom and wafer plating was torn up pretty badly too, sir. Probably heavy machine gun. Twenty millimeter, we suspect. One more burst of that and the fuel cells would have been penetrated."

"Wonderful," mumbled Virgil.

"The engines are shot. One had a cracked block; the other threw a rod. All the pistons were burned, the oil was cooked, no viscosity whatsoever, and the cooling system is even worse."

"Told you I could drive," Virgil whispered to Jack.

"I ran a check on the sonar and radar. They were about the only thing still operational on the boat. Checked out. No gremlins. Sir?" said the mate, looking up from his notes. "If I may?"

"Go ahead."

"Sir, that boat, well, I mean it's a miracle it's still afloat. It was hit with some really heavy stuff. I've never seen anything shot up so bad. And one thing's for sure. No other doper carries the kind of weaponry that hit them."

"Then who?" interrupted Dickerson.

"I dunno," said the mate, looking at Jack and Virgil. "Maybe what they say is true. Maybe it was a submarine."

The Coast Guard captain bristled at this suggestion. "That's preposterous," he said. "No submarine can do ninety knots."

"You're right," said Virgil. "This one was doin' more like a hundred and twenty."

"Now you are talking fairy tales," said the captain.

"Look, you dumb bastard! I had the engines of that hundred-thousand-dollar honey running red line for over twenty miles, and that imaginary submarine was closin' on us every inch of the way."

"Gentlemen!" interceded Dickerson. "We're not going to get anywhere calling each other names. Now, I've got a request on to the Air Force to run some surveillance over the area. If necessary, they can get satellite photographs. That should dispel any doubters. We should be hearing from them soon. I made the request when the Coast Guard spotted you limping into port."

Jack and Virgil moved into a corner of the interrogation room.

"I still don't think these clowns believe us," said Virgil.

"You're right," said Jack. "But there may be another way."

"What do you mean?"

"Later," said Jack.

The phone in the interrogation room rang. Dickerson answered it.

"You're sure, Major?" said Dickerson. "What about the satellite photos? I see. You checked with the Navy? Uh-huh. Well, thank you very much, Major. Yes, sir, I will. Goodbye."

The look on Dickerson's face was not encouraging. He paced around the room with his hands clasped behind his back, finally stopping in front of Jack and Virgil.

"So? What'd they say?" asked Virgil.

"All the surveillance, both flyovers and satellite, proved

negative. No sign of a submarine. Navy hasn't got anything operating in that area either."

"Now what?" said Jack.

"We'll get you another boat," said Dickerson.

"Why? So we can get blown out of the water this time?"

"We'll put more armor plating on and several recording devices. Infrared, the latest in Starlite, videotape, and stills."

"Well, I'm not going back out there unless you beef up *my* weaponry!" said Jack.

"What would you like?" said Dickerson, with a questioning raise of his eyebrow. "A fifty-caliber machine gun?"

"That'll do just fine," said Jack.

"We can't mount one of those monsters on a cigarette," said Dickerson.

"You could mount one on one of the new Popeyes," offered the Coast Guard captain.

Jack and Virgil seemed surprised by his cooperation.

"Popeyes?" said Dickerson.

"Yes," said the captain. "Twenty-eight-hundred horse unlimited catamaran. Prototype."

"Catamaran?" said Dickerson. "I thought a catamaran was a small sailboat with twin hulls."

"You're only half right," said the captain. "Catamaran refers to the hull design. Twin hulls aren't exclusively used on sail craft. In this case it's a modification of the hull design, applied to an offshore powerboat. I know the fella who builds them," he continued, winking at Virgil and Jack.

"Why the change of heart?" asked Jack.

"Well, somebody shot up your boat. And if it's a submarine, I'd like to get a good look at it too."

"All right," said Dickerson. "We'll make arrangements to get you another boat. In the meantime, you'll have to go through the regular routine."

"Meaning?" said Jack.

"You'll have to go back to your cell until a judge sets your bail."

"When will that be?" asked Virgil.

"Oh, around five this afternoon."

"Around five?"

"Take it easy," said Dickerson, signaling for the jailer. "You boys look as if you could use some sleep."

Jack and Virgil spent the next six hours napping in the jail. Neither really slept. The hubbub of the detention cell, plus thoughts of their narrow escape, made them restless. Still they were able to grab a few hours' rest, and around six their lawyer made bail.

Domino and Cody were waiting with the lawyer on the sidewalk outside the station. Jack and Virgil came down the station steps and greeted them.

"Your court appearance is the end of the month," said the lawyer, looking at Domino. "She put up the bar as bail. You blow town, she loses all of it."

Jack and Domino said nothing. They just embraced.

The lawyer left them to their reconciliations and handed Virgil his card. "If you have any questions, here's where you can reach me."

"Thanks," said Virgil, watching the lawyer drive away in his BMW.

"Thank you, too," said Virgil, placing an arm over Cody's shoulder.

"You want to keep that arm?" said Cody.

"Yes, sir," said Virgil, shoving both hands into his pockets.

"All right," said Cody. "Everybody in the car. We've still got to stop at the dock."

During the ride back to the dock, Domino and Jack remained silent. They rode in the back of Domino's convertible, each lost in his own thoughts. Cody pulled the car up to the dock and they got out to inspect the damage to the boat.

Two members of the Drug Task Force were still on board when they arrived. They had stripped the *Domino* of its gear, which they had laid out along the dock.

Jack and Domino were first to arrive at the mooring, and it was a sad sight that greeted them. The Blue Water catamaran lay bows-up in the water, its stern having sunk to the bottom of the marina.

"You Grigsby?" said one of the Task Force members. "Sign here for your property," he continued, shoving a clipboard at him.

Jack glanced at the dock. Only a few items had been salvaged before the *Domino* sank. There was Jack's old Coleman cooler, some flotation gear, life vests, and the scuba equipment.

Jack came up short on the count of the scuba tanks. "We had four tanks," said Jack. "Where's the fourth tank?"

"Oh," said the narc. "That one's being held in the prosecutor's office. Sign here."

Jack scribbled his name, and the Drug Task Force member left the docks.

"Damn," said Cody, looking at the bullet holes in the bows. "Looks like you guys ran into a buzz saw."

"And then some," said Virgil.

"I'm sorry about what I called you," said Domino.

"It's all right," said Jack.

"It's just that I was so scared. You forgive me, Jack?"

"Domino, it's all right," said Jack, kissing her.

"Ah, Jesus," said Cody, posturing. "I've got better things to do than stand around and watch you two."

"Come on," said Virgil. "Help me get this stuff aboard the *Ice Bucket*."

"Why not?" said Cody. "The atmosphere here is getting a bit maudlin."

"You're going out again, aren't you?" asked Domino.

Jack hesitated. "Yeah," he said. "They're getting us another boat."

"I don't suppose there's anything I can do to stop you."

Jack thought about his answer. He remembered how some guys used to react to stressful situations in Vietnam, how they couldn't stand it while they were there, yet once away from it, they couldn't wait to get back. Life took on a whole new perspective, a vitality, an intensity that couldn't be matched. Jack suspected his feelings about working for the FBI fell within the same boundaries.

"Don't ask, and you won't have a problem," said Jack.

"I don't know whether I can stand the waiting."

"Only a little longer, Domino," said Jack, taking her hands. "Call it crazy, but Virgil and I will never get another chance like this in a lifetime. We're both scared shitless when we're there and bored to death when we're not. Do you understand?"

"Yes," said Domino, shaking her head. "You *are* crazy, you and Virgil. And I'm crazy too, because I guess I'll have to learn to live with it."

"Can we go back to the Wharf Rat now?" asked Jack with a smile. "I'm starved."

Jack and Virgil left the Wharf Rat just as the early evening crowd began to gather. Jack bade Domino good-bye, feigning exhaustion, and headed for home.

"Boy, you must be tired," said Virgil, "leaving Domino alone on a Friday night."

"I'm not tired," said Jack. "I just don't want her to worry."

"What have you got up your sleeve?" said Virgil with a sly grin.

"We're going to make another run tonight," said Jack, starting up the engine of their junker Chevy.

"In what?" said Virgil. "We haven't got a boat, remember?"

"We have the *Ice Bucket*," said Jack.

"The *Ice Bucket*? Man, you are out of your mind!"

"That sub that tailed us last night was looking for dopers. Dopers run cigarettes, not tubs like the *Ice Bucket*."

"Oh, very clever, Mr. Grigsby."

"We'll just take her out for a little midnight snooping," said Jack, taking the turn for the docks. "I want to get a damn good look at who was tailing us before we make another run."

In the deepening dusk, the *Ice Bucket* set out into the Gulf. The last stubborn rays of the sun baked the western clouds a pastel orange. To the north a squall line cut toward the coast, the dancing lightning giving the Coast Guard reason to issue a small-craft warning.

But the *Ice Bucket* was heading south, away from the squalls and into a greater danger. Virgil corrected their course once they cleared the Cape of Romano and took a heading of 090. Now they entered the waters where they had first been tailed by the mysterious submarine, and both Jack and Virgil grew still as they increased their surveillance.

"See anything?" said Virgil, manning the helm while he monitored their aging radar.

"Nothing," said Jack, scanning the waters with field glasses.

"Say, Jack," said Virgil, with a puzzled look.

"Yeah?"

"What are we gonna do if we find one?"

"Follow it."

"In this tub? Hell, she'll barely make twenty-five knots!"

"Just get a rough fix on their heading and we'll guess it from there."

"Oh, that's a good idea," said Virgil, beginning to doubt the reasoning behind the voyage.

Jack reached into a storage locker, and pulled out two M-11s and bandoliers of ammunition.

"Hey," said Virgil, glancing away from the helm. "Where'd you get those? I thought they went down with the *Domino*."

"Dickerson had these planted on board," said Jack, strapping on the shoulder holster.

"Slip mine on for me," said Virgil. "Things are getting hairy now."

The *Ice Bucket* headed into the labyrinth of Ten Thousand Islands. Here navigation was particularly difficult. Their radar bounced off islands that were there and some that weren't, the pattern on the screen hazing and jumping with the ground clutter.

"Shit!" said Virgil. "You sure you want to do this?"

"Yeah," said Jack.

"Brother, if we kiss one of these coral reefs, this thing'll go down like a cement block."

"Then you'd better keep a sharp eye," said Jack, continuing to search the sea.

The tired diesels of the *Ice Bucket* began to sputter. Virgil feathered the throttles and the engines seemed to respond. Virgil throttled back and the engine began to smooth out.

"Christ," said Virgil. "I hope we don't conk out here. I'd hate to paddle home tonight."

At first Jack thought his eyes were playing tricks on him, as though he were following a school of fish whose scales reflected the light. But the sun had set, and the moon had yet to rise, so what was that strange light running just off their port beam?

"Virgil," said Jack in a hoarse whisper.

"I see it," said Virgil, correcting their course.

The light ran below the surface, no more than ten or twenty feet, and slowly, the danger of the reefs keeping their speed at a minimum.

Jack walked up to the bow of the *Ice Bucket* and waved Virgil in the direction the light was going.

"What do you think?" whispered Virgil.

"That's got to be our boy," said Jack.

They tailed the light for nearly a half hour, then about two nautical miles out from the Triangle Island, the light simply vanished.

"Where, where?" said Virgil frantically.

"Uh, left five degrees," said Jack.

"Ya see anything?" said Virgil, monitoring the radar.

"No," said Jack, banging his fist on the gunwales. "Cut the engines."

Virgil throttled back, and the diesels backfired to a stop. The *Ice Bucket* drifted with the waves while Jack bent his ears toward the sea. Virgil opened a hatch and cupped a hand to his ear. All he picked up was the lap of the waves against their hull.

"Ahh, come on, Jack," said Virgil in his normal speaking voice. "We ain't gonna find those—"

Jack's first thought was that they had run aground, plowed into one of the coral reefs, but they were too far off the island for that. Then the sickening sound of the hull being torn out from under them registered. The sub had come about in the dark and now cut across the *Ice Bucket* square amidships.

Water began to blast into the bilges and smother the *Ice Bucket*'s engines. Still hot from running, steam began to pour off the blocks just before they cracked.

Both Jack and Virgil were thrown off their feet, knocked onto all fours, and slid toward the stern.

The *Ice Bucket* was going down fast. In his momentary panic, Virgil grabbed the fishing tackle as he made ready to go over the side.

"Fuck the fishing tackle!" said Jack. "Grab the scuba gear!"

Virgil joined Jack at the aft locker and grabbed swim fins and mask as Jack frantically screwed the regulators onto their remaining scuba tanks.

Jack could feel the sub passing under them. The keel of the *Ice Bucket* must have been riding on the saw blades of her forward ram. It was probably the only thing holding the boat out of the water.

Jack and Virgil just managed to get into their swim fins and masks as the *Ice Bucket* went down. The water of the Gulf surged about them, a bubbling, frothing current that was laced with floating and sinking debris.

Deck chairs, coolers, fishing tackle, floats, seat cushions, were caught in the undertow. Jack and Virgil were pummeled by gear fighting for the surface or heading for the bottom. Both their face masks were ripped off, and Virgil's nose was bloodied. They struggled free of the suction and swam to the surface.

"Now what?" said Virgil, clearing his mouthpiece.

Jack trod water and ran a three-hundred-and-sixty–degree search. He found what he wanted just east of where the *Ice Buc-*

ket had gone down. The mysterious light had reappeared and was beginning to surface.

"Dive!" said Jack, clearing his mouthpiece.

"What?"

"Just dive, you dope," said Jack, pushing Virgil underwater.

Jack and Virgil had submerged a few feet when the cigar breeched the surface. The weight of their M-11s and ammunition aided their dive, but they still had to force themselves to stay underwater. The searchlight now sweeping the surface told them to stay put.

It was odd the way the light bent as it struck the surface of the Gulf and surprising how much it revealed. They would have to dive deeper if they wanted to avoid detection. Their ears began to notice the pressure as they neared the fifty-foot level. They swam in opposite directions of the searchlight, which seemed to run in precise patterns.

Jack and Virgil heard the first burst as a kind of muted thumping, the muzzle blasts of the Baretta 70 bouncing off the surface of the Gulf. The slugs slamming into the water made a peculiar sound before their heads mushroomed, sharply stopping their velocity.

The volleys of machine gun fire tore up the waters where the *Ice Bucket* had gone down. Jack prayed they didn't have any hand grenades on board, for a few of those over the side would act like miniature depth charges, and the concussion of the explosion would split Jack and Virgil's abdomens from crotch to Adam's apple.

The firing seemed to slow, and the cigar began to make a sweep of the area with periodic bursts of machine gun fire dotting the waters as it ran. Jack and Virgil swam away from the sub until the firing stopped. They allowed themselves the luxury of rising a few feet to a point where offsetting their buoyancy wasn't such an effort, and watched the submarine move off toward Triangle Island.

Jack gave Virgil the signal for surfacing, and, taking care to rise with the ascent of their air bubbles, the pair broke the surface. Jack could see the silhouette of the submarine as it closed on Triangle Island. Then, just as he expected it to correct its course for docking, the sub submerged.

"Come on," said Jack, swimming after the diving sub.

Virgil spat out his mouthpiece. "Are you crazy?"

"Hurry up, or we'll lose them!" said Jack, swimming after the sub.

"I don't even know how much air is in these tanks," said Virgil.

"Well, there's only one way to find out," said Jack.

"Oh, no!" said Virgil, reluctantly following Jack. "There are sharks out here, ya know."

Chapter Ten

CAPTAIN NEMO

THE WATER of the Gulf was cool and black. Virgil could barely make out Jack swimming just ahead of him. Jack homed in on the light from the submarine. The lumens sprayed out in an odd halo from the bow of the sub and silhouetted its strange shape in the dark water. But the light was fading, and the sub was putting distance on Jack and Virgil. Yet just as it seemed it would fade from view, the sub slowed to all stop.

"Come on," said Jack, beckoning Virgil to swim faster. "This is our chance," he continued, shoving his mouthpiece into place.

Virgil reached the point where Jack had submerged, and he cleared his mouthpiece. Virgil spat the device out of his mouth when he felt something grab him. Then Virgil realized it was Jack's hand, and not the jaws of a hungry shark.

Jack surfaced and trod water beside Virgil.

"Jesus!" whisper-shouted Virgil. "Don't do that!"

"Will you hurry up?" said Jack. "They've stopped just ahead of us."

"Jack, they just sunk our boat. What the hell are *we* gonna do?"

"Follow them," said Jack, submerging.

"Ah, this is stupid," said Virgil, following Jack into the lurid water.

The water was actually clear, but the available light was so poor that it appeared murky, as though clouded by some kind of eerie silt. Jack and Virgil swam toward the sub, which was still submerged some fifty yards ahead of them.

They came up port side aft of the sub, and Jack was awed by what awaited them. It was approximately fifty feet long, cigar-shaped, with an abbreviated conning tower that looked as if it had been designed to hold drag down to the barest minimum.

Jack and Virgil approached the sub cautiously. The light from the bow of the sub filtered back aft, but shadows still shrouded the boat. It held steady fifty feet below the surface, a man-made Moby Dick, beckoning the nearby swimmers for a closer look.

Jack was first to the side of the sub. He touched its hull and found it to be remarkably smooth, with a kind of polished skin. It felt like the inside of a teflon-coated skillet.

Jack and Virgil moved forward, stopped at the bow planes, and located the hydrofoils, which could snap down, rather like aircraft landing gear. But it was at the bow where they found their greatest surprise.

At first Jack thought the boat was sinking, but the amount of air seeping out of the bow was not sufficient to send the boat to the bottom. Jack ran his hand along the hull. The bubbles were almost microscopic and formed a kind of slick. Then it dawned on Jack. That's how they developed all that speed. The hull was covered with some kind of polymer, and the bubbles acted like a superlubricant, moving the boat through the water at incredible speeds.

Jack would have proceeded further up the bow, but he saw the ports built into the side of the hull. He could just make out the lenses peering out into the water. Closed-circuit cameras, no doubt, and Jack motioned Virgil to fall back toward the stern.

They swam toward the stern and held on to the aft bow planes in order to maintain their depth. Jack was wondering what their next move would be when he saw something move in front of the sub. Virgil and Jack watched in awe as two massive doors in front of the bow of the submarine opened before them.

The underwater doors yawned open, and light poured from within. The submarine waited for the man-made underwater hatch to open completely before making turns for slow ahead. Jack and Virgil hung on to the stern planes with all their might as the pull of the water threatened to drag them into the suck of the props. Jack could feel his swim fins being buffeted about by the turbulence of the boat's screws and dug his fingers into the slick surface of the stern planes.

Jack and Virgil found that they could cut their own drag by facing head-down into the wake of the sub. They could feel the wash of the microscopic air bubbles coming off the bow as it cut down on their own body drag and made it less difficult to hold on.

The sub jockeyed a bit before angling toward the open under-water doors, and Jack and Virgil rode along, wondering where the sophisticated vessel would take them.

They passed through the doors, and the stern had barely passed the juncture when the hatch began to close. The water was now bathed in light from above, but Jack and Virgil were hidden by the blowing of the sub's ballast tanks, which surrounded them in a wash of bubbles. The props were slowing to all stop, but the suction was still dangerously strong and would have been sufficient to pull both of the hidden scuba divers into the blades, where they would be pulverized.

Finally Jack felt the pull of the props diminish, and he and Virgil swam away from the sub toward the side of what appeared to be some kind of dock. The sub gave a quick thrust and moved forward, deeper inside Triangle Island.

Jack and Virgil held their position some twenty feet below the surface. In the bright light filtering down from above they could see each other quite clearly. Virgil shrugged his shoulders and made a questioning signal to surface. Jack nodded, and the pair cautiously rose toward the lights above.

* * *

Jack and Virgil's scuba regulators spat angrily as they broke the surface near the dock, yet the hubbub in the interior of Triangle Island covered their noisy arrival. At first Jack's vision was blurred by the water clinging to his mask, but when he removed it, the mammoth proportions of the island's interior came into view.

"Jesus!" whispered Virgil.

The intruders trod water against the wall of an underwater dock that led out into the Gulf. Jack and Virgil could see that they were actually inside a kind of lock, and the sub they had followed inside was moving up a sea-level canal that ran nearly the length of the island.

Above Jack and Virgil the ceiling of the underground grotto rose in a nearly perfect arch, the wash of endless waves having carved out the interior of the island sometime after the formation of the continents. The ceiling was covered with stalactites, some of which were over thirty feet long. Jack estimated that the ceiling rose about ninety feet from the sea-level floor.

They began to swim carefully toward the exit of the lock connecting with the Gulf. Jack and Virgil reached the far end of the lock and pulled themselves up, even with the edge. The canal connecting with the lock was bordered by docks approximately thirty feet wide, covered with supplies and support equipment.

The sub they had followed had come to a stop some two hundred feet ahead of them in the canal. There it had docked behind three other such vessels, which were being tended by a number of men all wearing what appeared to be some kind of uniform.

Virgil tapped Jack on the shoulder and pointed to the opposite side of the canal dividing the island in half. There was another sub, this one twice the size of the one they had followed, and another sub, of approximately the same size, docked behind it. Work crews crawled about these larger models, and the flash of arc welders danced over the walls of the grotto.

Jack gave Virgil an elbow and pointed to the end of the canal at the far end of the island. There rose a three-story structure, which straddled the canal and appeared to be constructed to blend in with the island's natural formation. Concrete had been poured to lay the foundation, yet the upper tiers of the structure were laid on ledges of solid rock that seemed to mold to the island's contours.

"Who do you suppose they are?" whispered Jack.

"Who cares?" said Virgil. "We'll let the Federal boys worry about that. Come on! We've seen enough. Let's get outta here."

"Okay," said Jack, stuffing his regulator back into his mouth.

Jack and Virgil started to descend. Their descent was accelerated by the pull of a strange current. Jack felt the pressure of the water against his body and knew something was wrong. Virgil was caught by the current, and the drag was such that it held him fast against the bottom of the lock. Jack was pulled down next, and even his strength was no match against the draft of the whirlpoollike pull. They lay helplessly on the bottom of the lock. Had it not been for their scuba tanks, both would have drowned.

Now the force of the escaping water was such that the turbulence tore the masks off their faces. Jack and Virgil had to press their regulators into their mouths lest they lose those as well.

Jack felt the rush of the water begin to abate, and his head come above the surface. They now sat on the floor of the drained lock in a quagmire of seaweed and stranded sea life.

"Welcome to Triangle Island," came a voice from above them.

Jack and Virgil looked up at the top of the lock and into the barrels of several Baretta 70's. There was a sickly-looking man leaning on a cane at the edge of the lock.

"Come up the ladder on this side of the lock," said Vicente Villa.

Jack and Virgil looked around. The exit of the lock was now sealed by two huge metal doors, and with their only exit to the sea cut off, they stood up and put their hands over their heads.

"Ah, shit!" said Virgil, spitting out his regulator. "We've had it!"

"If they want us dead," whispered Jack, "they'd have shot us to pieces the minute we came out of the water."

"Come up the ladder, gringo," shouted Villa.

Jack and Virgil got up and slipped out of their swim fins and tanks.

"Don't tell them anything," whispered Jack. "The less they know about us the longer they'll have to keep us alive."

"Gotcha," said Virgil.

"Leave your equipment and get up here!" ordered Villa.

"Friendly fella, ain't he?" said Virgil, testing the rungs of the ladder.

"*Dios condena,* gringos," said Villa, watching Jack and Virgil climb.

Jack and Virgil came up the ladder of what they discovered to be a dry dock. They reached the top of the cement wharf and were welcomed by several men wearing camouflaged uniforms and wielding Baretta 70's.

Villa gave Jack and Virgil a disdainful appraisal. He said something in Spanish that brought amusement to his comrades, then took his cane and poked at the bulge under Jack's arm.

"What es dat jou have under jour hacket, señor?"

Villa nodded, and one of the guards quickly stripped Jack and Virgil of their M-11's.

Villa examined the M-11's, screwing on one of the sonics suppressors, which he pulled from the bandaleros. "Es a very nasty weapon, señor. Who were jou planning on chooting?"

"You'll do for openers," said Jack.

The bolts on all the Barettas clacked back.

"Es a very stupid remark, señor," said Villa, signaling his men to lower their weapons.

Villa's cane whistled through the air. It caught Jack off guard. The blow struck him on the right ear, and for an instant the ex-linebacker lost his temper. The submachine guns tempered his wrath.

"Jou keep de smart remarks to jourself, señor," said Villa. "Jou savvy?"

Jack didn't answer, but leveled a calculating stare at the sickly Latin and wondered how it was going to feel when he broke both his legs.

An electronic beeping broke the tension-filled atmosphere. Villa reached into a pocket of his combat breeches and took out a small communicator. Someone spoke Spanish briefly, and Villa pocketed the device.

"Dees way, señors," said Villa, indicating the direction with his cane. "The comandante wants to speak with you."

The men with the Barettas shoved Jack and Virgil deeper inside the subterranean complex.

Jack and Virgil slogged along in their soaked clothing, taking in surroundings. The canal they had entered was bordered on both sides by cement walkways. Four cigar-shaped minisubs lay in bays docked parallel with the canal. Two larger subs were docked in the same manner on the opposite side of the canal. The walkways lining the canal were stacked with construction materials, giving the place the appearance of a subterranean shipyard.

Uniformed workmen busied themselves with the supply of the minisubs, while others formed construction gangs that worked on the two larger subs on the opposite side of the canal. Jack looked about and could see the ceiling of the cavern and the lighting fixtures that had been installed. Yet he could find no substation or generator that supplied the power.

"Look at that," said Virgil.

Jack looked toward the far end of the canal. There was the structure he had seen previously, only it loomed more ominously than before. Like the rest of the complex, the headquarters was fashioned of cement and its tiers molded into the island.

Jack turned his attention back to the docks as they passed the minisubs. A work crew was repairing the damage to the last sub in dock, and Jack recognized the paint embedded in its forward saw ram. It belonged to the *Ice Bucket*. Jack made a mental promise. The first chance he got he was going to pack the sub's bilges with C-4 and blow it out of the water.

"Dees way, gringos," said Villa. "I don't want to keep the comandante waiting."

Members of the repair crews stopped working when Jack and Virgil passed. They all stared at them in silence, as if watching condemned men being taken to the gallows.

The armed entourage surrounding Jack and Virgil reached the main doors to the headquarters. Aesthetics had been avoided during construction, no material wasted; function had obviously been the main concern.

Two sliding metal doors opened, and the group was met by a security guard protected by a small pillboxlike bunker. Villa spoke something in Spanish to the guard. After he had verified the entrance code, a second set of doors opened. Jack and Virgil were escorted inside.

Now the Spartan architecture was replaced by relative opulence. The floors were covered with wall-to-wall carpet, air conditioning was piped into every hallway. The walls of the lobbylike entrance were covered with murals with the predominant theme: propaganda. All manner of bloody heroics was depicted, and at the center of each mural seemed to be a bearded man, leading a charge, who resembled a revolutionary both Jack and Virgil recognized. Fidel Castro.

"Castro?" said Virgil to Jack.

This time Villa's cane cracked Virgil across the side of his skull.

"You will never mention that traitor's name again," said Villa.

Virgil winced under Villa's blow.

"The hombre jou see here is our glorious comandante, Rudolfo Cordova," said Villa, almost coming to a position of attention. "Jou will treat him with the greatest respect."

Virgil didn't reply. He just rubbed the side of his head, which was already beginning to swell, and hoped he could get in a few licks on Villa before Jack broke him in half.

Villa instructed the group to enter into the lifts at the far end of the lobby. Jack and Virgil were separated for the ride to the third tier. Each was accompanied by two armed escorts. Villa chose to stay with Jack. The ride up was quick, and the doors of the lifts opened onto the nerve center of the entire complex.

A bulletproof glass wall separated the hallway from the computer and communications center. Inside, teams of technicians monitored radio transmissions of the coastal authorities, both federal and state, as well as the local jabber between dopers. There was another group of technicians, these involved with an entirely different form of radio traffic, and Jack wondered what concern the comandante could have with commercial shipping in the area.

The escorts prodded Jack and Virgil down a hallway away from the communications center. Now they entered the most grandiose section of the headquarters: the comandante's living quarters. There were security guards stationed outside the main entrance. Villa had to repeat several codes, and then the guards admitted only Villa and the gringos. None but a trusted few ever entered the comandante's quarters armed.

Jack and Virgil entered the main salon and were amazed by what awaited them. The room was styled after a Spanish hacienda, and they stood on the outer edge of a courtyard. A balcony extended all around the courtyard, giving the comandante more rooms than he could possibly use. There was a fountain in the center of the courtyard, with live shrubs and landscaping fed by skylights that had to have been cut down from the very surface of the island. There were birds living in some of the trees, and their warbling seemed to indicate they were quite content with captivity. Jack and Virgil walked into the courtyard and studied the balcony and the rooms adjacent to the ground and upper floor.

Jack was just finishing his examination when he saw a bearded man step out onto the balcony. It was the same man they had seen in the propaganda murals in the lobby. At first Jack had thought the man in the murals had been exaggerated, the charisma a fantasy of the artist, but this fellow looking down on them from above was everything in the murals and more.

The comandante had a way of examining people that made

them squirm under his appraisal. He motioned for Villa to bring the intruders closer so he could make a better analysis. It was not often that any Anglos had evaded one of his cigars, and the comandante was anxious to meet them.

Jack could understand Virgil's earlier remark. The comandante did indeed resemble Fidel Castro. He came down the steps of the balcony, dressed in the familiar fatigues Jack had seen on the other men. Yet the comandante's dress, like any field-grade commander Jack had known in Vietnam, was of a better fit—tailor-made, no doubt—and it added an air of authority, which was precisely the intention.

The comandante was smoking one of his ever-present Cuban cigars as he sauntered across the courtyard. He stopped before Jack and Virgil, rocking on the heels of his highly polished jungle boots, and locked his free arm behind his back in a position of parade rest.

"These are the two?" the comandante asked Villa.

"Yes, Comandante."

"What are your names?" said the comandante.

"Jack Grigsby."

"Virgil Fullenkamp."

"So you are the Anglos who have breeched our security," said the comandante in almost accentless English. "Very impressive, gentlemen. You are to be congratulated."

"Thanks," said Jack, glancing about the hacienda. "This is quite a layout you have here."

The comandante gave a shrug of his shoulders. "It will do for now," he said. "Tell me," he continued. "How did you manage to shoot up one of my cigars so badly? The smugglers in these waters rarely have such weaponry, and then they do not use it so well."

"Shoot up what?" said Jack, feigning ignorance.

"Don't patronize me, señor. We have several photographs of the incident, the clarity of which would astonish you."

Jack winked at Virgil. "Trade secret."

"Is that so?" said the comandante with a brief smile. "That

is a very funny remark, señor. But you will find my sense of humor very short-lived.''

Jack and Virgil glanced at each other. It was obvious they were dealing with a ruthless man who would think nothing of having both of them shot.

"But come, gentlemen," said the comandante, changing his demeanor. "Let us not, as your expression goes, get started on the wrong foot. This way, please. There is much I wish to show you."

Jack and Virgil followed the comandante across the courtyard to one of the doors under the balcony. The door itself appeared to be part of the hacienda, made of wood, with the classic rounded sills. Jack expected to enter an office or library perhaps. What awaited them was totally unexpected.

The sound of surf greeted Jack first, that and the smell of salt air. Virgil was next inside the door and no less surprised. The comandante led them out onto a catwalk that overlooked the eastern side of the grotto. Here the sea washed in under the island through a natural cavern. The force of the waves through the cave opening was being harnessed by some kind of machinery. Teardrop-shaped floats were fixed into a device that could turn the motion of the sea into electrical energy.

The comandante took pride in describing how the machinery functioned, as it was his design and kept the island supplied with more than enough power to sustain even his grandiose plans. The wave generator was remarkably quiet and located at the mouth of the grotto behind a net of camouflage to keep any curious boaters at bay.

Jack noted the surroundings of the cave leading out to the sea, which formed the eastern opening of the grotto. His military training had taught him to look for escape passages everywhere, yet the security measures taken at this location were almost as stringent as those leading into the submarine docks.

"Come along, gentlemen," said the comandante. "There is so much more."

Villa pushed Jack and Virgil off the catwalk and back inside the courtyard. There they proceeded to another floor, identical to the one they had just exited. Now they entered the realm of high tech on Triangle Island. The room was spacious, double-tiered, and softly illuminated. Video display terminals glowed around both tiers, with technicians monitoring everything from weather satellites to shipping traffic. Then Jack recognized the room. It was the same room they had passed on their way to the comandante's quarters, only now they viewed it from Cordova's private entrance.

The comandante explained the capabilities of the room, which seemed to have no limit. He initiated some of the displays himself, taking great pleasure in bringing up the room's projection screen, which dominated the far wall. On this screen he could call up a map of the world, then zoom in on any particular zone, emphasizing intricate details, with shipping routes and cargos taking premier importance.

"What's this all for?" asked Jack.

The comandante smiled. "In due time, Señor Grigsby. This way, please."

They came back into the now familiar courtyard and exited another door on the hacienda floor. Now they came into the living quarters for the cadre. This area had been designed in the same manner as the comandante's quarters, only on a much larger scale. The comandante explained that he didn't want to appear more privileged than his men. He led Jack and Virgil around the facility, taking care to show them the kitchen, mass dining room, library, and theater.

"What do you need so many men for?" said Virgil.

Again the comandante avoided their inquiries, and took them back inside the hacienda. Yet another door opened into what appeared to be a large laboratory. Men dressed in spotless lab coats were cutting cocaine and bagging the potent substances for sale to dealers all over the United States. The comandante was particularly evasive on the particulars of distribution and sale and became irritated at Jack's incessant questioning.

Jack's and Virgil's imaginations were running wild upon their return to the hacienda, yet the comandante would offer no insight as to why he was hiding inside Triangle Island. It was Jack's ultimate conclusion that the comandante was out to corner the market in drug trafficking. The comandante scoffed at his speculation and led them through another door.

Now they came out on a balcony that overlooked the submarine docks. The comandante corrected Jack, telling him the vessels tied up at the docks were not submarines but cigars, engineered by him personally and designed to do battle with the cigarettes of the dopers who had such a profitable business running cocaine past the coastal authorities.

The newer models on the opposite side of the canal were merely larger versions of the two-man cigars, capable of the same speeds, but with a much greater plan in mind.

Jack stood on the edge of the balcony overlooking the panorama below. Obviously some kind of genius was at work. The engineering involved was overwhelming. That, coupled with the fact that the entire construction had been completed unnoticed, was a tribute to Cordova's brilliance. Still there was the overriding question—"why?"

"What are you?" asked Jack, looking at the comandante with a measuring stare. "Some kind of modern-day Captain Nemo?"

For a moment the expression on the comandante's face was unfathomable, then the force of his ego became evident, and he postured regally on the balcony, looking down on the work crews crawling about his brainchild.

"*Muy bueno,*" said the comandante. "Come, gentlemen. You must be exhausted after your ordeal. Vicente, see that they are fed, and receive a good night's rest."

Villa nodded a confused acknowledgment to the order.

"Sleep well," said the comandante, disappearing back inside his hacienda. "I will have a surprise for you in the morning."

* * *

Jack and Virgil sat in a secluded corner of the main mess hall. Vicente Villa was talking with two guards on the opposite side of the mess hall. The guards held machine guns on Jack and Virgil while they ate. Neither man had much of an appetite.

"So, you think they'll give us a cigarette and a blindfold before they stand us up against a wall in the morning?" asked Virgil.

"I don't think so," said Jack. "They'd have shot us to pieces in the dry dock if they wanted to do that."

"What, then?"

"Probably work us over a little bit. See what we know."

"Oh, that's nice," said Virgil. "Just what I need. Get my face reduced to Silly Putty."

"You can't tell them anything," said Jack emphatically.

"Ah, not that name, rank, and serial number shit?"

"Afraid so."

Virgil leaned over the table to whisper to Jack. "I say we tell 'em we're workin' for the FBI. That if we disappear, this place will be crawlin' with Feds."

"Goddamn it!" snarled Jack through clenched teeth. "You do that and we both get our throats cut in two seconds. We *are* missing, dumbass, and there aren't no Feds here to save our bacon."

"Oh," said Virgil, easing back into his seat.

"Now, do what I say. Just like over the pond. If Charlie couldn't get you to talk, he figured you knew something, and he'd keep you alive. Talk and you're as good as dead."

"Yeah," said Virgil, "you're probably right."

"You know damn well I am!"

"All right, Jack," said Virgil. "We tough it out. Airborne!"

"Ranger!" said Jack.

Villa thumped his cane on the table. "That's enough!" he said. "This way."

Jack and Virgil followed Villa out of the mess hall and

into the barracks. It was much more spacious than any military facility Jack or Virgil had ever seen, with a cubicle for each man, affording a luxury neither had known in the service: privacy.

Jack and Virgil, however, were stuck in a single cubicle, handcuffed into bunk beds, and left with an armed guard.

"Sleep well," said Villa, laughing as he left them with their guard.

"Funny guy," said Virgil, wrestling his handcuffed hand around the bunkpost.

"Yeah," said Jack. "A real comedian."

"If we get out of this mess . . ." said Virgil.

"Yeah?"

"That bastard's ass belongs to me!"

"Sorry, good buddy," said Jack, rolling over to a more comfortable position. "You'll have to stand in line."

Strangely, the night passed all too quickly for Jack and Virgil. They almost fought off sleep. The few fitful hours they did manage to doze only made them curse their sleep for shortening the hours before the comandante arrived with their "surprise."

Jack's thoughts were mainly of Domino and whether he would ever see her again. He thought of the worry she would have to endure, and the sickness of separation. The same sickness that was now haunting him.

Virgil tried to rechannel his fear into courage, but found the ploy unsuccessful. He was growing sick with fear, a fear he had never really experienced before. In Vietnam his devil-may-care attitude saw him through many a firefight, yet now he could not summon the grit that had once been his forte. Perhaps it was because they were being held prisoner and he had no means to fight back. Or maybe it was just age; the recklessness of his youth had waned, and now he had to suffer the indignities of fear and all its awful consequences.

Finally sheer exhaustion overcame them both, and they fell

into a dead sleep. So deep was their sleep neither would recall even dreaming. Small consolation, for with the dawn would come the real nightmare.

"Get up!" screamed Vicente Villa, stirring Jack and Virgil from their sleep. "The comandante is waiting!"

Chapter Eleven

LOST WITH ALL HANDS

WHEN DOMINO failed to raise Jack on the telephone, she rousted Cody out of bed and forced him to drive her down to the docks. There her worst fears were realized. The *Ice Bucket* was gone.

"Oh, Cody," said Domino. "Something awful has happened. I just know it."

"Calm down," said the unflappable bouncer. "Let's contact the Coast Guard before you go jumping to conclusions. They probably just had an early charter and left port before we got here."

"Where's the phone?" said Domino.

For Bill and Melinda Jensen the holiday in Florida was the first they had taken in five years. With their health club turning a substantial profit, they had rewarded themselves with a trip. Now, away from the crowds and the hubbub of Miami, they were going to get in some snorkel and scuba diving and bask in the warm Florida sun.

Bill and Melinda had rented a thirty-footer and the necessary gear in Goodland and, taking the dockmaster's advice, had motored out to Ten Thousand Islands to do a bit of spear fishing.

They anchored off one of the larger islands, checked their tanks and dropped over the side. The water was unusually warm and nearly crystal-clear. Small schools of fish darted out of their paths as the pair descended toward the coral fauna awaiting them below.

Melinda collected shells on the bottom, taking care to avoid the pitfalls of some amateurs. They had dived in the Gulf before, on their honeymoon some eight years before. When Melinda sighted the wreck, she wasn't sure whether or not to believe her senses. She picked up some stones off the bottom and clacked them together to attract her husband's attention.

Bill swung about and saw his wife, perhaps fifty feet to his right and signaling frantically for him to join her. Worried that she might be in danger, Bill swam vigorously to her side. There Bill saw what had caused her distress.

The boat was a forty-six–foot sportfisherman that had been cut in half. Both sections of the boat lay close to each other on the bottom. At first Bill speculated that the boat had struck a reef and had gone down, then realized they were in over fifty feet of water, with no coral rising more than ten feet from the bottom.

The vacationers swam cautiously toward the boat, expecting to find some grisly remains of the crew, but the boat was empty. A quick swim from stern to bow produced no bodies; only the ship's name remained to offer any clues. They realized the ship had not been in the water long. The bilges were still leaking air bubbles, and oil from the engines stained the water around the boat. They swam up to the helm and checked the lockers. They found the ship's log, and Bill signaled to Melinda to surface.

The two vacationers began their ascent with the log book of the *Ice Bucket*, haunted by thoughts of what had befallen the crew of the sunken ship.

The Coast Guard station on Marco Island was telling Domino Monet that no one had reported the *Ice Bucket* missing, when the call came in from Bill and Melinda Jensen. They confirmed the *Ice Bucket*'s registration number and pinpointed the location of the wreck. The lieutenant on duty still did not verify the disappearance of the ship, recalling the reports that vacationers had turned in before. Still, he did relay the information, taking care to note that the sighting had yet to be verified, and until such time as the boat was located, they had no recourse but to consider the ship still afloat.

Domino demanded to know the coordinates of the wreck, and although this was contrary to normal Coast Guard procedure, the lieutenant gave her the suspected position. Domino and Cody chartered a boat from one of Jack's rivals at the wharf and gave him the position they wanted to search. An extra fifty dollars saw the captain off without his crew, and the sportfisherman began to trace the same run the *Ice Bucket* had taken the night before.

Domino and Cody arrived at the site of the sinking and found the Coast Guard and the Jensens at anchor on the scene. Two scuba divers from the cutter were just going over the side when Domino's charter pulled up beside the cutter.

"You'll have to leave the area," said the captain of the cutter.

"I'm the woman who phoned about this," said Domino, scanning the waters above the wreck. "I'm related to the skipper of the boat."

"Heave to aft, then," said the captain. "We'll let you know if we find anything."

"Thank you," said Domino.

The divers from the cutter spotted the wreck the minute they broke the surface. It was right where the vacationers had said it would be, and both divers glanced at each other, somewhat surprised at the condition of the boat.

They made a thorough examination of the *Ice Bucket*, both marking down the ship's registration number as a hedge against misidentification. They worked their way aft from the bow, stopping to take note of the hole ripped through its hull.

One of the divers began to photograph the wreck, while the other looked for casualties. After remaining on the site of the wreck for about a half hour, the divers surfaced.

"Did you find anyone?" shouted Domino.

The divers shook their heads "no," spat out their regulators, and climbed into the cutter's skiff, then up the gangway to the main deck.

"What did you find?" shouted Domino.

"Please, miss," said the captain of the cutter, coming down from the helm to meet with the divers.

"What did you find?" asked the captain.

"It's down there, all right," said the first diver.

"What happened?" said the captain. "Hit a reef?"

The two divers looked at each other as if the captain might think they had taken leave of their senses.

"Well, it hit something," said the second diver, unzipping his wetsuit.

"What do you mean?" said the captain.

"I want some of the boys in photo analysis to take a look at the photographs before I say," said the second diver.

"All right," said the captain. "Mark the location with a buoy," he continued. "Make all preparations for getting under way."

"What?" screamed Domino. "Aren't you going to look for survivors?"

"That's what we're going to do now," said the captain. "If you like, you can join in the search."

For the next six hours, the cutter, the Jensens, and Domino's charter searched the waters around Triangle Island, but no bodies were found. A few floating cushions, a deck chair, and Jack's Coleman cooler were all they fished out of the Gulf.

"They could have swum to one of the islands," offered Domino, over the radio.

"That's entirely possible," replied the captain. "I've got a helicopter coming in now."

They kept sweeping the area, sometimes covering the same coordinates twice in hopes of catching something that might have been overlooked on the initial search. But as the sun began to fall, so too did the hopes of the search party.

The comandante monitored the activities of the search party from inside the communications center of his complex. A closed-circuit television camera with a telephoto lens set atop the island kept watch on the small flotilla as it continued to search for the lost seamen.

"Close the camouflaged door on the cavern leading to the wave generator," said the comandante.

"But sir," said one of the technicians, "that will cut our power resources nearly in half."

"It can't be helped," said the comandante. "The search party is dangerously close. Tell the men on the docks to stop assembly. That should cut back on usage."

"Sí," said the technician.

Jack and Virgil stood at the back of the communications center, but they could still see the monitors, and the picture projected on the display screen ate at their insides. Jack could see Domino and Cody standing on the stern of the charter, each searching the waters for the bodies they hoped they wouldn't find. Jack wondered what kind of mental agony Domino must be enduring. No worse than his own, he suspected.

The comandante kept monitoring the situation personally. He glanced back at Jack and Virgil, as if he had some lurid plan for their demise. "You gentlemen have caused me a great deal of difficulty," he said, turning back to the monitoring screens. "More than I thought possible. Possibly enough to upset my timetable."

"Things are tough all over," said Jack.

The comandante would not allow the gringo's remarks to disturb his concentration. The authorities were much too close for him to leave his command post for an instant. Besides, there was much he needed to know from the Americans before he disposed of them, and a few wisecracks were not going to cut short their existence. Not just yet, anyway.

The sun was slipping into the western Gulf when the captain of the cutter called off the search.

Domino was on the radio the moment the order reached her. "We haven't searched all the islands," she stated.

"Miss Monet," said the captain of the cutter, over the radio.

"Our helicopter made a thorough search of every island within ten miles of the wreck sight and found nothing."

"They could have been injured," replied Domino.

"Yes, you could be right. We'll have to continue the search tomorrow. It's much too dangerous in these waters at night. Now, please, return to port, and we'll pick up the search patterns again at first light."

Domino had no choice but to agree. She slumped down on the aft couch of the charter and stared blankly at the sea. Cody sat down beside her and put his arm around her shoulders.

"Oh, Cody," said Domino, placing her head on his shoulder. "We've just *got* to find them." She looked up into Cody's steel-blue eyes. "We'll find them, won't we?"

Cody gave Domino a somber look. This was no time to be patronizing, and the big bouncer knew it. Cody drew in a deep breath, then sighed. "If we don't find them tomorrow," he began, "then you'd better get used to the idea that we never will."

"No!" wailed Domino, beating on Cody's chest.

Cody let her cry and vent her frustration. Her struggling was short-lived. The nerve-racking search had drained her of all energy, and Cody cradled Domino in his arms and let her weep herself into an exhausted sleep.

The comandante kept Jack and Virgil in the communications center until the last of the search party had cleared the area. He then ordered the camouflaged doors to the northeastern cavern opened so that the wave generators would again come up to full capacity.

"Now then," said the comandante, examining Jack and Virgil with a calculating gaze. "I wish to ask you some questions."

Vicente Villa and an armed guard pushed Jack and Virgil back into the familiar courtyard of the comandante's hacienda. They were escorted up to the balcony of the hacienda and through a door at the top of the stairs.

Villa wedged his cane between Jack's legs and shoved him

into the room. Jack fell face-first onto the floor with his hands cuffed behind his back. Jack caught his breath and struggled to his feet. Virgil was next through the door, driven to his knees by the butt of a Baretta 70 delivered over his kidney.

Jack looked around. They were in some kind of laboratory, quite sophisticated from the looks of the equipment, with chemical stores and caged animals lining the walls.

"Vicente," said the comandante, entering the laboratory. "Where are your manners? Get our guests some chairs."

Villa pulled two chairs up next to one of the lab tables, then opened some drawers and took out leather straps, which he fastened to the arms and legs of the chairs. "Sit down."

Both Jack and Virgil hesitated. The guard gave Jack the butt of his Baretta in the back of his ribs, and the barrel across the back of Virgil's head. Both winced and dropped into the chairs.

Villa yanked Jack's hands painfully high, in a move Jack suspected might dislocate his shoulders, then felt his hands pulled down behind the chair, where they were held fast by a leather strap. Next his thighs were secured with straps just above the knees. The procedure was quickly repeated with Virgil.

Villa opened a drawer containing surgical instruments. These he placed on a table before Jack and Virgil. This deliberate display was part of the psychological warfare the comandante would employ to pick their brains. The ploy was already working. Jack and Virgil had broken out in a cold sweat.

Villa produced hypodermic syringes, which he waved just under Virgil's eyes.

"Too bad we do not have any sodium Pentothal," said the comandante, examining the surgical instruments. "It would make things so much easier. But no matter. You will find Villa most able in the means of interrogation. You may begin, Vicente."

Villa moved toward Virgil first. Physical size had nothing to do with a man's endurance. He chose Virgil only because he was closer to the tray of instruments.

Virgil pulled at his restraints when he saw Villa approach

him. Villa carried a roll of adhesive tape, which he used to further immobilize Virgil's hands. He took a hypodermic syringe and stuck it into a vial. He drew up enough of the liquid to fill the syringe. He grabbed hold of Virgil's index finger and began to insert the needle under the fingernail.

Virgil's arm exploded with pain. It felt as if a charge of electricity roared through his hand, up his arm, and into his neck. Virgil screamed as Villa injected the substance. Now the pain was multiplied tenfold. Virgil tore at his bindings. His writhing was so violent that he overturned his chair. Finally Virgil's nerve endings were cauterized and he was given a momentary respite from his agony.

"This can go on all night," said the comandante. "If you like, we can inject directly into the eye. You will find that most distressing. Unless you want to cooperate."

"You do what you want," said Jack, sneering at the comandante's threats. "We talk, you'll kill us anyway. That just means I won't be around to see the fireworks."

"Fireworks?" asked the comandante, signaling Villa to stop his interrogation.

"Yeah," said Jack, continuing the bluff. "You'd be amazed what you can do with five or six pounds of C-four plastic explosive."

The comandante sat down on one of the laboratory stools and thought about his captive's remarks. Most likely it was a lie, designed to save the gringos from the pain of the interrogation. Still there was the possibility. . . .

"And just where did you plant the explosives, Señor Grigsby?"

"Let's just say it will be interesting to see you try to get one of your precious cigars out through those underwater doors."

"I could easily dispatch a team of men to disarm the charges," said the comandante, calling Jack's bluff.

"Be my guest," said Jack.

Now the comandante began to pace about the laboratory. He still doubted the gringo's claim, yet he could not risk an explosion. The days until he initiated his operation were few, and he could not afford any interruption of his timetable.

"Anyone can say they have laid mines or explosives," said the comandante, turning on Jack. "How did you set them?"

"Oh, fuck you!" said Jack. "I won't tell you that. Brother, you must think I'm an idiot. But I *will* tell you this much, Captain Nemo. I could have used Bessemer blasting caps with a magnetic trigger. Could have used trip wire and contact triggers. Could have used trip timers with delay fuses. Could have used circuit triggers. Then again, I could have used Play Dough for the dummy charges, and when they were disarmed they would detonate the real charges I placed behind them. You want me to go on?"

The comandante's fingers tapped rhythmically on the tabletop. "You are a very resourceful man, Señor Grigsby."

"I hope he blows yer fuckin' balls off," Virgil said, grimacing with pain.

Villa raised his cane to clout Virgil when the comandante intervened. They went to a far corner of the room.

"We may have a larger problem here than I expected," said the comandante.

"He's lying!" said Villa. "He says dese things to save hees life."

"That is a risk I cannot take," said the comandante. "I must give the matter some thought. We are critically short of time, and I cannot afford any delays, real or implied I fear there is only one quick way out of this situation. Take these two back to the barracks. I will deal with them tomorrow night."

"But dat es when are cheduled to take the new prototype out for eets chakedown cruise," said Villa.

"Precisely," said the comandante, turning to smile at Jack Grigsby. "It will be a simple matter, then, to call the gringo's bluff."

Domino Monet tossed in her bed. A half sleep tormented her with wandering nigh ⁱres that were all too real. In them she saw Jack going down with the *Ice Bucket,* Jack trapped, gasping for air with an arm or leg caught in the wreckage. The deeper Jack sank in the water, the deeper Domino fell into the nightmare.

Domino wrestled with the bedding, reaching out, grasping for Jack, yet he always seemed just out of reach, begging her to save him. She saw Jack slipping deeper into the turquoise water, which suddenly grew black as it swallowed up her lover.

The scream that tore Domino from her nightmare did not return her to reality. For a moment she thought she was still on the Gulf, and even the friendly surroundings of her loft did not bring her around. Finally, her senses began to clear, and she groped about the bed for her robe. The feel of the robe gave Domino comfort, and she hugged herself in an effort to gain some sense of security.

Domino paced around the loft, realizing there was no point in going back to bed. She would only begin to dream again, and the nightmares had become too much to bear.

She went downstairs and made herself a cup of coffee. She kept trying to bolster her confidence by imagining scenarios in which Jack and Virgil somehow survived. But each bitter drama always ended the same way, and now even Domino's indomitable spirit was begining to weaken.

Jack and Virgil had been missing for over twenty-four hours, and with each passing hour the likelihood of their being found lessened. Tears began to well up in Domino's eyes. She was about to start crying again when she heard a knock at the door.

Wiping her eyes, Domino crossed her upstairs living quarters, wondering who had gotten inside the downstairs bar. She left the door locked and peered through the peephole. "Cody?" she called.

Domino opened the door and found the bouncer, dressed in jeans, deck shoes, and a windbreaker. "Thought you might like some company."

"Yes," said Domino. "Come in. Can I get you a cup of coffee?"

"Thanks," said Cody, following her into the kitchen.

Domino was filling Cody's cup when she finally broke

down. Yet she found no relief in crying. She was haunted by the uncertainty of the situation and wondered if she could ever accept the possibility that Jack and Virgil were gone forever.

"Come on," said Cody, offering a shoulder. "Pull yourself together. It's time to get dressed."

"Get dressed? For what? It's barely three in the morning."

"Get dressed," said Cody. "I'll buy you breakfast."

"Oh, Cody, I'm not hungry."

"Get dressed anyway," said Cody. "I want to get another charter and an early start."

Agent Dickerson was sliding his hand down the soft flesh of his wife's abdomen when the phone rang. At first he considered ignoring the sound. The kids were away for the weekend, and this was the first time he and Linda had been really alone in months.

"You'd better answer that," said his wife with a smile. "I'll give you a good seven minutes after you're done."

Dickerson returned her smile and answered the phone. "Hello? Yes, this is Agent Dickerson. . . . Cody who?"

"Carnes," snarled Cody into the pay phone at the marina diner. "We met before, in the Wharf Rat Saloon. You were passing yourself off as some kind of repairman."

"How did you get this number?"

"Never mind how I got the number. Did you know that Jack Grigsby and Virgil Fullenkamp are missing?"

"Yes," said Dickerson tersely.

"Well, what the hell are you doing about it?"

"Everything we can. We've got several agents on the case, the Coast Guard will pull in extra ships today, and I've ordered another helicopter to join in the search. But you must realize that this sort of thing can happen in the smuggling trade. We've had cases before where our operatives disappeared for days, even weeks, then turned up unharmed. The smuggling business isn't a nine-to-five job, you know."

"Yeah," said Cody, whose knuckles were tightening around

the receiver. "Well how many of your *other* operatives had their boats ripped out from under them?"

There was a long pause.

"Not very many," admitted Dickerson.

"Well, you listen to me, Mister Federal man. If those guys don't turn up soon, I'm coming after your ass, and if I can't hang you legally, I'll do it on my own."

"Threats aren't going to help anyone," said Dickerson. "Now, if you'll just listen—"

The line had gone dead.

Dickerson gave a deep sign and hung up.

"What's wrong?" asked his wife.

"Everything," said Dickerson, shaking his head.

"Come back to bed."

"Can't," said Dickerson, heading for the shower. "Damn!" he said, stopping at the bathroom doorway. "Of all the operatives we've used, I was sure those two would come through."

Domino and Cody sat in a booth in the marina diner. A few other fishermen had straggled in, wiping the sleep from their eyes as they washed down Danish with coffee strong enough to wake the dead.

"We'll go at first light," said Cody.

Domino nodded and kept stirring her coffee. "Do you think there's a chance?"

"There's always a chance," said Cody, taking her hand.

"Tell me the truth, Cody."

Cody hung his head to avoid Domino's penetrating eyes, then took a deep breath before confronting her again. "We'd better find them today."

The search party had swelled to an armada on the second day of the search. Nearly all the pleasure craft from the marina joined in sweeping the Gulf, though few held any hope of finding the men alive.

Agent Dickerson, disguised as a Coast Guard lieutenant, rode the first of two cutters that combed the area where the *Ice*

Bucket had gone down, but even their sophisticated gear and experience was not enough to turn up any bodies.

By three o'clock in the afternoon the pleasure craft began to give up the search. Other priorities, and no results, were taking a heavy toll. For most, the sea had just laid claim to two more souls. Even Cody began to doubt. Only Domino remained steadfast in her belief that Jack and Virgil would be found alive.

By sunset the search party had narrowed down to Cody's charter, the cutters, and one helicopter, and they had given up hope.

Cody was on the radio talking with the captain of the cutter. The captain informed Cody that they were returning to base. Domino tore the microphone from Cody's hand and begged the captain to continue the search.

"I'm sorry, miss," said the captain. "I can't authorize that. Returning to base. Out."

Domino and Cody remained at the sight of the sinking until the failing light left them no recourse but to return to the marina.

"We'll go out again tomorrow," said Domino.

"All right," said Cody, though he knew the effort to be pointless.

"They're still alive," said Domino. "I just know it."

All during the search the comandante had monitored the boats encircling Triangle Island. Only with the coming of nightfall did he authorize the reopening of the camouflaged sea doors to the cavern, and then only because power reserves were running dangerously low.

Now he had another problem to surmount, calling the gringo's bluff. The comandante had sent a detachment of scuba divers to inspect the underwater doors leading to the subterranean canal. His instructions had been specific. This was to be only a reconnaissance. The divers were to touch nothing. If they saw something suspicious, they were to photograph it and do nothing more.

The divers had found nothing, yet the comandante did not

test the situation by opening the sea doors. The gringo seemed too knowledgeable in the applications of explosives, and the comandante dared not accept the gauntlet. Not alone, anyway.

"Bring the gringos to the cigar docks in one hour," he ordered. "I wish to speak to them before we embark on our mission."

Virgil sat on the edge of his bunk, his injured hand cuffed to the bedpost. The throbbing in his finger was extending to his hand, and he massaged the injured appendage, though it had little effect on the pain.

Jack lay in the bunk below, mulling over their chances for escape. Two guards, armed with Baretta 70's, blocked each exit on opposite ends of the barracks. Jack rolled back over on his bed, his sullen expression hidden in the shadows of the bunk. Jack gave a gentle kick to the rack above him.

"How're you doing up there?"

Virgil winced as a new volley of pain tore up through his hand. "Not bad," he said. "Could be worse, I suppose."

"Yeah," said Jack, turning toward the guards. "We could be dead."

"You think they bought your story?"

"Had to. They stopped the interrogation and we're still alive."

"Yeah, but for how long?"

Jack was lost in thought for a moment, then his face filled with a confident smile. "Hey, Virge. You remember how we survived Tet?"

"Sure, we shot the shit out of anything that moved: So what's that got to do with this? We haven't got any guns."

"That's not what I meant. You remember that little saying we had, a play on the twenty-third psalm?"

"Yeah," said Virgil, grinning.

"How'd that go?" said Jack, with a broadening smile. "I think I forgot."

" 'Yea, though I walk through the valley of the shadow of death,' " began Virgil. " 'I will fear no evil. 'Cause I'm the meanest motherfucker in the valley!' "

"Damn right!" said Jack, giving Virgil's bunk another thump with his foot.

It was only momentary, but for a brief instant, the surge of adrenaline Virgil received from his recital gave him a respite from the pain in his hand.

"From now on we work on the same principle," said Jack. "Be sharp! Don't overlook any opportunity. If you see an opening, kick ass and haul ass!"

"Airborne," snarled Virgil through clenched teeth.

"Ranger," said Jack, curling both his hands into tight fists.

Chapter Twelve

THE *NAUTILUS*

JACK AND Virgil were taken to the cigar docks just before ten o'clock. There they found the comandante overseeing the final preparations of the large cigar they had seen at their capture. Work was also proceeding on another such prototype, while the smaller two-man cigars on the far side of the canal made ready for their night's run.

The comandante had changed clothes. Now, instead of the familiar jungle fatigues, he wore the blue coat of a naval captain. The jacket was overdecorated with gold braid, and he reminded Jack of a drum major.

The comandante motioned for the guards to bring Jack and Virgil forward, and they were ushered to the side of the prototype. The comandante took Jack's hand and shook it, then looked at Virgil's, now swelled to twice its normal size.

"I'll have the pharmacist's mate take care of that," said the comandante, then turned his attention to the cigar. "Isn't she magnificent?"

Neither Jack nor Virgil responded.

"There," said the comandante, pointing forward on the cigar. "You see, Señor Grigsby. You really inspired the name."

Jack looked forward on the bow. Just above the bow planes

and the retractable hydrofoils was the boat's name. The *Nautilus*. "I don't understand," said Jack. "How did I—"

"You were the first one who likened me to the character from the Jules Verne novel," said the comandante, posing regally. "I thought it most fitting that I christen my flagship with an appropriate title."

Jack was not impressed. To him it was an insult to use the name of the *Nautilus* for such grisly purposes. Apparently the comandante's ego was even larger than he first surmised.

"Come aboard," said the comandante. "There is much I wish to show you."

The guards on the dock rehandcuffed Jack and Virgil so their hands were in front, and turned them over to seamen armed with 9 mm pistols and blackjacks. They crossed the narrow gangway and stood on the foredeck of the cigar. The comandante was quick to join them and began to point out highlights of the ship's design.

"This is not a submarine," he began. "It is a cigar! It is submersible, but it can exceed the surface speed of any submarine, in any navy, anywhere in the world. The boat measures just under seventy-five feet, with a ten-foot beam. Conditions below are cramped, but comfortable. Come, let me show you."

Virgil and Jack followed the comandante around the conning tower. There the comandante ordered their handcuffs removed, with a reminder to them that if they attempted to escape they would be shot. Jack and Virgil nodded in understanding and followed the comandante up the rungs in the side of the conning tower to the flying bridge.

The bridge was cramped, with barely room for two men. The comandante gave a brief description of the communications devices, before he opened the hatch below their feet. Jack and Virgil were first down inside the *Nautilus*.

The interior of the sub was bathed in an odd red light. Specifically designed for surfacing at night, thought Jack.

"We are now still above decks," said the comandante, joining them inside the cramped confines of the conning tower.

"Here you see the cigar's sting," he continued, pointing to the sophisticated weaponry pointing toward the bow.

There was a small contour chair facing a 20 mm cannon and two 7.62 mm Gatling-type guns. Both sat behind a hatch that could be opened upon the boat's surfacing.

"We keep these inside," said the comandante. "I found that placing weapons on the deck increased drag coefficents to unacceptable levels. Follow me," he continued, descending down the hatch into the boat's midships.

Jack and Virgil climbed down the ladder into the command center. Both wondered why the comandante was giving them the Grand Tour, but they kept their questions to themselves. No sense in irritating the petulant Latin.

"Here, gentlemen, you see the nerve center of the cigar—the helm, navigational supports, and weapons control center. You would be amazed at what you can buy on the American market. A few discarded guidance systems from your NASA people proved invaluable. Not to mention renovated surplus from your armed forces. A few misguided penny-pinchers in the Pentagon got me more hardware than even I could handle."

Jack and Virgil exchanged disgusted glances. "Probably picked up the entire lot C.O.D. from the classified section of *Firefight Magazine*," whispered Jack.

They followed the comandante forward, through a hatch in a bulkhead into the galley/laboratory.

"We do not have a cook on board," said the comandante. "Most of the food is freeze-dried or dehydrated. We purchase our food stocks from the same people who supply your astronauts. It seems Americans stockpile these foodstuffs in fallout shelters. The shelf life on some of these products is truly remarkable."

"Didn't we get in the same kind of mess, sellin' scrap iron to the Japs?" whispered Virgil.

"The laboratory is small but efficient," continued the comandante. "We save time by testing and cutting the cocaine here on board. You must remember, the money for my fleet comes entirely from the Americans' insatiable desire for this white powder. The faster the money comes in, the sooner I complete my mission."

Now Jack's and Virgil's curiosity nearly got the better of them. They were about to query the comandante when Jack shook his head no. It seemed the comandante was going to tell them a great deal. Better let him reveal what he would. They could figure the rest out later.

They passed through another hatch and bulkhead, into the captain's quarters. Jack expected to find a posh interior but was surprised to discover the room quite spartan. A suspended cot that could double as a desk, a few lockers, collapsible chairs, and a private head were the extent of the furnishings.

"What, no Jacuzzi?" said Jack.

There was a blank look on the comandante's face, then a hint of a smile. "You gringos," he said with a puzzled look, "have a strange sense of humor. This way, please."

Jack and Virgil followed the comandante forward into the crew's quarters. This was the largest section of the boat that Jack and Virgil had seen. Double bunks hung down from the sides of the hull, with small lockers separating each rack. But it was forward, in the bow, where the real surprise lay. At first Jack couldn't believe his eyes. They couldn't be, he thought.

"Now you see the real power of my vessel," said the comandante. "We carry six torpedos. Granted, they are small, but for their purpose, they are suited well."

"What might that purpose be?" asked Jack.

The comandante smiled. "In due time, gentlemen," he said. "We can also lay a very sophisticated mine, I might add. One of my own design. But enough of this," he said, checking his watch. "We must go now."

The comandante gestured for Jack and Virgil to head back aft, toward the command center. Now Jack and Virgil were stricken with the same anxiety that had haunted them since their capture, the feeling of imminent death lurking just ahead of them. Yet when they reached the command center, the comandante kept them on board. Jack and Virgil found themselves handcuffed to conduits running along the hull just outside the crew's head.

"What now?" said Virgil, listening to the engines of the cigar firing up in the compartment just aft of them.

"What do I look like," said Jack, "the social director?"

Virgil was about to ask another stupid question when a crew member came down the hatch into the command center, then aft, toward them. The crewman carried another hypodermic, and Virgil pulled away at the sight of the offensive weapon. The crewman rubbed Virgil's arm with alcohol, then gave him an injection. As the crewman left, the comandante checked in on Jack and Virgil.

"Make yourselves comfortable," said the comandante. "We'll be getting under way shortly. Then we will find out whether you really mined the ocean doors to the canal. For your sake, I hope you didn't, for if this boat goes to the bottom, you will die with the rest of us!"

The regular patrons at the Wharf Rat understood the "closed" sign on the door. The Naples *Daily News* had run the story about the sinking of the *Ice Bucket* and the disappearance of its crew. Everyone knew of Domino's relationship with Jack, and cards of condolence would soon swamp the Wharf Rat's mailbox.

Cody and Domino sat at the bar, observing a kind of solemn wake. Cody poked at the ice cubes in his drink, trying to think of some way to bring Domino to the realization that Jack and Virgil were probably dead. Domino stared into space, oblivious to her surroundings. She kept reliving the night before Jack had left, blaming herself for not making him stay, as though this self-incrimination were some kind of penance.

"I've come to a decision," said Cody, downing the remains of his Jack Daniels.

"We're not giving up the search," said Domino adamantly.

"No, we'll give it another day," said Cody, motioning for a refill. "What I meant was, I'm going to take their place if we don't find them."

"What?"

"I've already talked to Dickerson about it. They're bringing in a new boat, and I begin training day after tomorrow."

Domino's emotions were exhausted, yet she still managed a stunned expression. "Are you out of your mind?"

"Quite sane," said Cody, taking the bottle of bourbon from Domino and refilling his glass.

"Revenge!" said Domino in a scolding tone. "It's just cold-blooded revenge that motivates you, Cody Carnes."

"Oh, knock it off, will you, Mom! The only reason I said I would do it was to find out what happened to Jack and Virgil."

"You're talking about them in the past tense again," said Domino. "I won't have that!"

"All right, then, I volunteered so I could find them. Is that better?"

"No! I wish none of you had gotten mixed up in this awful business to begin with. I should have never agreed to let Jack go to work for the FBI. And now you want to make the same damn mistake. Jesus, you men and your stupid machismo!"

"Machismo's got nothing to do with this," said Cody. "Chances are the Federal boys will never find out where Jack and Virgil are. As far as the idiots in Washington are concerned, your friends are in the past tense. All I'm trying to do is prove your theory right. Now, shut up and get us something to eat."

Domino's eyes began to well up and she began to sniff. "Then you *do* believe they're still alive."

Cody's normal dour expression returned. "Those clowns have fallen into more shit, and come out smelling like a rose, more times than anyone I know. And this scrape is probably no different from the rest."

"I *knew* you thought they were alive," said Domino, trying to fix her face and the sandwiches at the same time.

"Here," said Cody, taking the knife away from Domino. "I don't want snot on my sandwich."

"Thanks, Cody," said Domino, giving the huge bouncer a tear-soaked kiss on the cheek.

"I still don't know why I'm doing this," said Cody, tossing Domino a small hand towel. "Those two bastards are probably sitting in some posh resort in South America, sucking up suds and laughing about all the reports of them being dead."

Jack and Virgil sat handcuffed to a toilet in the *Nautilus*'s head.

"This is another fine mess you've gotten us into," said Virgil.

"Me? Why, you dumb sonofabitch!" Jack snarled, trying to kick Virgil on the other side of the stool. "If you hadn't come up with that half-assed scheme to bilk money out of the VA, we wouldn't be here at all!"

"Well, since we are, you got any bright ideas?"

"Yeah," said Jack, peering through the open head hatch. "Never listen to you again as long as I live."

"Hey, this is no time to get bitchy. What's gonna happen the minute we clear those underwater doors and this thing doesn't get blown out of the water?"

"Well, they won't be able to shove us out the forward torpedo tubes. They're too small."

"Oh, that's a real comfort," said Virgil.

"My guess is they'll surface and dump us off somewhere in the Gulf."

"Buried at sea in my blue jeans," said Virgil, shaking his head in dismay. "Got any other pleasant thoughts?"

"Well I've only seen seven guys come on board, including 'Captain Nemo,' " said Jack, testing the pipes of the toilet.

"What did you plan on doing," asked Virgil, "pull the toilet out of the bulkhead and use it for a battering ram?"

"Something like that."

"Oh, we'll go far with that idea. That'll just us get to the bottom of the Gulf faster."

"You got any bright ideas, smartass?"

"Yeah," said Virgil, his eyes lighting up. "How about a little Mace in the face?"

"Mace? We haven't got any—"

Then Jack saw it, a common disinfectant someone had stuck behind the stool. A forgotten can of aerosol spray that might be their salvation.

"Can you reach it?" said Virgil, struggling with his handcuffs.

"Not with my hands," said Jack, grunting as he wrestled himself around so he might get hold of the can with his feet.

It took some doing, but Jack managed to pinch the can between the toes of his deck shoes and pull it up toward him. Virgil stuck his hand down, pushing on the bracelets of the handcuffs until they cut off circulation, but did manage to reach the aerosol can. Virgil took it from between Jack's feet and held it up so Jack could get hold of the would-be weapon. Jack and Virgil managed to maneuver the can behind the stool, where either man could grab it up and put it to quick use if the opportunity presented itself.

"What if the guard they send to take us out isn't armed?" asked Virgil.

"Don't make any plans," said Jack. "We play it by ear. You remember what our drill instructor used to say?"

"Right," said Virgil, training his eyes on the hatch of the head. "When all else fails, follow your nose."

Vicente Villa and the comandante were running down their departure commands. The seven-man crew had been handpicked for the first run of the superprototype and they could afford no slip-ups in routine.

"The crew stands ready, comandante," said Villa.

"Excellent," said Cordova. "Take the gringos forward."

Villa and the torpedoman left the command center for the head. Both were armed with 9 mm pistols, which they were ready to use.

Virgil saw Villa in the hatch first. He had to suppress a smile as he reached for the aerosol can. Virgil's hand was still swollen, and the vision of Villa writhing on the floor with disinfectant in his eyes was sweet revenge.

Virgil felt Jack's hand stop him from grabbing the disinfect-ant. Virgil looked at Jack, questioning his restraint.

"Not now," Jack whispered.

"Take them," Villa ordered the torpedoman while holding his pistol on Jack and Virgil. The torpedoman quickly uncuffed them from the pipes but did not see the spray can hidden behind the bowl. He cuffed Jack and Virgil together and shoved them out of the head.

"Move forward," said Villa, prodding Virgil in the back with his cane.

They moved forward through the bulkhead hatch and into the command center. There they were met by the comandante.

"I have ordered all the crew aft when we pass through the un-derwater doors," said the comandante. "You two will have the privilege of riding in the bow. If you have booby-trapped the doors as you claim, you will be the first to go."

The comandante motioned for Villa to see them forward, then sat back to study his navigational charts.

Jack and Virgil found themselves handcuffed to a mine rack in the torpedo room. Villa and the torpedoman left, sealing the hatch behind them.

"Why'd you stop me back there?" asked Virgil.

"We're still inside the island, stupid. How the hell would we get out?"

"Yeah? Well, if they toss us out in the Gulf, we'll have loads of fun swimming sixty miles back to the mainland."

"We have to wait," said Jack.

"You better be right," said Virgil, looking around.

"Hey, what are these things?" said Jack, looking at the v-shaped metal objects separated by rubber buff mounts.

"I dunno," said Virgil. "We were in the army, remember?"

Jack read the stenciled letters on the side of the v-shaped ob-jects: EXPLOSIVO PELIGROSO. "Jesus Christ," said Jack. "They're mines!"

"They're what?" said Virgil, pulling away from the olive-drab–colored objects.

"What the hell is he going to do with mines and torpedoes?"

"Christ, I don't know. Maybe he wants to play pirate?"

"Damn!" said Jack, lost in thought.

"I was kidding," said Virgil.

"Well, Captain Nemo sure isn't."

"Hell, that's crazy. That kind of crap went out with Captain Kidd. Why, the Navy would blow him out of the water the first boat he tried to hold up."

"They don't even know he exists," said Jack. "And he's just crazy enough to make it work."

"You know, you may be right," said Virgil, studying the torpedos. "Three guesses what ships he'd go after first?"

"Mother ships!"

"No shit, Sherlock. Why buy the cocaine when you can steal the whole load?"

"Yeah, then he'd turn around and blame the Coast Guard or bad weather or unseaworthy ships for the disappearances. Christ, he could make ten, maybe twelve million dollars a run."

"What was that?" said Virgil, feeling the cigar tremble.

"It's the engines," said Jack. "We're getting under way."

"Make turns for all ahead slow," said the comandante.

"Aye-aye, sir," said Villa.

The new prototype pulled out into the center canal and headed for the undersea doors.

"Open the vents," ordered Villa. "Two degrees down angle on the bow planes."

The helmsman complied with Villa's order, and the cigar slipped beneath the surface of the subterranean canal. Forward in the bow, Jack and Virgil heard the rush of water about the outside of the hull. It was an alien noise, and with it came an accompanying increase in the atmospheric pressure. Both Jack and Virgil remained silent, their eyes looking upward, mouths open.

"Watch your depth," said the comandante.

"Even bubble," said the helmsman.

The comandante drew a deep breath and looked at Villa. "Open the undersea doors."

"Yes, my capitan," said Villa without hesitation.

The cigar's sonar sent out the blips that bounced off the undersea doors. Computers on board the *Nautilus* relayed a command through the boat's sonar, and sensors built into the undersea doors triggered them to slide back.

The *Nautilus* moved through the water like some great mechanical leviathan, its aft screws turning so slowly that a diver could have counted the revolutions.

The comandante stopped working on his charts. The gunner, machinist's mate, helmsman, and torpedoman-miner all seemed to hold their breath as they neared the juncture of the undersea doors. Only Villa acted unconcerned, yet even he gasped when the cigar was buffeted with the rush of water created by the opening of the doors.

The *Nautilus* glided silently through the portals, yet no C-4 charges detonated. But the crew still did not rejoice. Not until they were a mile or more out into the Gulf did the atmosphere of tension seem to wane. Then it was back to the business at hand and the comandante's mission.

"Bring the gringos here," said the comandante with a vindictive smile. "I do not like being played for a fool."

There was a viciously characteristic sneer on Villa's face when the hatch to the torpedo room opened. The torpedoman-miner was first through the hatch and freed Jack and Virgil from the rack of mines.

"The comandante wishes to see you," said Villa, signaling Jack and Virgil aft with his 9 mm pistol.

The torpedoman-miner handcuffed Jack and Virgil together as before and pushed them back toward the command center.

"I think they're callin' our bluff," said Virgil.

"I thought we'd have more time," said Jack, taking a clout to his ribs from Villa's pistol.

The comandante was busy with his navigational charts when Jack and Virgil entered the command center. Upon seeing the gringos, the comandante set down his compass and faced them. Cordova's movements seemed animated, as though he were about to recite some speech he had rehearsed too many times.

"And to think I was taken in by such fools," said the comandante, posturing as he spoke.

"You mean, you didn't find the charges?" said Jack, continuing his ruse.

"You needn't continue such a foolish ploy," said the comandante.

"I don't understand," said Jack.

"Stop wasting my time!" said the comandante. "You two have caused me too many unnecessary delays. Granted, it was a clever scheme, but it only bought you a few extra hours."

"A few hours before what?" asked Jack.

The comandante smirked and faced the helmsman. "Prepare to surface," he said.

"Aye-aye, sir."

"Give them the deep six," said the comandante, turning back to his charts.

Both Jack's and Virgil's faces turned ashen. Virgil struggled with the handcuffs, while Jack wondered what it would feel like to drown.

Villa held his pistol on the gringos while trying to decide where to shoot them before they were gutted, tied to pig iron, and thrown over the side.

"Blow negative," said the comandante.

The helmsman was about to follow the order when Jack and Virgil recognized a familiar sound. It was the *Nautilus*'s sonar, and the signal indicated a vessel closing on the cigar.

"What is their heading?" snapped the comandante.

"One nine zero," said the helmsman. "Same as ours."

"Pleasure boat?"

"Possibly," said the helmsman, watching the sonar.

"It's a cutter," said Jack with a grin.

The comandante glared at Jack, then turned his attention back to the sonar screen. "Range?"

"One six double zero."

"Bring her up to periscope death," said the comandante, twisting the bill of his captain's cap about in classic submariner's fashion. The helmsman set his bow planes, and slowly the *Nautilus* began to rise.

The comandante pulled down the periscope's focus posts and fitted his eyes to the apertures. He swung the periscope about to one nine zero and confirmed the gringos' supposition. There, filling the lens of the periscope was a Coast Guard cutter.

"Down 'scope," said the Comandante. "Take her down to one hundred fifty feet keel depth."

The helmsman complied, and Jack and Virgil felt the angle of the cigar sharpen as they dived for the safety of the deep.

"Rig for silent running."

"Aye-aye, sir."

"It would seem you have been granted a reprieve," said the comandante in a hushed voice. "You lived a charmed life, Señor—?"

"Grigsby," said Jack. "My sister once said I was the luckiest bastard on the face of the earth."

"It is a shame you cannot work with me, Señor Grigsby," said the comandante, returning to the sonar screen to monitor the closing cutter.

"Oh, I don't know," said Jack, winking at Virgil. "Make me an offer."

"A gringo could never be part of our cause," said the comandante.

"Cause?" said Jack. "What cause?"

The comandante did not answer. He sat down in the captain-navigator's couch and gestured for the gringos to seat themselves on the deck.

"We will be some time slipping away from the cutter," began the comandante. "I suppose I can indulge you two with a little history. Besides, it will only be knowledge you will be taking to a premature grave."

Jack and Virgil, wrists still handcuffed together, pressed their backs against each other and eased themselves down to the deck. The comandante began his lecture.

"Our cause began in the very swamps you gringos call the Everglades. Initially my plan was to recruit men who were anxious to avenge the blunder of the Bay of Pigs. But these Latinos were only interested in some nationalistic dream, not the grand scheme of Central America, and I realized I would have to raise my own army to fulfill the great cause.

"We began by eliminating many of the locals as they made smuggling runs in and out of the swamp. Soon the revenues we were generating offered us greater opportunity and power. That's when I conceived the idea for the subterranean headquarters complex. A power base from which we could raid and profit from the cocaine trade and at the same time begin to initiate my plan for the cause.

"Two degrees to starboard," said the comandante, continuing to monitor the course of the cutter.

"And just what is your grand cause?" asked Jack.

The comandante smiled. "Let me say that this voyage will initiate my plan for the cause. If the mission is successful, we have only to wait on the completion of the second superprototype and we will be ready!"

Both Jack and Virgil wondered what mad scheme "Captain Nemo" had in mind, yet neither of their speculations even approached the grandiose plan the comandante intended to implement.

The captain of the Coast Guard cutter held his course steady with that of the submerged cigar. The captain kept his heading purely by whim, for he was not aware of the cigar and was only on a random search for the dopers frequenting the area.

Perhaps it was fate that kept the cutter's next two course corrections on line with the evasive heading of the cigar. That or the luck of the two captives. Whichever, the comandante was losing precious time, and the maiden voyage of the *Nautilus* had to be completed on a strict timetable. Otherwise, the comandante might not be able to keep his rendezvous for the cause.

The comandante stood in the cramped confines of the com-

mand center, stroking his beard as he monitored the sonar.
"What is he doing up there?" asked the comandante, looking
upward as if he could actually see the cutter's keel.

"Perhaps he hasn't seen us," offered Villa.

The comandante shook his head. "No, he's maintained our
heading on the last two course corrections."

"What then, Comandante?"

"I don't know," replied the puzzled commander, glancing at
the mission clock hanging on a bulkhead. "We must take the
risk. Five degrees starboard. All ahead two-thirds."

The crew of the *Nautilus* braced themselves as the helmsman
brought the boat to its new heading. All eyes locked on the sonar. For a moment it appeared as though the cutter had turned
with them again, then the cigar began to put some distance on
the troublesome intruder and a collective sense of relief swept
through the boat.

"All ahead full," said the comandante, returning to his
charts. "Maintain present heading until the cutter is out of sonar range."

"What are we to do with de gringos?" asked Villa, pulling
his pistol from its holster.

The comandante studied the mission clock, his charts, and
their present course. "I cannot risk any more delays. We still
must complete our shakedown of the boat and make our rendezvous. We can eliminate the gringos upon our return."

Villa was about to argue the point when he caught himself.
Villa could not allow his thirst for blood to contradict the
comandante's judgment. Besides, he could savor the manner of
the gringos' demise throughout the remainder of the voyage.
Their death, he vowed, would be particularly agonizing.

Jack and Virgil sat on the deck of the command center, exchanging glares with Villa. Both Jack and Virgil felt like death-
row inmates who had been granted a stay of execution.

"On jour feet," ordered Villa.

"Anything you say, General," said Virgil, struggling to his
feet.

"I will chut jour smart mouth," said Villa.

Jack stopped before ducking through the hatch leading to the boat's head. "Don't count on it," he said.

Villa's loathsome expression changed, but only momentarily. It was replaced by the gold-toothed sneer Jack and Virgil had come to hate.

"Enjoy jour cruise," said Villa, watching the torpedoman-miner handcuff Jack and Virgil back to the pipes of the head. "I will be back when eet es time for jour swimming lesson."

Chapter Thirteen

SHAKEDOWN

CODY AND Domino stood at the bar as Agent Dickerson, disguised once again as a refrigeration repairman, entered the Wharf Red Saloon.

"Sorry we have to meet like this," said Dickerson, setting a new compressor on the bar, "but since Mr. Carnes has volunteered to work for us, it is necessary to remain incognito."

"Let's cut the cloak-and-dagger stuff, shall we?" said Cody.

"Any word on Jack and Virgil?" asked Domino hopefully.

"I'm afraid not," said Dickerson, dropping down to install the compressor. "We've got the word out, but none of our contacts has seen or heard anything."

"There's still a chance," said Domino, biting her lip.

Dickerson glanced at Cody. "Yes," he said, hoping for help from the bouncer. "There's a remote possibility."

"How remote?"

Cody took Domino by the arm and forced her to face him. "I thought we agreed to stop all this speculation."

Domino looked at the floor. "He said there's a chance. And as long as there is a chance, I'll be damned if I give them up for dead."

"Have it your way," said Cody with a sigh of exasperation. "What do you have for me, Dickerson?"

"We've got your training schedule all set. Tickets at the airport, and we'll be bringing down the new boat as soon as you're finished."

"When do I leave?"

"Be at the airport at two this afternoon."

"Done."

"I don't think I'll be able to repair this here," said Dickerson, taking up his role of repairman. "Have to take it into the shop."

"All right," said Domino. "You'll let me know if there's any news?"

"Good or bad, you'll be the first person I call," said Dickerson, taking the cooling unit out of the Wharf Rat on a two-wheeler.

Domino watched him leave. She thought back to the last time Dickerson had been in the Wharf Rat, the day Jack and Virgil had made their first contact with Red Pardee. The thought began to haunt her, torment her. If only she had been able to talk Jack out of entering the trade.

"Guess I'd better go pack," said Cody.

"What?" said Domino with a start.

"I'd better get ready."

"Cody," said Domino, watching the burly bouncer head for the door.

"Yeah," said Carnes, stopping in the doorway.

"You don't have to do this for me, you know."

Cody thought a moment. "Yes, I do," he said. "See you in a few days."

The comandante had signaled another diving drill. Jack and Virgil were awakened by the sound of the klaxon sending the crew to their battle stations. The *Nautilus* slipped beneath the waves, and the now familiar rush of water began to engulf the boat.

"Shit," said Virgil. "My ass fell asleep again."

"Where you figure we are?" said Jack, rubbing his eyes on his shoulders.

"Who knows?" said Virgil, yawning. "Hell, he's changed course sixty-five goddamned times."

"South, I'll bet."

"Good as any other direction. What I want to know is the final destination."

"Just as long as it isn't the bottom of the ocean."

The hatch opened at the end of the drill. The comandante looked in. Jack reached for the can of disinfectant. Virgil already had a hand on it.

Vicente Villa appeared at the hatch.

"Take them forward," said the comandante.

Villa stepped into the head, and Virgil's grip on the can tightened. Jack nodded to Virgil to hold off, and Villa uncuffed them from the pipe. He pushed them out of the head, past the comandante and into the command center.

"What now?" asked Jack.

"Get up, gringo," snapped Villa.

Villa freed Jack and Virgil and prodded them to their feet. As they exited the head, the comandante and the first officer entered. "There, against the bulkhead," the comandante said. "Remove that plate to get to the relay station."

During their wait outside the head, Jack and Virgil studied the command center. As they were surveying the banks of controls, a short crewman wearing a grimy T-shirt entered.

Villa spoke to the machinist's mate, inquiring as to the performance of the engines. The mate informed Villa that as soon as some minor adjustments were made, the boat could attempt a high-speed maneuver. Villa acknowledged this and sent him back to his post.

The comandante came out of the head, and Villa informed him about the engines. The comandante seemed pleased. They had been plagued by some minor engine problems, but soon he could unleash the full power of the *Nautilus*. It was a moment the comandante had been anticipating.

"I trust you gentlemen are comfortable," he said with a smile.

"Yeah," said Virgil. "Four-star accommodations."

"You may remain here for now. Villa," continued the comandante, turning toward the helm, "prepare to surface."

"Aye-aye, sir," said Villa, first checking to see that Jack and Virgil were securely handcuffed, hands and backs together.

Jack and Virgil wondered what awaited them on the surface. As the *Nautilus* began to rise, Jack had second thoughts about stopping Virgil from employing the disinfectant. Maybe it would have been wiser to use the spray and blind Villa, then fight their way—to where? They were still underwater, and though Jack and Virgil knew a great deal about ships, they knew almost nothing about submarines. And from the looks of the command center, the comandante's cigar was extremely sophisticated.

No, thought Jack, continuing his assessment. They would have to wait until the boat was on the surface, near land and preferably at night. That just might give them an opportunity. That is, if the comandante kept them alive long enough to implement his plan.

The *Nautilus* broke the surface, and Villa opened the hatch to the conning tower. The comandante went up on deck first, while Jack and Virgil had their handcuffs rearranged.

Villa separated Jack from Virgil, but he left the handcuffs in place, locking their hands in front of them. The temporary removal of the bracelets gave Jack and Virgil a bit of relief.

"Up on deck," ordered Villa.

They exchanged apprehensive glances, then climbed up on deck to join the comandante on the conning tower. The fresh sea air was a relief for them, after they had been cooped up in the stale air of the head for so many hours. They found the comandante standing on the conning tower with a pair of field glasses, studying the horizon.

Jack and Virgil looked around hoping to get their bearings. All they found was seawater.

"I suppose you men are wondering where you are," said the comandante, lowering his glasses.

"That'd be nice," said Jack.

"We are now in the Caribbean."

"Wonderful," said Virgil, glancing over the side. "You gonna give us the deep six?"

The comandante smiled. "Not just yet, gentlemen. I wish to show you what my new prototype can do. It will amuse me to share the experience with you."

"The perfect host," said Jack, wondering what the madman's real motives might be.

"I'm glad you think so," said the comandante.

"You gonna tell us where we're goin'?" asked Virgil.

"In due time, gentlemen," said the comandante, bending down to shout through the open hatch. "Come right three degrees."

Cody Carnes arrived at Parris Island and was greeted by the same sergeant who had trained Jack and Virgil. Cody's training schedule was abbreviated, by his own arrangements with the FBI. If Cody was to locate Jack and Virgil, he had to do it soon; time was a commodity that could not be wasted.

The training sergeant was amazed at how fast Cody adapted to procedure. The bouncer was all business, paying particular attention to detail, especially during the tactics-and-strategy sessions concerning terrorist organizations.

Cody completed his marathon course in record time. The sergeant said Cody should have been a Marine. Carnes never bothered to tell him he had been, and he boarded a Navy jet for the flight down to Key West Naval Air Station.

At Key West, Cody was met by Lieutenant Shively. The lieutenant was impressed with the training record that had been cabled down from Parris Island, and she wasted no time in putting Cody behind the helm of the new boat just acquired from the Florida State Drug Task Force.

"Little long for a cigarette," said Cody.

"It's not a cigarette," said Lieutenant Shively. "It's called a popeye. Almost twenty feet longer than a cigarette and twice the horsepower."

"Twice?" said Cody, his eyebrows rising from under the frames of his chrome-lensed sunglasses.

"Twenty-eight hundred horse," said the lieutenant. "Get in. We'll take it for a run."

The engines of the catamaran lumbered to life. Lieutenant Shively nursed the throttles up until the very deck began to throb. Cody, never easily impressed, shook his head in disbelief. "Wow!" he said.

"Wait till you see how it handles," said Shively, setting her trim. The water around the dock of the popeye was suddenly transformed into froth, the Gulf surrendering to the awesome horsepower of the engines.

Shively took the boat out into the Straits of Florida and gave the engines their head. The popeye streaked across the sea, slicing a vector of spray off its transom as its speed topped one hundred miles an hour.

Cody had been on fast boats before, but never anything that could match the popeye. Carnes had to stoop down behind the wind screen, for the rip of the wind was too much for even his strength.

Lieutenant Shively gave him a crash course in handling, nothing compared to what she wanted to teach, but a lesson that would comply with the arrangements Cody had demanded from the FBI. By the middle of the afternoon she felt reasonably confident with the way the bouncer handled the boat. Still she was apprehensive about Cody's timetable.

"You know, you really are rushing things," she said over the thunder of the popeye's engines.

"Can't be helped," said Cody. "Got a couple of friends. Trained right here, as a matter of fact. I have to find them— fast!"

Shively looked at Cody thoughtfully. "A tall, big guy and a smart-mouthed little guy?"

Cody smiled. "You know Virgil?"

"Yeah," said Shively. "Read about them in the paper. They were nice fellas."

"I'm not dealing in the past tense yet."

"You think they're still alive?"

"Well, with your instruction and this boat, I'm damn sure gonna find out."

"I wish you luck," said Shively.

"Thanks," said Cody, changing their course to head back to the Naval Air Station. "I may just need it."

The accommodations were beginning to wear on Jack and Virgil. They had been at sea for two days, most of which they had spent in the head of the *Nautilus*.

The comandante had been deliberately evasive as to their final destination, but had taken Jack and Virgil into his confidence concerning the operation of the boat. He treated Jack and Virgil like long-lost acquaintances he wished to impress with his newly aquired hardware. It was a kind of ego enhancement, with Jack and Virgil playing the roles of id-polishers.

Jack and Virgil tried to keep their wisecracks to a minimum, for it seemed the more they patronized his swollen ego, the better their chances for survival. The ploy worked. Now, instead of being handcuffed to the pipes of the head, Jack and Virgil were allowed the freedom of the minuscule room, though their hands were still bound in front of them.

The hatch to the head opened, and Vicente Villa gestured for Jack and Virgil to follow him.

"De comandante wants you on de conning tower," he ordered.

"Thank you, my good man." Jack smirked as he passed Villa. "Give the doorman a tip, Virge."

"Blue Boy in the fifth at Belmont," said Virgil, winking at Villa.

Villa would have loved to pound the crap out of both the gringos, but they had come under the protection of the comandante now, and he wasn't about to cross his orders. At least, not yet.

The comandante was at his post on the conning tower when Jack and Virgil set foot on deck. He motioned for them to join him. Jack stood beside the comandante while Virgil squeezed in behind them.

"Now, gentlemen," began the comandante. "I must show you the capabilities of this machine. All ahead one-third."

The twin turbines of the *Nautilus* began to propel the boat forward through the turquoise blue of the Caribbean, the two-foot seas breaking over its computer-designed bow.

"Make ready on bow planes," ordered the comandante. "Make ready planes aft."

"Planes ready, sir."

"Lower and lock hydrofoils forward."

"Hydrofoils forward lowered and locked."

Jack could feel the rise of the boat as the hydrofoils lifted the bow completely out of the water.

"Lower and lock hydrofoils aft."

"Hydrofoils aft lowered and locked."

Now Jack felt the stern rise, but not nearly on the angle of the bow. They appeared to be riding on a three- to five-degree angle from perpendicular, bow up, stern down.

"All ahead two-thirds."

The turbines pushed the *Nautilus* across the water with ever-increasing speed, yet the boat seemed to have lost some of the sensation of speed. At first Jack and Virgil thought there was something wrong with the boat.

"It is a strange sensation," said the comandante. "We are still on the water, but our course is no longer subject to the beating of the waves. The pounding would prohibit running at any greater velocity. All ahead full."

Jack and Virgil clung to the handholds built into the sides of the conning tower as the *Nautilus* began to reach unprecedented speed.

"We are now running faster than even the Russian hunter-killer submarines," said the comandante proudly. "Not as fast as the smaller two-man cigars, but faster than any other submarine of its class in the world. All ahead flank!"

Now the sensation of speed became pronounced. The wind tore over the streamlined hull of the *Nautilus* and forced the comandante, Jack, and Virgil to duck down out of the ripping wash. Still, it was an odd sensation of speed. The turbines, though many times more powerful than the piston drive of Jack and Virgil's boat, were so quiet they seemed not to exist, as though the boat were being propelled by some magical force, a godlike power that the comandante seemed destined to command.

"Come left five degrees," ordered the comandante.

The planes of the hydrofoils were corrected, and the *Nautilus* bore left, yet the normal inertia seemed cut in half. Jack and Virgil found themselves leaning physically into a turn, when it was hardly necessary to do so. The boat merely responded to the command, and though their speed was exceeding seventy knots, those below decks were unaware of the change in course.

"It's so smooth," said Jack. "At this speed you expect some pounding, but there's nothing there. I feel like I'm flying."

"You are, in a manner of speaking," said the comandante. "Here, there is more. Let me show you."

The comandante opened a small hatch fitted forward in the conning tower. There Jack and Virgil could see a computerized helm. There was a VDT approximately four inches square and an abbreviated keyboard. No other nautical instruments were displayed.

"You see," said the comandante, switching the system on. "I can monitor any of the boat's functions from this station. I can even control the course, speed, and weapons systems from this simple station."

The comandante punched a complex code into the ship's computer through the minihelm, which relinquished command of the *Nautilus* to him. The helm in the command center could be overridden in the event of malfunction, injury to someone on the conning tower, or the need to dive. But for now, the comandante was running the ship.

"Let me show you some of the other features," said the comandante proudly.

His fingers danced across the keyboard of the minihelm. Jack and Virgil peered over his shoulder and watched the VDT. The images that flashed across the screen barely had time to register before the comandante tripped menu responses for the next series of commands. Jack and Virgil did manage to recognize a quick overlay of the boat and where the comandante moved the cursor, but they had no idea what the commands meant.

"There," said the comandante, gesturing forward. "Watch closely, for the wake of the wind will soon shear it off."

Jack and Virgil stared forward, puzzled by what they were to expect. At first Jack thought the boat had developed a mechanical problem. Then the odd-looking ooze streaming out of the vents in the foredeck began to solidify.

"What in the world?" said Jack.

"It's a compound mixed with seawater. If I wish to evade the detection of sonar, I simply rig for silent, lie on the bottom, and give the computer the command to commence camouflaging. The compounds are pumped up through the vents and begin to grow, very much like the chemical compounds one can buy in American novelty shops, only here on a much larger scale. The silhouette that would give away our position on the sonar screens is quickly disguised by these swelling compounds, and the boat simply takes on the appearance of ocean bottom."

"I'll be damned!" said Virgil.

"Quite possibly," said the comandante. "There! You see, the wake of the wind is already beginning to shear the substance from the hull. If we were submerged, the compounds would be ripped away in the same manner. We pump a small amount of solvent through the vents to eliminate drag, and the phantom of the bottom can continue its mission."

Jack watched the comandante punch commands into the minihelm. He realized the information they were receiving would probably go to the bottom of the Gulf with them, yet he couldn't help but develop an odd sense of admiration for the comandante. The fine line between madness and genius, he thought. Which way did the comandante lean?

"Yeah, well, that's nice," said Virgil, somewhat bored by the demonstration. "But how you gonna maneuver a great big tub like this?"

The comandante was momentarily incensed by Virgil's remark, then shook his head. Would he ever understand the American sense of humor?

"It will be necessary for one of you to stand in the hatch," said the comandante, "the other directly above him, ready to drop into the hatch the instant the boat noses over."

"Noses over?" said Jack.

"Yes," said the comandante, punching commands into the computer. "We will not have a second to spare once the sequencing begins."

"All right," said Jack, glancing at his handcuffs. "Probably get down the hatch faster without these."

The comandante smiled before turning back to the computerized helm. "You'll manage," he said.

He hesitated just before keying in the final ten-second delay entry. "Get ready."

The blare of a diving klaxon sent the crew to their secure stations. The computer's simulated voice was now giving the orders. "Zambullida! Zambullida!" cried the computer's voice synthesizer.

"Now!" shouted the comandante.

Virgil was first down the hatch, followed by Jack and then the comandante, who made the boat watertight.

"Hang on," bellowed the comandante over the blaring klaxon.

Jack and Virgil clung to the periscope, while the comandante made himself fast against a bulkhead.

The *Nautilus* suddenly lurched forward, as though it had struck some underwater reef or another ship of some size. The inertia was such that Jack and Virgil were nearly torn off the periscope.

"The sea speed brakes," said the comandante. "They deploy as the hydrofoils are retracted. The maneuver has to be completed by computer; otherwise the boat would tear itself apart."

"How fast does it happen?" asked Jack.

"We can slow from maximum speed to dive within two-and-one-half lengths of the the boat. Fast enough to evade even the French Exocet missles."

"Amazing," said Virgil. "Wonder what it looks like on the surface."

"Like a great humpback whale sounding," said the comandante. "But come, there is still more."

Jack and Virgil followed the comandante to one of the many computer consoles built into the command center. There the comandante seated himself behind a VDT and switched the device on. On the screen he could produce one or several views, via closed-circuit TV cameras, which could provide surveillance three hundred and sixty degrees about the *Nautilus*.

"When we were on deck," began the comandante, "I showed you how the boat can camouflage itself underwater, by blending in with the bottom. This ploy would be ineffective without this next device."

He punched in more commands, and a mysterious sound emanated from the forward torpedo room.

The comandante cut off the cameras giving the view forward for a moment, then switched them back on. Jack and Virgil were astounded by what they saw on the VDT. It was just off their bow, suspended in the blue-green water, and beginning to pick up speed.

"It can't be," said Virgil. "It's some kind of trick! A television trick?"

"No, gentlemen," said the comandante. "I can assure you that what you see out there is quite real."

"Unbelievable!" said Jack in an awed whisper.

The boat was indeed real, an exact duplicate of the *Nautilus*, hovering in the depths, yet moving at barely dead slow. The water around the submarine seemed to blur Jack's vision, and the phantom boat began to bend.

"Wait a minute!" said Jack. "That's not a real submarine!"

"You catch on quickly," said the comandante. "You're right. We carry two such boats on board. They can be fired from the forward torpedo tubes. Once deployed, the decoys act rather like underwater dirigibles. The ship fills with seawater by means of a small electric pump, which also serves as its propellant. The real *Nautilus* camouflages itself as part of the bottom while one of these slowly limps off, luring our adversaries away. It's ridiculously simple, really. We embed the fabric of the dummy ship with fine metal particles, and the sonar systems searching for our location see it as real!''

"Amazing!" said Jack.

"There is one thing more," said the comandante, punching in more commands to the computer. "Watch this."

The image on the VDT began to change as the *Nautilus* came around. They were now on a collision course with the decoy when something deployed forward again. The sound was not like the previous one, as the decoy was being deployed, but rather more subtle. Then the decoy was sliced in half by a volley of spears fired from the torpedo room.

"I got the idea for this from some artillery rounds designed for a hundred-five-millimeter howitzer. The rounds are called fleshettes and fire in basically the same manner. Of course, underwater one must use spears, and the range is not as far, but it is still most effective against scuba divers, especially those bent on sabotage.''

"You've thought of everything," said Jack. "But what's all this stuff for?"

"Soon, gentlemen," said the comandante, rising up from the computer terminal. "I find myself growing rather fatigued now. I will show you more after I have rested. Vicente!''

"Sí, Comandante."

"See these men back to their quarters."

Chapter Fourteen

OPERATION PANAMA

CODY BROUGHT the popeye up the western coast of Florida. He had already christened the boat the *Domino II* and, during the trip, had grown rather comfortable with handling the unlimited catamaran.

Cody's first stop was the site where the *Ice Bucket* had gone down. The lagoon had already become a tourist trap, with charters bringing sunburned patrons to the place where "the dopers met their fate."

It seemed as if everyone in Naples was cashing in on Jack and Virgil's demise. There was even someone selling nickel bags of coke, Baggies half full of powdered sugar with a ridiculous stencil showing the *Ice Bucket* blowing up in a huge fireball. Scuba divers were bringing up pieces of the *Ice Bucket* and selling them as souvenirs. A few other clowns were hawking T-shirts reading: "I survived the sinking of the *Ice Bucket*."

Cody toyed with the idea of popping the twin fifty-caliber machine guns hidden aft and blowing the lot of them out of the water. Carnes settled on blending in with the crowd, veering in an out of the mini-armada, though he really wasn't sure of his purpose.

At first Cody thought his eyes were playing tricks on him. The last few days had been hectic, and he had been cutting back on his sleep, but he was sure the object he saw dipping into the Gulf was a periscope.

The engines of the popeye bellowed to life as Cody tore off in the direction of his sighting. The mechanized thunder was such that all activity ceased among the sightseers. Those captaining the charters wondered who the owner of the popeye was, and their patrons were simply awed by the horsepower.

Cody homed in on the approximate location of the periscope, but the cigar had already slipped through the underwater doors of Triangle Island, leaving only the wake of its jet drive behind.

Cody studied his radar and sonar, but to no avail. He laid down a precise search pattern and continued monitoring his surveillance devices, but his search proved fruitless. Whoever or whatever was running just below the surface had disappeared.

Cody took the popeye on a course around Triangle Island. He studied the island as though it might reveal some clue to the disappearance of Jack and Virgil. Cody felt a strange feeling of déjà vu as he swung the popeye around the north end of the island. The area had been thoroughly searched by the Coast Guard, yet he couldn't help being drawn toward it. Why? he thought. Why do I keep coming back here?

The comandante's cadre, manning the controls of the communications center inside Triangle Island, were understandably nervous. With so many boats around, it had been most difficult to maintain the regular routine. Now they were faced with a new menace, this new boat, the big catamaran, with a captain who seemed more than just curious.

Orders had been issued to close the camouflaged doors of the sea cave. This would cut the energy capabilities of the wave generators, and thus work on the second prototype, as well as maintenance on the smaller cigars, had to be curtailed. Recordings were made of the catamaran searching the shores of Triangle Island. No doubt the comandante, upon his return, would be interested in the owner of the boat, for the captain of the catamaran had more than a passing interest in Triangle Island. His curiosity might be setting a dangerous precedent.

"Take down the catamaran's registration number," said the

technician, studying one of the monitors. "Find out who owns it."

Domino stood on the wharf where the *Ice Bucket* used to moor and tried to fight back the tears. She was waiting for Cody to arrive with the new boat, yet was still tormented by the disappearance of Jack and Virgil.

Now even Domino's indomitable spirit was beginning to falter. It had been days since the *Ice Bucket* had gone down, and still there was no word on Jack or Virgil. Domino had thought she would have heard something, some word that might have bolstered her hopes, yet no news had come forth. Domino was reaching the point where she would have to face the truth. Still there was a glimmer of faith, a deep-seated hope that would not die. It would be the long shot of long shots for them to still be alive, and the sight of Cody rumbling into the Naples docks firmed up her faltering conviction.

"Any word?" called Domino expectantly.

"Nothing concrete," said Cody, tossing her a line.

Domino made the popeye fast to the dock and waited aft for Cody to toss her another line. "What do you mean 'nothing concrete'?"

"Ah, it's probably stupid," said Cody.

"What's stupid?" demanded Domino.

"I'll have to go back out there tonight," said Cody, rubbing his face. "After that circus is gone."

"What circus? Damn it! Will you tell me what's going on?"

"Sure," said Cody, picking up from the helm his gym bag with the M-11's.

"Well, I'm waiting."

"I'll tell you," said Cody, "but you're not going with me."

"The hell I'm not."

Cody stopped on the wharf and looked at the defiant expression on Domino's face. He gave an exasperated sigh. If he left her behind, she'd just get a charter and follow. It would be dangerous, but simpler, if she were on board the popeye instead of tagging along.

"All right," he said. "You can go."

"When do we leave?"

"Soon as I get some sleep. I'm damn near dead on my feet."

"Tomorrow?" asked Domino apprehensively.

"No, I'm not that tired. We'll leave at sundown."

"Good," said Domino.

"Yeah?" said Cody, raising his eyebrow. "We'll see about that."

Jack and Virgil were awakened by the sound of Vicente Villa's voice. He was shouting something in Spanish up the open hatch to the comandante. Apparently seawater had seeped through the seal of the conning tower's computer terminal, and commands now had to be shouted below decks.

"Now what?" asked Virgil, wiggling around inside his clothes, which by now were growing quite ripe. .

"We must be close," said Jack.

"Close to what?"

"Where we're going."

"Where's that?"

"How should I know?"

"Gee, thanks!"

The hatch to the head was open a crack, allowing them a tantalizing glimpse of activity at one end of the command center. From what Jack could make out, the comandante was undertaking the repairs of the computerized helm himself.

Jack glanced at his watch. Depending on their easterly or westerly location, they were nearing sundown. The question was, where was the sun setting?

The comandante completed the installation of a backup unit on the conning tower, and activity aboard the *Nautilus* returned to normal.

Vicente Villa poked his face inside the head to check on the gringos. Jack put a ready hand on the disinfectant spray. Villa smiled.

"De comandante wants to see jou," he said.

The torpedoman-miner was missing, and another crewman had taken his place. Jack recognized him as the machinist's mate.

"What's up?" asked Virgil, spotting the difference.

"Wherever we were going," whispered Jack, "we're there."

Villa held his 9 mm pistol on them as they came out of the head. Villa was still suspicious of the pair, despite the comandante's taking them into his confidence, and if either made any attempt to escape, he'd blow them apart.

"Up top," said Villa, gesturing with the pistol.

Jack and Virgil made their way up the ladder, to the conning tower. There they found the comandante scanning the horizon with a pair of binoculars.

"Make ready forward," the comandante punched into the computer. "We are here," he continued with a smile.

"Where is here?" asked Jack.

"Take a look around," said the comandante, returning to his surveillance. "You'll figure it out."

Jack and Virgil searched the horizon. The sun had just set, and the sky's orange luster ended abruptly where it met the sea. There was an eerie noise that cut through the settling mist. Foghorns. They seemed to be all around.

Jack's eyes adjusted to the light. He saw the silhouettes; the horizon seemed to be dotted with them. Ships of all sizes, but they were not moving; they seemed to be waiting, but waiting for what?

Jack shifted his attention toward the shoreline, which was still some miles away. It couldn't be Florida, he thought. The shoreline seemed almost devoid of lights, save for one glowing center of activity, and there the lighting was equal to that of Miami Beach at night.

Now Jack saw the ships lying ahead of them. They were strung out in a great line, as if some gigantic schoolboy had arranged them in his bathtub, and all the ships were headed directly toward the brightly lit shoreline.

"Jesus," said Jack, dumbfounded. "it's Panama!"

"Precisely," said the comandante, watching not the shoreline but the sky.

"The canal?" asked Virgil.

"Another brilliant geographer," said the comandante, punching "come left three degrees" into the computer. The *Nautilus* came to a new heading, one that would keep the string of waiting ships on their starboard beam.

"You may remain on deck," said the comandante, lowering his binoculars, "but only so long as you remain quiet. To scream for help would not only be foolish but quite fatal as well. Do we understand each other?"

"We do," said Jack.

"Good," said the comandante. "All ahead one-third."

The *Nautilus* ran smoothly through the water, its ultrastreamlined hull barely leaving a wake as her turbines pushed her silently toward the entrance to the Panama Canal.

Jack pondered one of a hundred different scenarios the comandante might be planning. Their earlier thoughts, that the comandante was planning to use the new prototypes to sink mother ships and steal their cargoes of cocaine, seemed tame compared with the grandiose plans he must be harboring.

The *Nautilus* passed one of the ships farthest out in the waiting line, a Norwegian freighter using the canal to save it the long and risky voyage around the Horn. Those standing watch on deck never saw the mysterious vessel pass by and, even if they had, most likely would have mistaken it for some large variety of marine life.

The comandante seemed preoccupied with the sky rather than the sea, and for good reason. Jack could see that the air space above the entrance to the Canal was patrolled by helicopters and probably turboprops as well. Security had to be tight around the Canal, because of the worldwide terrorist threats. How, then, was the comandante going to breech the gap and enter the canal?

"Clear the bridge," ordered the comandante.

Jack and Virgil quickly complied. They slid down the hatch

into the command center, where Villa awaited them with his ever-ready pistol. The comandante was next down the hatch, and made the boat watertight.

"Take her down to thirty-five–feet keel depth," ordered the comandante.

The helmsman complied, flooding the tanks and taking the *Nautilus* beneath the waves and out of the sight of an approaching surveillance plane. The comandante smiled as he clung to the hatch ladder, a cunning smirk that emanated from a feeling of invincibility. His eyes seemed to sense the surveillance plane, tracking it as passed overhead.

Villa signaled the all-clear, and the comandante ordered up angle on the bow planes to bring the boat to periscope depth.

"What about de gringos?" asked Villa.

"Let them watch," said the comandante, turning his captain's cap around in classic u-boat fashion before peering into the aperture of the periscope. He focused the lens and studied the rangefinder. "Come right two degrees," he said. "Prepare to make a mating run."

"Aye-aye, Capitan," said the helmsman, making the course correction.

"Steady as you go," said the comandante. "We'll make the run stern to bow. Range—eight hundred yards."

Jack and Virgil watched the helmsman hold steady on course. They surmised that the sub was making a run on one of the ships lined up to enter the canal. The question was why.

"Range," said the comandante. "Six hundred yards. Hold steady on present course. Down scope."

Villa brought the scope down, and the comandante swung his cap back around, covering his thinning thatch. Sweat was beginning to gather in his beard. The tiny gleaming droplets picked up the various colors reflected off the computer screens lining the command center.

"Cameras on forward," ordered the comandante.

Villa complied with the order, and the twin closed-circuit TV cameras mounted in the bow presented them with an awesome sight. They were coming up aft of a large freighter, its twin screws turning just enough to maintain position against the current and tide. The water was reasonably clear, but murky enough that even the sharpest lookout would not see the approaching *Nautilus*.

"Take her down to forty-five–feet keel depth," ordered the comandante.

The helmsman complied, and the *Nautilus* began its run on the freighter.

"What the hell are they going to do?" asked Virgil.

"Just be quiet and watch," said Jack.

The comandante studied the monitors with intensity. "Forty-feet keel depth."

The *Nautilus* came up ever so slowly, the helmsman dividing his attention among the depth gauge, sonar, and television monitors. They were being being buffeted by the wash from the freighter's screws, but the helmsman held steady on course.

"Thirty-five feet," said the comandante, whose face was nearly pressed against the television monitors. "Prepare for mating," he continued into the ship's intercom.

"Ready forward," came the voice of the torpedoman-miner. "All stop."

Jack and Virgil watched, transfixed, as the bow of the *Nautilus* rose to gently kiss the keel of the freighter. On board the freighter the slight thump was felt by most of the crew, but no one suspected anything unusual. This close to shore, the ships often ran into floating debris of one kind or another. The mate standing watch on deck assumed it was driftwood and spat over the side before continuing his rounds.

"Mating complete?" asked the comandante.

"Check-mating," replied the torpedoman-miner.

"Flood tanks," said the comandante.

The *Nautilus* dropped away from the keel of the freighter. All eyes trained again on the television monitors. At first Jack and Virgil didn't understand the cheering of the crew and the broad smile of the comandante. Then they noticed the odd yellow shape attached to the freighter's keel.

"Jesus Christ!" whispered Jack. "That's a mine!"

"Yeah," said Virgil. "But that can't be a mother ship, not lined up to go through the Panama Canal. And why would he want to blow it up out here?"

"I don't think he's going to blow it up out here," whispered Jack as the cheering died down in the command center. "I think he'll wait until it gets *inside* the canal!"

"Holy shit!" said Virgil. "Christ, he could hold up half the goddamn world like that."

"Now you're catching on," said Jack.

"Man, this guy ain't so crazy as he seems."

"Jettison mine," ordered the comandante.

"Aye-aye, sir," said the torpedoman-miner.

Jack and Virgil, now more confused than ever, watched as the yellow mine fell away from the hull of the freighter.

"All ahead two-thirds," said the comandante.

"Got it all figured out, haven't you, smart guy," whispered Virgil sarcastically.

"This was just a practice run," said Jack. "The real fireworks will come later."

"Whatever you say, Sherlock."

Jack was about to speak to the comandante, when he saw him conferring with Vicente Villa. Villa looked over at Jack and Virgil while the comandante whispered his instructions. Villa smiled, his gold inlays glistening in the light of the command center.

"Look at that slick sonofabitch smile, would ya?" said Virgil.

"Yeah," said Jack. "Bastard looks too happy to suit me."

"Dees way, gentlemen," said Villa, pointing with his pistol.

"Guess he's taking us back to our luxury suite," said Jack.

"Could be worse," said Virgil.

"I've got a feeling it will be," said Jack, stepping through the hatch.

Cody and Domino stood in the trio couches at the popeye's helm. Once again, they had come back to the site of the sinking of the *Ice Bucket* not to look for survivors but drawn by some strange magnetism. Sea pilgrims paying homage to missing comrades.

"There aren't as many today," said Domino as they rounded the southern tip of Triangle Island. Cody could see only three pleasure craft above the wreck of the *Ice Bucket:* the scuba divers, who had nearly stripped the wreck bare; the T-shirt salesman; and a charter carrying an Ohio family suffering from motion sickness.

"No," said Cody. "In a few days no one will even remember this spot."

"I will!" snapped Domino vehemently.

"So will I," said Cody, the tone of his voice indicating that he needed no reminder.

"Sorry."

"It's all right," said Cody. "Where to now?"

"I dunno," said Domino, studying the irregular terrain of Triangle Island. "There's something about that place," she continued, her voice becoming almost mystical. "I can't put my finger on it. I just *know* it had something to do with Jack and Virgil's disappearance."

"Women's intuition," scoffed Cody.

"Call it what you want," said Domino, studying the sea charts and the overlay of the island.

"There are thousands of islands like this. That's why they call this place Ten Thousand Islands. So what's so special about this one?"

"I don't know," said Domino. "It just is."

"Do you want to go ashore again?"

"No. But I do want to go around it again."

"Yeah," said Cody, correcting the helm. "That'll make an even dozen."

The surveillance crew had been monitoring the arrival of the ships to the site of the *Ice Bucket* since before dawn. Tension inside the command center of Triangle Island had been on the wane with the decrease in the numbers of ships returning to the site. But now that pesky unlimited catamaran was nosing around again, and faces pressed against the television monitors, studying the movements of the popeye. The catamaran had become a daily visitor, and since it patrolled so close to the island, the camouflage doors leading to the wave generators had to be closed, which cut power supplies back to the barest minimum.

Progress on the second large cigar prototype had come to a standstill, and technicians worried over the comandante's displeasure upon his return. He would expect to see major progress on the assembly; instead, the boat would show only a few cosmetic changes.

"Damn that catamaran!" grumbled one of the technicians, watching it round the northern end of the island.

The communications crew chief knew it was time to risk a transmission with the *Nautilus*. His first two hailing calls went unanswered, but the third got through, though static garbled some of the transmission.

Vicente Villa answered the call, to the crew chief's relief. The comandante had left strict orders that he was to be contacted only in case of emergency, and it was often difficult to decide what the comandante might consider an emergency.

The crew chief detailed the problem with the catamaran, and Villa wasted no time in giving an answer. The crew chief was to dispatch a squad to gather intelligence on who the owners of the boat might be, their place of residence, and possible motivation for frequenting the waters around the island.

The crew chief reminded Villa about the comandante's standing order to avoid contact with the local populace but was quickly countermanded by Villa, who demanded that the chief follow his orders.

The crew chief would comply with the command and handpick the team himself. There were those in the command who blindly followed the comandante's orders, and zealots would not break ranks to obtain the information they needed.

"No hostages," said Villa. "The squad is to reconnoiter and return. No one is to see them."

"Understood," said the crew chief, cutting off the transmission.

* * *

The comandante was taking one of his infrequent naps when Villa concluded his conversation with the crew chief. The comandante rarely slept for any length of time, preferring to nap when his driving ambition was drained by normal fatigue. Only the helmsman heard the transmission, and he concurred with Villa's decision. The helmsman knew how the comandante's mania for following orders could sometimes blind him of the need to question command dogma, and this was one of those situations. No sense in arousing the wrath of the comandante over a situation that could just as well be concluded with calculated discretion.

The helmsman smiled at Villa as he came to his next course correction. Villa did not respond. He maintained an aloof posture with cadre and crew, and the helmsman was no exception. After all, the helmsman knew who was *really* in charge.

Jack and Virgil adjusted their sleeping positions in tandem. Being handcuffed together for some time had developed in them the same sense of oneness as a set of Siamese twins.

Jack was half asleep, and an all-too-vivid dream woke him suddenly. He squinted and tried to wink the sleep from his eyes. His back was cramping again, and in adjusting his position he nearly roused Virgil.

Jack shifted his mind to pleasant thoughts. Domino. The Coast Guard would have pronounced us dead by now, he thought. But would Domino believe them? Even if they found the wreck, would she give up hope? No, probably not.

Then a new train of thought interrupted Jack. How could he have been so stupid? If the Coast Guard found the wreck of the *Ice Bucket,* they'd be bound to search Triangle Island. Then they'd find—

Jack's newfound enthusiasm quickly waned. If the Coast Guard had found the operation inside Triangle Island, the comandante would have heard of it, and they had received no transmissions from the island giving any such information. No, as far as the authorities were concerned, Jack and Virgil no longer existed.

Now Jack's thoughts returned to the day they fished Phil Lanard's arm out of the shark's belly. No doubt the same fate awaited them.

Jack tried to work out some plan of escape, yet each new scheme ended with the same result—failure. Jack sat up a bit and glanced out of the cracked head hatch. Activity aboard the *Nautilus* had slowed with the comandante asleep, yet something just outside the hatch caught Jack's eye.

How could he have been so blind? thought Jack, sitting up to get a better look through the crack. There they were, inside a hanging locker, just against the bulkhead. Escape vests. Granted, there were only enough for the crew, but Jack's plan didn't include them.

Jack eased himself back into a more comfortable position and thought through his plan. Escape hinged on how long the comandante planned to keep them alive, and, more important, how close to a landfall they would be if he didn't. If the comandante took them topside to give them the deep six, then they had a chance. Granted, it was a small chance, but between the disinfectant spray and the escape vests, it just might work. All they needed now was the right opportunity.

The *Adele Bristol*, like many of the rusting freighters employed by Colombian smugglers, was of Liberian registration. The *Bristol*'s bilge pumps worked around the clock to keep the listing hulk afloat. Its engines were a mechanic's nightmare, and its navigational instruments almost nonexistent, which was typical of the flotilla that sputtered their way up the Caribbean with holds bursting with marijuana and cocaine.

The *Bristol* had broken down twice on the run up from Colombia and now, as they neared the rendezvous, it looked as if the ship was going to break down again. The captain of the *Adele Bristol* left command of the helm to his mate before going below to supervise the repair crew. The *Bristol* was still just outside the United States' twelve-mile limit, and the current would not bring them into the territorial waters for some time to come. Enough time, the captain hoped, to complete the repairs below.

The bosun standing watch caught a glimpse of the silhouette on the horizon. At first he thought it was a doper, but they were too far out from shore, and way south of the rendezvous for anyone in the trade to make contact. And the shape of the ship. What was it? A new model of oceangoing cigarette?

The bosun of the *Adele Bristol* was about to signal the bridge, when the strange ship on the horizon simply disappeared into the setting sun. It must be the sun playing tricks with my eyes, thought the bosun, continuing his watch. Nothing to worry about. Just be glad you're not below trying to fix those god-damned engines.

"Dead in the water," said Villa. "A perfect target."

"Sweep the area for any other vessels," said the comandante, peering through the periscope.

"Area clear," said Villa. "Do we take her?"

"Yes," said the comandante. "This will make a good test ship."

Jack and Virgil could hear the goings-on through the cracked hatch of the head.

"What ship?" whispered Virgil. "The ones that were lined up to go into the canal?"

"Naw, we've been moving for too long. Couldn't be in the same waters. Besides, this has been a shakedown cruise. My guess is that we're somewhere in the Gulf again. Probably heading back home port."

"The Gulf!" said Virgil. "Jesus, that means we could be close to home."

"Don't get your hopes up," said Jack. "We could be two hundred miles out to sea for all we know. Now, be quiet, and let's just listen."

The comandante pushed open the hatch to the head. "Come, gentlemen. I want you to see the full capability of my proto-type."

It was the machinist's mate who freed Jack and Virgil from

the pipes. As before, the cuffs remained in place, but they were allowed the momentary luxury of having their hands shackled in front of them, a welcome relief from the contorted positions they had been holding.

Jack was first up the ladder to the conning tower. Grigsby calculated the distance to the locker containing the escape vests. Easily within arm's reach. The question was how they would get above decks.

The air on the bridge was clear and fresh and laced with an aroma Jack and Virgil thought they might never sense again—land! Both Jack and Virgil scoured the horizons, trying to conceal their hopeful glances from the comandante. Like poker players dealt a pat hand, they reacted to the sight of the islands. The landfall was still miles away, but at least they knew there was a chance.

"Yeah, I see it," whispered Jack, pushing Virgil's elbow out of his ribs.

The comandante pulled his field glasses down from his eyes. He mistakenly assumed that Jack was referring to the *Adele Bristol*. "Yes," he said, studying the freighter. "It is not much of a ship, but it will serve my purposes. Prepare to dive."

Jack and Virgil dropped back down the hatch. They passed Villa, who sat grinning at them from behind the gunner's console, located forward inside the conning tower. Villa's appearance was particularly heinous, the contemplation of his weaponry having generated his gruesome expression.

"He's in a good mood," whispered Virgil, following Jack down the ladder to the command center.

The comandante made the *Nautilus* watertight and slid down the ladder. He pulled off his binoculars and gave the orders to dive. The helmsman took the ship down to fifteen feet, while the comandante adjusted the periscope.

Jack looked about. All hands were preoccupied with making the run on the *Adele Bristol*. Jack reached up and tugged on one of the escape vests inside the locker. The vest did not move, held in place by Velcro strips set into the sides of the locker. "Cough a couple of times," Jack whispered to Virgil.

Virgil glanced back and caught Jack's meaning and, without overplaying the ploy, coughed loudly enough to cover the sound of the Velcro strips being torn away.

Jack grabbed a vest out of the locker. Next he stepped toward the head and reached around behind the hatch to hide the vest between the hatch and the bulkhead. With this accomplished, he stepped back to his position below the conning tower hatch and behind the comandante.

"Come right two degrees," said the comandante.

Jack and Virgil watched as the comandante made the same run he had taken on the freighter heading into the Panama Canal. The *Nautilus* crept up on the *Adele Bristol* and set a mine just short of the freighter's bow. With this accomplished, the comandante ordered the sub to bare off the *Adele Bristol*'s starboard beam and surfaced.

"Would you join me on the bridge?" asked the comandante, enunciating his demand with a drawn 9 mm pistol.

Jack's hopes sank with the sight of the pistol. The escape plan employing the disinfectant spray and the life-vest seemed all for nothing now. Jack figured they were about to suffer the same fate as the crew of the *Adele Bristol*.

"Guess we're gonna get to play captain and go down with the ship," said Virgil.

"Yeah," said Jack. "Right now, I'd trade places with two first-class ticket holders on the *Titanic*."

Chapter Fifteen

RETURN TO THE MEKONG DELTA

THE CIGARETTE out of Naples was navigating without running lights. When the doper failed to find the *Adele Bristol* at the rendezvous, he began to search the Gulf for the mother ship. Such delays were an expected part of the trade, and it wasn't the first time the *Bristol* had failed to make a rendezvous.

The cigarette, an unnamed forty-footer, was cruising along at forty knots when the doper sighted the *Adele Bristol*. The mother ship was dead in the water, which explained the missed rendezvous but not the strange craft off her starboard beam. The doper cut his speed and let inertia take him in for a closer look.

Jack led Virgil up onto the bridge. The comandante kept close watch on them as he came up through the hatch. Jack could see the *Adele Bristol* off to port. The decks of the freighter were strung with working lights as the maintenance crew worked below to repair her engines.

The comandante ordered the *Nautilus* to come about until their bow faced squarely amidships of the *Adele Bristol*. "You will detonate on my command," said the comandante into the intercom.

"What?" said Jack.

"If you call out a warning," said the comandante, "I will

shoot you and your friend without hesitation. Do you understand me?''

Jack nodded and studied the comandante as he prepared to sink the helpless ship. Whatever respect Jack had developed for the comandante over the course of the journey had now vanished. The expression the comandante wore now was not that of some misguided genius but of a demented madman.

''Detonate!'' ordered the comandante.

The explosion came in two stages. There was a sudden swell of seawater all around the bow of the *Adele Bristol*, followed by a geysering orange-red fireball that engulfed the forward hull.

The crewmen on the deck of the *Adele Bristol* were knocked off their feet by the explosion, and when they regained their footing they felt the ship going down by the bow. Those caught below decks, working on the engines, were swallowed inside a raging fireball, which raced through open hatches. Agonized screams emanated from below decks as men with their clothes on fire ran from the man-made hell they would never escape.

The doper out of Naples witnessed the explosion. He stood at the helm of his cigarette, bathed in the orange glow of the burning *Adele Bristol*. The doper's reaction was as heartless as that of other men in his pitiful profession. What luck, he thought. The mother ship is sinking. I may not be able to salvage the cocaine, but I can make a quick killing in free ''Square Grouper.'' The doper gunned his engines and moved in. Soon, he hoped, the water would be littered with the familiar cubic bales of marijuana that wash up on the beaches of southern Florida when mother ships get caught inside the twelve mile limit and deep-six their cargoes to avoid capture by the Coast Guard. Floating bundles of Square Grouper would be worth a fortune, and he wouldn't have to part with one cent in buy money. The doper threw caution to the wind. He was anxious to play his part as sea vulture and did not see the *Nautilus*, now shrouded in smoke from the burning *Adele Bristol*.

Jack could just make out the crew scrambling over the listing decks. Some crawled out from the hold, where the blast had been magnified. Their noses and ears ran with blood from the concussion of the mine. A few stumbled over the side, while others collapsed on the deck.

"Not a very pleasant sight, is it?" said Jack, leveling a condemning glare at the comandante.

"An unfortunate necessity," said the comandante. "In order to support my cause, it is necessary for me to test the weaponry of the boat."

"Fuck you and your cause!" said Jack, watching foundering men drowning in the Gulf.

The comandante's finger tightened on the trigger of his pistol. Then, just as he was about to pump a round into Jack's belly, his mood changed dramatically. "If you knew of the cause, you would understand," he said.

"I'm listening," said Jack.

The comandante shook his head. "This is not the time, nor the place. Perhaps when my business is finished here."

The doper out of Naples closed on the *Adele Bristol*. The mother ship was listing forty-five degrees to starboard when the cigarette came into the brightest light of the flames. He had thrown all caution to the wind in his approach and now lay less than a hundred yards off the *Nautilus*'s starboard beam but shrouded by the wall of smoke drifting off the *Bristol*.

At first Virgil thought his eyes were playing tricks on him. Then the light evening breeze cut a swath through the smoke pouring off the *Bristol,* and Virgil knew he wasn't viewing a mirage. He nudged Jack and nodded in the direction of the cigarette.

Jack moved to block the comandante's view of the cigarette, his mind racing with the possibilities. Swimming in handcuffs and clothes would not be easy, but if they could just reach that cigarette, there was a good chance they might be able to slip away.

Jack turned and saw that the comandante was almost mesmerized by the sight of the burning *Bristol*. It was as though he were living out part of the drama that would unfold when he implemented the plan that would see him triumph for "the cause."

Jack wondered if the skipper of the cigarette would fish them out of the water, or shoot them as he knew the comandante planned to do. There was no time for questions, only action.

Jack nodded at Virgil. Virgil winked back. Jack came in high, Virgil came in low. The comandante felt Jack's first blow, but not the second. His nose was smashed, while Virgil wrestled the 9 mm pistol from his hand. The comandante slumped over in the conning tower.

Jack glanced down the hatch into the command center. No one had seen or heard the commotion over the explosions now thundering through the *Bristol*. Virgil was about to leap out of the conning tower and into the Gulf when Jack stopped him and motioned downward.

Virgil could see the forward firing doors of the *Nautilus* open, and he knew that if they jumped for it, Villa might see them and chop them to pieces in seconds. Leaving the comandante unconscious on the bridge, the Vietnam vets climbed down the aft ladder of the conning tower and slipped quietly over the side.

"Comandante," came the call over the conning tower's intercom. "Comandante. We are awaiting orders," came the voice of the helmsman.

Virgil held on to the 9 mm pistol as they floundered around in the Gulf. He was making little progress and was forced to shove the pistol down in his shorts. Jack lead the way into the smoke of the *Adele Bristol*. The fouled air made the swim even more difficult than Jack imagined, but within a few minutes they were within thirty yards of the cigarette, which sat waiting for the crew of the *Adele Bristol* to abandon ship.

Jack could see the doper standing on the foredeck of the cigarette. It looked like they could come up aft, climb over the transom, and take the boat by force.

The swim began to exhaust both Jack and Virgil. They both swam with a spastic sidestroke, necessitated by their shackled hands and slowed by the drag of their clothes. Jack was first to the transom of the cigarette. He wrestled himself up on the stern, then turned and whispered to Virgil.

"Let me have it," said Jack.

Virgil trod water, pulled the 9 mm out of his shorts, and handed the weapon up to Jack. Jack took the pistol, shook the water from the automatic, then, holding the breech between his teeth, climbed into the cigarette.

The doper didn't hear Jack, didn't see him; he just felt the cold steel of the muzzle of the 9 mm poke him in the back of his head. Jack swung the doper around until his nose filled the barrel of the pistol. "Turn this tub around," said Jack. "And get your ass back into the swamp as fast as you can."

"Hey, wait a minute!" said the doper, hesitating, his greed still overshadowing his reason. "There's a fortune to be made here tonight!"

"Do you see that?" said Jack. He pushed the doper's face with the muzzle of the 9 mm toward the *Nautilus,* now visible between puffs of smoke. "Well, if you don't haul ass, that thing will blow you, the mother ship, and any other boat in the general vicinity clean out of the water!"

The doper didn't need any more encouragement. He knew how many locals had disappeared lately, and joining their numbers in Davy Jones' Locker was not among his plans for the night.

Both Jack and the doper slid toward the helm. Virgil was just hauling himself into the cigarette when the doper fired up his engines.

"Move!" snarled Jack, shoving the pistol into the doper's ribs.

Villa was climbing out of his gunner's couch in the conning tower when the cigarette off the *Adele Bristol*'s bow fired up her engines. Vicente had some difficulty in opening the hatch to the bridge, as the comandante had fallen on top of it.

Squeezing through the half-open hatch, Villa found the comandante just regaining his senses. Blood poured from his broken nose, and most of his front teeth had been loosened. *"Tu viejo zonzo,"* said Villa, pushing the comandante off the hatch.

Villa helped prop up the comandante, who was still too

groggy to take command of the ship. Villa took the comandante's field glasses and scanned the area for the escaped gringos. In a moment he located the fleeing cigarette and its two passengers.

"Full astern!" screamed Villa into the intercom.

The helmsman complied with the order, and the *Nautilus* began to back away from the sinking *Adele Bristol*.

"Torpedo room!" shouted Villa. "Prepare to fire tubes one and two!"

"Tubes one and two ready."

"Fire!"

The torpedoes flew out of the forward tubes and steaked for their target. The warheads ran true. The *Adele Bristol* was broken in half by the force of the blast. Crewmen leaping over the side were blown into pieces. Others were cut down by the hull, which had been rendered into huge chunks of shrapnel.

Villa sprayed the water around the fast-sinking *Adele Bristol* with the Gatling guns. He could leave no witnesses who had seen the *Nautilus*, especially those who had such a healthy head start.

"Come right to 090. All ahead flank," said Villa, then ordered the torpedoman-miner to take his place in the gunner's couch.

The doper, a small-timer named Larson, heard the deafening explosion behind them. He turned and glanced back to see most of the midships of the *Adele Bristol* go up. Twin geysers of burning oil and twisted debris rose into the night sky, a miniature volcanic erruption that tinted the waters of the Gulf bright orange.

"Jesus!" said Larson, shoving on his throttles. "What the hell is that?"

"Never mind," said Jack, pushing the 9 mm into the small of his back. "Just get this thing through Ten Thousand Islands and into the swamps as fast as you can."

"Here they come!" said Virgil, peering off their stern with a pair of field glasses.

The *Nautilus* opened up with 20 mm fire, the tracers coming every fifth round, and burning bits of crimson flew past the gunwales of the fleeing cigarette. Larson stood at the helm, hands locked on the wheel, and stared open-mouthed at the closing *Nautilus*.

"Jesus Christ!" bellowed Jack. "Take evasive action, you goddamn fool!"

Larson continued to look aft. The 20 mm cannon began to get the range. Soon the rounds would slam into the cigarette, and they would suffer the same fate as the *Adele Bristol*.

"Virgil! Take the wheel!"

Virgil looked at his infected hand. The injections had taken their toll. His hand was still swollen to twice its normal size, and circulation had all but been cut off by the handcuffs now cutting into his flesh. "Can't feel my hand anymore, Jack. You'll have to do it."

Jack shoved Larson off the helm. The doper fell to his knees but could not take his eyes off the submarine.

"Lower forward hydrofoils," ordered Villa, watching the comandante wipe the blood from his face.

"The Americans?" asked the comandante through a mouthful of blood. "Where have they—"

"We are closing on them now, my comandante," said Villa. "Lower aft hydrofoils."

The engines of Larson's cigarette were tired and in need of repair. Both began to misfire as the boat topped one hundred miles an hour. Jack could see the shorelines of Ten Thousand Islands just ahead. If they could just reach the maze of islands before the *Nautilus* closed the gap between them. But Grigsby's wish was unfulfilled. Two 20 mm rounds caught the stern of the cigarette. Jack felt Larson fall up against his back, then slide down his legs until his head rested against his calves.

"Get off me, you dumb bas—"

Jack could feel the warm ooze of entrails on the backs of his legs. He reached back with a free hand and unhooked Larson's intestines from the butt of the 9 mm pistol stuffed inside his belt. The feel of Larson's guts made Jack want to retch, but the fire from the *Nautilus* quickly sobered him to his task.

"You okay, Virgil?"

"Shit!" said Virgil, peering over the stern of the cigarette. "They hit the hydraulics on the trim."

"That's not all," said Jack.

Virgil turned around and caught a glimpse of what was left of Larson. A 20 mm round had cut through the stern, bounced off a turbo-charger, and caught Larson square in the back. The slug had cut him in half, and his entrails lay all over the blood-soaked deck.

"Jesus," said Virgil, looking back toward the *Nautilus*. "Well, good buddy, you better do something fast. He's on hydrofoils now."

"Only a couple of miles to the islands," said Jack.

Virgil peered up from the stern, over the windscreen. He gauged the distance they had to cover. "We ain't gonna make it," he said.

"The hell we aren't!" said Jack, taking the tachometers of the cigarette deep into the red.

"Call the island!" said the comandante, pulling himself to his feet. "Dispatch two cigars to cut off their escape."

"Already ordered, my comandante," said Villa, offering his commander no help. "Why don't you go below and care for your wounds."

The eyes of the Latin madman seemed to swell almost out of socket with rage. The comandante sucked air through clenched teeth as he pushed Villa away from the helm. "No," he snarled. "You go below. I am still in charge of this vessel!"

"As you wish," said Villa, sliding down the hatch to the command center.

"Villa," snapped the comandante.

"Sí, my comandante."

"Open up with Gatling guns, and see that your marksmanship does not fail me!"

"Sí, mi comandante."

Jack was having some difficulty handling the helm. The handcuffs made it awkward to set what was left of the trim and manipulate the wheel.

"Virgil!" Jack shouted, "can you manage the trim?"

"Hell, yes," said Virgil, stepping over the mangled remains of Larson.

Blood smeared across the comandante's face from the wash of the wind across the *Nautilus*, making his wounds appear more serious than they actually were. Plasma seeped into his beard and down onto his uniform. Like some Mephistophelian demon, the comandante rode the bridge, his eyes burning through the night, his outstretched arm seemingly able to move the course of the *Nautilus*. "Come right two degrees," he bellowed, and the *Nautilus* bore down on its evasive quarry.

Villa adjusted the straps of his firing couch and peered into the Starlite scopes mounted on the Gatling guns. Jack and Virgil darted in and out of the sight's eerie green light, giving Villa only a split second to squeeze off a burst.

Jack rode the helm, ripping course corrections that threatened to fracture the cigarette's Kevlar hull. The buffeting was such that Larson's corpse kept sliding across the decks, lubricated by his own blood.

The Gatling guns opened up. The night was scored by the line of crimson phosphorus, the tracers providing Villa with enough light to spot his target without the Starlite scopes.

Jack realized they were not going to reach Ten Thousand Islands. He looked quickly aft for anything that might slow the *Nautilus* down. Larson's corpse lay against it—a spare five-gallon gas can.

"Virge!" shouted Jack. "If we're going to burn up the water, let's do it for real!"

"Gotcha covered," said Virgil, leaping toward the gas can.

Virgil stayed low, as the tracers were now just above the boat's windscreen, and Villa was beginning to get the range. Virgil lifted the gas can and nearly passed out from the pain in his injured hand. Virgil poured about half the contents over their stern, then took out his lighter and set the gas ablaze.

The Gulf exploded in flames behind the fleeing cigarette. Virgil kept pouring the gas over the stern until the flames began to catch up with the cigarette. Virgil then tossed the three-quarters empty gas can over the stern.

The comandante saw the flaming water and was giving the order to take evasive action when the starboard hydrofoil hit the gas can. The concussion of the explosion nearly blew the comandante off the bridge. The hydrofoil buckled, with its planes bent out of trim, and the *Nautilus* came down bow-angled into the Gulf.

Villa managed one last burst before the bow slammed into the water. One of the outer torpedo doors was blown open by the force of the sea plowing into the hull. The starboard hydrofoil, already damaged from the blast, ripped off its moorings on the bow plane. The comandante managed to stay with the boat at the cost of several broken ribs, and those below, save for Villa, faired little better.

The torpedoman-miner had been killed, crushed by several mines torn loose from their moorings. The helmsman had been thrown from his couch and had a wicked gash torn in his scalp. The machinist's mate was frantically trying to shut down the turbines, which were still running wide open and threatened to push the *Nautilus* to the bottom of the Gulf.

Jack and Virgil screamed jubilant war whoops. They had seen the explosion and could now see the silhouette of the *Nautilus* highlighted in the burning water.

"Did you see that!" said Virgil, forgetting about the pain in his hand. "Blew his ass sky-high!"

Jack was about to roar his approval when a volley of Gatling gun fire tore over their heads.

Both Jack and Virgil ducked down behind the windscreen, momentarily shocked speechless by the shooting.

"Can't be coming from the *Nautilus*," said Virgil, peering over the gunnels.

They were coming in on Jack and Virgil's flank. Two cigars dispatched by the comandante's radio signal were now going to avenge the destruction of the prototype.

"Get on the trim quick!" shouted Jack, bearing the helm

away from the cigars and toward the islands. "Kick it into place!"

"We might just make it," said Virgil, gauging their distance to Ten Thousand Islands. "If we can just maintain this distance, we might be able to lose 'em. Stay in the shallows, where they won't be able to follow with the hydrofoils."

"Right," said Jack, veering hard off from the cigars and bearing down on the first of the atolls forming the maze of islands.

The cigars split their formation. One cigar slowed its intercept speed and dropped down into the water to run in the shallows with the cigarette, while its companion continued to run in the deeper water on hydrofoils and cut off their escape into the Everglades.

Jack could see the cigars' ploy, but kept to the shallows. He knew they had no chance in outrunning the sophisticated minisubs. Their only hope was in outmaneuvering them.

The trailing cigar, now running without the use of its hydrofoils, could not gain on the cigarette, but it could maintain the same pace. The gunner began to open up, laying down a murderous barrage that tore up the water around the commandeered cigarette.

"There! Through there!" shouted Virgil, pointing to a gap between two islands. "I'll handle the trim. Just like we did with Lieutenant Shapely."

Jack nodded his understanding and brought the helm of the cigarette to bear. The boat came up out of the water and onto the narrow sand bridge between the islands. Jack and Virgil both felt their feet leave the deck as the bow became airborne upon impact with the sandbar. Their stomachs reacted with the weightless sensation, and their hands kept them from flying over the bow. Virgil maneuvered the trim so as not to damage the props, and the inertia of the boat took them across the short landfall and back into the Gulf.

The cigar corrected its course to match the maneuver, but the minisub drew far more water than the standard eighteen inches of the cigarette, and when the bow struck the sandbar, rather than rising up to an apogee to clear the obstruction, it dug in. The drag of the hull, combined with the weight of the craft, left them beached, with their engines and props churning the Gulf into a sandy froth.

Virgil gave out another war whoop. "That's two down, and one to go!"

The flanking cigar began to open fire, though its marksmanship was hampered by a bad angle, and the islands now offered the cigarette plenty of cover. Still they maintained the chase. The comandante was now in communication with them, and his orders were adamant. The gringos were to be stopped at all cost.

Jack kept weaving between islands, sandbars and reefs. He never held the same course for more than a hundred yards. The cigar maintained its flanking, maneuvering in deeper water, where it could keep pace with the cigarette.

The Florida coast came into view and, more important, the Everglades. Jack set his course directly for the swamps. The flanking cigar brought all its weaponry to bear. The scrub palm withered under the murderous rain of lead. The small islands that had been Jack's and Virgil's salvation began to deflect rounds, which ricocheted wildly before whining into the Gulf.

A deflected round slammed into the starboard engine. Oil spewed over the red-hot manifolds and ignited.

"Jesus!" shouted Virgil, taking his good hand off the trim. "We're on fire!"

Jack only glanced over his shoulder. He kept the engines running wide open. The swamps were barely a mile ahead, and the cigar was already cutting its speed. The minisub could not follow them into the Everglades. Fumes inside the starboard turbo-charger detonated, spraying the stern of the cigarette with burning fuel. Virgil made a pathetic effort to extinguish the flames with the onboard fire extinguisher, but the wash of the wind provided the fire with more oxygen than Virgil could ever hope to smother, and he abandoned the effort, to join Jack at the helm.

"We gotta abandon ship before the gas tanks blow!" bellowed Virgil.

"We've got to make the swamps first!" Jack shouted back.

Virgil watched the fire now consuming the fiberglass engine covers, which were liquefying from the heat. The port engine, the only one supplying any real power, began to misfire. Jack tickled the throttle to maintain what little thrust remained. The cigarette cut through the silt leaching out from the swamps. The boat cut a smoky wake through the brown swamp water staining the turquoise Gulf. It was a welcome sign. If they could just nurse another mile out of the boat, they'd be in the Everglades.

The stern of the cigarette reacted to an explosion. The port engine had thrown a rod and both props were now dead in the water.

"Paddle for it," coughed Jack, over the smoke pouring from the stern.

"Are you crazy?" said Virgil, grabbing Jack by the shirt sleeve. "I ain't goin' down with this tub."

Virgil tumbled headlong over the side, dragging Jack with him. They both went ass-over-elbow into the swampy water just as the gas tanks detonated. The force of the explosion split the cigarette in two.

Jack could see the water above them. It was a burning inferno. Holding their breath until their lungs threatened to burst, Jack and Virgil swam underwater toward the swamp. They came up, sweeping the water about them, to grab a lungful of air before descending once more to escape the floating fire.

Maneuvering underwater in their clothes while handcuffed was still no easy task, but after about thirty seconds of swimming, they reached an area where the oil and gas had not spread, and surfaced.

Both were gasping for air and clung to each other for buoyancy. The water behind them was still alive with flames.

"Maybe they'll think we went down with the boat," said Jack.

"Don't count on it," said Virgil, nodding in the direction of the flanking cigar.

Jack turned and could see the cigar, about three hundred yards to the southeast. The two crew members were up on deck, inflating a small skiff. In minutes they would have the outboard engine fixed to the inflatable skiff's stern and would come to carry out the comandante's last order.

"Come on," said Jack, tugging on Virgil's shirt. "Swim for it."

"Strip first," said Virgil. "At least get your pants off. We'll swim a helluva lot faster without them."

It took what seemed like hours to wiggle out of their jeans, but with them gone, they did swim faster and with less effort. Jack kept a wary eye on the cigar. The crew had the skiff inflated and were mounting the outboard. Jack turned and looked toward the swamp, now tantalizingly close.

The bottom came up quickly. Jack and Virgil had kept their deck shoes, which protected their feet from the coral bottom. They were quickly up to waist-deep in the shoreline water and were straining for the safety of the swamp.

Jack and Virgil caught a bit of luck, a sandbar. Like an outstretched hand it reached out into the Gulf. Here the water was no more than a few inches deep. It would allow them to run for the cover of the Everglades.

Jack and Virgil covered the last two hundred yards to the edge of the swamp in world-record time. They literally dived into one of the salty estuaries emptying out of the swamp and were swallowed up by mangroves and cabbage palm as the crew of the cigar fired up the outboard motor on their skiff.

White ibises took wing as Jack and Virgil slogged through the stand of pine and cabbage palm.

"Jesus!" said Virgil. "We might as well send up a fuckin' flare."

"Pipe down," said Jack, wading through the swamp. "Look for cover."

Virgil followed Jack into the Everglades. They lay down in

the salty water lest they startle more of the wildlife and give away their position.

The cigar carried an extra crew member, making a search party of three. One man rode the outboard motor, another sat midboat, while the third took up a position in the bow. All were armed with Baretta 70 shorts and would follow their orders: shoot to kill. The inflatable skiff entered the Everglades, where the white ibises had been flushed.

Jack and Virgil passed small islands of pine and cabbage palm surrounded by seas of swamp grasses and lily pads. Frogs, fish, herons, and snakes moved out of their path. Jack and Virgil took cover behind one of these islands to catch their breath and locate their hunters.

The cool water felt good on Virgil's injured hand. Jack peered through the cabbage palm and saw the skiff slowly moving into the swamp. Jack reached back for the 9 mm automatic stuck in his belt. He pulled the weapon out, cleared the clip, and washed the silt and muck from the weapon before reloading.

"Here," said Jack, handing the weapon to Virgil. "You had better take this."

Virgil took the pistol with his good hand. "What are you going to use?"

Jack held up his manacled hands. "These," he said, pulling on the single chain length holding the handcuffs together.

Virgil looked around. Holding the pistol under his armpit, he reached down, took a handful of muck, and spread it over his upper body. Jack did the same.

Virgil could feel the cool ooze slide down inside his shirt and the mud hanging from his eyebrows. He looked at Jack, who now looked more like a piece of floating marsh than a man. It was then the feeling struck Virgil—that raw, invincible sensation, coupled with rush after rush of adrenaline, a feeling he hadn't experienced since they were last in the Mekong Delta.

"You know, this may sound funny," whispered Virgil, "but I feel like I'm at home in here."

"Me too," said Jack, looking toward the skiff like a gator

eyeing his prey. "Now let's show those bastards what it's like to hunt the Viet Cong in their own backyard."

The two pieces of swamp slid down into the water. Jack and Virgil moved through the grass and lilies, with only their noses and eyes above the water. Their heads were covered with mud, heron droppings, and grass. A small frog leaped onto Jack's head, but he did not wisk it away. Perfect camouflage.

The skiff glided into the swamp. The prop of the outboard began to foul on lilies and grass almost immediately. The crew haunted by phantom targets that never materialized.

Jack and Virgil set their ambush. Each slid off the skiff's heading until they flanked the inflatable, and the men on board, who were ready to shoot the first thing that moved.

Jack moved first. He slapped the water with his arm, then dived under the surface. Slugs from the Baretta 70's slammed into the water behind him. Jack swam through the maze of lily roots until he came up aft of the skiff.

Virgil came up out of the water just high enough to sight the automatic. Even if the crew had been looking right at him, it was unlikely they would have seen him. He was barely fifteen feet off the skiff's bow when he pumped two slugs into the man amidships. Virgil threw three more into the man in the bow, then dropped down in the water, knowing he wouldn't get a chance to nail the helmsman.

Virgil marveled at how fast the muzzle velocity of the machine gun was arrested by the water. The slugs penetrated no more than a foot, before falling harmlessly to the bottom.

The helmsman was shoving in another clip to his Baretta when something breeched out of the swamp water and flew over the stern of the skiff. The helmsman felt something metallic around his neck just before he was dragged over the side.

The helmsman held on to his Baretta, thinking he could shoot whatever had grabbed him from behind, but the surprise pull into the water left him without a lungful of air, and he quickly let loose of his weapon to try and grab on to something that would take him back to the surface.

It was a gruesome way to kill a man, and Jack took no pleasure in it. Using the handcuffs as a kind of garrote, Jack half strangled him and let the swamp water finish him off. The helmsman expired, with a smashed larynx, and lungs full of water.

Jack surfaced, grabbed on to the side of the skiff, now running red with blood, and searched for Virgil. He was nowhere in sight. Suddenly the swamp exploded just off the bow. Virgil came up coughing and choking, spitting swamp water while trying to catch his breath.

"Shit!" gagged Virgil. "You sure took your sweet time about that! Christ, I almost drowned!"

"Why didn't you come up for air?" asked Jack, helping Virgil into the skiff.

"What? And get my head blown off? I had to wait until you took out that third guy. I knew I'd never take out all three of them."

"Well, you nailed these two pretty good," said Jack, shoving the corpses over the side.

"Let's get our asses home," said Virgil, inspecting the outboard.

"How much fuel do we have?"

"Just enough," said Virgil. "But we stay on the shoreline all the way home. I don't want to run into any more of them damn cigars."

"Me neither," said Jack, jumping out to tow the skiff back to the sea. "Damn! I can't wait to see Domino."

Chapter Sixteen

AWAY ALL BOATS

THE HARBORMASTER had seen Jack and Virgil come into port in bad shape before. Often it was the result of some drunken run out into the Gulf with a load of equally drunken women. But the sight of them in an inflatable skiff, covered with mud, blood, handcuffed, and without their pants, was something quite original.

"Damn!" said the harbormaster, watching Jack help Virgil up the dock ladder. "What the hell happened to you? Everybody gave you up for dead."

"Have you got that pair of lock cutters around?" asked Jack.

"Sure," said the dumbfounded harbormaster.

"Would you mind getting these off?" said Jack, holding up his manacled hands.

"Well," said the harbormaster, studying their appearance. "You boys aren't in trouble with the law, are you?"

Jack stepped up to the harbormaster and glared down at him with bloodshot eyes. "Get those cutters," snarled Jack, "or I'm going to kick your ass into the middle of next year!"

"Yes, sir!" said the harbormaster. He disappeared into his shack and returned with the lock cutters.

In a moment, Jack and Virgil were freed of the handcuffs. Jack led Virgil down the dock to where their junker Chevy was still parked. They jumped inside and, after some jimmying, Jack had the wreck hot-wired and sputtering to life.

"First thing we do is get you to a hospital," said Jack, looking at Virgil's badly swollen hand. "Then I'll call Domino, then those assholes with the FBI."

The resident on duty at Naples Memorial Hospital was stitching up an eleven-year-old who had received a jackknife for his birthday, and had promptly carved up three of his fingers, when Jack and Virgil dashed into the emergency room.

"Sit down," said the resident, noting Jack and Virgil's unusual appearance. "I'll be with you in a moment."

"You have a phone?" said Jack, standing pantless before the injured boy's mother. "It's a local call."

"Yeah," said the resident, finishing with the boy. "Over there. Now, what seems to be your problem?" he continued, wondering about his next muddied, bloodied patient.

Virgil held up his swollen hand, now badly infected. "Ya got a Band-Aid and a shot, doc? We're kind of in a hurry."

Jack was dialing the Wharf Rat, when the resident plunged Virgil's hand into an antiseptic bath. Virgil lifted off the floor when the solution penetrated his wound. The resident called for a nurse, who took Virgil's temperature, pulse, and blood pressure. The pressure was low, pulse and temperature high.

"Nobody's answering the phone," said Jack, somewhat concerned.

"Try Domino's private number," said Virgil, wincing as the resident cleaned the finger that had taken the injection.

"How did this happen?" asked the resident.

"Uh, I tripped in my garage," said Virgil, wiping his blood-soaked sleeve on his nose. "Say, you suppose you could scare us up a couple pairs of pants?"

"Get them a pair of scrubs," said the resident. "And call John down in the lab. Tell him I'm going to need some samples run."

The nurse nodded. She knew what the resident meant and went to the nearest phone, out of sight of Jack and Virgil, and telephoned the police.

"Nobody's answering her private line either," said Jack anxiously.

"You'd better stay here with that hand," said the resident, glancing toward the nurse. "There's a good chance it could go gangrenous."

Jack turned and saw the nurse on the phone. Her startled expression told Jack all he needed to know. "Okay, doc, give him a shot and some pills, and we'll be running along."

"Well, it's not that simple. You see—"

The resident's words were cut off by Virgil's good hand catching him around his throat, while Jack caught him from behind in a hammerlock.

"Look, Dr. Kildare," said Jack through clenched teeth. "We haven't got time to hang around here answering stupid questions from some flatfoot stuck on weekend duty. Now, give my friend here a shot and some pills, and we'll be on our merry way. Otherwise, it'll be you needing emergency medical treatment."

The resident grimaced, and Jack tightened his grip. "I can't help the man in this position," said the resident.

"Then do it!" said Jack, releasing the resident.

The resident watched as Jack retrieved the nurse, who had already made the call to the cops. When Jack and the nurse returned to the treatment room, the resident was about to administer an injection to Virgil.

"Hold it!" said Jack, examining the vial from which the resident had prepared the injection. "Now, I'm not real sure what this is," said Jack, reading the bottle, "but it sure as hell isn't an antibiotic!"

"It's a new compound," said the resident nervously.

"Bullshit!" roared Jack, grabbing the nurse by the back of her neck. "Inject her, then."

The resident hesitated, then put the syringe down and took another from the cabinet. "This will sting a bit."

"He had better get up and walk out of here," said Jack, "or you'll be joining him on the floor."

"This will help," said the resident. "But I suggest you secure further medical attention. If you don't, there's a damn good chance he'll lose that hand.''

"Thanks, doc,'' said Virgil, wincing as the resident pushed the needle into his buttock. "Send us a bill.''

Jack tossed Virgil a pair of scrub pants he took from a nearby locker, and the pair trotted out the back of the emergency room just as a Naples cruiser pulled up at the front door.

"Couldn't get an answer on either line?" said Virgil.

"No,'' said Jack, jumping into the junker and hot-wiring a start. "Where the hell would she be this early on a Saturday morning?''

"I dunno,'' said Virgil, cradling his injured hand.

"You going to be all right?'' asked Jack.

"Fine,'' said Virgil. "We better beat it. There's John Law now.''

Jack looked back at the hospital. There he could see the resident pointing in their direction. Jack backed the car out of view, took a shortcut across the parking lot, and by the time the auxiliary officer got to the back door, they were gone.

The front door to the Wharf Rat was locked and the shades uncharacteristically closed. Jack pounded on the front door, shouting for Domino to open up, while Virgil tried to peer through one of the side windows.

"Jesus!'' said Virgil, managing to see inside.

"What?'' said an apprehensive Jack.

"Kick it in,'' said Virgil.

"Do what?''

"Just kick it in!'' shouted Virgil.

Two panes of glass and a hinge gave loose with Jack's fourth side kick. Shoving the door open, Jack and Virgil were shocked by what awaited them. Furniture was strewn about the dance floor, and broken glass crunched underfoot as Jack and Virgil stepped cautiously inside.

"Christ!'' said Virgil, assessing the damage in the dim light. "What hit this place? A hurricane?''

"Domino!" Jack called out. "Domino! It's me, Jack! Damn it, where are you?"

Jack and Virgil moved further inside the Wharf Rat. They were about halfway across the bar when they found the body. It had fallen under some smashed furniture and was lying in a small pool of blood.

"Oh, no," said Jack, tossing the furniture off of the body.

Jack rolled the corpse over and was relieved, as well as stunned, by the appearance of the body. It wasn't Domino, as Jack had feared, but a man, of Spanish descent. His nose was broken, as was his neck. The head of the corpse was contorted, and lay with its ear on the shoulder of the body.

"Who the hell is he?" said Virgil.

"I don't know," said Jack, now sick with worry. "Domino!" he shouted. "Domino!"

Muffled moaning came from behind the bar. Jack vaulted over the bar, sending glasses and fifths flying. There, lying in a pool of blood, was Cody Carnes.

Beside Cody lay another man, of the same ethnic background as the first, his head split open like a ripe coconut.

Cody moved and groaned again, making an effort to get up. Jack dropped down beside Cody and tried to assist him. Cody wheeled about in a blind rage and grabbed Jack. Both of Cody's massive hands grabbed Jack by the throat and started to close.

"Get him off me!" said Jack, his words squeezed off by Cody's viselike grip.

It was all Virgil and Jack could manage to push the bouncer back on the floor while they screamed their names. At first Cody didn't seem to comprehend, then he shook off the effects of his concussion and let go of Jack.

"Christ!" said Virgil, catching his breath. "It's us, ya goddamn fool."

"Where's Domino?" gasped Jack, rubbing his throat.

"They took her," said Cody, managing to get up on all fours.

"Who took her?"

"There were six of them," said Cody, reaching for a bar rag

and wringing out the ice water over the welts on the back of his head. "Came at me so fast—"

"Where did they take Domino?" asked Jack, starting to breathe a little easier.

"I don't know," said Cody, continuing his ice bath. "Last thing I heard was comandante something. That mean anything?"

"Yeah," said Jack solemnly. "It means he's a dead man."

Jack got up and headed for the door.

"Where you goin'?" said Virgil.

"You know damn well where they took her."

"Triangle Island? But we haven't got a boat."

"I do," said Cody, struggling to his feet.

"You?" said Jack. "Hell, you're in no shape to go anywhere."

"You want to try to stop me?"

Jack thought a moment. They needed a boat and a backup. Cody could supply both. Besides, there was no time for argument.

"All right," said Jack, "if you feel up to it."

"I don't, but I'm going anyway. Come on. My car's out front."

Jack, Virgil, and Cody were about to leave when Dickerson and Ames came through the front door. The agents were shocked by what they saw: the body lying in the pool of blood, Jack and Virgil covered with mud and blood, and Cody coming toward them from behind the bar, carrying a sawed-off pool cue.

Ames pulled his service revolver. Dickerson intervened. "What happened?"

"Never mind what happened," said Jack, starting for the door.

"I'm afraid we'll have to ask you to stay," said Dickerson, reaching for his piece. "Now I'll ask you again. What happened?"

Jack turned and faced Cody and Virgil. "Don't say a word,"

he whispered. "That's why the comandante took Domino. To keep our mouths shut. If we talk, she's as good as dead."

Cody and Virgil nodded their agreement.

"We're in a bit of a rush," said Jack, continuing toward the door.

Cody and Virgil followed along behind him.

Ames lowered his service revolver and pointed it at Jack. "Freeze!"

Jack stopped only momentarily, then he shook his head. "What are you going to do, G-man? Shoot me?"

"We can't help you if you won't cooperate," said Dickerson.

"Thanks, we don't need any help."

Dickerson looked around the bar. "Where's your girlfriend?"

"None of your fucking business!" said Jack.

"She's been kidnapped, hasn't she?"

"I said it's none of your fucking business!"

"Wait a minute," said Dickerson, blocking Jack's path. "We can help you, but you have to give us some information."

Jack thought the offer over. Perhaps Dickerson was right. The FBI was the best trained outfit in dealing with kidnappers. But Domino wasn't being held for ransom. She was being held captive by a bunch of revolutionaries, ultraradicals, who would slit her throat at the first sign of American authorities.

"No, you can't," said Jack solemnly. "Not where we're going."

Jack stepped around Dickerson, who reached out to physically restrain him. Jack caught Dickerson with a wicked left to the midsection. Ames was turning his weapon on Jack when the pool cue whistled through the air. The weapon caught Ames's arm and the revolver flew across the floor.

Ames's karate-kick was parried by Cody, who followed up with three swift kicks to the crotch, which left the agent wheezing on the floor. Virgil and Jack managed to wrestle Dickerson to the floor and strip him of his weapon.

"All right," said Dickerson. "I won't call my people, but at least take me along. I have a good deal of knowledge in such matters. Believe me! I can help.''

Jack thought about it for a moment. "Okay," he said, "but this clown stays," he continued, pointing to Ames.

"Agreed," said Dickerson.

"All right," said Jack. "Handcuff that guy to the bar, and let's get out of here."

Cody dragged Ames over to the bar, where he handcuffed the gasping man to the foot rail, then dashed out the front door to join Jack, Virgil, and Dickerson inside the agent's car.

"Where to?" asked Dickerson.

"To the dock where my popeye is moored," said Cody. "And step on it. They can't be more than five or six hours ahead of us."

Jack and Virgil briefed Dickerson and Cody on their fantastic odyssey. Their story held both men spellbound.

"And you mean to say, this entire complex was constructed under an island just off the Florida coast?" said Dickerson.

"You'll get to see for yourself," said Jack, pulling up at the dock. "All right, Cody, where's your boat?"

"Wait a minute," said Dickerson, running around to the trunk of the FBI sedan.

Dickerson opened the double lock and lifted the trunk. There was a steel case, padlocked, which he opened. Inside the case was a veritable arsenal—M-16's, tear gas, gas masks, flak jackets, and a variety of pistols and ammunition.

"Oh, a Boy Scout," said Virgil, reaching in to grab a flak jacket. "Be prepared."

"It doesn't hurt," said Dickerson, pulling out a bull horn. "Now then, where are we going?"

"You'll see," said Jack.

"Over here," said Cody, motioning the trio down the dock.

Now the harbormaster was even more confused. Jack and Virgil had arrived in strange fashion, and they were departing in even stranger fashion. And the sight of all those guns made him really suspicious. He wasn't taking any chances. He stepped inside his shack and called the police. Damned if he was going to see the boats of those who paid their dock fees shot up by a bunch of maniacs who were probably involved in the drug trade.

Cody was already firing up the engines of the popeye when Jack, Virgil, and Dickerson arrived. Virgil tossed a flak jacket to Cody, then leaped aboard. "Hope it fits," he said.

"Find a seat aft, wise guy," said Cody, waiting for Jack and Dickerson to board.

"Helluva boat, Cody," said Jack. "Where'd you get it?"

"At your friendly neighborhood used-boat dealer," said Cody, glancing at Dickerson.

"Holy shit," said Virgil, popping the aft fifty-caliber machine guns from a hatch similar to what they had used on the *Domino*. "Why the hell couldn't you give *us* a boat like this?"

"Just got it a week ago," said Dickerson with a shrug.

"Nice name for it," said Jack quietly. "Let's go."

"Where?" asked Cody, pulling away from the dock.

"Ten Thousand Islands," said Jack.

"Where the *Ice Bucket* went down?" said Cody, throttling up.

"Yeah," said Jack. "How'd you know?"

"Lucky guess," said Cody, roaring out of the Naples harbor.

Work gangs crawled over the *Nautilus*. All work on the cigars and the second prototype had been halted, in order to repair the damage to the boat's bow. The *Nautilus* had to be made seaworthy. The very success of "the cause" depended on it.

The comandante had ordered the destruction of the beached cigar and sent its crew to take their own skiff to retrieve the second, whose crew had been killed by Jack and Virgil.

The comandante still felt he could fullfill his destiny, but only if he moved swiftly. He had taken the girl hostage as a hedge against keeping the gringos' mouths shut. As long as he had her, they would do nothing. Now he set all his concentration on the task that lay ahead. "The cause" would not be denied.

Cody opened up the popeye and they flew down the coast. The unlimited catamaran was nearly half again as long as the *Domino,* with double the horsepower.

"I wish you'd let me call in my people," said Dickerson. "You go off half-cocked and you're liable to get Domino killed."

"That island has got a surveillance system that would make the CIA drool," said Jack. "You bring an army of agents in there, and they'd cut Domino's throat in two seconds. The only way we can get close is to look like every other idiot out on the Gulf. Cody can fake engine problems just off Triangle Island. Virgil and I will slip over the side and swim ashore. We know what the complex looks like and precisely where to go. Besides, we aren't exactly new at this sort of thing. We went on plenty of search-and-rescue missions in Vietnam."

Dickerson cocked his head questioningly. "It's your funeral."

"No," said Jack, slapping a magazine into his M-16. "It'll be theirs."

Cody began to cut his speed as they approached Ten Thousand Islands. The popeye's bow settled back into the turquoise blue of the Gulf. It was a familiar course and Cody brought the *Domino II* in east of Triangle Island, so as not to arouse suspicion.

Jack, Virgil, and Dickerson crouched down behind the gunwales while Cody stalled the engines. The popeye began to belch blue smoke from engines running on too rich a fuel mixture, and finally sputtered to lifelessness.

Cody played out the drama, cursing and swearing as he strode to the aft engine compartments, and lifted the hatches to inspect the feigned engine problems.

"How about letting me go with you?" asked Dickerson.

Jack and Virgil looked at each other, wondering whether they should take the risk. "What do you say?" said Virgil. "He's no rookie, you know."

Jack thought a moment. It was not his own life he was risking—it was Domino's. Jack's mistrustful attitude toward authority almost overruled common sense. Dickerson was an expert at such things, plus they might be able to use the additional fire power. "All right," said Jack. "But I'm calling the shots. You see me screw up somewhere, you say so. But the final decision is mine. If anybody is going to be responsible for Domino's life, it's going to be me!"

"Agreed," said Dickerson, pulling off his tie and suit coat. "Here, let's make a small raft of life jackets. We'll put the rifles and ammunition on them."

"International orange on a blue sea?" said Jack. "Hell, we might as well set off a flare."

"Here," said Cody, tossing the trio a blue seat cushion from the aft couch. "Use that. It'll float, and blend right in."

Jack nodded, while Cody continued to work on the engines. "See anything?"

Cody stood up to mop his brow and glanced at the island. "Nothing. Go over the stern behind me."

Jack was first over the side, with Dickerson and Virgil right behind him. Virgil tossed the seat cushion to Jack, while Dickerson handed down the weaponry. In a moment, all three were in the water and swimming for Triangle Island.

Cody watched them go, then went forward to send out a distress signal, just in case anyone on the island was monitoring his presence. "Good luck," Cody whispered watching the would-be commandos approach the island.

A hundred different scenarios raced through Jack's mind as they approached Triangle Island, each tinged with the vexing possibility of Domino's death. Jack began to wonder if Dickerson had been right. Maybe he should have employed the FBI. No! His initial instinct was right. An army of agents would only alert the comandante. Besides, there was no time. Whatever grandiose plans the comandante harbored would have to be implemented now. He couldn't risk "the cause" on Jack's and Virgil's improbable silence.

The salt water felt soothing on Virgil's hand as they approached the shore of Triangle Island. He glanced over at Agent Dickerson, who was swimming next to him. The man from the FBI seemed nervous, and Virgil wondered whether they were being accompanied by a desk-top commando.

"We'll get inside the island through the sea cave and onto the catwalk above the wave generators," said Jack.

Grigsby's remarks intrigued Dickerson and made him increase his kick, propelling the trio with their seat cushion full of armaments up onto the rocky shore.

Jack was the first ashore and was quick to arm himself with an M-16. Jack hid behind some cabbage palm and waited for Dickerson and Virgil to come up behind him.

"We're in luck," whispered Jack. "They've only got the camouflaged netting over the mouth of the cave. The sea doors are open. Come on."

Dickerson followed Jack along the shore line, with Virgil taking rear guard. They reached the mouth of the cave and crawled under the netting. Light reflected off the water washing into the cave and illuminated the wave generators. Jack hugged the wall of the cave while wading waist-deep toward the catwalk suspended above the wave generators.

Dickerson was awed by what he was experiencing. In all of his ten years of service with the department, he had never seen such a spectacle. "My God," he gasped.

"This is nothin'," whispered Virgil. "Wait till we get inside."

"Knock it off," said Jack, slinging the M-16 over his shoulder.

Dickerson and Virgil watched as Jack climbed the treacherous algae-covered rocks up to the catwalk. There he climbed over the safety railings and signaled for the others to follow. Dickerson was next and was forced to kick off his regulation black leather oxfords, as he could not climb with them on. Virgil brought up the rear and used Jack's lowered M-16 sling as a hand grip. He wrapped the sling around his good wrist, and Jack lifted him up to the catwalk. Dickerson was impressed with this show of strength.

"Strong mother, ain't he?" whispered Virgil.

"This way," said Jack, climbing the catwalk above the wave generators.

Jack's stomach began to hollow out as they reached the top of the catwalk. Stealth now became their ally. Dickerson tapped Jack on the shoulder and handed him a suppressor for the M-16. Jack screwed on the suppressor and reached for the door that led to the command center of the under-island complex.

The door was locked. Dickerson waved Jack off, reached into his hip pocket, and produced a small wallet containing lock picks. It took some time, but Dickerson finally tripped the lock, and Jack slowly opened the door.

After a quick search of the entrance the trio stepped inside, lest the sound of the waves inside the sea cave fanfare their entrance. Jack's eyes darted about, his hands causing the muzzle of the M-16 to follow instinctively. The long hallway leading into the heart of the complex was strangely devoid of activity. Jack worked his way down one side of the hallway, while Virgil and Dickerson worked the other.

Jack was first to reach the command center, and peered inside. The machines' magnetic hum was all that greeted him. The command center was empty. Chairs were pushed away from computer consoles, and radar screens and half-finished logs lay on the floor.

Jack swung back against the wall. Had the comandante abandoned the complex? Perhaps everyone was down on the docks. No. They would never leave the surveillance screens unattended. Then what?

Jack signaled Dickerson and Virgil closer. Virgil poked his head inside the command center. "Where the hell are they?" he whispered.

"Let's find out," said Jack, taking the lead down the hallway.

They took the familiar route to the comandante's quarters. They too were deserted. Jack was about to continue his search when he noticed something on the carpeted floor. Blood.

Jack poked a finger into the spot and found it still moist. Jack's worst fears surfaced. He pictured Vicente Villa taking the same bizarre pleasure in torturing Domino that he had shown with Virgil. Cooler heads prevailed.

"Keep up your search," whispered Dickerson. "You don't know that belongs to your girlfriend."

The grisly thought somehow bolstered Jack's spirits. Maybe Dickerson was right; he didn't know. They continued the search.

Jack burst into the mess hall, with Dickerson and Virgil right behind, brandishing M-16's and ready to cut down their would-be assailants in a hail of muffled lead. But the mess hall, like the computer center and the comandante's quarters, was empty.

Jack was about to move on when Virgil's arm caught him from behind. Virgil nodded in the direction of his discovery.

Jack turned and saw a leg protruding from the exit leading to the cadre's quarters. The trio dashed across the mess hall and kicked open the exit. A corpse lay in a pool of its own blood. A portion of the cranium had been blown away, along with most of the victim's face. He had been shot from behind and probably on the run, for either the force of his momentum or the velocity of the round had knocked him half through the exit doors.

Now the eerie silence inside the complex gripped the would-be rescue team with apprehension. Jack bolted over the corpse and raced down the connecting hallway for the balcony overlooking the subterranean docks. Dickerson and Virgil followed.

Jack kicked open the doors to the balcony and came out ready to shoot, but a smoky silence was all that awaited him. Dickerson and Virgil came out, to find Jack frantically searching the docks below for any sign of life.

Dickerson was awed by the subterranean complex, shrouded now in a haze of smoke. He could just make out the stalls where the cigars had once been moored, and the smoldering wreckage of the second half-completed prototype. Bodies littered the docks and a few were floating in the water. Dickerson noticed bullet holes in the walls of the living quarters behind him and concluded they must have been the result of a tremendous firefight.

"Come on," shouted Jack, dashing for the lift down to the docks.

Dickerson and Virgil followed Jack in what became a frantic, but fruitless, search for Domino. Dickerson got a flash review of the complex as they continued the search, and became caught up in fascinating thoughts of the man his operatives referred to as the comandante. How could anyone conceive of, much less put into operation, such a complex?

By the time they reached the docks, Jack had discovered over fifty bodies, some gasping their last breaths, but none that could shed any light on what might have happened. Jack kept shouting out Domino's name, as though he still might find her among the carnage, but the echo of his voice was his only answer.

Jack stopped next to the only remaining boat left at the docks, the half-completed prototype, which had been stripped for parts. A few of the work crew had been shot where they labored, which gave Jack a reasonable explanation for the carnage. "Goddamn banana republic mentality!" cursed Jack, kicking one of the corpses lining the docks.

"What happened?" asked Virgil, joining Jack beside the smoldering prototype.

"A mutiny," said Jack, lowering the muzzle of his M-16. "I'll bet Villa was behind it, the sneaky sonofabitch."

"Okay," said Virgil. "But where are they?"

"Gone to fulfill the comandante's great cause?" offered Dickerson.

"Yeah," said Jack scornfully. "And what might that be?"

"Not a what," said Dickerson, "a where."

"Stop talking in riddles," said Jack. "We haven't got the time."

"You're exactly right," said Dickerson, raising his M-16 on Jack and Virgil. "I'm afraid you'll have to let me call in my people."

"You can't nail both of us," said Virgil, stepping aside to flank Dickerson.

A short muffled burst cut off Virgil's tactic. Virgil could feel the whine of the lead flash past his upper arm and tear up the water behind him. "I'm prepared to kill both of you for what's at risk," said Dickerson.

"And what might that be?" asked Virgil.

"We haven't got time to discuss this!" shouted Jack. "All right, asshole, we're with you. What now?"

"Get back to the boat, and get on the radio," said Dickerson, still holding his weapon on them. "If the *Nautilus* is as fast as you say it is, there isn't a moment to lose."

Jack was about to run back to the boat, when he looked at the muzzle of Dickerson's M-16, still pointed at him. "You can put that down," said Jack. "We'll play it your way from now on."

"All right," said Dickerson, lowering the weapon. "Let's go."

Chapter Seventeen

THE DEEP SIX

JACK LED the sprint back through the complex. The lift to the top of the command center seemed agonizingly slow. Dickerson was first out of the lift, with Jack and Virgil right after him. They raced down the hallway toward the door leading to the catwalk, and back down to the wave generators. As Dickerson passed the communications center, he stopped and looked through the window.

The computers were running their usual scans, and the place abounded with radios. Dickerson was about to open the door, when he felt Jack's hand lock around his wrist.

Jack had pushed his face up against the window of the communications center and peered down at the inside of the door. "I wouldn't do that," he said, pointing in the direction of his interest.

It was a small charge, probably no more than a half pound of C-4, but enough to blow the communications center, and the first person who entered, into oblivion.

"Right," said Dickerson, taking his hand off the doorknob. "Let's get back to the boat."

Cody was still feigning engine problems, when Jack reached the mouth of the sea cave.

"Cody!" bellowed Jack, waving furiously. "Pick us up."

Cody cleared the engines, fired up the popeye, and ripped the helm hard to starboard to bring him to shore in seconds. Jack, Dickerson, and Virgil waded out to meet the boat. Cody cut the engines long enough to help pull the trio over the transom and out of the water.

It was the concussion of the blast that reached them first, a shock wave comparable to the bombs dropped by B-52's in Vietnam. Jack turned in horror toward the fireball. The mushroomlike cloud rose above the Gulf, a fiery froth licking orange flames that belched a cloud of black smoke that obliterated the sun and shadowed the sea.

The blast was some distance away, perhaps five or six miles down the coast, and Cody was on the throttles of the popeye before Jack could shout instructions. Cody opened up the engines of the unlimited catamaran and veered in and out between small island obstructions, leaving Triangle Island in their wake as they sped toward the now-smearing cloud from the explosion.

In the distance Jack saw the line of tracer ammunition. It seemed to move in a path ahead of the explosion and came from opposite directions, as though two boats were engaging in a firefight. Jack's stomach began to knot. The mutiny, the bloody evidence of which they had uncovered inside Triangle Island, was obviously not over. Whoever the warring factions were, they were ahead of them, with Domino apparently being held as a pawn in a desperate game both parties were determined to win.

"This is a priority message," said Dickerson into the radio. "Clearance code: X-ray, tango, zulu, eight, niner, six. Repeat: X-ray, tango, zulu, eight, niner, six."

"Roger, and confirm your priority code," came the voice over the radio. "What is your message? Over."

"Have reason to believe a submarine will attempt to rendezvous at the Atlantic mouth of the Panama Canal to sink or sabotage shipping entering the canal. Currently in pursuit of submarine, projected location: twenty-four degrees fifteen minutes north, eighty-two degrees twenty minutes west," said Dickerson, checking the satellite navigation system.

Jack's eyes narrowed at Dickerson's transmission. Jack surmised that the comandante was on some kind of suicide mission, and his concern for Domino multiplied tenfold. "Can't this thing go any faster?" shouted Jack.

"We're going a hundred and forty now," bellowed Cody. "I push it any harder in these waters and we'll splatter ourselves all over the side of one of these Mickey Mouse islands."

Jack cursed under his breath and checked his M-16, then turned his attention toward the battling boats ahead. They were closing on them now, but would they get there in time?

Cody increased their speed, nursing the throttles forward. Dickerson was on the radio again, this time calling ahead to Key West Naval Air Station to scramble a Marine Sea Spotter Chinook and Cobra gunships to intercept the southward-bound submarine.

Next Dickerson radioed the Coast Guard, diverting two cutters from their normal duties and ordering them to close for what Dickerson saw as a pincer's maneuver. Dickerson had to cut off the prototype before it had a chance to escape into international waters. There it might elude the search aircraft and complete its mission of madness.

"Go forward!" shouted Dickerson to Jack. "Raise the weapons midships."

Jack looked over the windscreen. There, neatly concealed, was a hidden gun mount very similiar to what he had seen on the *Domino*. Jack pulled on goggles, slung the M-16 over his shoulder, and climbed out over the windscreen to midships of the racing popeye.

Built-in handgrips were all that kept Jack from being torn off the bow by the rip of the wind. Jack opened the hatch, then ducked as the wash of the wind tore the hatch cover off. The cover slammed into the windscreen, scoring and cracking it badly, before hurtling back over the stern, narrowly missing Virgil, who was now popping the aft fifty-caliber machine gun.

Jack crawled down inside the specially designed gun mount and eased into the abbreviated chair fitted behind twin fifty-caliber machine guns. The size of the popeye allowed such awesome weaponry, and Jack set the bolts of the fifties before adjusting his sights.

"There they are!" shouted Cody, taking a hand off the trim momentarily to point.

Jack swung the muzzles of the fifties around to pick his target, then realized his dilemma. Which boat would he shoot? The two cigars trailing the *Nautilus*, or the prototype itself?

Cody flew past the wreckage of one of the cigars hit by the fire of the *Nautilus*. There was little left of the sophisticated craft, save for a few floating remnants of ship surrounded by a slick of oil staining the blue of the Gulf.

Dickerson searched the frequencies on the radio, until he picked up the communication in Spanish between the remaining cigars. Each of the minisubs was laying down a murderous barrage of Gatling gun fire on the *Nautilus*, which began to pull out of the maze of Ten Thousand Islands and into the Gulf.

Dickerson was awed by how these minisubs handled. The instant the *Nautilus* made its break for the Gulf they began to rise out of the water, buoyed up on their hydrofoils as they matched the speed of the prototype.

"Open it up!" shouted Virgil from the bow.

Now the combined horsepower of the popeye's engines came to bear. The cigars and the *Nautilus* were fast, but they could not outrun the *Domino II*. The unlimited catamaran kept pace with the fleeing flotilla, then slowly began to overtake it.

Dickerson kept monitoring the radio traffic among the boats, each captain taunting the comandante while their gunners enunciated their threats with burst after burst of Gatling gun fire. Suddenly the cigar closest to the *Nautilus* opened up with its 20 mm cannon, shearing off a piece of the prototype's conning tower.

Dickerson, monitoring the radio transmissions of the *Nautilus* heard it—the scream of a woman frightened out of her senses by the fusillade now bombarding the *Nautilus*.

"She's on the *Nautilus*!" screamed Dickerson over the roar of the popeye's engines. "Take out those cigars!"

Jack didn't question Dickerson. The *Nautilus* was taking a

terrible pounding, and firing from its conning tower had ceased. It was obvious the boat was running for its life. Jack took a bead on the cigar closest to the *Nautilus* and prayed he was doing the right thing.

The first burst was high, and Jack adjusted his sights. The next burst he drew down on target. The water all around the cigar began to erupt into hundreds of geysers, each a fifty-caliber round homing in on its target.

The second burst from Jack's fifties tore into the forward hydrofoils. Jack held the barrels steady and let the momentum of the cigar take it into the heaviest machine gun fire. Slugs tore through the outer hull and into the gunner's couch, cutting the gunner in half. The last of the burst caught the cigar midships, detonating the ammunition and fuel cells. The subsequent explosion blew a temporary crater of water in the Gulf and sprayed the adjacent area with a hail of twisted metal.

A few pieces of the detonated cigar bounced off the side of the popeye but did no significant damage. Cody maintained his speed and course and moved up on the remaining cigar, which was redirecting its fire at the popeye.

Cody began to veer his course, pulling away from the fire while Jack and Virgil laid down a withering barrage on the cigar. The crisscrossed fire of the aft single fifty and Jack's duals sheared off the hydrofoils, and the cigar nosed over into the Gulf at a speed even its superstructure was never designed to endure.

The physics of mass and velocity completed what firepower had begun. The last cigar tore itself to pieces as it slammed into the Gulf, made rock-hard by their own velocity. It appeared as though some huge canister of napalm had been dropped from the sky and splattered over the sea. The battle seemed to wane with its fiery consumption.

Cody was first to notice it, and he eased back on the throttles. Though the *Nautilus* still appeared seaworthy, its speed had slowed considerably. "What happened?" asked Cody.

"I don't know," said Jack, letting the fifties cool but still keeping them at the ready. "Pull alongside. She looks as if she's gone dead in the water."

Dickerson kept trying to contact the *Nautilus*, urging them to acknowledge his signal, but the prototype did not respond. It slowed to a stop and began to list slightly to starboard.

"Pull alongside and we'll board her," said Jack, climbing out from behind the fifties.

Virgil left his emplacement as well and joined Jack and Dickerson as they waited for Cody to bring the popeye alongside the derelict.

"Ahoy aboard the *Nautilus!*" Dickerson said through his bull horn. "FBI! We're coming aboard."

There was no response to Dickerson's hails. Dickerson tried the radio, to no avail. Cody brought the popeye alongside the *Nautilus*, and Jack jumped aboard with a rope and his M-16 at the ready. No one appeared on deck. Jack made the popeye fast and signaled the others aboard.

Cody stayed with the popeye and watched Virgil and Dickerson join Jack on the listing deck of the *Nautilus*.

"This way," said Jack, heading for the conning tower.

Twenty mm cannon fire had damaged the prototype badly, and Jack was shaken by the appearance of the boat and the fact that there were no signs of life. Jack struggled with the hatch leading down inside the conning tower, which had also sustained damage.

The hatch opened and Jack peered down inside. Still no sign of life. "Domino?" Jack called hesitantly. "Are you down there? Domino?"

Jack thought he heard someone crying. It was a woman's cry. It had to be!

Jack was about to leap down the hatch when Dickerson restrained him. "Here," said Dickerson, handing Jack his service pistol.

Jack handed Dickerson his M-16 and dropped down the ladder, hitting the deck with both feet after barely breaking his drop with his hands, and instinctively leaped to the side, landing with his back against a bulkhead. Jack whipped his pistol

about, searching for his would-be adversary, but found no as-
sassin lurking inside the ship.

Jack spotted Domino. She was curled up in a corner of the
command center sobbing, her face buried in her hands. Jack
was about to dash to her side, when he stopped himself. The
boat was not yet secure, and the training he received in Vietnam
would not allow him to make a foolish mistake, even with
Domino so close.

Jack crept along against the side of the ship, hugging the hull
as he made his way toward Domino. As he walked, the drama
of the mutiny began to take shape. There on the floor of the
command center was the body of Vicente Villa. He had been
shot several times and lay in a pool of blood. Beside Villa,
slumped over the helm of the *Nautilus,* was the comandante.
He appeared to have been shot in the back.

Now Jack forgot routine and rushed to Domino's aide. She
was whimpering, drained of energy, and curled up in a fetal position. She screamed when Jack embraced her and, for a fleet-
ing moment, could hardly believe her eyes. "Jack? Jack?
Jack?" she kept repeating, as though she were living some kind
of dream and expected to wake at any moment.

"Yes," said Jack, cradling her in his arms. "It's me."

"It is you," said Domino, grabbing Jack and escaping her
nightmare. "Oh, God, it is you!"

"Yes, Domino, it's me. Believe it."

"Oh, Jack, take me home. Take me home, now."

"All right," said Jack, pulling them up to their feet.

"Not just yet," came the voice from behind them.

Jack turned, shielding Domino with his body, and holding
his pistol behind his back.

The comandante sat up at the helm, his captain's tunic
stained with blood and a 9 mm pistol in his hand. His eyes were
weary, glazed, and seemed not to focus. "There is still time,"
said the comandante in a guttural rasp.

A pair of bare feet began to climb down the hatch ladder behind the comandante. It was Dickerson. A few tell-tale drips of
water fell from his pants leg and onto the deck. The

comandante's head turned slightly. He brought his 9 mm to bear. Jack could see the shot would go straight through him and kill Domino as well.

"Tell the man coming down the hatch that if he takes another step I will shoot both of you," said the comandante, bracing himself against the helm.

"You hear that?" said Jack.

"Give it up, Cordova," said Dickerson. "The war is over."

The comandante smiled. "No, señor, the battle has just begun. Now, get off my boat!"

There was a moment of hesitation on Dickerson's part, then slowly, he began to climb back on deck.

"Close the hatch," coughed the comandante.

Jack could hear the hatch close above him and felt Domino's fingers dig into his arm. Still no respite from her nightmare. Jack studied the comandante. Blood gurgled and bubbled out of the exit wound in his chest. Probably a lung wound, thought Jack. Wait him out. In a few minutes he'll bleed to death or drown in his own blood.

"Start the turbines," managed the comandante.

"Sure," said Jack, pocketing his pistol and giving Domino a reassuring squeeze. "What happened?" he continued, staring at the corpse of Vicente Villa.

"Es cochino traidor," said the comandante, spitting on the corpse. Blood-laced spittle ran from the comandante's mouth. "He would abandon the cause, only for profit."

The comandante seemed to wobble in his chair. There was a strange sense of finality to his speech, as though he knew he was about to die. Jack eased his hand down toward his pistol, which he had kept hidden from the comandante, then hesitated. The comandante's weapon was still pointed at Domino. If Jack shot him, there was a good chance the comandante might get off a last shot.

Jack worked his way around the command center until he was just to the left of the comandante and pretended to fiddle with the controls to the turbines. "Tell me about the cause," said Jack, looking for an opportunity.

"We could have brought the world to its knees," said the comandante, reveling in the possible glory. "Now? Now it is all ended."

"You were going to blow up the Panama Canal?" said Jack.

The comandante scoffed at Jack's remark. "A stupid terrorist tactic. The canal is good to no one damaged. No, we were to use the prototypes to mine ships entering the canal, radio in our demands, then our troops, in a coordinated effort, would simply take control of the Canal Zone."

"I still don't see how that would humble the entire world," said Jack, waiting for the opportunity to act.

"Don't be so foolish, señor. Once in control of the Canal Zone, I would begin negotiations with the Soviet Union."

Jack seemed a bit puzzled. "You don't strike me as a comrade."

"You are right. I'm not. But if the West thought I was negotiating with the Soviet Union, they would have no other choice than to deal with me."

"Yes, but to what end?"

"The complete removal of American forces from Central America."

"The American government would never allow that—"

"Faced with the possible loss of such a strategic location to the Soviet Union, a direct threat to their national security, I'm afraid they would have no choice."

"But the U.S. government has always had the best interests of Latin democracy in mind—"

"Ha!" replied the comandante, coughing up some blood. "*Their* best interests in mind. No, the only one to decide the fate of Latin America is a Latino."

"And you figure you're the one to do the job."

"I am. Did you not see what I accomplished with my under-island complex? With my direction, Central America would have enjoyed a new prosperity, its proper place in the world."

The comandante misinterpreted Jack's expression. Jack was appalled by the comandante's mad scheme, not awed, as the dying genius thought.

"It would have worked, too," said the comandante, staring at the corpse of Vicente Villa, "had it not been for Vicente's greed."

"And what was his plan?" said Jack, taking a pensive step further down the command center.

The comandante shook his head, still unable to comprehend the stupidity. "Vicente wanted to abandon the cause, to keep playing modern-day pirate. He would have continued to strip the locals of their precious white powder. He wanted the money, only the money."

"His idea made more sense," said Jack.

"Then you are as foolish as he was," said the comandante disdainfully. "There are more important things in this life than money."

"Your glory, for instance."

"Not my glory, señor, the glory of all Latin America!"

"You really believe you could have pulled it off, don't you," said Jack, drawing the comandante's attention away from Domino.

"I can still do it," strained the comandante, infuriated by the gringo's doubt. "Start the . . . Start the turbi . . ."

The comandante's pistol fell from his hand. The weapon discharged, but the round slammed into one of the computer consoles, shorting out a few circuits. Domino screamed as Jack wheeled about, pulled his pistol, and grabbed the comandante from behind.

The comandante was slipping closer to death with every second. Jack had thought that given the opportunity, he could shoot him, but now, having the means of his revenge, he could not bring himself to assassinate the helpless man. Jack picked up the pistol, ejected the clip and the round in the chamber, then tossed the weapon to the far side of the command center.

"Come on," said Jack, stepping to help Domino to her feet. "We're getting out of here."

At first Jack thought it was some kind of warning that had been triggered by the comandante's gun's discharging, then he noticed where the red lights and alarm emanated, the console in front of the comandante.

Jack hurried Domino to the ladder leading to the conning tower and climbed up to open the hatch. Dickerson helped Domino up onto the conning tower. Jack was about to abandon the *Nautilus* when he was drawn back, down the ladder to the dying man who had once ordered his execution. Perhaps there was a part of Jack's personality that even he himself didn't understand. Perhaps he wanted to save the comandante to show the world true genius. Or perhaps he just wanted him to stand trial for all those poor wretches he had sent to the bottom of the sea. Jack wasn't sure, and there was no time for pondering his motivation. He dropped below decks and dashed toward the comandante.

The comandante lay over the helm, barely clinging to life. Jack was trying to lift him out of his seat, when the man turned and looked at him. "Leave me," said the comandante. "I would go down with my dream."

Again Jack tried to lift him.

"Leave," said the comandante, whose voice had faded into a whisper. "The automatic scuttling device has been armed. You have only a short time to get clear of the boat."

Now Jack heeded his words. He left the comandante at the helm and leaped up the ladder, out of the hatch, and onto the conning tower.

Cody had brought the popeye alongside, and Dickerson had already helped Domino on board. She was sharing embraces with Virgil when Jack jumped down from the conning tower.

"Clear away!" shouted Jack, leaping down into the popeye. "The boat's rigged to blow any second."

Cody shoved the throttles forward, and the popeye tore away from the doomed prototype. Domino fell into Jack's arms and joined Virgil and Dickerson at the stern to watch the drama unfold.

Cody had put about five hundred yards on the prototype when the scuttling device triggered its first charge. The stern went first, a ripping explosion that broke the back of the *Nautilus*.

A second charge detonated forward, an orange fireball that swallowed the ship in a fiery inferno that swept the boat from bow to stern. The *Nautilus* went down slowly, slipping beneath the waves bow-up, almost a final good-bye before slipping into the deep.

An air of melancholy swept over the popeye as it headed back toward Naples. Jack stood with the others on the stern, watching the slick of oil burn, marking the place where the comandante had given his treasure the deep six. It was as though they were all paying homage, watching the pyre burn. Jack rendered the appropriate eulogy.

"Good-bye, Captain Nemo," he said.

SUSPENSE...
ADVENTURE...
MYSTERY...

John D. MacDonald's
TRAVIS McGEE SERIES

TAF-17